THE DAY OF THE DRAGON

Written by

Alex Phillips

MAPLE
PUBLISHERS

The Dawn of the Dragon

Author: Alex Phillips

Copyright © Alex Phillips (2023)

The right of Alex Phillips to be identified as author of this work has been asserted by the author in accordance with section 77 and 78 of the Copyright, Designs and Patents Act 1988.

First Published in 2022

ISBN 978-1-915796-66-0 (Paperback)
       978-1-915796-67-7 (eBook)

Book cover design and Book layout by:
   White Magic Studios
   www.whitemagicstudios.co.uk

Published by:
   Maple Publishers
   Fairbourne Drive, Atterbury,
   Milton Keynes,
   MK10 9RG, UK
   www.maplepublishers.com

Contents

Prologue

Deep into the vast forest of the Zalhara Timberlands, an eerily calm breeze whistled through the branches of the trees. At their highest peaks, amongst the canopies, the gentle yet arid winds echoed throughout that area of the forest as no animals or creatures dwelled in that section to mask the creaks and moans of the swaying branches. Under normal circumstances at this time of year, this part of the forest would be almost lifeless on account of the intensely dry air blowing from the southeast.

On the forest floor however, the sounds of the winds were being drowned out by the trudging of hundreds of heavy boots, firmly pressing down into the ground beneath them. This was then followed by the squelching noises that came as the mud clasped to the soles of the boots when they were ripped out of the earth. Occasionally, this was also subsequently accompanied by grunts, partly from exhaustion due to carrying bulky backpacks over their shoulders and wielding binoculars, guns and swords on top of the thick boots, but partly from frustration because any noise that was made was unintentional since careful efforts and steps were being taken to be as silent as possible.

Thick beads of sweat trickled down the foreheads of the men and soaked into their uniforms for they had almost traversed their way through the Zalhara Timberlands which, at just over one million acres in area, was one of the largest forests in the world. It was a forest that was situated in the country of Lyrasia, yet none of the men that had hiked their way through the immense forest were from Lyrasia. Instead, they had journeyed their way from overseas, from their home country of Entritica. Their reason for doing this was that they were at war, one that had started only six months ago when their enemies from a country called Etracova which lay far beyond Lyrasia, had announced their intentions to invade and take over Entritica. These foes were a terrorist organisation known as Chimera.

For almost twenty years, Chimera had kept a stranglehold over the country of Etracova and ruled over it with an iron fist, but they had never stepped beyond the boundaries of Etracova or made any attempts to spread their dominance until six months ago when they declared war with Entritica. It was believed that this coincided with rumours of a powerful new leader stepping up to guide the faction. Even so, it was still a curious decision for them to target Entritica which, despite its small size, was still viewed as one of the global superpowers compared to Etracova which was not nearly as technologically or economically developed and was considered one of the poorest countries in the world.

Nevertheless, the soldiers of Entritica had travelled all the way to Lyrasia to combat the threat that Chimera posed, never underestimating them for a second. They were determined to protect their home country and their families that lived there and had clashed with Chimera repeatedly in the last few months with the Zalhara Timberlands serving as their battlefield. Thus far, the superior weapons of Entritica had given the soldiers an advantage and they had been able to force Chimera into retreating farther back into the forest and closer to Etracova. Their next battle could potentially win them the war early.

The soldiers knew this would soon be approaching when the commander raised his arm high in the air indicating for them to stop. It was a signal they had seen several times and it only ever came when the recon squad had spotted the enemy ahead with their binoculars and alerted the commander. They knew they had to prepare their weapons in case of a desperate ambush from Chimera, so they got to work reloading their guns and sharpening their swords, being sure to maintain the cover of the trees for safety.

During this period of respite before the attack, it was common for some of the soldiers to feel anxious, particularly some of the younger ones. One of the commanders, Richard Bennett noticed this in one of his comrades, Bradley Butcher, whose hands shook as he honed his blade. He placed his hand reassuringly on his shoulder.

"Hey, not much farther to go," Richard calmly stated. "Just one more push. Then you'll be able to see your sweetheart, again."

Bradley nodded as his hands slowly started to steady. "I've made up my mind. Once this is all over, I'm proposing to Gill," he declared.

"Wow, really? That's a big move," Richard acknowledged with a chuckle.

"Yup. I know it's just been over a year. Hell, I was going to give it at least another three years before even thinking of marriage. But I guess war really makes you realise how short life can be," Bradley rationalised.

"Amen to that. I was around your age too when I married Victoria so if you need advice, just let me know," Richard said, gesturing towards himself.

"Ah, cheers," Bradley answered appreciatively as the shaking of his palms ceased, his resolve strengthened. It had become a part of the pre-battle ritual for each of the soldiers to remind one another of who and what they were fighting to protect. "You must miss her like mad. And Nathan too."

"Yeah, I'd give anything to be with them right now," Richard sighed solemnly. "It's his birthday today, can't believe I'm missing it..."

"He's sixteen already?!" Bradley exclaimed. "Wow, it only feels like yesterday when I saw him and Thomas together in the halls during first year!"

"Not surprising really, you've only just left school yourself," Richard quipped. "The horrors of war – no child should have to experience that."

"Well then, let's fight to make sure that doesn't happen," Bradley declared as both men finished priming their weapons.

They looked around for the chief commander who still had his attention towards the transceiver in his hand. He looked around at each of the soldiers and rapidly shook his head, signifying that he was still waiting for the signal to advance from the reconnaissance squadron.

As they waited, Bradley took the chance to query Richard further. "Rich, you know how you were mentioning that it was Nathan's birthday today? Well, I was wondering, what was the birth like?"

Richard's head briskly turned to face Bradley. "Oh wow, you're even considering-"

"Pretty much," Bradley confirmed. "I knew I wanted to be a dad one day but after all this, better sooner than later! Thought it'd be good to ask what your experience was like when Nathan was born. You know, what to do, what not to do...."

Richard cleared his throat, taken aback by Bradley's request. "I'm not actually sure I'm the best person to ask on this one," Richard responded hesitantly. "Nathan's birth was, well, quite a peculiar case..."

"I remember you saying he was born prematurely before. That's why I wanted to ask you as you've been in that situation. I'd want to know how to handle it so I could support Gill if the worst-case scenario happened," Bradley explained.

"I get what you're saying Brad, and it's good that you want to be prepared," Richard assured understandingly. "But what happened with Nathan was even more unusual than that."

"What do you mean?" Bradley asked him as his eyebrows furrowed in confusion and intrigue.

"Well yes, Nathan was born at twenty-six weeks," Richard described. "He was very frail and tiny and needed an incubator to keep him alive. But it wasn't the technology that saved him."

"Then what *did* save him?" Bradley enquired, growing increasingly more puzzled.

Richard frowned, agitated with himself. "I've said too much already. If I told you, you wouldn't believe me," he stated, his eyes widened as the words left his mouth. "Because I was there, and I still don't believe it happened."

"Try me!" Bradley challenged him stubbornly. "After all, you can't just say all that and leave me hanging now..." he pointed out to try and lighten the tone a bit.

After much reluctance, Richard released a deep breath and finally yielded to Bradley's persistence. He closed his eyes and bit his lip as he pondered where to even start with explaining the experience.

"I-I remember," Richard began, "it was three days after Nathan was born. H-he was still in the incubator and his condition was showing no signs of improving. Whenever she had even a shred of energy, Victoria was with him. She'd have been there the entire time if she could have. She refused to give up on him even with how drained she was.

"That day, I spoke to the doctors while Victoria was resting. They had to tell me that at this stage, Nathan had no chance of recovering and that if they kept him in the incubator for much longer, it would only prolong his suffering. They urged me to make the most painful decision that a parent could make." Richard's eyes showed signs of watering as he relived the experience. Just as his elder had done for him, Bradley reassuringly placed a hand on Richard's shoulder, giving him time to compose himself.

"So I went into the room where Nathan was," Richard carried on, trying to recall each detail. "I saw how weak his vitals were on the monitor and he was lying there, barely breathing. I just stood there looking at him, my son.

One side of me was asking, 'how can I let him go?'; the other was asking, 'how can I let him keep suffering?' I wouldn't wish that on anyone, even my worst enemies. So I did something that I'd never done before in my life, even after losing my own family – I prayed. I prayed and I hoped against all odds that a miracle would happen to save Nathan's life.

"Then in that moment, all I heard was a long beeping sound. I opened my eyes to see the heart monitor had flatlined.

"I could feel my heart sink as I rushed to the door and tried to call someone, anyone, for help.

"But then, that's when *it* happened. When I heard the heart monitor start to fluctuate, I turned round and saw Nathan's body – only it was glowing black!"

Bradley's eyes widened in shock as Richard stated this. "His whole body was surrounded by a strange black aura! I could see it emanating from him, but it felt so cold and malicious. As I got closer, the sensation got stronger until it started to take shape in front of me, converging right above Nathan. It took the form of a dragon's head – and before I could do anything else, the dragon plunged right into his body!

"It created such a shockwave that it not only knocked me to the floor but also shattered the glass in both the incubator and the doors and destroyed the heart monitor on top of that. By the time I'd recovered, the doctors had arrived on the scene after hearing the alarm. They were asking me what had happened, but I didn't even know what to say about what I'd just witnessed…

"And then I heard it – crying. We all turned to the broken incubator to see that Nathan was crying. He hadn't made a sound since he was born, yet there he was, crying. He was alive! I couldn't believe it – we'd nearly lost him but that black aura, or whatever it was, saved him! The doctors said that this had never happened before and took him away from the splintered glass of the incubator to do any tests to monitor his health. But in that moment, all that mattered to me was that I had my son back…"

After Richard finished telling the story of Nathan's birth, there was a brief silence between the two men as Bradley processed what he had just heard.

"Well…I certainly wasn't expecting that!" Bradley admitted.

"Told ya," Richard replied. "Sorry that it's not what you were looking to hear. Nathan's birth certainly wasn't conventional – even for a premature one. After that incident with the black aura, Nathan made a full recovery and there's been no signs of his health deteriorating ever since."

"Well, that's good to know at least," Bradley said reassuringly. "Does Vic know about this too?"

Richard gulped and his pupils darted away from Bradley before he spoke. "I didn't tell her at the time..." he confessed. "Since Nathan seemed fine afterwards, I convinced myself that it was just a one-time miracle. So I didn't want to worry her needlessly."

"So when did you tell her?" Bradley quipped.

"Twelve years after."

"Twelve years?" Bradley repeated before taking a few moments to reflect, all the while keeping an ear out in case the call to battle was issued by the commander. Suddenly, Bradley realised something. "Wait a minute! That's the time when –"

"Yes, that's right," Richard confirmed solemnly. "It wasn't long after *that* incident – I'm sure you're familiar with it. When Nathan told us how he'd felt at that time, the way he described it, it was the exact same sinister sensation I got from the black aura. After that, I had to let Vic know, in case it ever happened again. So that we could be there for him."

"I'm sorry," Bradley whispered. "I'd only heard rumours about it back at school, but if I'd have known that it was affecting him that much, I..." Bradley shook his head regretfully. "I should have intervened..."

"You weren't to know," Richard muttered. "In the end, Nathan's turned out just fine. He's got good friends and he has me and Vic, we'll be there to help him through anything."

"That's what's important," Bradley agreed. "But boy, didn't know you had such a flair for the dramatic – *I could feel my heart sink*," the young soldier playfully teased Richard for his story-telling quirks to brighten the mood.

"Oi, cheeky little..." Richard laughed off with a nudge to Bradley's arm. "Sorry I couldn't be of more help on this one. You're better off asking someone else if you're after experience with a premature birth. I've only experienced it one other time in my life and that was when I was really young – when I was still in Etracova and still had my family. I had a –"

Suddenly, the commander bellowed out to Richard, Bradley and the other soldiers, "ORDER, ORDER!!" Immediately, every soldier stopped their conversation and gathered round the commander for his booming announcement.

"We've got confirmation from Recon – Chimera is straight ahead, only fifty yards away! They're at a standstill, so it looks like we'll be the ones to make the first move!

"Luckily, although they have weapons, they still have no artillery! Our strategy is to approach them and as soon as we have them in our sights, we shoot them down! They'll have no choice but to retreat and we can force them out the forest! We keep pushing them back until they're back into Etracova! From there, we can take out the group's leader and win the war! Is everyone ready?!"

The men all cheered in unison before they continued their march through the timberlands, their guns cocked and loaded for the instant they spotted a Chimera soldier. Each soldier kept their eyes peeled and listened out for any hint of movement, human or otherwise. Their steps became instinctively slower and lighter the closer they got to Chimera's expected location – despite having a clearer idea of what to expect from their enemies, the feelings of anxiety of Richard and the other soldiers remained the same. As they progressed further to that point, they could feel a chill in the air carried forward by a gentle gust of wind that seemed to strengthen ever so slightly with each step traversed. Though Bradley withstood the cold air without flinching, he noticed Richard shiver from the breeze and even spotted goosebumps forming on the back of his hand.

"Hey, you okay?" Bradley questioned, wondering if the nerves had gotten to Richard. Contrarily, the elder soldier promptly set him straight.

"I'd be a pretty lousy soldier if I was stopped by a breeze like this – besides, you're a million years too young to be worrying about me!" Richard declared defiantly. Bradley grinned in response at his display of guts and pressed onwards alongside his comrades.

Then for the first time that day, a shadowy figure could be spotted from afar, lurking in between the trees. There was no mistaking it, they had found Chimera and each soldier raised their gun ready to fire.

Using the surrounding tree trunks as cover, the soldiers that carried pistols and shotguns like Richard and Bradley crept close to where the figure was for a better shot, while any soldiers with sniper rifles were able to comfortably keep a wider distance. The soldiers that dared to get closer to the figure were able to see more and more masked Chimera soldiers concealing themselves using the forest surroundings.

Once the commander was satisfied that everyone was in position, he gave the order to attack. Richard, Bradley and the soldiers in the frontline were the first to strike as they took aim and fired their bullets at the figure hiding behind the tree. For a brief instant, Bradley winced as he felt the winds ahead intensify amidst the shot and once the gunfire ceased, he looked up to his surprise to see that the shadowy figure was still standing, unscathed.

"How? How did we all miss?!" Bradley grunted out of frustration.

"Calm down!" Richard advised him. "The snipers should be able to take care of it."

Just after he'd said this, the shadowy figure's head popped out from behind the tree trunk and three snipers quickly had it in their line of sights, knowing it would be a certain kill. They each pulled their triggers and the bullets rapidly zipped towards the target.

However yet again, a brief but powerful gale reverberated throughout the timberlands, the ominous chill of the air drawing out goosebumps on the skin of the soldiers and once more, the figure could be seen without a scratch, leaving the soldiers stunned.

"What's going on?!" Richard wondered, becoming concerned.

"Is it the wind, knocking our bullets off course?" Bradley theorised.

"That shouldn't be possible!" Richard snapped. "Our guns and bullets should be able to cut through them! The winds aren't that strong!"

But Bradley wasn't sure of this claim. Looking back, he was certain that the force of the winds increased dramatically at the point when the bullets should have made contact.

It was then that the most inexplicable thing happened. The shadowy figure ahead stepped out from his hiding place and stood out in the open like a sitting duck. And he wasn't the only one. Richard, Bradley and the other soldiers watched bewildered as one by one, more and more masked Chimera soldiers revealed themselves and stood together in unity.

"What are they doing?!" one of the soldiers shouted. "Do they have a death wish?!"

"Something's not right..." Richard commented as he watched the soldiers ahead, gesturing arrogantly at them. "They're taunting us, even though they have no guns of their own. It's like they know something that we don't..."

"Should we consider retreating for now?" Bradley pondered, also believing something was afoot.

"Men!" the commander interrupted. "I've just had a crucial update from Recon! The leader of Chimera is right ahead and approaching!" Richard, Bradley and the other soldiers turned towards the commander, astounded to hear this announcement and knew what this meant. "We're not turning back now! If we kill her, we can end this war! We might not get another chance like this! Keep pushing through them! It's just one last wall to break through!"

With that, a deafening uproar spread throughout the forest as the soldiers launched a full-scale bombardment upon Chimera, unleashing an onslaught of bullets towards the masked soldiers. Richard paused briefly between the gunfire as he spotted clusters of bullets being propelled in all directions as if they were ping pong balls bouncing off a sheet of glass. Some were impaled into tree trunks, splintering them on impact while others landed limply into the mud below. Then he saw all the Chimera soldiers still smugly standing together, no casualties present. His instincts were telling him that something was very wrong and they were proving warranted. Once the commander could see that his soldiers were starting to run out of ammunition and that the guns were having no effect, he knew he had to change tactics.

"Charge them!" he ordered the rest of the men.

On command, Richard, Bradley and the other soldiers drew their swords and ran towards the enemy. In turn, the masked soldiers went on the offensive, drawing their own weapons and rushed to engage. Richard and Bradley could feel the force of the winds against their faces as they closed in on Chimera. It was strong, but it shouldn't have been enough to repel bullets. Yet it did have a foreboding, sinister energy to it that made the hairs of every soldier stand on end.

Finally, the soldiers clashed with one another. The winds carried the clattering of steel and the roars of the warriors upwards to the highest points of the trees. Initially, the numbers on each side were practically even as each soldier tried to gain an advantage. Richard, though inexperienced as a soldier, used his wisdom and outsmarted his opponents by swiping mud into their eyes with his sword to blind them before taking them out, demonstrating a knowledge that exceeded what his potential would have otherwise suggested. Meanwhile, Bradley was younger and quicker, able to outpace his enemies while striking them down with deadly ferocity.

Things looked to take a turn for the worse when the masked soldiers were able to ambush and kill the commander. There was no time to mourn the loss though as Richard and Bradley chased off the surrounding enemies and Richard was quick to take charge and lead the soldiers. He ordered his comrades to work in groups to try and outnumber individual Chimera soldiers. He instructed several of the soldiers to fake a retreat and lure some of Chimera away from this gusty area towards the snipers. From there, he took the transceiver from the commander's blood-stained corpse and ordered the snipers still watching from afar to shoot down any Chimera soldiers that followed their withdrawing comrades.

After employing these strategies, Richard and the other soldiers were able to recover and gain ground. Several Chimera soldiers took the bait and chased after the seemingly fleeing soldiers only to be struck down by the snipers' bullets as planned. This reduced the amount of Chimera soldiers that were fighting in factions, allowing Bradley and the others to outnumber them and whittle their numbers down even further. They also borrowed some of Richard's strategies of using the surroundings to their advantage, such as forcing enemy soldiers to get tangled in vines, using nearby rocks as a weapon and parrying any enemy attacks so that they struck down their own brethren.

Bradley was able to even the score by striking down Chimera's own commander. From this point, it became clear that while Entritica's forces had been trained for battle to ensure that they were prepared, Chimera's own soldiers mostly consisted of amateurs. Entritica were able to adapt after the death of their commander thanks to Richard's improvisation, but in contrast, Chimera were wholly unprepared for the same situation as, exhausted from the fighting, their tactics and teamwork fell apart and many of the masked soldiers started lashing out at any soldier they could find, attacking wildly. Richard, Bradley and their remaining comrades were able to slowly pick off any remaining masked soldiers, more and more blood soaking into the soil below before forcing them to retreat after Bradley struck one final soldier down.

However, in his triumph, Bradley made a rookie error in letting his guard down as the soldier was still alive and quickly shot up and lunged, ready to impale him. Luckily, Richard was quick to spot this and stepped between them, intercepting the attack and fatally stabbing the soldier who remained standing as Richard held his ground.

"Thanks Rich…" Bradley uttered gratefully. "Sorry…"

"Do we follow them, Commander?" one of the other soldiers addressed Richard as the winds continued to howl, accepting him as their new squad leader.

"Yes," Richard answered determined, huffing and puffing, as sweat and blood dripped down his forehead, still holding the terrorist's body upright. "Their leader is up ahead. We kill them and Chimera is finished!"

In that moment, the figure impaled on Richard's sword began to tremble and splutter as he coughed blood from his mouth, still clinging on to life. Then, the windspeeds built up and accelerated through the forest and blew at a force unlike anything the soldiers had felt to this point, breaking several branches and causing the trees to creak and groan. The soldiers staggered as the winds threatened to drive them off their feet and into the mud beneath them, some using their weapons for support to remain standing. Richard himself used the impaled man to stay upright, their foreheads touching each other as he did.

Richard then heard a muffled sound, almost like tittering, underneath the soldier's mask. He removed the mask to look into the eyes of a young, yet weary and bloodied man who began to cackle manically over the howling storm to the discomfort of Bradley and the others. Once his laughter died down, the man slowly spoke and sent a threatening warning to the soldiers:

"Y-you have n-no chance now!" he spluttered, blood trickling down his chin. "She's c-coming…M-Maris is coming…y-you're all…you're all d-dead…now…"

The man's head slumped down as he took his last breath and Richard stepped back, releasing his grip on the sword and watched as the lifeless body collapsed into the soil. The man's final words, the name Maris, echoed hauntingly in the minds of the soldiers while the winds continued to bellow before bizarrely coming to a screeching halt. The soldiers looked around them, hoping that the storm was truly over as the quietness seemed to settle in.

But this feeling of relief and tranquillity was only brief.

It was quickly overtaken by an overwhelming sense of despair within each of the men as the clouds above the trees turned from grey to jet black, completely blocking out any trace of light. While most of the soldiers, including Bradley, were unable to comprehend this feeling, it was one that was all too familiar for Richard. The intense darkness that currently loomed over them felt indistinguishable from the sinister sensation he had experienced from the black aura that potentially saved young Nathan's life – and it was unmistakable.

Richard heard a gasp from one of the soldiers who stumbled back into the mud behind him. He looked back at the man to see his face painted with fear, beads of sweat dripping, mouth agape and his eyes wide open, transfixed on whatever was ahead. The soldiers all slowly turned to see a hooded figure emerge from the shadows of the timberlands.

The hooded figure approached the soldiers gradually but assertively and had an undeniable presence that commanded the attention of every man there. They could feel their chests pounding as the figure got closer and closer to them, the warriors almost instinctively inching backwards with each step that the figure took, trying to get away from the malevolent frosty impulse that was emanating from this ghoul. This was nothing like any of the masked terrorists that Richard and the other soldiers had already fought. This presence was far more demonic, as if they were being confronted with the Devil or Death himself.

Unable to distinguish the full shape of the figure from the shadows, Richard raised his sword, its gleam now being the only shred of light in the persisting darkness. Almost immediately, the figure stopped in response to this, though the air of confidence remained the same. In his sword's reflection, he was able to uncover the face that was underneath the hood. He could make out pale skin, long crimson hair and despite the evil intent that flashed in the eyes, there was still a trace of feminine features in the facial structure.

There was no doubt. This was Maris – the leader of Chimera.

As Maris raised her hand, the winds reappeared and accelerated wildly. The soldiers cowered and shielded themselves as they detected the energy within Maris surging exponentially. Sensing the incoming danger, Richard briefly closed his eyes, let out a deep sigh in acceptance of his sudden responsibility as a leader and called out a hasty order:

"I'll hold her off! All of you, get out of here now!"

Before Bradley or any of the soldiers could act on Richard's command, Richard, positioning himself between her and his comrades, charged directly at Maris. In return, Maris swiftly motioned her arm in the direction of Richard and the soldiers.

In an instant, the force of the gales escalated dramatically, engulfing the soldiers that stood in their path, throwing them upwards into the air at speeds so fierce that their bodies slammed through the thick tree trunks, splintering both bone and bark on impact. The trees themselves were viciously ripped out of the ground as the storm evolved into a full-scale hurricane that drowned out the screams of the men who struggled fruitlessly before succumbing and perishing to the disaster's might, their bodies unable to withstand the intensity with which they collided into the earth below.

The hurricane continued to devastate the woodlands that lay before Maris, transforming a quarter of the entire forest into a wasteland strewn with debris, fractured tree stumps, torn leaves stained with blood and the corpses of the fearless soldiers who had failed to escape, crushed underneath the weight of the timber. What was once a peaceful and beautiful area of the forest had now been rendered into a mass barren graveyard for both plant life and mankind, permanently scarring the landscape itself.

Once the chaotic winds finally subsided, Maris who had stood calmly watching the destruction unfold, continued to advance forward, stepping over fragments of bark as she made her way. The remaining Chimera soldiers re-emerged from behind the area of trees that had been protected from the hurricane's annihilation of the forest by Maris' presence and followed their leader.

Hearing the sounds of Maris' footsteps crack the branches beneath her, Richard, whose body was being compressed by the weight of the fallen trees, began to stir, still barely conscious. His breathing was now disturbed as he could only gasp and wheeze underneath the tree's might, he could no longer move his body which was wracked with pain but could feel his head get lighter as blood trickled from his wounds.

As Maris came into his line of sight, he caught her eye and she briefly stopped to glance at him. Both stared at each other for a moment until Richard's vision began to blur, finally succumbing to blood loss. Maris then turned away and continued her path through the timberland ruins, her cult following behind her devotedly.

Slowly but surely, Richard's consciousness began to fade, with his final thoughts being of his wife Victoria and his son Nathan, hoping that he had done enough to protect them before everything turned to black…

Chapter 1

Three days later, at Silver Dawn Comprehensive School, a secondary school in the country of Entritica across the sea from Lyrasia, the halls and the classrooms were filled with an unsettling silence, accompanied only by the sounds of thick droplets crashing down onto the bricks and cobbles outside.

In the classrooms, the students and the teachers all had their heads bowed at their desks. Since the war began, it had become tradition for there to be a moment of silence whenever it began to rain, as a way of paying respects for the soldiers that were out on the frontlines fighting to protect Entritica, the rain serving as a symbol of the blood, sweat and tears that they sacrificed for the sake of their country.

In particular, one pale, sombre, red-headed student had his hand clutched around the locket that hung down from his neck amidst the quiet – Nathan Bennett. Praying during these moments had more significance for him compared to his classmates as he was the only one with a family member, his father, who was fighting in the war. Whenever he heard the splattering of raindrops now, it was a reminder of what his dad was up against.

The sound of the rain was then briefly drowned out by a bell that chimed four times in succession, alerting everyone that it was now 4 o'clock. Instantly, the students raised their heads and stood up from their desks, the silence now replaced by the clapping of footsteps eagerly making their way out of the classroom and the chattering of excited voices, mostly talking about their plans for the next two weeks. It was the end of term, meaning that the teachers and students were off for two weeks due to the Easter holidays, hence the majority, students and teachers alike, were even happier to finish for the day than normal.

Unlike the other students who rushed out of the classroom, Nathan sluggishly shuffled his way out which was noticed by the boy with messy black hair, the fringe drooping just above his eyes, that sat next to him. Without a word, they exited the classroom together. This was Nathan's best friend, Thomas Cartwright. He already knew why Nathan was so morose –

he had turned sixteen three days ago and it was the first birthday that his dad had missed. Add to that the fact that it had been raining almost constantly for the last three days and it was no wonder why his father's absence was playing on Nathan's mind more than usual. Words were not needed as Thomas was aware that Nathan didn't want to talk right now – but he hoped his company would help him even if it was just a little bit.

As both boys walked through the school corridors towards the exit, they passed by several other groups of students who were also delighted to be finishing for the next two weeks. Some students didn't notice them as they carried on with their day, however a few others either scowled or flashed dirty looks at them. Nathan and Thomas both disregarded them as they just wanted to get out of school now.

One specific pack of four lads, led by the burlier of the boys, and one apprehensive but tomboyish girl with short blonde hair, glanced back at Nathan and Thomas, and began whispering among themselves. Both boys started to slow down, keen to avoid them.

The leader of the group stopped altogether when another girl with black hair caught his attention as she left her locker and walked in the direction of Nathan and Thomas. As she passed them, she looked at Nathan and gave him a brief but sad smile before quickly averting her eyes again. Despite how short-lived it was, Nathan had managed to notice it. She was the only other student who smiled at them or showed them a look of something other than contempt. Without properly realising it, Nathan had instinctively looked back to see where she had gone.

"Nath, look out!" Thomas shouted.

Before he could even turn his head fully, Nathan was knocked flying off his feet and crumpled into a heap on the floor as the stocky boy brutishly barged past him in the direction of the dark-haired girl. As Thomas kneeled down to try and help his friend amidst the stifled sniggers of the rest of the gang, a humiliated Nathan looked back at their supposed kingpin who flickered a callous glare at him, the iciest one he had seen all day with not even a trace of a smirk on his face as he left in pursuit of the girl.

"Just ignore Ranjit," Thomas muttered trying to reassure him. "He's only going after Lucy anyway," to which Nathan nodded glumly, almost with concern upon hearing these words being uttered. Lucy Donovan was a fellow classmate who was timid but kind whereas Ranjit Ali was known around the school as a ruthless thug, despite being the same age as Nathan and Thomas. Many of the students and even teachers were wary of him.

Whilst Nathan tried to compose himself, the first thing that he checked on was the locket around his neck, his hand automatically wrapping around it tenderly to check that it was not damaged. The remainder of Ranjit's crew seemed to spot this as the three boys began mouthing something to the blonde girl. Thomas attempted to help Nathan up to his feet but his feeble arms were barely able to budge him and his legs ended up giving way before he also fell meekly onto the floor, leading to Ranjit's accomplices erupting into howls of laughter at the sight of this. In response to this uproar, the door of the nearby office was flung open as a man wearing glasses and a suit emerged, followed by a tall muscular boy with neat brown hair, dressed in a soldier's uniform.

"What's with all this noise?" the man demanded to know addressing the three troublemakers who suddenly went very quiet. "Dan, Denzel, Drew, I suggest you all head home before you get detention," he warned.

The three boys were quick to scurry away as the girl hesitated. It was then that the young man in the uniform spoke up.

"You're still hanging around with them Abbie? I thought you were better than that..." he chastised with a disapproving look on his face.

Abbie turned red with anger as he said this before she stormed off out the doors following the three other boys. Once they had left, the man with the air of authority around him turned to see Nathan and Thomas still sprawled on the floor.

"Nathan, Thomas, are you two alright?!" the man said as he rushed to help the boys up to their feet.

"Nathan...?" the young man in uniform uttered as he heard his name called out. The colour left his face as he turned to see Nathan being helped to his feet.

"We're okay Mr Jones, thank you," Thomas replied, his teeth gritted in frustration but the gratitude in his voice still shone through. Mr Jones was the headmaster of the school who also led the school's Combined Cadet Force (CCF) society on the back of his previous military experience, so he was able to command respect from most students with little difficulty.

As Nathan rose, he glanced up at the uniformed boy who sheepishly averted his gaze and bit his lip, as if unsure what to say. He was Nathan's cousin, Joshua Griffiths, older than him by two years. He was a prize pupil of Mr Jones, being one of the cadet officers in the CCF society, and had aspirations of joining the army once he left sixth form later that year.

"How did you end up on the floor? Was it Ranjit? You *can* tell me if it was," Mr Jones quizzed the boys, aware of Ranjit's reputation among the students.

"No, we just tripped," Thomas responded quickly, eager to brush the incident aside while Nathan stared pensively at Joshua, wondering why he looked so uncomfortable in his presence. He was accustomed to this reaction from other students around him, but not from his own cousin. Although a gap between them had formed in recent years as Joshua had thrown himself into his army training, it was never to the extent that he couldn't even look Nathan in the eye.

"Well, if you're sure…" Mr Jones commented, his brows furrowed as he gave a rueful smile, not fully convinced by Thomas' explanation. Unexpectedly though, he didn't push the matter any further. "I think you should both be heading home now," he said to both of them yet his head was looking directly at Nathan as he spoke. "You surely don't want to be wasting the start of your Easter break still in school."

"No, of course not," Thomas agreed. He moved to leave but stopped when he saw that Nathan was still stood there, his head pivoting as he examined Mr Jones' and Joshua's faces, one after the other – from the way their pupils flickered, he could tell that something was amiss. "Nathan," Thomas called, finally catching his attention. "Let's go," he pulled at his friend's arm, guiding him out towards the end of the corridor. Nathan looked back before exiting to see Joshua and Mr Jones watching them leave.

They silently made their way out of the school grounds, trying to cover themselves from the deluge of rain as they did so. As the drops continued to beat down onto the ground beneath them, Nathan thought about how Joshua and Mr Jones behaved around him; how Joshua practically shunned him; how Mr Jones specifically focused on him when telling them to go home; how both stayed behind to observe them leaving the building before they continued on with their own business. He spun the locket around in his hand as these concerns persisted in his mind. He couldn't get past how unusual these interactions were and there was a churning sensation in his gut. *Could these instances really just be coincidence?* he thought to himself.

As Nathan and Thomas approached the school gates, the former felt an unease wash over him. In the corner of his eye, Nathan spotted two shadows vanish behind the fence as quickly as they appeared. Instinctively, he held out his arm in front of Thomas indicating for him to stop.

"Is someone there?" Nathan called out, speaking for the first time that afternoon, his voice trembling as he did so. No movement or response could be heard over the rainfall that continued to pour down upon them.

"It's probably nothing," Thomas rationalised as the grey skies loomed over the school. "Nath, we need to hurry up else we'll get soaked."

Nathan wondered if Thomas was right. Maybe he really was just being paranoid, especially after the events just a few minutes ago and he could feel the rain getting thicker and heavier. They both continued to walk towards the gates, being sure to avoid the puddles that began to form on the pavement.

Once again, Nathan felt the same ominous foreboding sensation that he was being watched and when he looked at the fence, he was certain he could see the outline of a boy's head disappearing behind the bricks. His shaking subsided as his nerves turned to frustration and he ran ahead of Thomas, to his surprise, and dashed through the gates.

"Whoever's there, just stop hiding and come out!" Nathan shouted as he stood outside the gateway. He searched around, waiting for some mystery person to appear but it didn't happen and he could feel his surge of bravado declining again.

"Behind you, Nath!" he heard Thomas call out desperately.

Hearing this, Nathan went into a blind panic and quickly turned around, instinctively raising his scrawny arms to cover himself. Whether it be by intense nerves or the continuous rainfall, his vision was obscured as a mysterious figure reached out towards him and he clenched his eyes shut out of terror of what was about to happen…

"Oh, not you again!" Thomas groaned as Nathan heard his voice close by.

Nathan slowly opened his eyes to see that Abbie was standing smugly in front of him. He then heard the cackles of laughter coming from near the school walls and turned to see Dan, Denzel and Drew emerging from behind their cover. Nathan let out an exasperated sigh as it dawned on him that he was the victim of a prank once again.

"So what, Joshua called you out, now you take it out on me, the runt?" Nathan wearily probed Abbie, recalling how embarrassed she became after his cousin's earlier remark. Abbie Westbrook had only been at this school for several months after previously getting expelled and had already fallen into a bad crowd with Ranjit's gang who enjoyed regularly tormenting Nathan and Thomas.

"Sh-shut up!" Abbie spluttered as her cheeks ripened to a shameful shade of scarlet. She looked back at the other lads. "Alright, I've done your stupid dare, now what?" she asked them.

"C'mon, mess about with him some more!" Dan hissed to her from a distance.

"Seriously, just leave him alone!" Thomas yelled at Abbie and the others, his patience wearing thin.

Hearing Abbie and Dan's brief exchange, Nathan wondered what Abbie's dare was. He moved his hand over his heart, trying to calm it down as it furiously pulsated. It was then that he realised that something was missing from his chest – his locket! His pupils wildly darted to Abbie's hand and there, he could see the locket dangling from the chain which was clutched in her fist. While the chain was gold, the locket itself was a black circular shape with a brilliant golden dragon in the centre.

"Abbie," Nathan spoke firmly but with a slight waver in his voice as he fought to control his emotions. "Give that back," he ordered softly, gesturing to her hand that was holding the locket. Thomas, who hadn't yet realised what Abbie had done, listened intently to Nathan's faint voice which was barely audible over the worsening rainfall.

"Oh, you mean this?" Abbie responded casually, raising her arm to hold the locket in front of Nathan's face as Dan, Denzel and Drew continued to egg her on. Thomas' eyes widened in terror as it became clear what Abbie had taken from Nathan who now had a steely, unflinching expression painted on his visage. "And why should I?" Abbie goaded as her fingers wrapped themselves around the shiny metal chain, toying with it as if it were any other trinket.

"I'm not messing around, Abbie," Nathan warned her, his voice getting lower as he witnessed Abbie playing with the locket and heard the jeers of the lads in the background, spinelessly hiding behind her. A tingle travelled down Thomas' spine as he could detect Nathan's anger silently building. "Give it back now," he stated once more.

"Seriously Abbie, do what he says!" Thomas barked, the crack of panic in his voice catching Abbie's attention.

"What's the big deal?" she asked perplexed. "It's just a necklace."

"That *necklace*," Nathan uttered, his teeth grinding together as the words left his mouth, "is the last thing that my dad gave me before he joined the war!" Abbie's expression softened upon hearing this, but Nathan continued, "It might mean *nothing* to you, but to me, that could easily be the last memory I have of him. So I'll ask you one more time." His voice now barely more than a whisper, Nathan made the final demand. "Give me. My *dad's* locket. Now."

After hearing Nathan's plea, Abbie looked down at the locket, softly unclenching her fist as she did so, rain dripping down her hair and onto the gold dragon. It was an unusual but beautiful design and as Abbie examined it with Nathan's words about his dad echoing in her mind, she looked at it in a different way than she did when she snatched it from Nathan's neck, a sense of shame brewing in her for not appreciating the value that it had to someone else. While Dan, Denzel and Drew continued to taunt from behind her, she looked back at them, her eyes once sparkling with a desire for approval now dulled to a scowl of disgust. Lastly, she looked back at Nathan, properly seeing the stony seriousness etched on his face for the first time. It wasn't just that though. Despite his feeble exterior, Abbie detected a dangerous energy exuding from within him which caused her arms to flare up with a cluster of goosebumps. She had never once thought of Nathan as intimidating before and yet here she stood before him, beads of rain and sweat trickling down her forehead. She couldn't explain why she felt this way but wondered if this was why Thomas was so insistent that she did what Nathan said. But now knowing how cruel her actions had been, she knew what she had to do.

"Okay," Abbie muttered to Nathan, nodding her head in agreement. "You can have it back. Here…"

Abbie lightly threw the locket towards Nathan, taking him by surprise. He threw up his hands to catch the locket but as it landed in his palms, moistened from the rain, it slipped straight back out, Nathan's relief turning to terror as it happened, and dropped down past the pavement and into the roadside gutter. Before either Nathan, Thomas or Abbie could act to prevent what happened next, the locket was swept away by the rapid current of rainwater until it disappeared down the nearby drain.

Nathan and Thomas rushed to the drain and desperately scrambled around on their hands and knees, trying to reach through the grate hoping that they could pull the locket back to the surface. Abbie stepped forward wanting to try and help but her body became paralysed by an overwhelming sense of shock and guilt for what she had just done and all she could do was watch. The seconds passed and Nathan could feel the sinking pit of despair and regret in his stomach as the slow realisation set in that he had truly lost his dad's locket. But this was soon replaced by an intense sensation bubbling within him, his heart beating so viciously that it felt like it would rip out of his chest, his blood boiling as the mocking laughter of Dan, Denzel and Drew rang through his ears, even over the smacking sounds of thick rain drops plunging into the puddles around him.

"I'm sorry, Nathan," Abbie squeaked remorsefully. "I didn't mean to-"

In that instant, everything went hazy for Nathan with only the image of his father's locket vanishing down the drain playing through his mind, accompanied by the relentless ridiculing cackles of the three thugs hiding away in the background, the noise seemingly getting louder and louder. Seconds later, there was another sound mixed in with the laughter that Nathan could make out. It was only faint the first time, but it was louder the second time. Then the third time, he realised it was the sound of his name being called. And then the fourth time, it even overpowered the laughter which was now replaced by a violent shaking felt through his whole body.

"NATHAN!!!!" Thomas screamed desperately. "NATHAN, STOP!!!"

Hearing this, the mist within Nathan's mind faded and with it, so too did the visions of the locket and the haunting sounds of endless laughter. In its place was the sight of Thomas' face, red with anger yet he could also see the concern in his eyes through the damp strands of hair that hung over them. Confused at first, Nathan slowly twisted his head to look in front of him before realising why.

Before him, he saw Abbie, face drained of colour and eyes wide open in shock. He saw his hand clasped onto Abbie's shoulder and she had her back against the school fence. Nathan had no recollection of how he got from pawing at the drain trying to retrieve his locket to pinning Abbie's shoulder to the fence, but horrified, he stumbled backwards, his body splattering into one of the puddles below.

Abbie stepped forward, still shell-shocked and unsure what to do, whether to help Nathan to his feet or to flee. In the end, her body seemed to seize up as she looked at Nathan sitting pitifully on the wet pavement and all she could do was mouth the words *I'm sorry* to him before she ran away, past Dan, Denzel and Drew without even acknowledging them this time.

Nathan and Thomas watched her retreat and scowled in the direction of the other boys who also took their leave but not before getting one final dig in.

"Looks like *Dragon Boy* is back! See you around, you *freak*!" Denzel taunted, the others laughing as they departed the scene, leaving Nathan and Thomas alone together again, Thomas looking down at Nathan who was still on the ground, his clothes soaked by the rain now.

"Nathan, what the hell happened there?!" Thomas demanded to know. Nathan paused for a while before answering as he tried to process what has just occurred.

"I-I don't even know," Nathan stammered. "E-everything just went black, I-I don't remember anything. Tom, w-what did I do?" he pleaded frantically.

Thomas shook his head before answering. "Well one minute, we were both trying to get your locket back; the next thing I know, you'd shot up and pushed her all the way to the fence! I tried to break you two apart but it was like you were possessed!"

Nathan thought back to how frightened Abbie looked. "Tell me," Nathan spoke, tightly closing his eyes as he did so, "please tell me I didn't hurt her!"

"No, she was just spooked. You didn't hurt her thankfully," Thomas reassured Nathan to his relief. "But it really felt like you wanted to," he added honestly, recalling a malicious energy emanating from Nathan during the scuffle. "I've never seen you that angry before."

Nathan knew Thomas was right. He looked back at the drain as water flowed in like a river and rain continued to bounce off the metal. All it reminded him of now was the pit of rage that stewed within him after he'd lost his dad's locket and been tormented by Ranjit's gang one time too many. Yet he felt it had been simmering for the last three days since his birthday, the consistent rainfall constantly reminding him of his dad's absence. *Is this the result of everything getting on top of him all at once?* he wondered.

"I'm sorry about your dad's locket," Thomas said compassionately. "You've got enough going on and if I was in your shoes, I'd have probably lost it too."

Nathan finally struggled back to his feet, but still downcast over the events of the day. "I just want to go home now..." he mumbled quietly.

"Yeah of course, we'll catch the flu if we stay out here any longer," Thomas replied trying to diffuse the situation, though now shivering as he felt his rain-sodden clothes compress against his skin. Before Nathan could leave, Thomas had some parting words for him. "Nath, if you need to talk or anything during the holidays, just text me or give me a call. I'll help in any way I can…" he expressed.

"Yeah I know, thanks," Nathan acknowledged appreciatively. "Same goes for you."

Both boys said their farewells before leaving the area. On his way home, Nathan tried to empty his mind of what had transpired earlier with Abbie and the rest of Ranjit's motley crew, but the thoughts continued to persist within his head. Eager to avoid the rain as much as he could, he ended up trying to run part of the way there, avoiding the puddles where possible before quickly getting a stitch in his side and having to rest until the aching went away. Never one to enjoy physical activity for this very reason, Nathan didn't actually mind the pain this time as it was a brief distraction from thinking about everything else. The rest of the journey home was more of the same with Nathan gaining a brief burst of energy until he succumbed to the agony of another muscle cramping up, as if he was plodding along for cross country until he found himself outside the door of his home.

Relieved to at last get refuge from the rain, Nathan threw the front door open, breathing heavily as he unloaded his backpack from his shoulders and wrung out any excess water from his clothes. Once he had composed himself, Nathan realised that something was odd – his mom hadn't come to the door to greet him as she usually did by now.

"Mom?" Nathan called out from the hallway. No answer. He wiped his shoes on the mat beneath him before removing them from his throbbing feet. He then warily made his way through the living room towards the kitchen and dining room. As he entered, he saw his mom, Victoria Bennett, sitting at the dining table with her back to him.

"Mom?" Nathan uttered softly to which Victoria turned round to face him.

"Nathan…" she squeaked solemnly, her face red and the cheeks under her eyes damp.

Taken aback to see his mother so upset, Nathan spotted something on the table in the corner of his eye. It was an opened letter in a crimson red envelope.

In that instant, Nathan's heart plummeted. He knew the significance of this envelope as it was a well-known custom to receive one only during a time of war in Entritica. It was something that the armed forces specifically sent out as condolences to the families of soldiers who had been killed in action. For a letter to be here in their house, Nathan knew it could only mean one thing.

"No…" he gasped, devastated.

"I'm so sorry Nathan…" Victoria sobbed as she burst into tears, confirming Nathan's worst fears. His father, Richard Bennett, was dead.

Nathan delicately moved towards his mom, embracing her as they both mutually mourned the loss of their departed husband and father.

❊❈❉❈❊

Chapter 2

Two weeks had passed since Nathan and Victoria had learned about Richard's death and the Easter holiday was now drawing to a close. After struggling to get their way through the holiday in the aftermath of their loss, there was one more thing that needed to be done.

During the break, they had been notified of a funeral service to be held in Richard's honour on the final Friday of the holiday. It was a custom in Entritica for the Armed forces to arrange the memorial for the fallen soldiers, partly to pay respect for how they had died in service for their country and partly to take away from the families of the deceased the burden of arranging the funeral themselves.

Today, the day of the memorial to Richard had finally arrived as Nathan and Victoria, both dressed in mournful black, sombrely sat in their hearse which travelled towards the cemetery. Nathan gazed out the window and although it was not raining today, he could see the gloomy clouds shrouding the sky, high above the mountains that circled their province like a fortress. Sensing a movement on the seat beside him, he glanced back to see Victoria's hand resting on the seat but outreached towards him. Nathan placed his own hand in Victoria's palm and she squeezed it affectionately, both silently consoling one another since anything that could be said at this point between the two had already been done so over the last fortnight. Now they just had to support each other on this day for Richard's sake.

Once the hearse had reached the destination, the driver opened the door for Victoria and Nathan to exit where they were greeted by two family members wearing suits – Victoria's older brother and Nathan's uncle, Clint Griffiths, along with his son and Nathan's cousin, Joshua. Clint embraced his sister Victoria as Nathan and Joshua could still only awkwardly acknowledge each other.

"I'm so sorry," Clint whispered as he hugged Victoria.

"I really miss him…" Victoria sighed into her brother's shoulder.

"We all do Vic," Clint echoed. "We all do…"

"To think our roles would reverse like this," Victoria joked darkly, stifling a sob as she tried to mask her sorrow.

"I know, I know," Clint responded with a sad smile. "Both lost our parents. Now our partners. And so young too," he pondered reflectively. "Anyone would think we were cursed or something..."

"Can you stop with that today or are you trying to set me off?" Victoria sarcastically asked as she wiped at her eyes.

"Right, sorry," Clint said as he let go of her. "Wish I was better at this."

Victoria looked at Nathan. "Make sure your phone's turned off before we go in," she ordered.

Nathan nodded and took his phone out of his pocket ready to switch it off. As he did so, he saw a sole message on the screen from Thomas that said *Thoughts are with you today Nath* to which he took a few moments to appreciate before clicking the phone's power button. He then walked into the cemetery along with his remaining family, staying close to Victoria with both her and Clint in between him and Joshua.

Once they walked through the gates, Nathan noticed that the cemetery was filled with a massive amount of people for one ceremony, women carrying flowers and wreaths, adorned in black dresses and veils while the men wore courteous suits, something that he found odd given that Richard had no other close friends or familial ties. He searched around to see if he could recognise any of their faces, but he couldn't.

"Mom, who are all these people?" Nathan asked her with a puzzled expression.

"I-I don't know," Victoria retorted, equally perplexed as she too surveyed the area. "Richard was always about family before anything else, I have no idea how he'd know many other people, let alone this many. Do you know any of them, Clint?"

Similarly, Clint was also unable to provide an answer. However, as Nathan looked to see Clint's reaction, he saw Joshua fidget uncomfortably in the corner of his eye, his face again turning pale as he pursed his dry lips together.

"Do *you* know anything about this Josh?" Nathan questioned.

Joshua's eyes widened nervously upon being asked this and as Victoria and Clint also turned to look at him, he seemed to clam up before the four of them were welcomed by another familiar face.

"Joshua, Nathan, it's good to see you both, all being considered of course," greeted Mr Jones, their headmaster, as he approached them.

"You're here too, sir?" Nathan retorted, taken aback at seeing him here.

"Indeed, I am Nathan," Mr Jones acknowledged before turning to Victoria. "I'm so sorry for your and Nathan's loss, Mrs Bennett. You have my sincerest condolences," he said to her kind-heartedly as he shook her and Clint's hands.

"Mr Jones, do you know why there are so many people here for Richard?" Victoria asked him, still trying to take everything in.

Mr Jones' face turned red when questioned about this, seemingly embarrassed. "W-were you not informed?" he responded and as he said this, Nathan spotted his eyes briefly shift to Joshua's direction who, again, averted his gaze. After an awkward but brief silence, Mr Jones explained, "I apologise, it seems there has been some miscommunication. I helped to organise this ceremony along with current army officers to allow families and loved ones to pay respects to *all* the soldiers who recently passed away in service. So while it is a memorial for Richard, it is likewise a memorial to honour his fellow soldiers and comrades who also lost their lives. And all of their names are engraved on that stone plaque in tribute to their sacrifices."

Mr Jones pointed out the tablet as he spoke which was erected in the middle of the cemetery. Nathan's eyes followed the headmaster's finger to see the tablet standing tall above the crowds of mourners. Although he couldn't read them from this distance, he could make out numerous carvings in the stone, neatly arranged in columns. Mr Jones and the two parents continued to talk but as they did so, their voices became fuzzier and more distorted to Nathan as he could only concentrate on the sheer number of inscriptions that he could estimate. Eventually, as Mr Jones managed to amicably settle any misunderstandings with Victoria and Clint, Nathan snapped out of his trance and uttered two words so quietly that they were barely a whisper:

"How many?"

This didn't go unnoticed by Victoria who called out his name, "Nathan…?"

Turning to face Mr Jones, Nathan elaborated on his question. "How many were killed?" he requested bluntly. When Mr Jones hesitated to answer, Nathan insisted on knowing. "There's over a thousand people here. Something big must have happened to warrant a gathering this size. How many soldiers were killed?!" he demanded desperately. Mr Jones regarded Nathan sympathetically before finally answering.

"Over three hundred..." he commented regretfully.

A disconcerting silence washed over Nathan, Victoria, Clint and Joshua as this information sunk in, their minds flooded with horrifying thoughts as they tried to fathom or rationalise how so many soldiers could have perished.

"I'm sorry to have to tell you this," Mr Jones continued, intent on breaking the tension.

"Do you know anything about how this happened?" Nathan quickly questioned, his mind frantic with scenarios of what could have caused this.

"I'm afraid I don't," Mr Jones answered gently as he shook his head. "I too, was shocked by how many had been killed, but sadly, these are the unfair realities of war."

"And when did you find out about their deaths? About my dad?!" Nathan asked, almost as if interrogating his headmaster now.

"Nathan, calm down," Victoria interrupted but Nathan remained adamant in wanting to know this.

"I remember, that last day before the holiday," Nathan recalled aloud. "You were really pushing for me to go home that day. Did you know then?"

After pausing for a while, Mr Jones finally sighed and answered Nathan's question. "Yes, I only found out that same day," he confessed, "I'm sorry, it didn't seem appropriate for you to hear it from me..."

Upon hearing this, Nathan's eyes darted to where Joshua was standing. Seeing the guilty expression that was plastered across his face, Nathan's suspicions were confirmed.

"You knew too, didn't you?" Nathan boldly accused his cousin. Victoria and Clint also looked at Joshua who initially became flustered, but after Mr Jones reassuringly placed his hand on his shoulder, he accepted that he couldn't hide the truth any longer.

"I'm sorry, Nathan, but it wasn't my place to tell you either," Joshua explained, finally speaking to him for the first time. Feeling betrayed and abandoned by his cousin, Nathan's resentment erupted into an outburst.

"So is that why you've been avoiding me?! Out of guilt for being a liar?!" Nathan exclaimed angrily, his heart beating rapidly and his breathing heavy as he struggled to contain his frustration. "And what about all the other times this year when dad *was* away?! I know how much joining the army means to you, but where the hell were you when I needed you?!"

"Nathan, that's enough!" Victoria sternly insisted as she sensed that things were getting out of hand. "Let's not do this here. Not today," she told him, her voice softening now. "Today's about respecting the fallen. We can resolve anything else later, okay?"

Hearing her words and not wanting to make a scene at the ceremony that would honour his father, Nathan nodded in agreement to Victoria's proposition. However, he still glared coldly at a now ashamed Joshua, still unable to forgive him for hearing of his father's fate before him. With the sight of his cousin making him angrier though, he turned away only to face the memorial tablet once again. Amid a mixture of emotions upon seeing the place where his dad's name was etched from a distance, he felt compelled to go there and see the names for himself.

"Mom, do you mind if I get a closer look at the tablet?" Nathan asked Victoria. "I just need to get some space for a bit…"

"Yes, of course," Victoria replied gently as she gave her blessing. "I'll come and find you there before the service starts."

Nathan agreed and thanked Victoria before wandering away from the group while Joshua and Clint were now talking with Mr Jones about Joshua's intentions to enlist in the army after finishing sixth form in a few months. Nathan made his way towards the giant plaque, meandering past various groups of mourners and families, mostly consoling one another over the losses of their loved ones.

It wasn't the only thing he heard from the crowds though. While making his way across the cemetery, Nathan's ears picked up specific things that were being muttered by certain individuals. On one instance, he heard mention that the Entritican government had intentionally sent the soldiers to their deaths as part of a failed strategy. Another voice claimed that the opposition had a hidden weapon that had wiped out their forces on the battlefield. There was even speculation that the Entritican armies had been sabotaged by their own weapons' suppliers. Nathan tried to block these opinions out. His mind had tormented him enough over these last two weeks of what could have happened to his dad and unless anything was confirmed for definite, he had to take anything he heard as mere rumours. Yet, the amount of different conspiracy theories spiralling around was curious. No matter how much he tried to think otherwise, part of his mind was still telling Nathan that there was something more to the situation than he knew.

As he approached the memorial tablet, Nathan did spot another person covered by a cloak at the foot of the stone slab, head covered by a hood but raised up as it looked up and down along the engravings. While the presence of a hood was unusual as there was no forecast for rain today in spite of the grey clouds above, Nathan just took this to be another bystander, lost in thought as they paid respects to a fallen relative and didn't consider him too much as he moved closer to look at the inscriptions.

This, however, turned out to be a mistake as the cloaked figure turned round suddenly and rushed backwards as Nathan was in his blind spot, accidentally knocking him to the ground. The figure seemed anxious and fidgety as they debated what to do until finally extending a hand out to Nathan who was dusting the grass clippings off from his body. Looking up and seeing the hand, Nathan reached out and accepted the help. He felt no annoyance towards the stranger – instead, he blamed himself for just assuming that they wouldn't move from where they were standing. But as the figure helped Nathan to his feet, he caught a brief glimpse of the face underneath the hood. He knew that he recognised that face and before the figure could make a hasty exit, Nathan held his hand firmly, preventing the stranger from escaping much to their shock.

"You…you're Bradley Butcher, aren't you?" Nathan whispered quietly. The figure was left wide-eyed and speechless so Nathan continued. "It's me, Nathan. Nathan Bennett. We went to Silver Dawn together, but I was three years below you." Still, the figure didn't respond as the colour faded from his face, almost in a stunned paralysis. "You remember, right? You know, the-" He hesitated before finishing his sentence, his teeth gritted as he tried to repress painful memories. "The *Dragon Boy*?" he uttered reluctantly.

At last, the figure responded to Nathan's questions. "Y-yeah I remember you. And yeah, it's me, Bradley," Bradley confirmed in what was no more than a hushed murmur.

"You joined the army after you left school," Nathan recollected aloud. "Is that why you're here? Did you know my dad? Richard Bennett?" he continued to bombard Bradley with questions. Hearing Richard's name and triggered by memories of fighting alongside him, Bradley stumbled over his words but Nathan caught a look in Bradley's eyes that gave the truth away. "You did know him, didn't you?!" he exclaimed eagerly. "Please, I need to know what happened to him! How did he die? Who killed him?" he pleaded, desperate for answers while he sub-consciously tightened his grip on Bradley's hand.

Again though, Bradley froze upon being interrogated like this, breathing rapidly as he dealt with the trauma that he experienced in the previous battle. Trying to calm him down, Nathan examined the young man closer and realised that underneath the cloak, Bradley's other arm was missing. Seeing this, Nathan attempted to relax his approach.

"Sorry, I didn't mean to spook you," Nathan said reassuringly. "If possible, I'd like to know, did you know my dad well?" he asked in a much gentler tone, his grip on Bradley's hand softening, yet still remaining firm.

Bradley's heavy breathing began to settle as he saw Nathan compose himself more. Now that the pressure on him had seemingly lessened, he was able to find his words easier. "Yes, I did," he answered after a brief pause. "We joined at around the same time when the war started, but he was like a mentor to me. When he learned that I came from Silver Dawn like you, he took me under his wing. To him, I was probably a reminder of you."

Nathan couldn't help but smile after hearing this. "Did he talk about me and Mom much?" he requested, keen to hear of how Richard coped during the war.

"Oh, all the time," Bradley responded, now smiling back at Nathan as he reminisced about his time with Richard, his shields starting to lower. "We both used to talk about our families before we went into battle. I'd talk about my Gill and he'd always gush about you and Victoria. It was our incentive to endure and survive. He really thought the world of both of you and he was one of the bravest men I'd ever met – a true leader."

Nathan beamed with pride at hearing these words, knowing that his dad constantly had his family on his mind and in his heart. It brought him a peace deep down that he had not felt for the last two weeks since his passing.

"Are there any other soldiers around here who have stories about my dad?" Nathan asked. "I'd love to hear some more."

As he finished his sentence, Nathan caught Bradley's glowing expression darken once more, the smile vanishing from his face and his eyes almost zoning out. This surprised Nathan since he thought the earlier tension between them had been resolved.

"It doesn't have to be loads of them," Nathan elaborated, hoping he hadn't said something out of turn. "Even just one other soldier that dad was friends with would be enough."

Again, Bradley failed to respond, only managing to quiver his lips slightly. Confused, Nathan looked around briefly to see if any other soldiers, whether disguised or not, were nearby. But he didn't see anybody. Then all of a sudden, an epiphany struck Nathan as he glanced back at the sheer volume of names that were listed on the tablet that towered over him. When his eyes returned to a shaken Bradley, it dawned on him why he had come here.

"Are you the only survivor?" Nathan whispered to him.

Although Bradley did not answer, his reaction confirmed Nathan's theory as his face turned paler than ever before and sweat started to pour profusely from his brow underneath his hood. Taken aback by this realisation, Nathan's clasp on Bradley's hand went limp, and in a panic, Bradley yanked his hand free of Nathan's grip to clutch his chest as his breaths became quicker and heavier.

"I sh-" Bradley stuttered between gasps for air. "I sh-shouldn't have c-come here!"

Nathan watched Bradley as he hyperventilated, unsure what to do as he himself was reeling from the revelation that Bradley was the sole survivor. He sympathised with Bradley for what he had withstood, but similarly, the mystery over what they had been up against had thickened even further and this may be his only chance to uncover the truth.

"Bradley, please," Nathan pleaded one more time. "What happened out there?"

Bradley jerked round to face Nathan, his eyes now frantically bulging from his face. "Richard died protecting me! Okay?!" he cried out, unable to contain his guilt and emotions anymore. "They all did! I s-shouldn't be here, I should be w-with them! I-I'm sorry!" he gasped as he held back tears of grief.

Nathan pitifully regarded Bradley, a man broken by war standing before him. As Bradley turned away to make his leave, Nathan regretfully accepted that he would be unable to provide anything more substantial about what he'd barely survived against, not in his current state. So he reluctantly opted to let Bradley go – but not before giving some parting words to him.

"Bradley," Nathan called out to him which made Bradley stop in his tracks, though he did not look back at him. "Thanks for sharing what you did about my dad. It meant the world to me. And thanks…for being there for him when he needed you."

After hearing Nathan's heartfelt message, Bradley slightly turned his head to look at him one more time. Nathan was only able to see his eye from the side, but he could make out the tear drops that were gliding down his cheek. There were no more words exchanged between the two of them, just an unspoken understanding of the pain they both felt in their hearts on this day. Once the moment had passed, Bradley departed, hood and cloak draped over him, as Nathan watched him disappear into the crowd.

By himself once more, Nathan turned towards the memorial, his eyes following the massive lists of names from the top to the bottom, searching for his father's name in the mix. Eventually, he found it towards the left of the tablet at the same height as his shoulder, engraved in glorious gold – Richard Bennett.

Seeing the name in that moment, Nathan instinctively reached out towards his chest, only to feel the crushing disappointment when he remembered that his father's locket was no longer there. He bit his lip as he tried to block out any thoughts and memories of his dad that might make him break down in tears, fighting the overwhelming urge to do so – he had secretly promised to himself that he would be strong for his mother today. Instead, his mind drifted back to speculation of what could have caused this day to happen, to have brought about the deaths of countless soldiers. Knowing now that only Bradley survived, Nathan contemplated the conspiracies that he had heard previously from the other mourners. Rather than dismissing them this time, he began to question whether there was a grain of truth in there somewhere.

While he concentrated on this, it was a temporary relief from the pain that he felt, a distraction. To Nathan, it felt good to not feel that anguish and, in his mind, he began to rationalise that this was the only way to come to terms with losing his dad. He knew he needed answers and if nobody was going to tell him the truth of what really happened, he decided that he would uncover it himself.

"Nathan, are you okay?" he heard a voice call out to him. Nathan snapped out of his trail of thought and saw his mom standing behind him. He meekly nodded his head to her.

"Is the ceremony about to start?" Nathan asked.

"Yeah, there's about five minutes now," Victoria confirmed. "I came over to see how you were. I know things got a bit heated earlier with Joshua. Look, it must have been really difficult for him to know that about your dad and have to keep it from you. It was *my* responsibility to tell you, not his, so please don't be too hard on him for that. But you did mention that he hasn't been around to help you much recently." Nathan's eyes widened after remembering that he did blurt this out. "You haven't talked much about school over the last few months and you must have had a lot on your mind with Richard not being here. Have you been okay there? Is there anything that I need to know?" she questioned, concerned.

"No, I've been okay," Nathan quickly answered but felt a pang of guilt in his chest as the words left his mouth. He hadn't told Victoria about his and Thomas' recent run-ins with Ranjit, Dan, Denzel and Drew as he felt she had enough going on with Richard's absence. He certainly hadn't mentioned anything about his unexplained outburst towards Abbie after losing the locket, partly because he learned of his dad's death only less than an hour later. This time, Victoria stepped closer to Nathan and placed her hands affectionately on his shoulders so that she could look directly in his eyes.

"Please, Nathan. If there's *anything* you ever want to tell me, you can," she declared. "You've been so quiet this holiday since losing your dad, and I know you're trying to be brave for me but you *don't* have to do that. You're my only son and I promised Richard that I would protect you and I won't let you or him down. Please don't bottle everything up like you did before. I can't lose you too…"

"And I can't lose you," Nathan agreed, his eyes unblinking as he faced his mother. After a moment's silence between the two, both pulled the other in for an embrace, holding each other tightly but tenderly. "I will be okay, Mom," Nathan whispered reassuringly to her, a smile of relief spreading on Victoria's face as they hugged. She directed her eyes towards the area of the memorial that Nathan had been looking at and saw the engraving of Richard's name there.

"You found his name…" Victoria uttered as they each released one another. She then carefully stepped towards the engraving, placing her hand affectionately over Richard's name. Nathan watched her as she closed her eyes and muttered a few words quietly to herself. They were faint but Nathan could just make out what she said:

"Goodbye my love…I swear I'll protect Nathan…"

Victoria stepped away from the tablet as she and Nathan heard a bell sound in the distance. Nathan looked back to see the crowds of people start to shuffle in the direction of where Mr Jones was standing at the plinth a few yards away from the memorial.

"It must be starting," Victoria realised. "Nathan, we should go and find Clint and Joshua." But having seen Victoria make her promise to Richard's engraving, Nathan wanted a chance to do the same thing.

"Mom, can I just have a quick moment to-" he asked, stumbling over his words and gesturing towards his father's name. Luckily, Victoria was quick on the uptake.

"Yes, of course," she replied, respectfully stepping aside to give Nathan a brief moment alone by his dad's engraving. Nathan, like Victoria did, placed his hand gently over the carving, his fingers stroking over the scores that had been cut into the stone.

"Dad..." he muttered, pausing for thought as he searched for the words submerged deep in his mind and speaking again once they had surfaced. "I-I will protect Mom...l-like you would have wanted..." he stammered anxiously. "A-and..." he thought to himself as he remembered his earlier turmoil, before Victoria's interruption, about all the possible reasons for Richard's death and what or who could have been behind it. With the potential conspiracies swirling around in his head, a surge of conviction brewed within him. "And I swear I'll find out who did this to you!" he vowed fiercely, his head lifting upwards to look upon the other names honoured on the tablet, their gold tint now illuminated by the sun that poked out from behind the clouds for what felt like the first time in weeks. "To all of you..." he finished decisively.

With his promise made, Nathan returned to Victoria as they walked together towards the funeral service organised by Mr Jones, the clouds starting to shift bit by bit as the sun shone its light down upon them. Nathan intended to get through the rest of the day as originally planned, but after the service was completed, he knew what he would do next. He had a renewed purpose - investigating the secrets and mysteries surrounding the deaths of these soldiers, to find out who or what they were fighting and hunt out any evidence that may suggest foul play. No matter what, he was determined to find the truth because right now, although he couldn't explain why, it felt like the last meaningful thing that he could do for his late father, Richard Bennett...

⊶⊷⟨⟩⊶⊷

Chapter 3

It had been three days since the mass memorial service had taken place for Richard and the other fallen soldiers. Nathan was quickly getting into his school uniform as the sun began to rise from outside his bedroom window. The Easter holiday had now ended which meant it was time to return to school. Nathan rushed down the stairs, buttoning his shirt up as Victoria waited for him at the doorway, holding his bag containing his books for him.

"Are you really sure you want to go back today?" she asked him curiously. "Mr Jones told me that you could take some more time off until you're ready to return," Victoria reminded him, feeling that it was too soon for him to go to school in the wake of Richard's death.

"Well, I'm ready now," Nathan stated determinedly as he took his bag from his mom.

"And you're *sure* you don't want me to give you a lift to school?" Victoria offered once more.

"Yeah, I'm sure," Nathan answered frankly. "I could do with the walk. Fresh air will do me some good."

"Okay, just be careful then," Victoria accepted as Nathan stepped outside and made his way down the driveway, waving goodbye to his mom as he passed the car. "And don't push yourself too hard!" she called out before he disappeared from her view.

As soon as Victoria was out of sight, Nathan hastily pulled his phone out from his pocket and started looking through the news bulletins on the internet. On his journey to school, each time he clicked on the link to an article related to the war, it came up with the same message, *'domain no longer exists'*. Nathan had expected this by now but was getting frustrated. The past few days had taught him that any active internet reports about the war were scarce, not being able to find any reference of the incident in which his father and hundreds of other soldiers were killed, something that he found peculiar given that Entritica was involved in the war.

The only thing of note was that the country they were warring with was Etracova. It struck a chord with Nathan as he knew that it was where his dad had originally been born. Other than that, Richard hardly ever spoke of his time there besides a few stories from his childhood that he retold to Nathan when he was young. Then again, Richard was only young when he left Etracova, so he'd just assumed that he had very few memories of his homeland, especially as his father had always told Nathan that Entritica was his home. But Nathan knew that Etracova was a poor country and not a global superpower so couldn't understand why there would be so much secrecy around the war. Nevertheless, it wasn't going to deter him.

Nathan started to think about the different rumours that he heard at the funeral and, clutching at any straw that he could find at this point, decided to try typing them into the search engine. He keyed in the words 'Etracova leader' but found nothing. He typed in the phrase 'terrorist organisation' and not a scrap of luck. He fingered out the sentence 'army betrayed by Entritican government' and still no result.

Fortunately, it seemed like Nathan may have found a lead after coming across an active article related to his fourth search, 'ammunitions supplier'. The article was titled 'Arms Dealer Sells Out Entritica?!' which immediately caught his attention. Nathan eagerly read through about how the Entritican army's chief weapons supplier, Ali Ammunitions Ltd. had stopped providing weapons to them and even speculated about whether they had betrayed their country by making a secret deal with Etracova, the enemy.

However, before he could read any further into the reasons for suspecting this, his phone froze and then a message popped onto his screen, saying that the connection was interrupted. When he tried to refresh the page, just like with the other previous websites he had tried, Nathan was dismayed to see the message *'domain no longer exists'*. Vexed, Nathan shoved his phone back into his pocket as he approached the school gates. If the articles being unavailable over the last two days hadn't been questionable before, then the speed in which that last website was taken down definitely roused his suspicions.

On his way towards the courtyard at the west side of the school, he received a text message from Thomas letting him know that he was running late because he and his mom were stuck in traffic. While he keyed a response into his phone, his eyes darted upwards from the screen as something caught his attention nearby.

He saw Denzel and Drew talking quietly with one another, the latter with his hand gently on Denzel's shoulder and looking downward towards his stomach. Nathan noticed that Denzel had a black eye and was clutching his ribs, seemingly in pain. As his curiosity peaked, Nathan was unable to take his eyes away from the two boys. Unluckily for him, this got noticed by Denzel who didn't take kindly to being spied on and stormed towards him with Drew trying to calm him down once he realised what was happening.

"What do you think you're looking at Bennett?!" Denzel hissed at him, wincing from the discomfort in his ribs with each step he took. Nathan, feeling bolder than usual since Ranjit wasn't around and seeing that Denzel was weakened, decided to bite back.

"Well since you asked, where'd you get that massive shiner?" Nathan responded coolly. "Ranjit finally getting sick of you?"

Both Denzel and Drew were taken aback by this comment and Nathan could see that it struck a nerve with Denzel as his face went bright red and he fumbled over his words. Drew then had to restrain Denzel who tried to intimidate Nathan by lunging forward at him, but this failed when he stumbled down to his knees, his ribs racked with pain. Even Nathan got concerned seeing this, realising that the injury to Denzel was quite extensive. Denzel looked up at Nathan from the ground to see a pitying look on his face and this only riled him up more.

"D-don't look at me like that, you freak! As if you're better than me!" Denzel huffed furiously as Nathan gazed down at him. "We all know what you are, *Dragon Boy*! I haven't forgotten – about you 'attacking' Abbie that day..." Nathan's eye twitched and a bead of sweat trickled down his forehead as he got reminded of the incident, still feeling guilt despite not being in control of his actions in that moment. "It'd be so easy, you know. To tell everyone that you did this to me. They'd all believe me...with your track record, you'd be gone from here in an instant," Denzel threatened and even Drew seemed unnerved by what he was telling Nathan. It was then that a voice called out from behind them.

"You really are pathetic, playing the victim like that," the voice spoke, full of contempt.

Before she came into view from behind Drew, Nathan recognised the voice as Abbie's but it still took him by surprise to see her there. Yet his reaction didn't compare to Denzel's and Drew's with the former scrambling away from her on his hands and knees, his face drained of colour after seeing her and the latter nearly jumping out his skin by simply hearing her voice.

"Nathan, stay there. I need to talk to you," Abbie quickly said to him before turning her attention back to Denzel and Drew. "As for you," she growled scornfully at Denzel who stared feebly back up at her, "just so we set the record straight, nothing happened that day as far as I'm concerned. So if you spread any 'rumours' about what happened with me and Nathan, I'll deny it. And if you try to push him around like you did Ben, you might just get another black eye to match!" she harshly warned.

Nathan was stunned that Abbie defended him the way that she did, but relieved to know that he wouldn't have to put up with being the centre of gossip among the other students again if she meant what she'd said. Denzel staggered back up to his feet, nearly in tears as he struggled through the stinging sensation in his ribs. As Denzel waddled away from them, Drew shook his head and looked back at Nathan.

"I'm sorry..." he murmured to Nathan, another thing that left him flabbergasted. Before he could process Drew's apology though, he was distracted, along with Abbie and Drew, by the sound of Denzel's voice yelling across the courtyard.

"Stay the hell away from me you snake! I want nothing to do with you!" Denzel shrieked angrily.

Nathan, Abbie, Drew and many other students in the background turned to see Denzel storming away from Dan who it seemed had just arrived at school and looked to be pleading with Denzel as he followed him. Drew sighed regretfully before pursuing them himself, leaving Nathan and Abbie alone with each other.

It had been a whirlwind morning for Nathan in terms of his interactions with Ranjit's cronies from seeing a wounded Denzel, hearing Drew actually apologise to him and witnessing a possible fallout between Dan and Denzel. He didn't have much time to process all this though as he awkwardly turned to look at Abbie, the same girl he had unknowingly pinned against a wall over two weeks ago. Despite this, she had just stood up for him against the three boys she was previously united with which was the biggest surprise to him of them all. Similarly, the typically brash Abbie also seemed unsure what to say as she bashfully stared at Nathan.

"I feel I'm missing some context here, what was- ?" Nathan asked, struggling to finish his sentence and resorting to gesturing in the direction that Denzel and Drew had wandered off to.

"O-oh right" Abbie responded nervously. "I had a fallout with them during the holiday about a week ago. Denzel shoved my little brother Ben to the ground and...well-"

"You gave him the black eye?" Nathan deduced.

"I gave him the black eye," Abbie candidly confirmed.

"I know Denzel was out of order doing that, but don't you think you went a bit too far? He was clutching his stomach a lot just now," Nathan wondered to which Abbie's forehead scrunched up in confusion.

"His stomach?" she asked puzzled. "I only punched him in the eye. I didn't even touch his stomach."

"Really?!" Nathan exclaimed in response and then went quiet as he tried to make sense of it in his head.

"I swear, all I did was punch Denzel and hurl insults at them! They all cleared off with their tails between their legs and I took Ben home with me," Abbie explained hastily. "I've not even seen them until today and I'd been trying to avoid them well before that since...well that day with your locket..." she finished ashamedly. "That's what I wanted to talk to you about-" she was about to say until Nathan interrupted abruptly.

"Ranjit!" Nathan blurted out in realisation, finally breaking from his trail of thought.

"Ranjit?" Abbie repeated for clarity's sake.

"It must have been Ranjit who gave Denzel a beating to his ribs," Nathan rationalised.

Abbie briefly considered what Nathan had just said. "I mean, I can certainly see him doing that, but are you really that certain?" she asked him.

"No doubt," Nathan answered decisively. "I know first-hand what Ranjit's capable of. And Denzel got real jumpy when I mentioned his name. Then there was Denzel and Dan arguing after that," he continued to speculate. "I bet that Ranjit saw the black eye that you gave Denzel and forced Dan into telling him what happened. He wouldn't like knowing that one his 'boys' was beaten up by a girl – and gave him a beating as punishment!"

Abbie tilted her head and raised her eyebrows, convinced by Nathan's reasoning.

"You training to be a detective or something?" she remarked, somewhat impressed – he had a good understanding of how Ranjit thought.

"Well I suppose I've had some practice recently," Nathan glumly admitted. "I've been trying to find out who or what killed my dad."

"Oh…" Abbie uttered sensitively as her expression softened. "I-I had no idea. I'm so sorry Nathan…does anyone else at school know?"

"Seems like it's only Mr Jones, Joshua and Thomas for now. Bit of a relief, really," Nathan answered as he thought of Denzel's earlier comments.

"Yeah, probably for the best that it happened after the end of term," Abbie blurted out. Upon hearing the words that left her mouth, her eyes widened in horror as she realised how they sounded and cupped her face with her hands feeling mortified. "O-oh god! I-I didn't mean it like-" she began to say but Nathan stopped her.

"I know, I know," he reassured Abbie. "I remember not knowing what to say to Josh when he lost his mom. I get it."

Abbie regarded Nathan for a moment, appreciating him for not judging her for her slip-up. "Look Nathan, I wanted to talk to you about your dad anyway as I have something that you might want back," she said as she reached in her bag and unzipped one of the pockets.

To his shock, Nathan watched as Abbie pulled something familiar out of her bag and held it out to him – his dad's locket.

"H-how did-?" Nathan spluttered, feeling overwhelmed as he saw the sun's reflection bounce off the gold dragon emblem of his dad's keepsake once again.

"After w-…what happened that day," Abbie explained carefully. "I felt awful after I did it. So after you'd left and I'd lost Denzel and them lot…I went back to the grate it went down. Long story short," she continued, stifling an embarrassed laugh as she did so. "I ended up going down the drain after borrowing a screwdriver from my dad's toolbox. And luckily I found the locket lodged in another smaller grate." Nathan was still quiet throughout as he stared at the locket, still in disbelief that he had been reunited with it. "I-I would have returned it to you sooner but…w-well I didn't know where you lived and I don't have your phone number," Abbie added. "But I just wanted to try and put things right. So…here," she finished, extending her arm further, beckoning Nathan to take the locket.

Still bewildered, Nathan gently retrieved the locket from Abbie. He held the chain of the locket in the palm of his hand, checking it over for any scratches after its excursion into the sewer but was delighted to see that it was unspoiled. He bit his lip as his thumb stroked the golden dragon, trying to contain his emotions before closing his eyes tightly and bringing the locket close to his chest.

"It really is a beautiful locket," Abbie commented as she watched Nathan. "You'll have to tell me where it came from one day."

"It came from Etracova," Nathan answered still clutching the locket near his heart. "My dad grew up there before coming to Entritica by himself when he was fourteen. This locket was one of the few mementos he had from his childhood." He opened his eyes again to properly take in the locket's design. "He once told me that the dragon is seen as a symbol of protection in Etracova and its golden colour represents hope, even when surrounded by the darkness…" Nathan explained thoughtfully as he examined the black border around the dragon.

"I see…" Abbie responded, trying to think of something more meaningful to say. After a few moments of silence, she cleared her throat and said "Well, I'm glad you have your 'hope' back..."

Nathan finally took his eyes away from the locket and turned to look at Abbie. "Why did you do this?" he asked her. "To go this far…even going into the sewer to get it-"

"Like I said, what I did to you that day was awful and I just wanted to make things right," Abbie answered sincerely.

"But after how close I came to atta-" Nathan spoke but unable to finish the last word, gulping on his feelings of shame. "I mean, aren't you afraid of me?"

Abbie gently shook her head at Nathan's question. "When it happened, yes I was spooked, but I could tell something was off with how you were," she clarified. "Like, I knew that it wasn't in your nature to do that. I know a good person when I see one, especially because I don't know many like that."

Nathan gave her a sad smile and glanced at the locket once more. He then unhooked the latch in the centre of the chain and draped it round his neck before fastening it again. He felt an immediate sense of comfort wearing the locket once more. His neck had felt bare and empty for the last two weeks, but now it felt uplifting to have this memento of his dad back where it belonged.

"Thank you," Nathan said to Abbie, not only referring to her returning the necklace but also for forgiving his previous actions and not viewing him in a negative light because of it.

"A-also," Abbie continued shyly. "If there's any way I can help you with, y-you know, finding out information about your dad, j-just let me know, okay?"

Nathan nodded gratefully in response before he was interrupted by the sound of Thomas' distant voice getting closer.

"Sorry I-I'm late! The traffic was mental!" he huffed, short of breath from rushing down from the school gates. As he approached Nathan, he was confused by Abbie's presence. "W-what's she doing here?" he questioned, only remembering the locket incident. While Nathan and Abbie stumbled over their words trying to explain, Thomas noticed that Nathan was once again wearing the locket and was quick to understand the situation. "Oh, you guys made amends?" he presumed, struggling to hide his tone of amazement.

"Yeah," Nathan confirmed to Abbie's appreciation. "I'd say we have…"

In that moment, the school bell rang indicating it was time for the students to go to their classrooms before assembly. Seeing some of the other students shuffling towards the building, Nathan knew they had to get moving too.

"We'd better go," he decided. "I'll see you around Abbie," he bade farewell to her before hurrying off with Thomas towards their lockers.

"Yeah, see you," Abbie called as the two boys departed. Thomas, still trying to comprehend what had gone on in his absence, tried to get information from Nathan.

"Did I miss much this morning? When did Abbie suddenly start trying to be friends with you?" he asked curiously. Nathan, focused on getting through the next part of the day – his classes – chose to postpone telling Thomas the full story.

"You missed a lot but there's no time now. I'll fill you in at lunchtime," Nathan replied decisively as they entered through the school doors towards their classes, normality finally resuming for them, something that Nathan cherished now more than ever after the last two weeks…

Chapter 4

Later that afternoon, the cafeteria and lunch hall were alive with the chatter of students, catching up with their friends and reminiscing about their school break after a long morning of classes. The sounds of their laughter could be heard from the open windows outside by Nathan and Thomas as they met one another for lunch outside on a creaky wooden bench in the courtyard with no other person in sight.

As intended, Nathan told Thomas about the events from that morning, starting with his frustrations of finding very little information relating to the war. He then led on to his confrontation with Denzel and being sure to highlight the injuries that he had, including his theory about Ranjit being the person to leave him in that condition.

"Threatening to frame you for causing his injuries?!" Thomas commented about Denzel with disgust in his voice. "That's low even for them!"

"It's not surprising, they've always had it out for us thanks to Ranjit," Nathan responded casually. "Never mind that, Ranjit injuring Denzel – do you think that's what happened too?"

"Oh, from what you've told me, definitely!" Thomas agreed, remembering Nathan's details about Dan and Denzel arguing. "We both know what he's capable of!"

Nathan nodded before finishing his update with the conversation he had with Abbie and how they had reconciled.

"So, she just…gave you the locket back? No tricks or anything?" Thomas questioned.

"Pretty much," Nathan confirmed. "Like I said, she was the one who chased Denzel away and even said she'd deny the incident ever happened. She really had my back there."

"Strange," Thomas responded, still confused. "Sorry, I'm still trying to get my head round it all. I get that she's had a fallout with them…but going as far as defending you? I mean, isn't she worried that Ranjit might get back at her for doing that?"

"No, I don't care about that anymore," a voice spoke from behind Thomas.

Nathan and Thomas both jumped up in shock and turned to see Abbie standing behind the bench, listening to their conversation.

"Geez, will you stop doing that?!" Nathan exclaimed as he put his hand on his chest to try and calm his breathing.

"Doing what?" Abbie chuckled casually.

"Appearing out of nowhere," Nathan stated. "It's putting me on edge, I keep thinking it might be Ranjit or his gang again."

"Right, sorry. I'll try and work on that," Abbie responded as she casually walked round to the other side of the bench and jumped over the back onto the seat next to Nathan, the planks of wood squeaking as she landed.

"How did you know where to find us?" Thomas asked her.

"Because, well…you guys *always* have your lunch here," Abbie pointed out to him.

"Oh yeah…" Thomas replied coyly.

An awkward silence descended upon the group for a few seconds with the two boys unsure what to say next now that Abbie had intruded into their chosen safe space. Detecting this, Abbie nervously cleared her throat to speak again.

"Why do you both do that anyway?" she asked curiously, keen to disrupt the tension. "Why not come into the canteen with everyone else?"

"Well…it's because we're not exactly *welcome* in there," Nathan answered honestly to which Abbie gave him a sad but understanding look.

"Yeah, the rest of the school sees us as freaks thanks to the rumours that your *friends* spread about us," Thomas bitterly added.

"Those guys were *never* my friends," Abbie retorted resentfully before taking a breath. "Look, I came out to see you because I wanted to give you some more information about Ranjit, Denzel and the others," she explained. "But for what it's worth, I'm not exactly a guest of honour in there either."

"Oh right," Nathan uttered, unsure what to say to Abbie's admission. He decided to focus on the information first. "Well, what did you find out?"

"Okay so I took the chance to spy on each of them during my break time," Abbie explained. "Firstly, Dan and Denzel still look to be at odds.

They sat apart during class and weren't with each other at all during the break which is very unusual."

"Denzel's still angry then," Thomas summarised bluntly.

"But Drew seems to be acting as their go-between," Abbie continued. "I saw Drew consoling Denzel first but after they split up, I followed Drew until he met up with Dan. They were talking for a bit about Denzel and Ranjit. But when Ranjit showed up, they both went quiet. They're treading on eggshells around him, even more so than normal – I think something's *definitely* happened between them over the holidays. Like, they were both scared, but it felt like there was some tension between Drew and Ranjit. He told Drew to clear off and he seemed like he really wanted to bite back but was holding his tongue. After Drew left though, Ranjit seemed to be putting pressure on Dan to do something – I didn't get to hear what that was though."

"Weird to think of those three being apart. You didn't see one without the other two at one point," Nathan remarked.

"I bet that's intentional on Ranjit's part," Thomas theorised. "Likely so he can drip poison in their ears easier…"

"Makes sense," Abbie agreed. "Anyway, the last thing I saw was Ranjit taking a phone call and he got real shifty about doing it, even telling Dan to get lost. Sadly, I couldn't get close enough to hear who he was speaking to but it sure was suspicious," she finished.

"You don't think it was his brother, do you?" Thomas guessed.

"I doubt it, it felt way too secretive," Abbie replied. "That's as much as I could get, I thought I'd let you know," she said to Nathan.

"Right, thanks," Nathan acknowledged and briefly mused about what to say to her next. Despite her assistance today, he still felt uneasy around Abbie given who she had associated with before. Aware of this, he knew what he wanted to ask next. "Sorry, but-" he began, pausing to think how to choose his words delicately. "Y-you said that Ranjit and the others were never your friends. So *why* did you hang around them for as long as you did?"

This time, Abbie leaned forward as her shoulders unconsciously stiffened and some of the colour in her face faded. She went quiet for a moment and Nathan and Thomas watched her as she twiddled her thumbs before she finally gave Nathan an answer.

"…because I was scared too," Abbie murmured, ashamed.

"Of getting hurt?" Thomas quizzed with a confused look. "Because it sounds like you can handle yourself in a fight with them," he recalled hearing of her giving Denzel the black eye.

"No, not that. I didn't care about getting hurt that way," Abbie clarified. "Ranjit found out what my family were like and I didn't want the rest of the school getting word of it. It had happened at my previous one and several other girls bullied me for months because of it. It was horrible and I felt like I couldn't turn to anyone about it. Then when I finally stood up to Harriet, the leader of the pack, I was the one who got expelled!"

"What?! How is that fair?!" Thomas cried out, appalled.

"Yeah that's way too hars-" Nathan was about to say until a brief thought about the words Abbie used crossed his mind. "Hold on. When you say *stand up* to them, what did you do?"

Abbie awkwardly bit her lip and looked away from Nathan and Thomas before responding.

"I-I might have broken her bra..." she started to say, slowly turning to face them again to see their reactions. As she saw them stare curiously at her, aware that there was more to it, she sighed. "And her nose..." she admitted, embarrassed.

"Yep, that's more like it," Nathan remarked casually as he rolled his eyes.

"Still, it sounds like that Harriet deserved it if you ask me..." Thomas added.

"Well regardless, I didn't want to go through that again. And when Ranjit confronted me with what he knew about my family, he threatened to spread it round the school if I didn't do as he said...so I just caved..." Abbie confessed guiltily.

"He likes having power over others..." Thomas muttered gloomily.

"I know," Abbie concurred. "He and the others used that against me to get me to do things I didn't feel comfortable doing..."

"Like taking my locket that day..." Nathan realised aloud. To this, Abbie meekly nodded with an expression of pure shame on her face. "What is the deal with your family then?" he asked her curiously, his voice and posture slowly softening now.

Again, Abbie hesitated before giving a reply, however she was quicker to open up this time, her posture relaxing bit by bit in the presence of Nathan and Thomas.

"M-my mom and dad drink…like a lot…" she confessed. "And it leads to arguments between them. Not all the time of course…but when I hear it, it's really bad…and then there's the uncomfortable silences that can last for days where you're afraid to say the wrong word around them. I'm not sure which is worse…"

"I-I had no idea. I'm sorry you have to put up with that," Nathan empathised.

"Yeah, that's awful," Thomas agreed sadly. "Do you think they'd be better splitting up?"

"Yeah, I do," Abbie replied. "I wish they would but sometimes, I think they thrive on the drama of it all. It's so selfish, Ben shouldn't have to be around that!"

"Oh god yeah, your brother!" Nathan remembered. "How does he deal with it, being around that environment?"

"Well it upsets him, naturally," Abbie answered. "I try to keep him away from it as much as I can, especially when they start shouting. In fact, that's what I was doing that day, taking him to the park to get out the house until things settled, when I came across Denzel and the others. They were giving me grief for blanking them after…well, you know," she recalled, haunted by her past actions. "Anyway, I told them to get lost but they just kept pestering me and even started insulting Ben, calling him a baby. Then Ben swore at them – must have picked it up from mom and dad's arguments. It did shut them up though…"

"And that's when Denzel pushed him?" Thomas deduced.

"Yeah," Abbie confirmed. "When he did that, I just saw red and…yeah, I punched him. He just fell to the ground and scurried away with the other two. Thankfully Ben was okay, but he shouldn't have had to see me do that…"

"You care for your brother a lot," Nathan noted with a kind smile which took Abbie by surprise at first before she smiled back in return.

"He's only six and…well half the time, I feel like I look after him more than mom and dad do," she revealed. "He needs me. Yet at the same time, I need him too. He's what keeps me going, especially when times are hard. And when Denzel pushed him, it just triggered something in me…"

"Yeah, a mean right hook!" Thomas joked.

"Well, not just that," Abbie said as she tried to hide a smirk. "It hit me how much time I'd wasted hanging around those jerks these last few months and all just to avoid feeling alone again. How pathetic could I get?" she continued reflectively before looking directly at Nathan. "Seeing him push Ben, I realised that I felt the same way that you must have felt after losing your locket. It means a lot to you just as Ben means the world to me. And you lost it because of *me*. So in the end, I was no better than Denzel or Ranjit or any of them. And Ben's the person I want to be better for so I knew I had to make a change."

Nathan nodded approvingly. "I think anyone can make a change if they really want to," he asserted. "And how do you feel now? You know, without Ranjit and the rest of them?"

"Free," Abbie declared confidently. "And I think Denzel and the others probably resent me for that."

"Good. Let 'em. That's their problem…" Thomas remarked coolly.

Abbie took a moment to look out at the field that lay before them, basking in the newfound peace that she felt. As the three sat quietly on the bench, the sounds of the other students could be heard again from the windows of the canteen, disrupting their own serenity which left Thomas feeling mildly irked.

"I just wish they'd keep that racket down…I'm glad I'm out here, they're far too loud," Thomas mumbled.

"Alright, just because you're sitting on a bench doesn't mean you have to *act* like an old man!" Abbie teased to lighten the mood.

"Oi, who're you calling an old man?!" Thomas replied indignantly.

"Careful what you say Abbie, or he'll whack you with his cane," Nathan jested.

This led to both him and Abbie bursting into laughter themselves and even Thomas couldn't help but chuckle at Nathan's cheeky comment – it was refreshing to see him laugh again. The three of them took a few seconds to calm themselves again before Abbie took the conversation in a new direction, geared towards the two boys.

"Well, you guys know my story now," Abbie pointed out. "So how about you two? Why are you guys fellow outcasts?"

Hearing this, Thomas raised an eyebrow, surprised. "I thought you'd know that from Ranjit and the others?" he questioned while Nathan started to fidget and shuffle uncomfortably, his head lowering as he looked downwards at his lap. Meanwhile, the clouds in the sky above started to shift and conceal the sun bit by bit.

"I've heard lots of different rumours, so I don't know or care which is truth or lies at this point," Abbie insisted. "You guys took time to hear my story, so I'd rather hear the real truth from your lips now."

"You're one of the few that have..." Thomas acknowledged gratefully. "In my case, when I was younger, I used to hear voices in my head." Abbie's eyes widened in surprise as she heard this, but she continued to listen to what Thomas had to say. "I didn't know why and I didn't know how to stop it from happening. But other kids stayed away from me because of that..."

"Okay..." Abbie uttered, briefly pausing to think what to say next. "If you don't mind me asking, what did the voices *say* to you?" she questioned curiously.

"They...u-uh..." Thomas stuttered as he ruminated back to his childhood. Abbie watched as he sighed and clenched his eyes shut, seemingly tormented by his past.

"Sorry, I didn't mean to pry," she asserted gently. "If it's painful for you, you don't have to tell me-"

"T-they'd tell me I was a monster..." Thomas interjected as Abbie went quiet again to allow him to speak and Nathan looked up for the first time since Abbie had asked about their backstories to listen to his friend. "They'd say I was unloved...and seeing how others reacted to me, I started to believe them..." It looked as though Thomas was about to say something more but after further reflection, his face winkled in distress as he decided against it. "There's more behind it but...I just can't-" he exclaimed.

"It's okay, you were really brave to share as much as you did with us," Abbie reassured as Nathan nodded his head in agreement. "That must have been horrible for you, I couldn't even imagine having to go through that. D-do you ever still hear them?"

"No, I haven't heard them for four years," Thomas answered. "I actually haven't heard them since I met Nathan," he added, turning to his friend as he did so. "Of course, the stigma still stuck with me ever since..."

"At least, Nathan's been there for you those last four years," Abbie highlighted optimistically which Thomas agreed with. "How did you, two, meet anyway?" she asked interestedly.

"Oh, we just happened to meet in class one day and hit it off there!" Thomas declared but almost overzealously. "Right Nath?" he addressed him, pushing for a response.

Doubtful of how to answer, Nathan turned to look at Thomas to see his eyes focused on him, quietly beseeching him to corroborate his assertion.

"Yeah, sure..." Nathan replied half-heartedly as Thomas' posture relaxed.

"Oh okay, thought there'd have been more to it," Abbie quipped. "What about you then, Nath? Why are you out here with us and not in there with them?" she asked Nathan, her head motioning towards the canteen where the other students still were.

Nathan's head dropped again upon being asked this and a silence descended upon the three as Nathan struggled to get even a few words out, with only a few rays of sunlight being able to escape through the cloud and beam down upon him. Trying to help his friend, Thomas jumped in on his behalf.

"It was a really difficult time for him," he explained to Abbie. "Not only did he get shunned by others after the incident, but he got cyber-bullied by, well, no prizes for guessing who..."

"Ranjit..." Abbie inferred, the contempt palpable in her voice as she spoke his name. Then she picked up on the other thing that Thomas had mentioned. "Wait, *incident*?" she repeated, confused while Thomas cringed, annoyed that he'd let that word slip. "What happened?"

"Do you really not know?" Thomas probed as Nathan now had his hands cupped round his mouth, trying to calm himself down while his breathing quickened erratically and his arms and shoulders were trembling.

"Like I said, I may have heard the truth already for all I know but I don't really trust anyone else's word at this point," Abbie reinforced. "It's Nath's version that I care about."

"Um, w-well...w-what happened w-was...uh..." Thomas stammered again but before he could find the right words, Nathan finally spoke up as the shadows of the clouds now completely obscuring the sun loomed over them.

"I nearly killed someone..." he whispered despondently, a sudden gust of wind blowing past and carrying his confession upwards, the brief echo of the words resonating hauntingly in his own mind...

Chapter 5

Abbie sat quietly as she processed what Nathan had just admitted to almost doing. Despite this, she never recoiled from him or showed any signs of feeling discomfort, a reaction that was foreign to Nathan. She just stared at him, patiently waiting – much to his confusion.

"S-so does that match with any of the rumours you'd heard about me?" Nathan questioned anxiously, still surprised by how calm she was.

"Might have heard that version before," Abbie retorted bluntly. "Now I want to hear the *full* story from the horse's mouth. I may have only got to know you properly in half a day but I can tell you're not a violent person. If you nearly *killed* someone, there must be more to it."

Nathan was again taken aback by this but did feel a warming sense of relief of not being immediately demonised swell within him as the clouds above continued to shift, allowing the sun to shine through once more. He turned to Thomas who was equally confused yet without saying a word, they mutually agreed to Abbie's request.

"Well, where do we begin?" Nathan quietly asked Thomas.

"So you were there when the incident happened?" Abbie addressed Thomas.

"That's right," Thomas confirmed. "Guess we'll start from the beginning. The incident happened four years ago in our first year here. It was in January and term had just started again – we were both eleven at the time, but not far off turning twelve," he described carefully. "Anyway, we both finished school late because we'd had detention and after that-"

"Ha, *you two* had detention?!" Abbie exclaimed in disbelief.

"Yeah, hard to believe, I know," Thomas muttered sarcastically. "We got into a scuffle with Ranjit who had only joined the school that week-"

"Why does everything bad at this school *always* come back to Ranjit?!" Abbie moaned as she rolled her eyes, exasperated.

"And Mr Jones, who was deputy head back then, put the three of us in detention for fighting," Thomas continued. "Ranjit got off scot-free though after the previous headmaster, Mr Nelson pulled some strings – he played favourites with those from wealthy families," he mentioned in response to Abbie's shocked expression while Nathan twitched at the mention of Mr Nelson's name.

"Mr Jones ended up letting us leave detention fifteen minutes early," Nathan interposed. "We left by the side entrance of the school where Curzon Close is," he recalled, the events and the scenery starting to form vividly in his mind, picturing the wiry fence that separated the school pathway from the cul-de-sac. "That's when we heard a girl scream…"

"A scream?" Abbie reiterated curiously. "W-who was it?"

"We ran over to where it was coming from and we saw Lucy being restrained by two men near a van," Nathan explained as he recalled her struggling whilst in their grasp.

"My god…" Abbie mouthed, her eyes wide with appalment at hearing this.

After taking a few moments to digest what Nathan had told her, she remembered the name that she heard Nathan use.

"Wait, Lucy? You mean Lucy Donovan?" she quizzed.

"Yeah," Nathan verified, thinking of when he'd briefly crossed paths with Lucy the day before the end of term, leading to him getting bowled over by Ranjit. "Like Ranjit, she'd also joined the school that same week. But at that point, she was seen as a minor celebrity around the school and the community."

"When she was younger, Lucy had appeared in some TV commercials for Dynochoc chocolate," Thomas added to give Abbie some more context.

"Oh! I remember those now, that's my favourite chocolate!" Abbie squealed excitedly. "Was that really Lucy?! I had no idea she was *so* pretty back then!"

"Back then?" Nathan remarked under his breath before bashfully going quiet again upon seeing Thomas smirking at him having caught his comment.

"Sadly, she stopped getting commercial gigs around the time she joined our school – something about her no longer being *attractive* enough for TV…" Thomas lamented. "But at the time, she and Ranjit joined the school with a lot of fanfare because of their fame and family background. I'm pretty sure that Mr Nelson wanted to use them to raise the school's profile…"

"I think we're getting off topic a bit," Abbie pointed out, trying to correct the course of the conversation. "What happened to Lucy with the two men?"

"Right, right," Thomas said apologetically. "Where were we? Oh yeah, the two men were trying to bundle her into the back of the van," he reminded himself.

"You don't think they were going to-" Abbie asked, her nose wrinkling as a repulsed look spread across her face.

"No, I don't," Thomas stated, trying to remember what the two men were saying as they heaved Lucy towards the van doors. "I remember hearing them using each other's names – Otis and Tobias – and Otis seemed to be the one giving orders. He said something about using her to get ransom money from her parents."

"I see," Abbie remarked, still feeling unsettled from hearing the story. "How much older were they? What did they look like?"

Thomas thought for a moment, trying to visualise the details of that afternoon. He remembered catching a glimpse of their pasty complexions as well as their matching blonde hair. Aside from Otis having a scruffier beard than Tobias, their visages and bone structures were indistinguishable from one another.

"T-they didn't look much older than teenagers, probably just turned twenty. And...y-yes, they were definitely identical, so they must have been twin brothers," he recollected. "T-they also had really thick accents, so not from around here, probably desperate for money."

"Okay," Abbie said, nodding her head and pursing her lips. "So what did you both do?"

"Well, Nathan was the one who acted quickly and called the police," Thomas admitted, his head motioning towards his best friend. "He did one of those silent distress call things."

"Something my dad taught me before starting at Silver Dawn – in case of trouble from strangers..." Nathan clarified.

"Oh," Abbie uttered, startled. "But if the police were called, then how did it lead to-"

"While Nathan was making the call, Lucy managed to break free from Tobias," Thomas elaborated. In his mind, he recalled how after Tobias covered Lucy's mouth to muffle her screams for help, she bit down hard on his hand forcing him to release his hold. "But then Otis was there to stop her..." he continued, clenching his fist as he remembered how Otis blocked her path, grabbed her by her hair and pinned her against the side of the van. "She was still resisting though..." he added, the image of Lucy kicking wildly towards Otis retained in his memory which culminated with her spitting in the kidnapper's face.

"And then?" Abbie pressed with concern in her voice.

"Then he slapped her..." Thomas answered angrily. The image of the back of Otis' hand catching Lucy's cheek, knocking her to the cobbles and drawing blood, evoked some very unpleasant memories for him.

"And before I could do anything," Nathan muttered, speaking once more. "*You* charged in to try and stop them..." he finished, glaring at Thomas with a vexed expression.

"What?!" Abbie yelled out in shock. "Thomas, what were you thinking?!! You were eleven! They could have killed you!" she reprimanded.

"I know, it was reckless! But when I saw him lash out at Lucy, I just snapped! I didn't even think..." he acknowledged sheepishly, thinking of how he rushed towards Otis, yelling frantically at him to get away from Lucy, and trying but failing to separate them.

"And you paid the price for it..." Nathan mumbled, grimly remembering how Otis effortlessly lifted the feeble Thomas off the pavement like an infant and proceeded to give him a brutal beating against the van.

Reliving that moment, Nathan felt a sense of guilt and helplessness in the pit of his stomach as he was able to do nothing but watch Thomas take blow after blow from Otis and just hope for the police to arrive soon to stop this. But hearing Thomas' pained cries from each punch and with each second that passed without the sound of a police siren, Nathan felt that powerlessness slowly transform into rage at seeing his best friend being attacked like this.

"So how did you all even get out of that?" Abbie questioned, bewildered at what she was hearing.

Both she and Thomas turned to Nathan expectantly for his version of what happened next. It took him a while to respond as he was still rattled about having to reminisce about this day, however he eventually summoned the courage to recount the incident.

"I knew I had to do *something*," Nathan explained quietly. He recalled Otis throwing a bruised and bloody Thomas back down in a heap onto the pavement and barking orders to Tobias to bundle a stunned Lucy into the van. Tobias seemed hesitant at first, especially when Otis said he needed to get rid of 'any witnesses' before heartlessly kicking a defenceless Thomas repeatedly, but he followed suit and tried to heave the dead weight that was Lucy towards the van's back doors. "They were both in danger and I didn't know how long it would be before the police arrived," Nathan rationalised, remembering how he desperately fumbled around him for anything that may help his friends when his hand touched a loose brick.

"Then I found a brick nearby…" he detailed, picturing in his mind how he struggled to lift it up, partly due to his own frailty but also a little due to his own inner reservations. These doubts quickly faded though upon hearing Thomas' wails of anguish and seeing Lucy being forcefully marched by Tobias closer to the rear of the van. Thinking fast, Nathan targeted the side mirror near the front of the van. "I aimed at the mirror, hoping that if I hurled the brick at it, the smash might scare them off," he elaborated. "S-so I chucked it…a-and…a-a-and…" he strained to recall what happened next, but any further recollections devolved into a haze. "I-I only remember b-blacking out…" he finished remorsefully.

"E-even when I was getting the life kicked out of me, I saw what happened," Thomas piped up. "You said you were aiming at the mirror, but…your aim was way off. You threw the brick with *some* force…and it smashed right into the side of Tobias' head!" he revealed to Abbie's astonishment, the sickening thud that he heard when Tobias' body slumped to the ground, which distracted Otis from pummelling Thomas further, still resonated in his mind.

"A-all I remember is th-throwing the brick," Nathan stammered anxiously. "Th-then it was like I z-zoned out…a-and when I came to, I j-just…s-saw him lying there…" he said, haunted by the image of Tobias spasming on the floor, blood pouring from his head and staining the brick. "O-Otis was just c-crouched over him…" he recalled, picturing Otis' face filled with fear, his lips quivering as he eyed Nathan, and also seeing the looks of shock from Thomas and Lucy as they struggled to their feet, trying to take in what had transpired. "I swear, I didn't mean for him to get hurt…" Nathan pleaded before lowering his head and falling silent again.

"We know Nath…" Abbie whispered reassuringly, placing her hand gently on Nathan's shoulder. "They got what was coming to them, targeting children like that! And besides, what you did saved Thomas *and* Lucy's lives! You should be a hero, not a pariah!"

"I agree, but sadly that's not what happened..." Thomas commented bitterly, speaking on his friend's behalf. "The police arrived before Otis could escape and arrested them – though they had to take Tobias to the hospital for urgent treatment. They took us home to our families but Nathan did get questioned about Tobias' wound, after forensics found his fingerprints on the brick. Thankfully, he didn't get charged for two reasons – One, me and Lucy both attested to the police that he acted in self-defence and out of necessity. And two, he was under the age of twelve so he couldn't be held criminally responsible."

"So that should have been the end of it, surely?" Abbie quipped.

"Unfortunately, the media got wind of it," Thomas revealed. "The incident went to court and when a crooked reporter working with the defence solicitors heard of Nathan's involvement, he sold a story that got published in the newspapers about how he was a danger to society for severely injuring Tobias and how he should be punished by the law. No mention of needing to defend himself or us. Just any underhanded tactic to help push the odds in the defence's favour and anything for a quick pay day..." he spat venomously.

"That's sickening!" Abbie hissed, outraged.

"That triggered the rumours at school," Thomas continued as Nathan's eyes were still vacantly fixated to the bench underneath him. "Of course, Ranjit jumped all over them...and the rest is pretty much history..."

Abbie shook her head in disbelief. "Didn't the truth ever come out?!" she protested. "That should have cleared his name!"

"It did come out in the end," Thomas replied. "The court case ended a few months' later with both Otis and Tobias being charged for attempted kidnapping, attempted murder and ABH. They ended up being deported back to Etracova. My mom was a former journalist but she went back to her roots briefly to try and help Nathan's cause. She published the decision of the case in the papers, including how Nathan had acted bravely to save us instead of painting him as some demon. The media didn't bombard any of us again after that...but at school, the damage was already done. Most of the other students believed Ranjit's exaggerations while others were still wary of him. The school's reputation suffered a lot thanks to the negative press at the time and a lot of the teachers, especially Mr Nelson, held that against Nathan," he explained, with Nathan once again shuddering at the mention of Mr Nelson. "Only Mr Jones still treated him like an actual human being..."

"Unbelievable..." Abbie mouthed. She then turned to look at Nathan. "I'm so sorry, you must have gone through hell back then..." she said empathetically.

"He did," Thomas confirmed. "As you can imagine, his mental health was at rock bottom during that time..."

At that moment, Nathan quickly lifted his head and broke his silence.

"No Tom," he interrupted, his words firmly spoken. "I can't...I'm not ready to talk about that," he insisted.

"Right, sorry. It's not my place to say..." Thomas squeaked remorsefully.

"It's okay, I get it..." Abbie reassured Nathan with a sad smile. Suddenly though, a thought crossed her mind. "Um, Nath?" she uttered cautiously. "Y-you said that you blacked out shortly before throwing the brick at Tobias, is that right?"

"Yeah...I literally don't remember anything between throwing the brick and seeing Tobias on the floor..." Nathan clarified.

"Okay," Abbie responded. "Because I was wondering...did you have a similar experience with me after I threw away your locket?"

As these words sunk in, Nathan's eyes widened with worry, realising that Abbie had a point. Just like the incident with Tobias, he recalled there being a gap in his memory from the point of losing his locket to snapping out of his trance and seeing Abbie pinned against the wall by his own hand. Gaging Nathan's reaction, Thomas could tell that Abbie may have hit a nail on the head.

"Are you trying to say that they're connected?" Thomas questioned, half intrigued but also half concerned about his friend.

"Well I think there could be a chance..." Abbie theorised. "I did find it unusual that Nathan was actually able to push me back that day. I mean, nothing personal, but..." she glanced at his thin, bony arms. "You're not exactly *strong*..." Nathan tried not to take offence but did inadvertently scowl at hearing this. Nevertheless, Abbie continued. "And...I've also seen you throw during sports...I find it hard to believe that you could pick up and throw a brick that far a distance *now*, let alone four years ago..."

"So you're saying that not only did he zone out both times, he also got a surge of power on each occasion..." Thomas pondered aloud. At this point, an unnerved Nathan rapidly stood up from the bench

"Okay, I think we're looking too much into this now!" he firmly asserted. "I was angry both times, I probably just had a surge of adrenaline...

and maybe it was just…so intense that I zoned out from it!" he rationalised unconvincingly.

"Come to think of it…" Thomas considered, pausing to mull over the events once more. "I might be mis-remembering but…after you threw the brick at Tobias…I definitely remember feeling a really sinister energy coming from you…and it was like there was a black mist coming from your body…" Nathan began to sweat uncomfortably upon hearing this.

"Wait, mist?" Abbie echoed, perplexed. "Sure, I get the sinister energy, but I'm pretty sure there was nothing black or misty coming from him when he pushed me."

"Yeah, that's true actually…" Thomas reassessed pensively.

"See?!" Nathan yelled exasperated, his patience starting to wear thin with the speculations. "I don't know what you're talking about with a black mist or whatever, but you were probably just seeing things! Otis really did a number on you after all! They were just two *different* incidents where I lost my temper and was pushed to my breaking point! There's no connection! I'm not some *demon*!!"

Gasping for breath, Nathan turned away from Thomas and Abbie, ashamed that he had erupted at them like he did. His pupils darted frantically around him as he looked out towards the field as Thomas and Abbie regarded him with concern. Despite his insistence to his friends otherwise, the possibility that he was not in control of those acts of aggression was something that deeply terrified him, especially with his history of being ostracised by others.

"Nath, we know you're not a demon," Thomas said, rising up from the bench to comfort his friend. "You're probably right, we were getting a bit carried away."

"Yeah, it was hypocritical of me to even say that. I lost my cool with Harriet and Denzel after all," Abbie reflected on both her past experiences as she too stood up. "You're probably just like me in that sense, both forces to be reckoned with when backed into a corner!" she laughed off, patting Nathan's back affectionately. "C'mon, let's all have a walk, get away from that bench for a bit and get some fresh air for a change," she suggested to which Nathan nodded approvingly, though the doubts about his unexplained 'outbursts' still weighed heavily on him.

Abbie led Nathan and Thomas towards the field. Compared to the courtyard which was mostly enclosed by the school walls, the air around the field was much more refreshing and the intoxicating smell of the surrounding grass was carried up through their nostrils. While Nathan and Thomas shuffled their way carefully through the trimmings with their hands in their pockets, Abbie strolled across them unreservedly, inhaling the aroma.

"Now that I think about it, you did always look miserable around Ranjit's crew," Thomas commented as he reflected on Abbie's previous demeanour. "This is the happiest I've ever seen you…"

"Well, it helps that I've always loved going to fields and parks, even when I was a kid" Abbie confided merrily. "They're like my happy place, somewhere I can feel free…"

"It's funny, I remember Lucy saying something along those lines to us once," Nathan chuckled in response.

"Oh, that reminds me!" Abbie exclaimed. "You also saved Lucy that day as well as Thomas. Did you guys become friends with her too?"

"Yeah, we did," Thomas answered. "We got close after what happened with Otis and Tobias. Plus, a lot of people shunned me and Lucy for associating with Nathan so the three of us had each other's backs."

"But she's not with you guys now…" Abbie remarked bleakly.

All of a sudden, the mood seemed to darken as Abbie caught the dejected grimaces of both Nathan and Thomas.

"Well, she…she stopped hanging around us at the start of this school year…after…" Nathan began before Thomas interjected.

"After she started dating Ranjit's brother, Kamran…" Thomas finished sullenly.

"Oh…yeah that…" Abbie uttered awkwardly. "It was a bit of a whirlwind romance when it happened. But to think they're getting married this summer, it's just crazy to even ima-"

"Wait, hold on," Nathan interrupted sharply, his head jerking round to look at Abbie's face. "Did you just say *married*?!"

Nathan and Thomas stared at Abbie, dumbfounded by what they had heard while her pupils shifted between the two of them, at a loss for what to say.

"Y-you guys didn't know…" Abbie realised slowly, feeling the guilt of having to break the news. "W-well, I suppose she hasn't really been very vocal about it at school…I doubt many others would know…"

"When did this even happen?" Thomas probed.

"I-I'd heard from Drew that the marriage was arranged almost immediately," Abbie replied.

"She'd have only just turned sixteen at that point!" Nathan cried aghast. "And isn't Kamran four years older than us?!"

"From what I can remember of Drew's account of things," Abbie reflected "their dad, Anil, wanted to get Kamran married because he was tired of him acting like a playboy."

"But why Lucy?!" Nathan questioned, frustratedly. "Why did it have to be her?!"

"I'm afraid I don't know that..." Abbie acknowledged until a thought crossed her mind. "Tom, you said Ranjit's family is wealthy earlier. Could that be why Lucy's gone with Kamran?"

"Hey, Lucy isn't like that!" Nathan snapped angrily before Thomas could even respond.

"Calm down Nath," Thomas remarked. "It could be the reason for all we know. She did shut us out pretty quickly after all," he reminded Nathan to his dismay. "As long as she's happy though..."

"If she is, she's hiding it well at school..." Abbie commented. "She's always sitting by herself at lunchtime before wandering off alone somewhere, no wonder she looks so miserable..."

Nathan's head drooped downwards to the ground as he heard this. Although they had now grown apart, it still hurt him to think that his former friend Lucy was alone and unhappy.

"Don't blame her, I'd feel the same way if I was associated with Ranjit and the rest of his family," Thomas grumbled. "I knew that they were rich but do they really have *that* much money to make it worth doing that – isolating yourself from everyone else?"

"Well, Ali Ammunitions is one of the biggest weapons companies in the world," Abbie explained. "And they're probably making more profit than ever since the war started."

While Abbie continued to talk, Nathan snapped out of his daze, one inflicted by concern for Lucy's wellbeing, his memories from earlier that day now triggered by Abbie's words.

"Abbie, what did you just say?!" he quickly blurted, his head jerking round to see her face.

Confused, Abbie responded by saying "Um, they're making more profit than ever since the war star-?"

"No, the thing before that!" Nathan clarified bluntly.

"They're one of the biggest weapons companies?" Abbie squeaked, looking over to Thomas as if wanting him to help somehow, but he merely shrugged his shoulders in bewilderment.

"Abbie, the name!" Nathan demanded impatiently. "What was the company's name?!"

"Oh, Ali Ammunitions," Abbie answered.

Hearing that name again, Nathan fixated on it for several moments, repeating it aloud over and over certain that he'd heard or seen it somewhere recently. Then it dawned on him. He had read about it only this morning…

"That's it!" Nathan exclaimed hastily to Thomas and Abbie who both listened intently. "The article I read this morning – the only one I was able to find! It was about Ali Ammunitions and how they'd stopped supplying weapons to our army! There was even belief that they've betrayed us and sided with the enemy!"

"Do you really think that's true?" Abbie asked surprised.

"Now that I know it's Ranjit's dad's company, I'm certain!" Nathan asserted desperately. "And if so, they'll know what killed my dad!"

"Hold on," Thomas interrupted to try and calm Nathan who was getting riled up again. "I hate Ranjit as much as you do but aren't you jumping to conclusions? Other than an article, you don't really have any other proof, do you?"

"It's the closest I've gotten to finding out the truth!" Nathan justified frantically as he clutched at his locket. "Every other article I tried to look at was taken down! I was lucky to even see that one before that got struck down too! It's the *only* lead I have!"

"Okay, okay I get it…" Thomas sighed. "I just don't want you doing anything rash."

"What, like charge in guns blazing against two kidnappers?" Nathan retorted sarcastically, silencing Thomas whose face turned red like a radish.

"I think he means, don't get into it with Ranjit," Abbie elaborated. "You've seen the damage that he did to Denzel. We don't want him doing the same or worse to you…"

"Look, I'm not *planning* to confront Ranjit," Nathan insisted as he pulled his phone out from his pocket. "I'm going to do more research into the company. I want to know just how involved they are with this war – and with what happened to my dad…"

Nathan's fingers typed furiously onto his phone's keypad but just as he was spelling out the words 'Ali Ammunitions' into the search engine, he was distracted by a notification on his social media account. He swiped across to another screen to read the post that had caught his attention.

"Guys, have you seen this?" Nathan questioned before Thomas and Abbie gathered around him to see the post that he was referring to, which read:

'Entritica will fall beneath the might of our divine leader...'

The three of them re-read the post a few times. Nathan analysed the statement over and over, trying to extract any clue from it as to who might have sent it. He also saw that it had only been posted a few minutes ago, yet there was already a stream of negative reactions and comments on the post.

"What do you think it means?" Nathan queried curiously.

"It's probably trolls..." Thomas dismissed. "Just keyboard warriors trying to stir up drama. They've kept themselves anonymous after all."

Nathan saw that Thomas was right as the profile that posted the comment was nameless and faceless. However, when he tapped on the link to view the profile information, he spotted something that he found familiar in the past activity.

"This account..." Nathan mumbled, his throat gulping as the words came out from his mouth. "It's one of the ones that was used to cyber bully me..."

"What?! Are you sure?" Abbie asked him gently.

"There's no doubt..." Nathan stated calmly as in one swift motion of his finger, he scrolled down on the screen and sure enough, the last activity on the account were comments towards Nathan from four years ago. Nathan's heart sank and Abbie's blood boiled as they read back through several remarks from this account, such as ones labelling him *'freak'*, *'demon'*, *'psycho'* and *'dragon'*. Abbie had had enough by the time she read three comments in a row that encouraged Nathan to *'kill yourself!'*...

"I can't look at them anymore..." Abbie declared disgusted as she paced around angrily on the grass. "To even say things like that...they're worse than pondlife!"

"Are you okay?" Thomas asked Nathan, aware that reliving this would be painful for him.

"I'll be fine," Nathan responded quietly, nodding his head multiple times in attempt to reinforce this to himself.

"You said you recognised the account," Abbie recalled. "Does that mean you know who sent that post just now?"

Nathan lifted his head to meet Abbie eye to eye. "Well…" he was about to start.

Suddenly though, the bell rang from afar, meaning that lunch time was coming to an end.

"Bloody hell, is that the time?!" Thomas cried out, alarmed at how quickly the hour had passed.

"There's still five minutes before the next lesson, what's the rush?" Abbie stated nonchalantly, confused by Thomas' anxious fumbling.

"I've gotta get my books ready and everything!" Thomas shouted frantically as he rushed towards the school away from Nathan and Abbie, treading his way over the grassy field in that direction. "I'll see you both later!" he called out to them from afar before vanishing off into the distance. Abbie turned to Nathan, as if silently searching for an explanation for Thomas' abrupt departure.

"He um…has Law next," he revealed awkwardly. "It's his favourite subject…wants to be a judge one day…" he added to which Abbie slowly nodded as if pretending to understand, though her face still gave away a look of perplexity.

"Okay…anyway, do you have to rush off too or do you still have some time?" Abbie asked Nathan, still casually strolling around the flowers.

"To be honest," Nathan said as he started to jig up and down on the spot. "I could do with using the restroom before classes start again."

"Ah, that's fair enough…" Abbie commented but Nathan detected the disappointment in her voice, fully aware that he was leaving her on her own.

"We can all hang out again tomorrow," he promised encouragingly, guessing that this was what she wanted to hear – an accurate assumption on his part as her eyes lit up immediately.

"I'll hold you to that," Abbie chuckled as her mouth curled into a grin.

Nathan said his goodbyes to Abbie before hurrying off towards the school, stepping over any patches of mud and dirt in between the blades of grass. Once back on the cobbled pathways, he headed to the left around the side of the building, knowing that there were toilets close by that area.

On his way there though, he passed the gymnasium and got distracted by the faint sound of a familiar voice, but he couldn't put his finger on who it was exactly. He heard it coming from behind a deep alcove in one of the walls. It was quiet, but he detected a panicked anger in the voice which piqued his curiosity so, choosing to hold his bladder, he crept carefully behind the wall to try and pick up what was being said.

"Look!" Nathan heard the voice hiss furiously. "I've done what you told me to do! I'm not doing it again, it's going too far now!"

Nathan then listened while the voice went silent as he heard another gargled noise distorted by static. From this, he guessed that the person he was eavesdropping on was talking on the phone. The next time the voice spoke, Nathan could sense the fear exuding from within it.

"No…" the voice whimpered, breaking as it did so before summoning the courage to raise his voice defiantly again. "No, I don't want to do this anymore! I'm not doing any more of those posts! I'm done! Just leave me alone from now on!" he finished before hanging up the phone.

Nathan made sure to stay hidden behind the wall as the figure emerged from the alcove. As he came into view, he saw that it was Dan who had been talking on the phone and watched as he sheepishly left, his body and legs trembling. Once he had disappeared through the school doors, Nathan finally stepped away from the wall, Dan's words about posts ringing in his mind. Convinced that it was Ranjit threatening him on the other end of that phone, it not only served to confirm his suspicions about Ranjit's involvement in the social media stunt from earlier but also fuel his own theory linking the entire Ali family to the potential treachery of Entritica's armies, including his late father…

Chapter 6

Three days later, on a gloomy Thursday morning, Nathan walked through the school gates to meet with Thomas and Abbie. As he passed several other students, he overheard mutterings about a slew of social media posts, again prophesying the downfall of Entritica, that had gone viral the previous evening. These included ominous claims that *'Entritica will burn'*, *'A new order is coming'* and *'Death to the King...'*

This wasn't new information to Nathan as he had already seen the posts himself that same night. It was the only noteworthy thing that had happened since Monday because he'd had no luck finding any more information or articles that may incriminate Ali Ammunitions – they were still getting struck down almost as quickly as they were uploaded. With all this in his mind along with his lingering suspicions towards Ranjit, his family and subordinates, Nathan believed that the time to take action was approaching.

"Nath, did you see them?" Thomas called out from behind as Nathan turned round to see him and Abbie run over towards him.

"Yeah I did," Nathan confirmed, already aware that they were referring to the online posts, "from the exact same account too."

Abbie detected the determined glint in Nathan's eyes. "Do you...do you have an idea of who it is?" she asked curiously – Nathan hadn't yet told them about the phone call that Dan had taken on Monday, choosing to wait for more conclusive evidence.

In that moment, Nathan's eyes darted towards the school gates where he saw a dishevelled and restless Dan shuffle his way through them. After three days with no new information and clutching on to the Internet posts and Dan's suspicious call from Monday as his only leads, his patience had finally run out.

"I'm about to find out..." Nathan stated resolutely as he marched over in Dan's direction. Realising what he was planning to do, Thomas and Abbie attempted to stop him.

"Nath, stop! You can't just cause a scene in the middle of the courtyard…" Abbie tried to remind him as she stood in his path to slow him down.

"I'm not going to fight him!" Nathan snapped as he struggled to get past Abbie. "I just want to get answers about the posts and what they mean!"

"I think someone may have beaten you to it…" Thomas commented as he looked off in the distance.

Initially confused by this, Nathan glanced in Dan's direction but quickly understood what Thomas meant when he saw his cousin Joshua confront Dan. They were too far away from them to hear what was being said, however they could see that Dan was fidgeting and staggering uncontrollably with each word that came out of Joshua's mouth.

"Are those cigarette burns on his neck?" Abbie questioned aloud.

Nathan squinted his eyes to see that Abbie was right. Dan's shirt collar was unbuttoned with his neck fully on display and he could make out that there were multiple tiny burns seared into his skin. There was a point where Nathan could see Joshua point towards Dan's neck to which the stocky student unconvincingly tried to cover the blemishes with his hand, as if they didn't exist. He seemed to be in a dazed state as he swaggered from side to side but even in that condition, Nathan caught a wide-eyed fearful look spread over Dan's face as he continued to argue with Joshua. Yet, it was as though he was looking straight through the prefect.

While Thomas and Abbie continued to observe Joshua and Dan, Nathan turned his head in the direction that Dan was facing, only to see Ranjit standing there with a menacing glare locked onto the situation brewing before him.

Suddenly, the surrounding students started to shout and cheer encouragingly. This drew Nathan's attention away from Ranjit and back to his cousin as Dan swung his fist towards Joshua who casually swatted it away, causing Dan to stumble to the floor. From the crowd, Drew emerged to try and help his friend back up to his feet. Nathan's eyes darted to where Drew had come from and saw that Denzel was there too, still clutching his ribs and making no move to intervene, though he had a conflicted expression on his face.

Drew tried to drag Dan away but he wriggled free and lunged wildly towards Joshua. However, Joshua sidestepped the attack effortlessly before wrapping his arm tightly around Dan's neck, slowly incapacitating him and drawing more roars of approval from the crowd of students. As Dan struggled feebly against Joshua's power, Nathan's eyes shifted back to Ranjit, just managing to catch him flash a look of disgusted disdain in Dan's direction before leaving him to fend for himself. After a few more seconds, Joshua released his hold and Dan leaned over, gasping for breath.

"I'm taking you to the headmaster's office," Joshua sternly told Dan before marching him towards the school doors, Dan no longer having the strength to resist him. As they passed Nathan, Thomas and Abbie, they each caught a whiff of the wretched stench of liquor emanating from Dan, their noses wrinkling out of revulsion from being in the vicinity of it. "Everyone to your classes now!" Joshua ordered to the groups of onlookers before disappearing inside the school with Dan. While many of the students began to lumber their way into the building, gossiping about the confrontation between Joshua and Dan and what it could all have been about, Nathan, Thomas and Abbie took advantage of the little time they had to quietly convey their own thoughts on the matter between them.

"Did you smell the alcohol on Dan?" Abbie hissed. "Even my parents don't reek that bad, how much did he drink last night?!"

"I don't know, but he didn't have those burns yesterday," Thomas remarked. "Even just one is painful and he had more than ten…"

"You've been burned by a cigarette before?" Abbie responded as Nathan silently listened, looking around him as he saw a desolate Drew in the distance. Meanwhile, Thomas rolled up his sleeve to show Abbie a pink carving of the word '*psycho*' on his lower arm.

"That's where Ranjit burned me when we were twelve years old…" Thomas revealed grimly while Abbie winced at the sight of the wound. "It took ages to heal properly."

"Goodness…d-do you think Ranjit's the one who burned Dan this time?" Abbie questioned.

"Hold that thought," Nathan interrupted as they were approaching the classrooms, not wanting the teachers to overhear them. "We can talk about this at lunch," he decided which Thomas and Abbie accepted before they each entered the class to start the school day.

****

Two and a half hours later, a weary Nathan left his maths class along with many other students for a brief fifteen-minute break. He'd barely been able to focus on his studies that morning as his mind kept drifting to the scuffle that Joshua and Dan had earlier, as well as the anonymous social media posts prophesying Entritica's downfall that had the school abuzz.

Heeding Abbie's words about the fresh air of the fields, Nathan decided to step outside for a while to see if it might rejuvenate him. On his way there though, he spotted Drew pacing agitatedly on the edge of the field, adjacent to the boiler room steps – and he was alone. No Denzel, Dan or Ranjit in sight.

Nathan saw an opportunity that he couldn't afford to pass up. If anyone was likely to know the truth of what happened to Dan and Denzel, it would be Drew and with none of his mates around to back him up, it was a perfect chance to get some answers from him. Nathan approached quietly, stepping carefully across the grass before catching a distracted Drew by surprise.

"What are you doing here?!" Drew loudly blurted out in a panic.

"I could ask you the same thing," Nathan retorted boldly. "Thought you'd be looking after Dan or Denzel – you know, tending to the injuries Ranjit gave them?" he added, recalling how Drew had been around when Denzel had confronted him with damaged ribs and also when Dan had scuffled with Joshua earlier.

Drew tripped over his words trying to deny Nathan's accusation. "I-I-I…I don't know what you're talking about…" he stuttered unpersuasively as his body language gave the entire truth away.

"Oh, don't play dumb!" Nathan barked impatiently. While his expression towards Drew was stern and uncompromising now, his mind couldn't help but think how backwards this felt. Before this, he'd have never even dreamed that he'd be the one unsettling one of Ranjit's cronies, rather than being intimidated himself. Nevertheless, the thought of finding out the truth about his dad's death continued to spur him on. "We both know full well what Ranjit's capable of! He doesn't give a damn about any of you! And I heard Dan talking to him on the phone three days ago! I know that Ranjit forced Dan to put those posts online!"

The colour drained from Drew's face as he was rendered speechless at what Nathan was saying. In the distance though, unbeknownst to the two boys, a head poked out from behind the wall of the boiler room. Concealed from their view, Lucy had been sat on the steps looking out over the field, enjoying her own privacy. But now, Nathan's interrogation of Drew had captured her attention and she watched on as Drew hunched his shoulders before attempting to flee.

"W-w-whatever you th-think you heard..." Drew stammered uncontrollably, fearful of cracking under the pressure. "Y-you shouldn't be getting sucked into business that's not yours. F-for your own sake, I mean..."

As he tried to make a hasty retreat, Nathan continued to berate Drew. "He's already hurt Dan and Denzel! It'll be you next!" he warned bluntly leaving Drew aggravated by the fact that he couldn't rebuke his words. "And are any of you really happy doing his dirty work?! Living like his puppets?!"

In that moment, Drew turned to flash Nathan a look, not of anger but of sheer terror. "It's better than being dead!!" he snapped defensively.

There was an icy chill in the air as Nathan silently processed Drew's words, an eerie silence descending upon them both. Before Drew could turn to leave though, Nathan calmly and gently uttered two words that shook him to his core.

"*Is* it?"

Drew didn't answer or bite back this time. To Nathan, it was almost as if Drew's expression had changed slightly. Although the fear was still very much there, his forehead was less creased, as if the earlier turmoil spread over every corner of his face had receded, even just slightly.

Conversely, Drew's last words to Nathan resonated in his mind, leaving him in a trance to the extent that he failed to stop Drew from escaping and realising only too late that he'd allowed the chance to get any more information slip past his fingers. He felt frustrated, yet Drew's feeble attempts at lying had all but confirmed his strong suspicions that Ranjit was the real mastermind behind the social media posts. Knowing he needed time to reformulate a plan, he decided to head back into the school to find Thomas and Abbie, completely unaware that Lucy was observing him as he left.

****

It wasn't until lunchtime that Nathan next reconvened with Thomas and Abbie, meeting them once again on the bench that looked out over the courtyard. The grey clouds shifted overhead as Nathan explained about his brief dispute with Drew a couple of hours ago. He mentioned how shifty Drew was regarding Dan and Denzel's injuries at Ranjit's hands along with finally revealing about Dan's curious phone call from three days ago where he refused to do any more posts.

"What?!" Thomas exclaimed in response to this news. "Why didn't you tell us this before?!"

"I had my suspicions about it, but it could have been a coincidence, so I didn't think it was worth mentioning yet," Nathan explained. "Then there were no more posts until last night and after seeing Dan stumble into school drunk with those burns and talking with Drew earlier, there's no doubt now – Ranjit's the one who pressured Dan into making those posts online."

"Yeah, I believe you," Abbie agreed, fully convinced now. "But why do it in the first place? Just to cause chaos?" she speculated.

"Who knows why he does half the things he does…" Thomas muttered. "Why bully us? Why stalk Lucy all the time? Why hurt those who are supposed to be his friends? As far as I'm concerned, he's not right in the head; tormenting and controlling others, making people miserable – you'd have to be pretty twisted to thrive off all that…"

"Well, I actually think there's more to it this time…" Nathan disclosed. "You remember before how I told you both about that article saying that Ali Ammunitions has stopped supplying weapons to our armies? And how they may have aligned with the enemy?"

"We remember," Abbie confirmed. "You definitely think that's the case now?"

"More than that! I think Ranjit himself is one of them!" Nathan declared his theory confidently to the alarm of Thomas and Abbie.

"B-but you said you've not seen any more articles about Ali Ammunitions since then…" Thomas reminded Nathan.

"Exactly!!" Nathan cried excitedly. "Just like with any news of the war! Any articles, all have forbidden access or just say 'domain no longer exists'. You don't think that's a *little* strange when it's *our* country at war? Like they're trying to *conceal* the truth?"

While still doubtful, Nathan's rationale was starting to make sense to Thomas and Abbie as they mulled over his words.

"Even if that *is* true about Ali Ammunitions siding with the enemy," Abbie spoke after a brief while, "why are you so sure that Ranjit is one of them?"

"When I heard Dan on the phone," Nathan began, "he was really trying to distance himself from Ranjit, saying he was going too far. And after I spoke with Drew earlier, it was like he was warning me to stay out of Ranjit's way. Not even in a threatening way – like he said, 'for my own sake'. Then when I asked Drew if it was worth being treated like his puppet, his words were 'it's better than being dead'…it just felt such a specific thing to say… and the look on his face too…it genuinely seemed like he was in danger…" Thomas and Abbie were silent as they processed what Nathan was telling them with an equal level of concern.

"You really think that Ranjit's been threatening to kill Drew and the others?" Thomas whispered anxiously.

"We know he's already harmed Dan and Denzel," Nathan reminded them. "It's not a huge leap from that to giving death threats. And with Ranjit, those threats may not be empty…"

Thomas and Abbie both nodded broodingly at this notion, unable to argue against Nathan's beliefs at this point. While not all the evidence was concrete, his logic behind each suspicion was connecting and sounding more and more logical.

"So, what now?" Abbie asked apprehensively.

Nathan thought for a moment as he weighed up the options in his head. In the end, he could only see one way forward but as he opened his mouth to answer Abbie, a voice spoke from behind the bench.

"You're not planning to confront Ranjit, are you?"

Recognising the voice, Nathan and Thomas shot up from their seat on the bench.

"Lucy?" a shocked Nathan uttered as he saw her standing behind the bench with her arms folded tightly.

"Well, are you?" Lucy meekly demanded, her eyes shifting nervously between Nathan and Thomas. The tension between the three of them was palpable, for this was the first time in around eight months where they had all been at their old hangout spot since Lucy had inexplicably stopped interacting with them.

"What do you want Lucy?" Abbie interrupted sharply after noticing Nathan's reluctance to answer Lucy's request. On the one hand, Abbie stared unflinchingly at Lucy while remaining seated on the bench. On the other hand, Lucy could barely bring herself to look Abbie in the eye, almost intimidated by the girl who had replaced her as Nathan and Thomas' friend.

This only irked Abbie more though as she presumed Lucy was looking down at her like the rest of the students. Lucy looked back towards the school where the cafeteria hall was, seeming even more on edge before turning back to Nathan.

"Can we talk somewhere more private?" she asked gently, addressing Nathan and Thomas. "It's important."

"Okay sure," Nathan agreed, still perplexed. "But where?"

"I know a place, just follow me," Lucy said as she shuffled over in the direction of the field. At this point, Abbie rose from the bench and rushed towards Lucy and got in her face.

"Anything you have to say to Nathan and Thomas, you can say to me too!" she asserted, causing Lucy to flinch and step backwards.

"Yeah, fine…" Lucy mumbled uncomfortably as she carried on walking.

Nathan, Thomas and Abbie wordlessly followed Lucy as she led them away from the courtyard and towards the field. As they headed further west of the field and away from the school, Nathan quickly realised that Lucy was taking them to where the boiler room was, recognising it from when he confronted Drew hours ago.

"S-so that's your new hangout spot now?" Thomas asked Lucy as he looked towards the boiler room steps that they were approaching.

"Y-yeah…" Lucy replied shyly. "It's one of the few places left where I can get away from everyone else – including Ranjit – and just draw and feel at peace again…"

"I thought you had that with us…" Nathan lamented sadly. Lucy didn't say anything to this but Nathan noticed her head lower upon hearing it. Once they reached the steps, Lucy made sure to check that they were all hidden out of view from the rest of the school before continuing their conversation.

"Okay, I'll cut to the chase," Lucy stated, directly looking at Nathan. "Don't confront Ranjit. You need to stop investigating him else he *will* hurt you and I don't want that to happen."

Nathan sighed as a realisation sunk in. "You heard me and Drew earlier, didn't you?" he guessed.

"That's right, I was here painting when you guys had your 'chat' – I heard everything," Lucy confirmed. "I spoke to Drew myself after that – turns out he was wondering whether to confide in me about the situation with Ranjit."

"And did he?" Thomas questioned curiously.

"Yes, he did," Lucy answered. "It sounds like you've guessed it already, but Ranjit is the one who attacked Denzel and Dan – and was behind Dan's anonymous posts…" Lucy's eyes were red as she said this, as if holding back tears. "If he can do that to his *friends*, I dread to think what he'd do to you if he knew you were meddling in his affairs. That's why I'm begging you Nathan – please stop investigating Ranjit!"

Taken aback and conflicted between Lucy's plea and his need to find out the truth about his dad's death, Nathan quietly mulled over what to do for the best.

"Why the hell do you even care?!" Abbie barked angrily at Lucy. "Didn't you abandon them for Kamran anyway?!"

Lucy's lips trembled as she had this accusation thrown at her. Her eyes started to water and she had to clench them shut with all her effort to stop the tears from flowing.

"I-I'm s-sorry…" Lucy apologised, her voice cracking as she spoke. "I-I swear, I never w-wanted to-"

"I won't confront Ranjit," Nathan interrupted, finally answering Lucy's plea. He saw a sensation of relief wash over Lucy's face upon hearing this but also detected the same reaction from Thomas and Abbie in the corner of his eye.

"Nathan…thank yo-" Lucy began to say but Nathan stopped her before she could finish.

"As long as you tell me whatever you know about Ali Ammunitions and their involvement in the war," Nathan announced to Lucy's surprise. "That's my condition. My dad died fighting for this country."

"Oh…I'm sorry Nathan, I had no idea…" Lucy said sympathetically with a gleam ridden with guilt for not knowing sooner shining briefly in her eyes.

"There's too much I don't know about his death," Nathan continued boldly. "And I *have* to know. So, if you really want me to leave Ranjit alone and if you're really as sorry as you say you are, then tell me what *you* know…"

Lucy hesitated to respond for a moment, but after considering Nathan's words, she timidly nodded her head, accepting his terms.

"W-what do you want to know?" she asked.

Nathan thought carefully about how to phrase his questions and took a big gulp before speaking, a mixture of emotions churning within him. Half of him felt relief and a sense of achievement that he could be closing in on the truth at last. Yet, the other half of him still wondered whether he was ready to hear it…

"Do you know if Anil tells Ranjit and Kamran about his job – you know, any dealings about his business and who he supplies weapons to?" Nathan began.

"H-he tells Kamran more than Ranjit," Lucy answered honestly. "Kamran never tells me the details unfortunately, but I know Anil has private meetings with him about any company contracts – he wants to get Kamran involved in the family business but I don't think he's that interested. There was one time recently though that I came to their house and caught Ranjit eavesdropping on one of their discussions – when he saw me, he got really sheepish and warned me against saying anything…"

"Okay," Nathan uttered as he listened to Lucy's explanation. "Has there ever been a time where Anil *did* tell Ranjit about what was happening with his company?"

"Well, there's been a few times when I've been over for dinner at theirs where Anil's talked openly about developments within the business at the dinner table – usually after he's had a few drinks – but they've only ever been in vague detail," Lucy clarified.

"Anything about the war itself? Like who we're even fighting against?" Nathan queried eagerly as Thomas and Abbie also listened intently.

"No," Lucy responded, shaking her head. "H-he's never mentioned anything about the war when I've been around…I'm as in the dark about it as you…"

"And anything to suggest he's stopped supplying weapons to our armies?" Nathan added. "Or that they've aligned with the enemy?"

"I-I'm not sure where you've got that from…" Lucy replied. "But I've not heard or seen anything to suggest that either of those are true…"

"Nothing?!" Nathan groaned, his frustration increasing. "No secret phone calls or anything like that?"

"W-whenever Anil takes a business call, he always leaves the room," Lucy admitted. "So, I wouldn't know…I'm sorry…"

Nathan bit his upper lip as he digested this information. It certainly wasn't what he'd hoped to hear as he'd wanted to find something conclusive. However, it had only created more questions for him as it had neither confirmed nor disproved his suspicions. After deep thought, the only piece of substantial news that he could dig deeper into was Ranjit's sneaky behaviour regarding Anil's and Kamran's business meetings. It certainly suggested that he had an interest there and given his recent violent behaviour towards Dan and Denzel and his influence regarding the previous social media posts predicting Entritica's downfall, it could be linked to any speculation of siding with the enemy.

"Okay then, I'll make this my last question," Nathan decided aloud. "Ranjit seems to have a weird curiosity about their meetings – do you think he could be working with the enemy himself?"

"You could try asking me yourself…Dragon Boy," a deep unfeeling voice spoke from behind Nathan.

A cold shiver ran down Nathan's spine as he heard the voice, one that turned his blood to ice at the sound of it and he witnessed the colour fade from Lucy's face before he, Thomas and Abbie turned around to find Ranjit standing menacingly behind him, towering over them. Instinctively, Abbie stepped in front of Nathan and Thomas, coming between them and Ranjit. However, Ranjit barely acknowledged them, instead focusing on Lucy who quivered uncontrollably with each step he took towards her.

"Get away from her!" Thomas cried out shakily which fell on deaf ears as Ranjit loomed over Lucy. Nathan placed his hand on Thomas' shoulder, wordlessly telling him to hold back. Concerned as he was for Lucy, he was far too curious about what Ranjit had to say and whether he'd disclose anything crucial.

"You really thought I wouldn't find you here?" Ranjit taunted sinisterly. "I have eyes everywhere, you know. Got to keep them on you – make sure you're keeping to the terms of our agreement. Can't have you tarnishing our family name by being a disobedient wife to my brother now, can I?"

As Lucy recoiled at these words, Nathan and Thomas also felt disturbed by how slimily they were spoken while Abbie had a thunderous look on her face, staring daggers at the back of Ranjit's head.

"And yet, here you are falling at the first real test of your loyalty to us?" he continued, his voice lowering to a haunting whisper. "You know what's at stake. We set you and your mother up for life, wiping out her *many* debts – and all you had to do was ditch these little freaks," Ranjit gestured, his eyes still focused on Lucy, at Nathan and Thomas who were stunned to hear this revelation. "And you can't even do that? Oh, how sweet Zara will be disappointed when she knows…"

"Lucy, is that true?" Nathan asked her. Lucy glanced over at Nathan, her mouth open but no words left them before looking down at the ground ashamedly as Ranjit sneered at her.

"Well, since you couldn't keep your end of the bargain," he spoke as he finally turned his head to see Nathan and Thomas in the corner of his eye. "You two are fair game now…"

Once she heard this threat, Lucy sharply raised her head towards Ranjit's face. "Please, I'm begging you! Just leave them alone!" she pleaded distraughtly.

By now, Nathan had heard enough of seeing Lucy squirm and saw no other way of getting answers about the war. He stepped past Abbie towards Ranjit who raised his eyebrows as though slightly startled by this.

"Fine by me!" Nathan impulsively declared as Thomas, Abbie and Lucy watched on, concerned. "I know exactly how you've been treating Drew and the others."

"Oh, is that right?" Ranjit snarled.

"Yeah, it is," Nathan snapped. "And I want to know exactly what you know about this war!"

"Nathan, don't!" Lucy shrieked.

"Lucy, stay out of this!" Nathan advised sternly. "I don't want you getting hurt too!"

At the sound of this though, an evil smirk spread across Ranjit's face.

"Alright, you want to know about the war?" he repeated mockingly. "Then, these are my terms. If you have the guts to face me after school tomorrow, I'll tell you what I know."

Blinded by his desire to uncover the truth and without thinking, Nathan hastily responded to Ranjit's offer.

"Suits me!" he stated fiercely and as the words left his mouth, Thomas cringed because he knew Ranjit would not make matters so straightforward.

"Good, I'll meet you at Seppuku Bridge then," Ranjit proclaimed.

Other than an audible gasp from Lucy, Abbie looked on, perplexed, as an unsettling silence descended upon Nathan and Thomas, the colour in their faces fading from merely the mention of the bridge's name.

"Oh, did I strike a nerve?" Ranjit ridiculed arrogantly. Nathan didn't say anything, his earlier bravado now nowhere to be seen as he stared vacantly back at Ranjit, almost bewitched. From the glint in his sullen eyes, Ranjit revelled in seeing this and decided to push his buttons even more. "Well, if you don't show up tomorrow – I'll make sure *she* pays the price," he growled as he pointed at a scared and shocked Lucy. This time, an incensed Thomas defiantly stepped past Abbie to stand side by side with Nathan against Ranjit.

"No way we're letting you do that! We'll be there!" Thomas spat angrily which caught Nathan by surprise and snapped him out of his stupor. He still couldn't find the words, only managing to quietly nod in agreement with Thomas.

"Good. See you tomorrow…" Ranjit uttered ominously before striding past Nathan, Thomas and Abbie, only stopping to look back at a pale Lucy. He didn't say anything to her, he just stopped and glared, his eyebrows again raised.

Lucy hesitated for a while until she begrudgingly followed him. Nathan automatically moved to stretch his arm out, as though reaching his hand out to her in the hopes she would change her mind. However, the words failed to come out of his mouth once again, so he helplessly retracted it back, realising it was futile. All they could do was watch as Ranjit left them behind with Lucy in tow, the latter glancing back at them with regretful eyes. Once they had both gone, a frowning Abbie turned back to Nathan and Thomas.

"You two are as bad as each other!" she lambasted them. "What on earth were you thinking?! This is obviously some sort of trap!"

"If he's threatening to hurt Lucy, what else are we supposed to do?!" Thomas retorted. "Look, we have a day to figure out what to do. We'll figure something out, right Nathan?"

Thomas turned to Nathan who looked back, still in deep thought while the name 'Seppuku Bridge' continued to play in his mind. He was troubled by it, but the need to save Lucy from Ranjit's grasp and to also find out more about what was happening in the war that claimed his father's life ultimately overpowered this worry.

"Yeah, we will. After all, what's the worst that can happen?" Nathan finally spoke, trying to think optimistically.

The three of them heard the school bell chime in the distance, meaning that lunch period was coming to an end. They made their way back to the school, even Abbie, all exhausted by the events and developments of that day and with the upcoming confrontation with Ranjit playing on their minds.

****

Later that afternoon, after school had ended, Ranjit received a phone call just as he got into his pre-arranged limousine ride back home. He saw the name Cain appear on his phone and answered it as he took a seat next to a wrapped parcel.

"I was wondering when I'd hear from you next," Ranjit answered the call assertively.

"Your sharp tongue never ceases to amuse me," the mysterious Cain chuckled on the other end of the phone. "Have you gotten into your ride now?"

"I have," Ranjit confirmed.

"Good," Cain responded. "There'll be a parcel on the seat next to you. When it was delivered to your house, we included instructions for it to be put in the limo waiting for you. You can open it now."

Ranjit picked up the parcel next to him, removed the packaging and smiled wickedly. Inside the box was a jet-black locket in the shape of a dragon that had vicious red eyes.

"You've done good work spreading fear into the hearts of the public with those internet posts," Cain continued as Ranjit unhooked the chain of the locket and draped it around his neck. "You are one of Chimera now."

"Excellent," Ranjit remarked coolly. "What's my next mission?"

"Eager one, aren't we?" Cain laughed. "Well, thanks to your intel, we know that Entritica are trying to cover up our existence which was trivial to us – until now. Maris and the rest of our troops should reach the shores of Entritica by tomorrow night. The time is coming for the name 'Chimera' to be properly heard throughout Entritica, to make them realise that their only option is to submit to Maris' will. So we need to make a more powerful statement to show that our influence has seeped into the country – which is where you come in…"

"What do you need me to do?" Ranjit questioned bluntly.

"Make an example of someone. To show that Chimera is not to be trifled with. You understand what that means, yes?" Cain directed.

"Oh yes I do," Ranjit answered gleefully. He looked in his bag as he continued to talk. "In fact, I'm one step ahead as I've already got a victim lined up for tomorrow afternoon," he disclosed as he pulled a handgun from his backpack, twirling it around with his fingers.

"Good, I trust that you'll get the job done," Cain acknowledged with contentment.

Ranjit casually ended the call and shoved the handgun back into his backpack as the limousine continued on its way...

Chapter 7

The next morning before school, Nathan sat on his bed, wearing his uniform and looking pensively at the foreboding grey clouds outside his window. Just like yesterday afternoon, the ensuing confrontation with Ranjit weighed heavily on his mind, looming over him like a phantom. He tried to look beyond that point yet was unable to visualise anything that may come after the event – there was only Ranjit and then nothing. He couldn't explain why he felt this way, but it left him troubled.

Taking a deep breath and summoning his courage, Nathan finally stood up from his bed, his stomach churning uneasily as he did so. He draped his backpack over his shoulder and made his way downstairs where Victoria was waiting to see him off. He moved to hug her goodbye but could see from the distant look in her eyes that something was on her mind.

"Mom, is everything okay?" Nathan asked her, believing that she was still struggling to cope without Richard around. However, her response caught him by surprise.

"I've seen some posts online…about Entritica falling…" Victoria spoke after taking time to find the words. "I-is it true…?"

"How did you-" Nathan uttered, bewildered that she'd even seen them since she didn't have a social media account as far as he knew.

"You'd been quiet for the last few days…" Victoria explained sensitively. "I was worried that you were getting bullied like before…so I created an account online to see if that was the case…and that's when I saw the posts…"

"Oh, mom," Nathan gasped compassionately. "Please don't worry about them. They're just trolls spreading lies about the war. They're not even targeting me, I promise…"

"Okay," Victoria accepted. "I'm sorry, I didn't mean to invade your privacy. I just wanted to make sure that you were okay… I'd hate to think you were being tormented again like back then…"

Nathan embraced his mother tightly to reassure her. "I'm okay," he whispered gently. "*We* will be okay…" he emphasised, as though not just trying to convince her but himself too.

"I love you," Victoria told Nathan.

"I love you too, mom," Nathan echoed. "I'll see you when I get back home," he added before walking out the door, crossing the driveway and vanishing out of his mother's view.

He felt his insides stir chaotically like storm clouds once again as he got further from his home and Victoria, this time, with a sense of guilt mixed in with the earlier apprehension. He didn't enjoy lying to his mother regarding the seriousness of Dan's social media posts as there was no guarantee that they would be okay, as much as he hoped that they would be. Plus, the parting conversation that he'd had with her had only served to make him feel more conflicted about meeting with Ranjit that afternoon, the level of danger that he could walk into still being uncertain to him.

Twenty minutes later, Nathan walked through the school gates to the courtyard where he found Thomas waiting for him. With his hands in his pockets, he shuffled over to Nathan who recognised the perturbed expression on his face – for it was similar to the one that looked back at him in the mirror earlier that morning.

"Nath, are you really sure about meeting Ranjit later?" Thomas questioned nervously, cutting to the chase. Although he'd accepted the challenge yesterday, he was riled up when he did it. Now having had the evening to think over what he'd agreed to, he was clearly having regrets.

Similarly, Nathan's bravado from the prior afternoon when arguing with Ranjit was also absent as he hesitated to answer, giving Thomas hope that he would change his mind. Before Nathan could reply though, Abbie arrived on the scene.

"What are you going to do this afternoon?" Abbie abruptly demanded, focusing on Nathan who again went quiet. After several moments of uncomfortable silence , Abbie disapprovingly shook her head and continued. "Look, if you're dead set on going after Ranjit and actually have a plan, I'll help in any way I can. But I don't think we *need* to do this. I'm convinced that this is a trap," she rationalised with Thomas nodding his head in agreement.

"I know. I feel uneasy too," Nathan reluctantly admitted. "But he was also threatening Lucy if we didn't show up. We can't just leave her in danger…"

"Ranjit isn't going to hurt me," a voice called out from behind Nathan.

The eyes of both Thomas and Abbie shifted past Nathan who also turned around to see Lucy walking over towards them.

"You sure you're safe to talk to us again?" Thomas remarked, not forgetting how on edge she was in Ranjit's presence.

"He's not coming in today," Lucy revealed, seeming more relaxed as a result. "I heard that he was feeling unwell but I'm pretty sure it was a lie to skive school."

"Skiving? That doesn't bode well for later..." Abbie noted aloud, focusing on Nathan as she said it, something that he was aware of as his eyes darted downwards away from her uncomfortably upon hearing this.

"Nathan, Ranjit never had any intention of hurting me. Kamran wouldn't allow it to happen and he knows that. He only said that to get both of you to agree to face him and it worked," Lucy explained which left Thomas feeling even more embarrassed for losing his cool and taking the bait.

"So, you don't need us to *save* you after all?" Abbie snidely summarised. Her scorn didn't go unnoticed by Lucy who was irked by this but chose to overlook it.

"That's right, I'm not in any danger," Lucy confirmed. "Nath, Thomas, I'm begging you both, please don't confront Ranjit!"

Nathan heard her plea, however he couldn't stop thinking about the unsettling words that Ranjit had whispered to Lucy yesterday, detesting the idea of her being emotionally blackmailed.

"You're certain that you're not at risk?" Nathan queried doubtingly.

"Yes, that's what I'm telling you!" Lucy insisted overzealously.

"The reason I'm asking," Nathan elaborated, unable to hide the concern in his voice, "is because I remember what Ranjit was muttering to you before – about your mom's debts. Are you being pressured into marrying Kamran?"

Lucy sighed before she answered his question. "Nathan, I understand it's hard for you guys to believe," she responded, a hint of agitation slipping out in her words. "But dating Kamran was *my* choice. He bumped into me last summer and I didn't even know he was Ranjit's brother at that time. We got to talking, bonded over our relationships with our parents – his dad, my mom – and that's how we hit it off."

"Lucy, I can accept that," Nathan interrupted. "But that wasn't what I asked you. Dating is one thing, but *marriage*. This soon. Something feels off." While Lucy didn't reply to this, Nathan heard an audible gulp from her throat, one that suggested that she knew what he was saying was true. "Is Ranjit or Anil pressuring you into marrying Kamran? Or even Kamran himself?" he asked her. Again, Lucy didn't respond, her face remained steady, giving away no visible signs to suggest that Nathan had hit the mark. "If they are, can't you tell your mom what's really happening?" he added, trying to find a way to help her.

This time, Lucy automatically averted her gaze from Nathan, biting her lip in the process. Knowing Lucy to be a terrible liar, Nathan realised what was actually happening.

"Your mom's the one pressuring you, isn't she?" he deduced as Thomas and Abbie watched the interrogation curiously. To their surprise, Lucy looked up at Nathan and sheepishly nodded to confirm his presumption.

"M-my mom…arranged the marriage together with Anil," Lucy clarified. "Anil wanted the marriage…hoping it would get Kamran to mature more so he could entrust him as the heir to the company. My mom *needed* it…for the money…"

"So it's no different that when she was forcing you into acting and modelling back in the day…" Thomas grunted irately, recalling how she had featured in the Dynochoc commercials while still only a kid. "What kind of mother does that to her daughter?! Can't she earn the money herself?!"

"I-I never wanted to leave you two," Lucy confessed, turning to Nathan and Thomas in turn while Abbie scowled at her resentfully. "Before we returned to school after the summer, Ranjit threatened to hurt you both and put a stop to the marriage if I continued to hang around with you. He didn't want anyone from his family to be associated with…in his words, *'freaks'*. I told my mom all this hoping that she'd support me. But she flipped out and ordered me to do as Ranjit was saying…" Nathan and Thomas struggled to hide their disgust at what they were hearing. "She told me that if I didn't go through with the marriage, they wouldn't support us, meaning she wouldn't be able to afford her loans and our house could get repossessed…"

"That shouldn't be your burden though…" Nathan asserted, still horrified. "You're only sixteen!"

"It is what it is…" Lucy acknowledged begrudgingly. "I can't just let her lose the house and she's got nowhere else to go, so I have no other choice…"

"Meaning you can't be around us anymore because of your mom…" Nathan summarised sadly. "She never liked us much anyway…"

"I'm sorry, really I am" Lucy apologised. "But I promise you, I'm not in any danger with Kamran or any of his family, even Ranjit. So please don't put yourselves in harm's way on my account!"

"Well, that's a relief to hear," Thomas commented. "Sorry Nath, but now we know this, I definitely don't think we should go."

"I'm with Thomas. It's not worth the risk and there's nothing to gain from facing Ranjit now," Abbie reasoned. "If you still insist on going Nath, I'll have to tell Joshua – or your mom…" she boldly warned, to Nathan's surprise and displeasure.

With his friends backing out of facing Ranjit due to this new information, along with the idea of causing unnecessary distress to his mother by walking into such a potentially precarious situation, these factors were finally enough to sway Nathan's resolve.

"Alright, you guys win…" Nathan yielded reluctantly. "I won't confront Ranjit later…" Thomas, Abbie and Lucy all breathed a collective sigh of relief after hearing this, as though an unseen weight had been lifted from each of them.

"Thank you," Lucy said gratefully. "Look, I've said what I've needed to but I have to go now. I know Ranjit won't be in today but Dan, Denzel and Drew still are. If either of them sees me with you guys and tells Ranjit, then…"

"I get it, you're still trying to protect us from him…" Nathan recognised. "I still hate that you have to sacrifice your friendship with us to do that… but I don't want you and your mom to be made homeless either…" he commented, pitying not just Lucy, but himself for not being able to come up with a solution for her. The only thing he could think to offer was support should she ever need it again. "Just know that we are here if you do need someone to turn to…"

Lucy was taken aback by Nathan's words, not knowing how to react immediately. She opened her mouth to speak but seemed to choke on her own words. Instead, she settled for silently forcing an appreciative smile towards Nathan, one that masked the pain she felt deep down, before leaving the group behind once again.

"There she goes, leaving you both high and dry again..." Abbie grumbled cynically. "You're being far too nice to her after the way she's treated you..."

"And you're being a bit harsh on her," Nathan retorted. "She just told us how none of this was her choice. She's always had a turbulent relationship with her mom, you should know what that's like." Abbie guiltily pursed her lips together as he reminded her of this, fully aware that he had a point.

"Yeah, what's your beef with Lucy?" Thomas queried. Just as Abbie wavered when asked this, the school bell rang and the surrounding students started shuffling towards the school doors.

"It's nothing, just ignore me, I was way out of line..." Abbie responded, throwing her hands up in the air as she hurried past Nathan and Thomas towards the school, avoiding the question. Both boys looked at each other, puzzled by Abbie's reaction but knowing they couldn't do much about it now, they followed the rest of the crowd into the school.

"Well at least we know we're not having to see Ranjit now. I feel like I can actually breathe again now," Thomas commented optimistically, just before they entered the building.

"Yeah, same here," Nathan agreed, starting to feel a bit more at peace. Once inside, they each split into different directions, heading towards their respective lockers to put their books away before the morning assembly. As he reached his locker, Nathan pulled the key from his pocket and turned it in the lock before pulling the door open.

To his surprise, he found a single post-it note at the bottom of his locker. This was unusual for Nathan – he knew that he'd left his locker empty before he left school yesterday. Quickly putting his bag inside, Nathan took the note and unfolded it to find a scruffily written message which read:

If you want to know how daddy dearest died, I'll see you at the bridge at half 4 – if you have the balls, Dragon Boy - Ranjit

Reading the mocking message, Nathan's mind fell into a state of turmoil once more. Memories of his father flooded back to him, but the one that stood out most was his final moment with him – before he went to war. He remembered how Richard asked him to protect Victoria, bequeathing the locket to him. Nathan automatically clutched his locket as he recalled his father telling him how proud he was of him prior to his departure.

The despair soon turned to anger though as Nathan's blood bubbled while he reminded himself of the funeral one week ago and seeing how many soldiers had perished along with his father. Ranjit's cruel note resuscitated his resolve to discover the truth about what happened, believing deep down that he had to take any chance that came along to do so. Resolutely, he scrunched the note up in his fist and furiously slammed his locker door shut…

****

Much later, at the end of the school day, Nathan left his final lesson along with Abbie at 4pm. After reading the note from Ranjit, Nathan had been distant throughout the day and this hadn't escaped Abbie's notice. When he rushed past his locker, Abbie hastily tailed him.

"Nath, you okay?" she called out to him with concern, catching his attention. "Where are you going?"

"I'm just going to the toilet," Nathan replied nonchalantly.

"Oh!" Abbie uttered, surprised yet relieved. "Okay then, I'll wait for you!" she added fervently with an overenthusiastic grin on her face.

"Okay then," Nathan echoed calmly as he quickly disappeared into the men's toilets.

Abbie looked down at the ground as she anxiously waited outside the toilets for him for about five minutes, long after the majority of students had left the building already. She jerked her head upwards as she heard the sudden scraping sound of a door scratching against the floor as it opened, thinking that Nathan was finally emerging from the toilets.

Instead, the creak came from the other side of the corridor and to her disappointment, she saw Joshua exiting Mr Jones' office. Abbie scowled at him before turning away towards the bathroom door, hoping for Nathan to come out. However, Joshua had caught her dirty look out the corner of his eye and strode over towards her.

"Last time I saw you here, you were scurrying off with Ranjit's lot," Joshua stated sternly, remembering how Abbie was still hanging around with Dan, Denzel and Drew three weeks ago. Abbie avoided his gaze while he reminded her of this. "Now I've seen you lingering around Nathan all this week. What's that all about?" he demanded to know.

"Oh, so you *do* pay attention to him then?" Abbie snapped sarcastically.

"Don't get lippy with me Abbie!" Joshua cautioned her sternly, forcing her to hold her tongue with all the effort she could muster.

"For your information," Abbie sighed through gritted teeth and a vein pulsating on her temple, still not looking at Joshua. "We made peace at the start of this week. I'm done with Ranjit and the rest of them…"

"Yeah, right," Joshua remarked sceptically. "If I find out you're messing Nathan about-"

Before he could finish his warning, Abbie's head shot up, having finally run out of patience, and stared Joshua dead in the eyes.

"Messing him about?!" she yelled incredulously, shocking Joshua as she defiantly stepped towards him. "You've got *some* nerve saying that! You're supposed to be his family, yet where the hell have you been these last few weeks when he's still been grieving for his dad?! I've been here for him more the last five days than you've been for the last sixteen years he's been around!" Joshua became more and more flustered as Abbie continued to unleash her tirade on him. "What, cat got your tongue?! You might be the headmaster's pet with your army training and your martial arts trophies, but don't you *dare* lecture me on messing people about when you can't even be there when your own cousin needs you!!"

"Abbie?" a voice called out from the corridor.

Abbie and Joshua turned around to find Thomas who saw the two red faces staring back at him – Abbie breathless and angry with wild eyes while Joshua was speechless and wide-eyed in embarrassment. After an awkward silence among the three, Joshua sheepishly slinked away from the two of them.

"Oh yeah, now look who's scurrying off!" Abbie jeered at Joshua just before he escaped out the door while Thomas rushed over to calm her down.

"What the hell was that about?!" Thomas questioned, trying to make sense of what just happened.

"He just set me off," Abbie waved off dismissively, though still seething. "And where were you anyway?"

"I just had Law and I stopped behind to ask Ms Woo some questions," Thomas explained before shaking his head, exasperated by the situation. "Never mind that, have you seen Nathan?"

"He's in the toilets," Abbie answered, idly pointing to the bathroom door with her thumb. When hearing this however, a worried expression slowly spread over Thomas' face.

"In *those* toilets?" Thomas reiterated.

"Yeah," Abbie replied bluntly.

"H-how long has he been in there?" Thomas demanded frantically.

"About ten minutes now, why?" Abbie revealed, now bewildered as to why Thomas was asking this.

"There's a window in there…" Thomas stated, a gravely serious tone in his voice.

Abbie didn't immediately understand what Thomas meant by this – until she remembered what was meant to happen in around twenty minutes, looking fearfully back at Thomas. Now both on the same page, they stormed into the toilets, hastily checking each of the stalls, kicking the doors open only to find them all empty. They then turned their attention towards the bathroom window which they were terrified to see was left ajar, all but confirming their worst suspicions…

"This is bad!" Thomas panicked aloud. "This is really, really bad!!"

"Why would he do this?!" Abbie desperately tried to reason. "I thought we'd agreed not to go! Why would he go somewhere so dangerous alone?!"

"We can't let that happen!" Thomas declared, racing out of the toilets as fast as he could with Abbie closely following him.

Unbeknownst to the two, Joshua was still outside mulling over Abbie's scathing comments, sitting on a bench with her words playing on his conscience. He snapped out of his trail of thought though when he heard Abbie and Thomas burst through the school doors.

"Maybe we're overreacting?!" Abbie suggested hopefully. "Maybe we're just imagining the worst when it may not even happen?"

"At Seppuku Bridge?! I hardly think so!" Thomas blurted as they both dashed past Joshua, so wrapped up in fretting over Nathan that they didn't even notice him. "There's a reason Ranjit chose that place!"

Joshua, having overheard what they'd just said, observed them as they vanished into the distance. Still bothered by what Abbie had said to him about failing his cousin, he decided to follow them from afar.

"Why that place then?!" Abbie gasped aloud as they rushed down the long winding drive towards the school gates. "I remember Nathan clammed up yesterday when Ranjit brought it up! What's the deal with it?!"

"When Nathan was getting cyberbullied after the Tobias incident," Thomas explained, puffing as he did so, "he confronted Ranjit and the others at Seppuku Bridge…and they gave him a vicious beating there. It's not a place Nathan or I want to revisit…and Ranjit is taking advantage of that…"

Abbie noticed an agonised expression on Thomas' face as they continued running, one that suggested there was still more to this story that he wasn't saying.

"Thomas, is there *anything* else that I need to know about this bridge?" Abbie asked him.

In that moment, Thomas stopped at the school gates, panting heavily as Abbie watched him, waiting for an answer. Unable to endure her suspicious eyes much longer, Thomas relented.

"R-remember how I said before that Nath's mental health really suffered that year because of the cyberbullying?" Thomas reminded her.

"Yeah...?" Abbie responded, nervously anticipating his reply.

"Well after that beating...and the torment from Ranjit and everyone else...it's the same place where Nathan tried to take his own life..." he confessed regrettably.

For a brief moment, Abbie didn't say anything as she just stared back at Thomas, horrified and still reeling from the revelation she'd just heard. Then she snapped back to reality, remembering that Nathan was going back to that same bridge to confront the same tormentor, fully realising the severity of the situation.

"We've got no time to waste then!!" she shouted determinedly before sprinting away from the school gates to Thomas' amazement. He was left to try and catch up with her, both of them still oblivious to the fact that Joshua was also pursuing them, equally unsettled by what his cousin could have possibly gotten himself into...

Chapter 8

As the now pitch-black clouds loomed menacingly above him, Nathan cautiously proceeded along the path and past the trees, his head hung low until Seppuku Bridge finally came into view. It was a small, dilapidated bridge towards the centre of a tiny secluded wooded area, above a narrow river and far from any nearby roads.

There were barely any signs of life around since the area had been left mostly abandoned for years. This was because Seppuku Bridge was known as a place where people, often local depressed students, would come to commit suicide, with a few reports of such incidents coming out in the news years ago. It was so infamous that whenever there was a local disappearance within the neighbourhood, the police would search Seppuku Bridge as the first port of call. With such a dark and haunting reputation, most people took care to even avoid the woods.

Looking at the bridge from a distance, repressed memories hazily flooded back to Nathan about the last time he had been here. Distorted images of the brutal assault that he had endured, one led by Ranjit, began to play over and over sporadically in his mind, leaving him unnerved. Nevertheless, he decided to press on as he tried to push such thoughts out of his mind and focus on finding out what happened to his father.

With the first steps he took toward the bridge, the recollections of the incident became clearer as he painfully recalled each punch and kick that connected with his head, his ribs and his limbs. After about ten steps, he saw a hooded figure emerge on the bridge which he assumed to be Ranjit. Spotting this, Nathan was now able to remember Ranjit's voice from back then, how he cackled about what he'd done to him along with some of the abusive taunts and jeers he hurled at Nathan:

"Freak!"

"Look at you, you're pathetic!"

"You should do the world a favour and just disappear!"

Channelling his strength to block out these cruel comments, Nathan snapped out of his trance and, learning from history, realised that he shouldn't walk into this confrontation unprepared. He looked on the ground around him, noticing a rock the size of a cricket ball protruding out of the soil. Nathan plucked it from the dirt and shoved it into his right trouser pocket as a contingency plan. He then gathered some of the surrounding soil and scooped it into his other pocket in case he needed it.

He then walked the last few yards in the direction of the bridge, each step he took now feeling heavier as the trauma of the prior incident remained with him, weighing him down. Nathan's final memories of the day were of him standing on the ledge of the bridge, his body wracked with agony from his wounds. A feeling of hopelessness and self-loathing washed over him before he clenched his eyes shut, blocking the memory out once more.

When Nathan opened his eyes again, he was standing at the foot of the bridge. And his tormentor Ranjit was standing in the centre to greet him.

"You must be truly desperate for answers to meet me here of all places," Ranjit acknowledged mockingly.

Before he could respond, Nathan heard a rustling noise behind him. He turned around to find himself surrounded as Dan, Denzel and Drew were standing there, blocking any chance he had of escaping. Just as Abbie had believed, this was a trap.

"Don't struggle. You may get out of this unscathed," Drew recommended. Although he took the advice on board and didn't resist, Nathan caught the reluctant expressions and hesitant body language from the three boys as they each placed a hand on his shoulders and back to march him further down the bridge as Ranjit observed.

"And after all he's put you through, you're all *still* doing his bidding?" Nathan asked rhetorically, unsurprised but disappointed. Dan, still sporting his burns, Denzel, still clutching his ribs and Drew, who had been powerless to prevent these events, each stayed silent at this, not even able to throw one snide remark at Nathan this time, like their spirits had truly been broken.

Nathan was led towards the centre of the bridge and, as ordered by Ranjit, Dan, Denzel and Drew held him in place against the railings.

"Well, this brings back fun memories," Ranjit sniggered cruelly, knowing full well that it was the exact place they had pummelled Nathan four years ago. Even though just being in this very spot plagued his mind with the chilling experience, Nathan refused to let Ranjit show that he was phased.

"So, are you going to tell me what you know? Or are you just going to waste my time?" Nathan snapped boldly, irritating Ranjit.

"Ah yes, you and that cousin of yours have both been snooping in my business this week, haven't you?" Ranjit spat coldly. Nathan raised his eyebrow curiously as he said this – the fact that Joshua had been investigating Ranjit too was new information to him. Did he also have misgivings about him? As this thought crossed his mind, Ranjit detected the surprise in Nathan's face. "Seems you didn't know that…such a shame that your own family is keeping you in the dark…" he taunted, trying to rattle Nathan who tried to disregard this but was secretly bothered by the implication.

"Then what's *your* family letting you in on?" Nathan demanded assertively. "You claim to know what killed my dad. So tell me. Now!"

"Very well, since you've come all this way, I'll indulge you," Ranjit conceded confidently as Nathan listened intently. "The truth is…that your dad along with many of Entritica's other soldiers…were killed by a hurricane…" he finally revealed.

Alarmed, Nathan took a moment to process what Ranjit had just told him. Unable to accept this explanation at face value, especially from Ranjit of all people, Nathan angrily disputed this declaration.

"I'm not playing games here Ranjit! I want to know the *truth*!" Nathan bellowed as Dan, Denzel and Drew struggled to keep him pinned against the bridge railings, baffled by the typically feeble boy's sudden surge of strength.

"Whether you believe me or not is up to you," Ranjit stated and shrugged off nonchalantly. "But what I've just told you *is* the truth! The hurricane happened over three weeks ago and devastated the Entritica forces, along with a quarter of the Zalhara Timberlands. Hell, it was so severe that there was only one survivor from Entritica…"

Hearing this, Nathan was reminded of when he saw Bradley Butcher at the mass memorial for the Entritica soldiers. He remembered how cagey he was when asked whether he was the sole survivor from the battle. After reflecting on this, Ranjit's assertions about the hurricane now had added weight.

"I-if what you're saying is true…" Nathan mumbled, still conflicted. "Then all those soldiers – my dad – died because of a freak accident? The enemy wasn't even to blame?!" He didn't know how to feel if this was the case, for it would mean that he had nobody to direct his anger, his unresolved emotions towards…

However, upon hearing Nathan utter these words, Ranjit began to cackle before this descended into demented, maniacal laughter which unsettled Nathan, along with Drew and the others.

"You really are clueless!" Ranjit taunted hysterically. "It was no *accident*! Maris is more powerful than you could possibly imagine!"

Nathan's eyes widened inquisitively as he heard the name that Ranjit disclosed. "Maris?!" he exclaimed, a sense of fulfilment surging within him as he supposedly reached a breakthrough. "You're saying this *Maris* is responsible for the hurricane?!"

"That's right!" Ranjit confirmed brazenly. "In fact, I'll let you in on a secret – Maris and her forces will arrive in Entritica tonight. When that happens, another disaster will occur."

Nathan recoiled at hearing this, horrified at the idea of the enemies, the ones that his father fought so hard against, making their way onto Entritican soil. He couldn't believe it and after remembering *who* was telling him this, he decided that he didn't have to believe it either.

"You're lying!" Nathan accused indignantly before scoffing at Ranjit's claim. "Of course, you're lying," he repeated as he shook his head. "No human is capable of that."

"Indeed, no *human* is," Ranjit agreed to Nathan's surprise. "But Maris is no human – Maris is a *god*! And when she arrives and the rest of Entritica finally realises it, they'll have no choice but to submit to her will as well!"

"You…you actually believe what you're saying, don't you?" Nathan remarked, having sensed the fanatical conviction in Ranjit's words. He was now unable to hide the anxiety in his own voice as Ranjit's behaviour left him feeling increasingly disturbed and he could feel from the tension in the air that Dan, Denzel and Drew were also rattled at seeing this.

"I do," Ranjit fortified, his voice lowering as he said it. "And you know what? So does the Entritican government – don't you think it's odd how there's been *no* news about the war these last few weeks?" Doubt once again filled Nathan's head at the mention of this. After all, this was one of the key frustrations he'd encountered when trying to look for any information about the war. "It's because as soon as they found out about the existence of Maris, they've been scared – because they know they're going to lose this war…"

For the first time, Nathan was unable to refute Ranjit's proclamations and fell silent as he tried to process everything he'd been told. Bit by bit, Ranjit's statements started to connect with what Nathan had experienced, his initial belief that they were gross fabrications now waning to despairing hope...

"Finally starting to dawn on you?" Ranjit jeered callously as he relished in Nathan's torment. "Well, I've graciously given you the answers you were searching for – but question time is over. As a chosen emissary of a god, it's time I fulfil my mission by delivering my message – only the ink will be *your* blood..."

In that instant, Ranjit drew the gun out from the pocket of his hoodie, alarming Nathan along with Dan, Denzel and Drew.

Elsewhere, an exhausted Thomas was struggling to keep up with Abbie as she sprinted in the direction of Seppuku Bridge, impatiently stopping every few seconds to make sure Thomas hadn't fallen too far behind.

"Tom, hurry up! The longer we take, the longer Nathan's on his own with that headcase!" Abbie yelled out, agitated, before quickly hurrying off again.

"I-I-I......I'm c-coming..." Thomas wheezed as he waddled uncomfortably after Abbie while Joshua continued to tail them both, keeping a far distance so that they didn't catch on to his presence.

Meanwhile, Nathan was frozen in terror as he watched Ranjit raise the gun and point it in his direction – he tried to shift his legs and jerk his arms, but it was as though his entire body was weighed down by an unknown force, powerless to move. Although his mind descended into a dazed panic, he did sense that Dan and Denzel's grip on his shoulders had loosened as they tried to comprehend what they were witnessing. This did not go unnoticed by Ranjit.

"Hold him still you idiots! His death will be for a worthy cause!" Ranjit growled at Dan and Denzel, however Drew stepped in front of the three boys to everybody's shock.

"You never told us anything about this!" Drew protested, gesturing at the gun that Ranjit still aimed threateningly towards Nathan. "This is all going *way* too far now!"

"Oh, where's this come from?" Ranjit jibed derisively at Drew, a bemused smirk spreading on his face. "You had no qualms about assisting me earlier..."

"*No qualms*?!!" Drew exclaimed incredulously. "You *forced* us to!"

"Ingrate!" Ranjit spat at him. "You do *my* bidding and my family will protect you – that was our agreement! You're either with us or against us! It's that simple!" Drew timidly gulped as Ranjit reminded him of this. "So…what's it going to be?" he challenged Drew who hesitated to respond, something that concerned Dan and Denzel behind him.

"Drew, what are you doing?!" Denzel hissed nervously towards his friend, his hand still resting limply on the shoulder of Nathan who was still in a state of mental paralysis as he helplessly watched things implode before him. Drew slowly turned his head to look at Dan and Denzel, the eerie silence being broken only by the tranquil sounds of the river flowing beneath the bridge, temporarily disrupting the chaos above it.

"Is this really what you guys want?" Drew asked them urgently. "To be complicit in a murder?!" The eyes of both boys shifted uneasily upon being propositioned with this question. They couldn't even look at each other for support, tension still remaining between them from earlier in the week.

"Drew, the other alternative is being victims…" Dan emphasised, trying to remind him of what was at stake. Upon hearing this though, Drew's pupils lowered to look at the burns on Dan's neck, seared into his skin by Ranjit himself. And then they shifted to Nathan, remembering the last words he'd said to him at yesterday's encounter…

"Like we're not already…" Drew pitifully acknowledged.

Hearing these words leave his mouth, the looks in Dan's and Denzel's faces changed, as though a spark that had long died out had reignited within their eyes. Not just those two but listening to Drew's outspoken epiphany had snapped Nathan out of his glossy petrified haze, his awareness of his surroundings fully returning to him as Drew's words echoed through his mind. Seeing their reactions, Drew felt an unwavering sensation swell within him, the conflict within his heart finally settled.

"There's only one way out of this…" he declared resolutely as Dan and Denzel listened to him, their bumbling body language still showing signs of uncertainty. "Ranjit," Drew addressed him as his head slowly turned back towards where he was. "This has to sto-"

Before Drew could even complete his sentence, the chilling sound of a gunshot reverberated loudly throughout the surrounding area. This echo was heard by Thomas and Abbie who had finally reached the outskirts of the woods, as well as Joshua who continued to keep a wide distance from them. Fearing the worst, Abbie promptly zoomed off towards the bridge without hesitation, leaving a tired Thomas behind as he limped along after her, trying to pick up his speed as he also recognised the gravity of the situation. Likewise, Joshua also quickened his own pace.

At this exact moment, Nathan's, Dan's and Denzel's ears rang with the crack of the gunshot as, in a state of horror, they watched Drew collapse backwards onto the ground, blood pouring from his shoulder where the bullet fired by Ranjit was lodged. The three of them stared at the downed Drew in shock as Ranjit stepped menacingly towards them.

"I warned you," Ranjit heartlessly uttered as he stood over Drew's body, looking down at him with disdain before lifting his head to look back at Dan and Denzel. "Well, what about you two? Choose wisely – either fall in line and follow me or fall at my feet like this traitor!" he pressured them, taking the time to reload the gun with another bullet and cruelly pressing his boot repeatedly into Drew's wound, causing him to gasp in pain and violently cough up blood. Despite trying to make a statement of his power, Ranjit had only enraged Dan and Denzel as they witnessed their friend's suffering.

"You son of a-!" Denzel shrieked furiously, ignoring Ranjit's wishes of holding Nathan in place and, before Dan could even stop him, lunging towards his oppressor in a frantic bid to save Drew before Ranjit could rearm himself. Ranjit, however, used his free hand to land a punch directly into the previously damaged ribs of Denzel, stunning him completely. As he was doubled over in agony, Ranjit drove his knee into Denzel, opportunistically targeting his ribs again which led to Denzel falling to his knees helplessly beside Drew. In spite of their previous arguments, Dan couldn't bear seeing his friend get hurt like this and also left Nathan behind to try and aid Denzel. Once more, Ranjit anticipated the incoming Dan and managed to catch him as he charged towards him, displaying his strength by lifting his enormous frame up into the air and slamming him into the ground along with Denzel and Drew, incapacitating Dan and driving the air out of him.

While this happened, Nathan feebly observed as Ranjit effortlessly dispatched his former cohorts. Even with everything that these three had put him through over the years, Nathan wished that he could do something to help them but looking at his puny arms, he knew he was nowhere near strong enough to be able to stop Ranjit. His arms dropped defeatedly by his trousers, his right one brushing the rock that was in his pocket. Nathan debated internally over whether to use this, however upon remembering how he nearly killed Tobias with a similar weapon and now seeing the merciless monster that Ranjit was becoming after shooting Drew, he couldn't bring himself to do it. Unable to think of any other options, he tried to flee from the scene in the hopes of finding help. Unfortunately, his legs trembled uncontrollably, leaving him able to take only small steps until Ranjit noticed him.

"I'll deal with you three turncoats later..." Ranjit warned the three battered boys before turning his attention to Nathan. Drunk off power, Ranjit marched over towards Nathan, ready to torment him even more. Seeing this, Nathan tried to frantically force his legs to move faster, even placing his hands around his left leg in a pathetic attempt to lift it.

In that moment though, his hand squished over his left pocket causing him to remember – the soil! Nathan quickly realised that if Ranjit got close enough, he could blind him with the dirt and take the opening to escape! Nathan thrust his left hand into his pocket to gather the soil in his fist as he watched Ranjit sinisterly approach him.

"Stay away from me!" Nathan cried out, hoping against all expectation that this would deter Ranjit, but naturally, it did not. Instead, he forcefully grabbed Nathan's right arm while he brandished the gun casually in his remaining hand.

"This is all your fault, you know?" Ranjit insinuated. "You turned them against me and now look at them..." he jeered as he glanced back to see Denzel gently place a hand on Drew to try and revive him.

"You branded me a demon for years!!" Nathan shouted as he tried to wrench his arm free from Ranjit's grasp. "Yet you're the one who's prepared to kill people – even your supposed friends!!"

"Hey, *you* made me do it! You planted the seed in their heads that made them defy me," Ranjit protested manically, wilfully trying to shift the blame and toy with Nathan's sense of self-guilt. "I'll dispose of them once I've killed you, but their blood will still be on your hands!" He looked around the bridge as he pinned Nathan against the railings whilst he struggled to free the fistful of soil from his pocket. "You nearly did the rest of the world a favour four years ago when you tried to take your own life here..." Ranjit icily whispered into his ears as Nathan winced at this disturbing reminder. "Now I'll finish the job and send you to hell with your dad!!"

His last mocking sentence egged Nathan enough to wrench his fist out of his pocket and in one swift motion, he irately hurled the soil straight into Ranjit's eyes. Ranjit recoiled as the dirt blinded him, but to Nathan's distress, he stubbornly did not release the grip on Nathan's arm. Taking advantage of a disorientated Ranjit, Nathan grabbed hold of his hood and yanked it further over his head, pulling it until the jumper was halfway up from his waist.

Yet, Ranjit writhed wildly while trapped under the hoodie and Nathan was too scrawny to be capable of containing his power. As a result, Ranjit shoved Nathan backwards and as he fell back, he bumped his head on the bridge railings, the impact leaving him stunned. His vision was cloudy, but he could make out the blurry figure of Ranjit wriggling free of his jumper and casting it down onto the ground, the Chimera locket that he received from Cain now on display. He staggered around blindly as he tried to wipe the soil out of his eyes.

"You little-!" Ranjit muttered angrily, sounding truly infuriated for the first time and dropping his self-assured frontage. "I'll make you pay for that!" he threatened as he cocked his gun. Nathan, though woozy, still had the wherewithal to remain silent, knowing that a blinded Ranjit would be listening out for any sounds that he may make. He was too dazed to move as he felt blood leak from the back of his head, so this was his only hope for survival...

Suddenly, just as it looked like Ranjit would detect where Nathan was, Abbie arrived at the bridge, seeing Nathan slumped against the railings and Ranjit looming over him.

"NATHAN!!!" she screamed out instinctively.

Nathan recognised her voice, instantly regretting his choice to come here as he realised that not only had he put his own life at risk, he'd needlessly endangered his friends as well. Before he could even call out to her or turn his head in her direction, Ranjit reacted faster at the sound of her outcry. Abbie watched in horror as Ranjit rapidly turned towards her and pointed the handgun in her direction, with his eyes still closed.

The sound of a gunshot pierced Nathan's ears once again and he powerlessly watched, mouth agape in a silent scream, as the hazy outline of Abbie's body plunged to the ground below.

An overwhelming numbness swept over him as he blamed himself for what he believed was Abbie's death. This then transformed into a brief searing rage before everything went black...

But from Dan and Denzel's viewpoint, while they were tending to Drew, they got distracted by the emergence of a sinister energy nearby. They turned to observe as Nathan's body rose to his feet, surrounded by a pulsating black aura as he stared down Ranjit who was still trying to wipe the dirt from his eyes.

In a sudden motion, the same boy who was too puny to even shove Ranjit back, stunned both Dan and Denzel as he inexplicably lifted Ranjit up from his feet and ferociously flung him into the bridge railings. An exasperated squeal escaped from Ranjit's lips as his bulky frame bent the metal bars upon impact and the force of the collision caused him to drop the gun through the railings where it splashed into the river underneath and vanished.

Just as Nathan towered over a downed Ranjit by the railings, the same place he himself had been subjected to a horrific beating years ago, Thomas finally arrived on the scene. Huffing and puffing but still fretting about the second gunshot, he hurried over to the bridge only to find Nathan raining down thunderous punches into Ranjit's face and abdomen. The black aura emanating from him captured Thomas' attention for he recognised the malevolent sensation he'd previously felt from its presence. Once he reached the bridge, he instantly realised what had triggered the extreme reaction as he saw Abbie in a heap on the floor.

"Abbie!" Thomas yelled frightfully before rushing over to her side. "Oh dear god, please be okay!" Thankfully, Abbie got up from the ground to Thomas' surprise and relief.

"I'm fine!" Abbie reassured, slowly getting to her feet. "I ducked as soon as I saw Ranjit point the gun at me…"

Abbie raised her head to see Nathan, teeth gritted and still imbued with an evil darkness, repeatedly thrusting his fists into Ranjit's body, each one paying him back for his cowardly assault four years ago. Catching a glimpse of Nathan's eyes, Thomas and Abbie saw only the whites – his pupils weren't visible! It was like he wasn't even in control of his own actions at this point, as if under the influence of some unseen malicious entity. The sight of Nathan acting this way made Abbie tremble with trepidation for her friend.

"I-is-is this the black 'mist' you mentioned before?!" she asked Thomas, turning to him for an explanation for the aura surrounding Nathan. However, he just stayed silent as he watched his best friend go berserk. "S-shouldn't we stop this?!" she yelped helplessly.

"What, stop him from beating up the psycho who tried to *kill* us?!" Thomas reminded her bluntly.

"If we don't do something, Nathan might kill *him* instead!!" Abbie insisted. Thomas considered this before he spotted Dan and Denzel still trying to save Drew, quickly deducing what had happened from the earlier gunshot.

"Look at what he's capable of! Scum like him are better off dead!" Thomas declared darkly, the disturbing admission leaving Abbie taken aback.

Meanwhile, Nathan continued his vicious thrashing of Ranjit who was rendered a bruised and bloody mess because of Nathan's enormous surge of strength. As he swiped downwards at him, he inadvertently caught Ranjit's locket with his hand and ended up hurling it backwards behind him. Thomas was alerted by the clatter of the black locket, disrupting his debate with Abbie. He stepped forward to examine it.

"Th-this is-!!" Thomas gasped, shaken by the sight of the locket that he was holding.

Preoccupied by the presence of this locket, neither Thomas nor Abbie realised that Joshua had arrived, running past them towards Nathan. Ranjit coughed violently because of the blows he'd endured before bursting into another fit of sadistic laughter. Nathan's bloodshot pupilless eyes twitched in response and his hand reached for the rock in his right pocket. He held it in his fist and raised it high above his head, ready to smash it down onto Ranjit until Joshua grabbed his hand to stop him.

"That's far enough, Nath," Joshua sternly told him, holding his arm back.

As Joshua's voice penetrated his ears, the black aura around Nathan slowly subsided before it disappeared and once he blinked, his pupils had returned to his eyes.

His vision gradually returned until, mortified, he was looking down at the bruised, beaten and bloody mess that was a grinning Ranjit. Nathan staggered backwards at the sight of him before catching a glimpse of his own knuckles tarnished with blood. Barely able to look at them, he turned away from them to properly see the rattled expression of the typically composed Joshua. They each spun round towards the centre of the bridge where Dan and Denzel were still cradling Drew while staring sheepishly back at them. Joshua walked over to where they were while Nathan glanced behind him to see Thomas and Abbie, also looking concerned by what they had witnessed. At the sight of Abbie, Nathan rushed over to her, a huge sense of relief washing over him.

"You're okay! Thank god you're okay!" Nathan gasped gratefully as he hugged her, repeating the words about three times. Abbie, still feeling shaken, was slow to react yet eventually reciprocated by reassuringly patting his shoulders.

"I'm okay, I ducked the shot..." Abbie whispered to him while she consoled him. As they separated, Thomas was there to clarify what had happened.

"You have no memory of what just happened, do you?" Thomas deduced, addressing Nathan who nervously shook his head in response. Thomas sighed, hating that he'd have to inform Nathan of what he'd done but knowing he couldn't avoid it. "W-well, as you've already guessed, you're the one who beat up Ranjit. But your eyes looked possessed...like you weren't even in your own body...and you were surrounded by a black mist or glow..." Nathan's eyes enlarged in astonishment at hearing this. "It was a similar sensation to what I felt from you that time with Tobias..."

"A-and I remember it from...that time where I took your locket..." Abbie added awkwardly, recalling how Nathan had briefly lost his memory between losing his locket and pinning her against the school fence.

"Only this time...it was the darkest I've ever felt it..." Thomas stated honestly.

Nathan stayed quiet as he processed what his friends were telling him. Eventually, as he looked at his knuckles once more, he was forced to accept the truth.

"So, these incidents...might be connected after all..." he acknowledged dejectedly. "But...why? What the hell is wrong with me...?" Nathan asked himself meekly, his voice cracking from frustration, to which neither Thomas nor Abbie could offer an answer.

After a while, Thomas placed his hand affectionately on his friend's shoulder. "Mate, you've been through enough today already. We'll get to the bottom of it somehow..." he uttered, trying to instil Nathan with some hope. He took another look past Nathan to see Joshua talking to Dan and Denzel as they crouched over a wounded Drew, Dan typing into his phone as he listened to what Joshua was saying. As his eyes darted back to the railings, Thomas frowned as he saw Ranjit beginning to stir again. "You were right about one thing though, Nath..." he told a perplexed Nathan as he clutched the black locket in his hand and made a beeline past him towards Ranjit. "Oi! Ranjit!" Thomas fiercely called out as he approached him to the disbelief of everyone, even briefly catching the attention of Joshua, Dan and Denzel. "I know what this amulet means!" Thomas revealed, holding the ornament outwards, dangling it above the ground. "You're working with Chimera, aren't you?!"

In the corner of her eye, Abbie caught Joshua's expression change to one of fright as the name Chimera was uttered by Thomas. She then watched him as he turned back to hurriedly instruct Dan and Denzel while Ranjit used the bent railings to pull himself to his feet.

"So..." Ranjit spluttered as a subdued laugh escaped from his mouth. "You know of them, do you?"

"I know them *well enough*!" Thomas snarled resentfully. "Are they the ones we're up against?! *Tell me*!"

Before Ranjit could even answer, Joshua barged back into the scene and quickly restrained the thug.

"An ambulance is on its way now! You three need to get out of here! I'll take this punk to the police myself!" Joshua barked frantically at them as he overpowered a weakened Ranjit.

"We can't just leave Drew! He's been shot!" Abbie retorted.

"He's still alive...we'll stay with him..." Dan called out to them having heard Joshua and Abbie's exchange. "Joshua's right, you should go. Let us take care of the rest..." he insisted as he and Denzel continued to cradle Drew in their arms.

"B-but..." Nathan uttered, still in shock from everything that had happened.

"Nathan! Vic's going to be worried sick about you! Just go home already!" Joshua yelled at him.

"Yeah, go tell her about what you did, you freak!" Ranjit jeered one last time before Joshua shut him up and marched him away from the bridge.

As Thomas and Abbie tried to beckon Nathan to leave, he took one last look at the railings that he'd hurled Ranjit into, seeing specks of blood on the metal and comprehending the damage that he'd done. Despite how much of the bridge was now dilapidated, Nathan knew from experience how strong the railings were – for it was he who had been beaten against them four years ago. He knew that some force was required to make them bend the way he had done but never imagined that he could be capable of a feat like that. The idea of having that level of power and not being in control of it, scared Nathan – and he knew he couldn't just ignore this now…

"Nath, you should probably hold onto this…" Thomas interrupted, placing Ranjit's black amulet into the palm of his hand. "Sorry, I just can't look at it right now," he added, shuddering as he spoke. "But we can talk about it tomorrow…"

"Yeah…sure…" Nathan murmured, unconsciously accepting the amulet, his head still in a haze with images of Drew's and Ranjit's injured bodies that kept playing over and over.

Appreciating that he was still deeply shaken by the experience, Thomas and Abbie led Nathan away from the area, leaving Dan and Denzel to wait with Drew for the medics to arrive. They had many questions from what they had witnessed of his mysterious power, however both knew those would have to wait. For now, they were just relieved that they had all survived Ranjit's wrath.

As for Nathan, the only thing that currently mattered to him was to get home – just as Joshua said – to see his mom again. Because right now, he needed her more than ever…

⚬═══◅❮❯▻═══⚬

Chapter 9

Rain started to pour down from the gloomy skies as Nathan shuffled down the road to his home, still in distress from what he had done to Ranjit under the influence of the mysterious black aura. Thomas and Abbie had been reluctant to leave him alone, only doing so once they had reached Nathan's street.

Once he finally got to the driveway of his house, Nathan froze up, hesitant from the thoughts of facing his mother after the events of that afternoon. As the rain started to worsen though, it ominously triggered memories of the day he found out about Richard's death – that day another instance when his body acted on its own and nearly attacked Abbie. Haunted by these reminders, Nathan closed his eyes and darted into the house to escape from the downpour and face the music.

He opened the door and as he closed it shut, the click alerted Victoria who called out her son's name.

"Nathan! Where have you been?! I've been worried sick about you!" Nathan heard her cry out from her bedroom, his eyes shifting to the hallway clock which read half past five, a whole hour longer than when he'd usually arrive home from school.

Hearing the panic in his mom's voice produced a pang of guilt within his chest. Victoria rushed down the stairs and into the hall where Nathan was standing, pale-faced and visibly rattled. Seeing this, she instinctively embraced her son to comfort him as Nathan tightly gripped her in return.

"Something's happened, hasn't it…?" she deduced, gently whispering into his ear. Unable to hide the truth, Nathan buried his head in Victoria's shoulder as he responded.

"I've done something really stupid mom…" Nathan confessed. Victoria patted his back in a calming manner.

"You'd best sit down then. I'll make you a drink," she suggested before she tenderly placed her hands on Nathan's cheeks and raised his head upwards so that his eyes met hers. "And then you tell me everything..." Victoria insisted, her pupils unwavering.

Nathan silently nodded to his mother's request and, after removing his shoes, he followed her through the living room to the kitchen where the dining table was. Upon examining the dining table, it was another familiar reminder of three weeks ago, when he spotted the letter that notified him about Richard's passing – only this time, his mother would be consoling him instead of the other way round. He sat in the same chair that he saw Victoria sitting in and waited while she boiled the kettle to make them both a coffee.

Minutes later, once drinks had been prepared and placed upon the table with coasters underneath, Victoria was sat beside him patiently waiting for Nathan to explain what happened. Once he'd found the words, Nathan told her about how he needed to know who or what had killed his dad which led to him detailing about how and why he'd confronted Ranjit at Seppuku Bridge. Even though she quietly listened to him, Nathan caught Victoria's eyes widen in horror as 'Ranjit' and 'Seppuku Bridge' were uttered in the same sentence. Nathan strained to describe the initial conversation that he'd had with Ranjit, however those memories seemed to be blocked by images of Ranjit's gun and his own actions in beating up Ranjit. Unable to overcome those visions, he couldn't retell that detail of the situation which was frustrating to Nathan because his instincts told him that there were some important details revealed during that discourse. Victoria did not pressure him to do so either – not at this stage. Instead, Nathan moved on to how Ranjit had pulled out a gun and ended up shooting Drew who had tried to stand up to him.

After hearing this, a horrified Victoria immediately rose from her chair and paced around frenetically with her hands clasped over her mouth until she turned to look at Nathan again.

"Why?! Why would you go to face Ranjit there – of all places – *alone*?!" Victoria pleaded, desperate to understand why her son would go into such a dangerous situation after losing his father. "After what you'd gone through there before – why risk bringing that all up again?! You know I can't lose you too!" she continued, her eyes watering as she painfully recalled the time Nathan had tried to take his own life after the cyberbullying that Ranjit had subjected him to.

"I know...I was being foolish..." Nathan conceded as his head drooped down in shame. "I-I just...I needed to get some closure after dad died...but after the funeral and seeing all the others that were killed too, I just felt even more lost...so when Ranjit claimed that he knew what really happened...I..." he raised his hands from beneath the table and cupped his head with them. "This is all just a mess..." he muttered to himself. However, Victoria had caught sight of his hands, particularly the blood on his knuckles.

"Nathan...that's not your blood, is it?" Victoria asked rhetorically, already guessing where the story was going next. She anticipated his next words as he paused for a moment, gathering his thoughts together before continuing.

"I remember..." Nathan began to recollect. "Ranjit had me by the arm...I couldn't escape...even after blinding him with dirt and his own hoodie... he just pushed me against the railings...and I was losing consciousness..." He felt the back of his head for the first time, noticed that it was damp and brought his hand back to find blood on his fingers. Victoria got up from her chair to find some tissue. She returned and carefully dabbed at the wound he'd received, all the time making sure that Nathan wasn't concussed and only urging him to carry on telling the story once certain that he was capable of doing so. "Anyway...the last thing I remember at that point was...Abbie arrived...and then a gunshot...I saw her fall down...and I just blacked out..." Nathan explained wearily as Victoria listened, still tending to his head.

"But when I came to...I saw that Ranjit had been beaten...by my hands...and I have no memory of it..." he recapped. "Abbie was okay in the end...she and Thomas told me that my body was acting on its own...like I was possessed...and it had a black glow around it..."

In that moment, Victoria stopped moving completely.

"A-a black glow...?" she echoed, trying to clarify what Nathan was saying.

"Yeah...that's what they said..." Nathan confirmed bluntly. "And the thing is...I don't think this was a one-off occurrence either...I also zoned out that time with Tobias...and Thomas said he felt the same sinister sensation that time too..."

There was an uncomfortable silence between them as Victoria walked away from behind Nathan, towards the kitchen counter and stared off in the distance, processing what she had heard from her son. After a while, Nathan spoke up again.

"Mom? Please…say something…" he called out to her desperately, not sure what she could be thinking. Eventually, Victoria let out a regretful sigh before talking once more.

"I had hoped this day would never come…" she confessed sorrowfully to Nathan's surprise. "I just wish Richard had also been here to have this conversation with you…"

"H-hang on…d-do you know something about this black glow?" Nathan questioned.

"I'm afraid so…" Victoria admitted. Putting aside her guilt, she turned back to look at her son. "I'm sorry Nathan, but it's about time that I told you the truth about that black aura…" she informed as she sat back down in her chair opposite Nathan, who curiously leaned in to listen to her. "You remember how your dad and I told you before that…you were born prematurely?" Victoria asked him to which Nathan nodded. "Well…it seems that you weren't given the full story back then…

"I only found out myself four years ago after…you tried to…at Seppuku Bridge…" Victoria croaked, still struggling to mention his suicide attempt due to the sadness she felt to think of her son being so unhappy. "Once Thomas, Lucy and Joshua brought you back home that evening, I remember you finally opened up to me and Richard about everything you'd gone through at school after what happened with that awful Tobias – the students' bullying, the snubbing from the teachers, even the vile comments from Mr Nelson!" Nathan winced as he was reminded of these experiences again. "Then you said that you felt an intense sinister energy within you when Tobias was hurting Thomas. I didn't think anything of it at the time – as far as I was concerned, you were just protecting your friend…"

"But after you'd gone upstairs to rest, Richard went out for a while. When he came back, that's when he told me – about *how* you actually survived such a premature birth…"

"W-was it really that serious…?" Nathan questioned, feeling unnerved.

"I was asleep when it happened, but from Richard's recount, he was told that you had no chance of survival – and was urged to remove you from the incubator to stop you suffering. Essentially, you were inches from death…" Victoria answered morbidly, causing Nathan to gulp. "That night, Richard told me…" she said before pausing for thought. "I'm trying to think how he described it…" she muttered aloud exasperated as an impatient Nathan waited. "Yeah, that's right," Victoria recalled, continuing on and only pausing to carefully choose her words. "As the heart rate monitor flatlined, he saw your body glowing with a black aura…and then…he witnessed that same aura form into a black spirit…in the shape of a dragon…which shot back into your body…and that's what revived you…as if you were never at death's door. Yes, that's how Richard told it to me…" she finished before examining Nathan, his expression of sheer disbelief and bewilderment apparent to her. "And I had pretty much the same reaction back then that you do now," she added sympathetically. Even with this, Nathan still struggled to process what he'd just heard.

"S-so…the reason I survived all those years ago…is because of this so-called black aura? The *same* one that possessed me to attack Tobias and Ranjit?!" Nathan exclaimed incredulously.

"Well…when you told us about the sinister energy you felt while Thomas was being attacked…your account of it matched what your dad experienced that day…" Victoria explained pragmatically. "This incident with Ranjit today…and how you felt before blacking out…did it compare to that time with Tobias…?"

Nathan quietly mulled these words over, even adding the incident with Abbie three weeks ago to the mix, something that Victoria was still unaware of. During each instance, Nathan had blacked out and, before regaining consciousness, acted uncharacteristically by attacking (or nearly doing so in Abbie's case) somebody. Thinking hard about each occasion, he remembered feeling a searing rage that overpowered him prior to fainting. Could this have been the black aura controlling him? After recalling what Thomas and Abbie had mentioned earlier about Nathan acting like he was possessed while beating up Ranjit, the mounting evidence made this prospect impossible to deny anymore.

Victoria's mention of the dragon that the aura had formed was also an unsettling revelation for Nathan, for he now connected this malicious presence to the reason for his tormenting school nickname of 'Dragon Boy', one that Ranjit had saddled him with . Deep within the recesses of these memories and this new information, the existence of this 'dragon' dawned on him – gradually, Nathan reluctantly started to accept what his mother was telling him as fact, finally nodding in response to her question.

"I…I get that this is a lot to take in…" Victoria whispered, trying to break the silence and gently placing her hand over Nathan's. However,

Nathan retracted his hand away from her before finally snapping out of his train of thought.

"Why didn't you or dad tell me any of this?!" Nathan demanded, his forehead wrinkled up in annoyance as he met Victoria's gaze. "You knew about this for the last four years! You should have told me about this dragon aura from the start! Who knows – we could have done something about it!" he blurted out angrily.

Victoria nodded understandingly at Nathan's outburst. "Richard and I agonised over this very thing when I learned about the aura..." she acknowledged. "When we'd discussed it that evening, it had only been hours after...you'd tried to..." Victoria choked up, still unable to say the next part of that sentence, instead moving on. "We...knew you were vulnerable... and were certain that telling you about the black aura would...push you back over the edge. We just couldn't do that to you after all you'd been through that year – you're our son after all. So, because there'd only been the two occasions with your birth and the Tobias incident, we decided that we'd only tell you if the aura ever resurfaced again, hoping it never would. And it didn't...until today that is..."

Nathan quietly turned away from Victoria, upset as her explanation provided little comfort to him right now. He then wearily stood up from his chair.

"I'm going up to my room..." he said distantly, his mind still in overdrive from the entire afternoon. "I need some time alone..."

Victoria, though concerned, respected his wishes knowing that he needed some space. She breathed a regretful sigh when Nathan left the kitchen and, once she heard the stairs creak as he made his way up to his bedroom, she stood up herself to clear out his backpack which he had left behind.

As Victoria removed the lunchbox from the bag, the black locket that Nathan and Thomas had taken from Ranjit, slipped out onto the floor, the clattering sound catching her attention. She knelt down to pick up the locket, turning it in her hand until she saw the symbol of the black dragon with red eyes – causing Victoria to let out an audible gasp and drop the locket back onto the ground.

Upon seeing this, she remembered a time when she and Richard were still teenagers and were getting close to one another. Richard had shown her this symbol before when he opened up to her about his experience with Chimera and his words echoed in her mind:

"This is the mark of Chimera. They're a satanic, terrorist organisation, infamous in Etracova and they're pure evil! They killed my whole family and destroyed my village – forcing me to flee here to Entritica. They've gone under the radar since then but during that time, they were known for wanting to conquer Etracova, spreading destruction and even kidnapping children – possibly to brainwash them into joining their cult..."

Then, Victoria recalled the point where she challenged Richard about his intentions to enrol in the army when the war began, with very few knowing what they were going up against. Again, Richard's cryptic retort stuck with her:

"I can't lose my family again!!"

It was the fear in his eyes and voice when he said it that lingered with Victoria. He looked haunted, and now that she had seen Chimera's emblem again, she believed she knew why. Richard must have had knowledge that he would be battling Chimera. And yet, he'd kept her in the dark about this. She couldn't fathom why he would do that, but the locket suggested one possibility. Even after creating a new family, Victoria knew that deep down, Richard had never truly dropped his vendetta with Chimera after they'd taken his first family from him. Had he really been so blinded by revenge that he'd risk his own life to stop them?

After stewing over this for about an hour, Victoria decided that she needed to ask Nathan about the locket. With it in hand, she made her way up the squeaky stairs until she was standing in front of his bedroom door. She softly knocked on the door before she called out to him.

"Nathan...can I come in?" Victoria asked courteously.

"Yeah, sure..." she heard Nathan murmur dejectedly on the other side of the door.

Victoria entered the bedroom as Nathan was on his phone, answering messages from both Thomas and Abbie who were asking if he was okay after the near-death experience at the bridge. Nathan looked up from his phone to see his mother holding the black locket in the palm of her hand.

"I found this in your backpack," Victoria explained carefully. "This... this belonged to Ranjit didn't it?"

Nathan nodded in response to this and as he did so, his hand automatically clutched his own golden locket which his dad had given to him.

"Do you...do you know that the organisation that this emblem belongs to is called Chimera?" she questioned.

"I'd never heard of them before, but Thomas mentioned that name to Ranjit, just before we left the bridge. So...you know of them too..." Nathan lethargically answered her.

"W-we're at war with them...aren't we?" Victoria deduced rhetorically. Again, Nathan nodded to confirm this.

There was still a tense atmosphere between the two of them after the revelation of the black aura. Victoria debated in her mind whether she should now mention Richard's history with Chimera but before she could say anything, Nathan finally broke the silence.

"You said earlier...that the aura hasn't resurfaced until today..." he restated, remembering the words she used earlier. "But that feeling of darkness that I felt towards Ranjit and Tobias? I've been feeling that ever since dad joined the army...I never thought about it until now because it was faint...but it was definitely there..." he revealed as his mother absorbed what he was telling her. "And it's been even more intense ever since he died...in fact, the aura nearly made me attack Abbie that day after I almost lost this..." he confessed to a shocked Victoria whilst he gestured towards the locket around his neck.

He twisted the golden dragon around with his fingers as he continued, reminiscing about the day his dad left – the same day he received this heirloom. "When my dad gave me this, I remember what he said to me, word for word," he said before reciting Richard's words to him. *'Nathan, in Etracova, where I came from before Entritica, the golden dragon on this locket is a symbol of protection and purity – it has many meanings whether it be to protect against the evils of the world or whether it's something as simple as protecting your loved ones. I want you to have it now. Not just because I want you to do your best to protect your mother, but because if you ever go back to a dark place again, I want it to remind you of the good person you really are – one who will do whatever it takes to protect the things that matter to him...'*

"I hear those words all the time in my mind when I go to sleep. They usually comfort me, even in my darkest moments," Nathan admitted earnestly, Victoria feeling her guilt mounting upon her. As Nathan carried on though, the volume of his voice started to rise, his anger and disappointment cutting through. "But right now, when I hear the part where he says *'dark place'* play in my head, it dawns on me – he knew. He knew of that wicked black aura within me all along and never once told me…he just buried his head in the sand, never giving me a chance to try and find a way to fix it! This should have been dealt with years ago – maybe then I wouldn't have been treated like a monster!! I mean, is there anything else that he's lied to me about?!" he ranted irately before turning away from Victoria and curling up onto his bed, visually shutting himself out from further interactions with her.

Feeling culpable for allowing Nathan's predicament to get to this point and believing she had let her son down, Victoria elected to leave him alone to digest the events and revelations of today. If she were to voice her beliefs over Richard's experiences with Chimera now, she feared it would only further tarnish Nathan's memory of his dad. Plus, she herself needed to make up her mind about what Richard's intentions were. She knew it needed to be addressed to give Nathan some sense of closure, but right now was not that time. After vowing that she will always be there for her son if he needs her, Victoria stepped out of his bedroom and quietly shut the door behind her.

Just as she was about to walk away from the door, Victoria remembered the final time she and Nathan saw Richard, prior to departing for war. It was Richard's parting words that resonated with her this time:

"You two are the purest lights in my life. I'll fight to the end to defend you both. Until I come back, please protect one another…"

She played these words over and over again in her thoughts, because just like Nathan said previously, it brought her comfort. Eventually though, the words resounded with Victoria in a different way, helping her to fully comprehend Richard's motives for joining the war. As her mind began to clear, it helped her to plan what she could finally say to make Nathan feel at peace with himself, almost like Richard sent this message to her from the beyond for this very purpose…

****

Elsewhere though, not far from the shores of Entritica during the dead of night, multiple naval ships made of reinforced steel had gathered and formed a barrier between the sea and the land. They had received reports that Chimera was on the approach and were ready to keep them out of their country. The waters remained calm as the privates hurried around the ships, making sure that the missiles were loaded and functioning whereas the men on lookout observed any developments through their telescopes.

After half an hour had passed, they detected a fleet of Chimera ships in the distance, mostly constructed of wood, and promptly alerted the rest of their forces. Every soldier quickly took their position at the armaments, ready to engage their enemies once they were in range and blast them out of the waters with their superior technology.

However, they wouldn't get the chance to launch the weapons – within seconds, the waves around the Entritican fleet grew increasingly more turbulent despite all weather reports to the contrary. The boats swayed vigorously back and forth, throwing the privates around and disrupting the trajectory of their missiles. Many of them clung desperately on to anything within range for dear life to avoid being thrown overboard into the sea. Once they had steadied themselves enough to pick themselves up from the deck, the soldiers noticed that a large shadow was being cast over them – and judging from the tremors in the ocean, the water was swelling up in one area just ahead of them.

As soon as the men raised their heads, they were left to despair at the sight of an enormous tsunami towering over them. They didn't even have chance to scream, for within seconds, the tidal wave came crashing down upon the ships at blistering speed. The almighty force of the water was enough to plunge the vessels and all aboard it down into the depths of the ocean – neither of which re-emerged to the surface...

When all was said and done, Chimera's fleet were the only ships that remained as the choppy waters returned to a tranquil state. Under the dark, murky sky and with their adversaries vanquished, the order to advance was given by Maris who led the ships at the front. On her command, the terrorists pressed forward unopposed until they set foot on the shores of Entritica. For a faction formed from a third world country like Etracova, to trespass into enemy territory was a feat worth celebrating for Chimera; conversely, it was a worrying sign of things to come for Entritica...

Chapter 10

Saturday morning arrived and a restless Nathan struggled to prise himself from his bed whilst a few beams of sunlight pierced past his curtains. He rubbed his eyes furiously to try and wake himself up but the headache he felt now from a lack of sleep left him feeling out of sorts. Throughout the night, he had been tormented by nightmares where he relived what he could remember of yesterday's incident at the bridge, namely Ranjit revealing the gun along with how he shot Drew and nearly did the same to Abbie.

Finally mustering the energy to get up, Nathan trudged his way towards the bathroom, his head pounding with each step he took. Once at the sink, he squinted his eyes as he squeezed a blob of toothpaste onto his toothbrush and brushed his teeth. His vision was still blurry as he rinsed his mouth and spat the solution down the drain. Nathan glanced up towards the mirror above the sink, hoping it would help to regain his focus.

However, in his sleep-deprived state, the face that looked back at him was that of his dad. Just like in his dreams, Richard was dressed in his army uniform which was the notable difference between the two, for being father and son, they shared a lot of characteristics such as their facial structures and the same red hair. There were still subtle deviations though, even with appearances given that Richard had more years on Nathan. The main parallel that Nathan picked up on was that they were both wearing the golden locket around their necks. This was the image of Richard that he'd seen just before he had entrusted Nathan with the locket.

Using the sink to steady himself, Nathan closed his eyes knowing that what he was seeing wasn't real – no matter how tempting it may have been to succumb to the illusion. Unfortunately, the throbbing in his head didn't die down which prevented him from being able to concentrate. When he opened his eyes again, he staggered backwards in fright as the hallucination he now saw was that of a bloodied Ranjit, still wearing the black insignia of Chimera, a painful reminder of the damage he was capable of inflicting under the black aura's influence. As he was breathing heavily from the shock, he heard a soft voice behind him.

"Nathan?" Victoria called out to him. Nathan quickly turned around to see his mother standing there, holding a glass of water and two tablets in her hands. "I-I heard you walking about upstairs and…well I thought you might need these after yesterday…" she explained.

Nathan heaved a sigh of relief and gratefully accepted the offer. They both went back into his room and sat on his bed as he washed the painkillers down with the water. Then, they sat together silently for a few moments until Nathan started speaking again.

"I'm still angry at you both for keeping this from me for so long…" he reinforced, much calmer than the previous day. However, he didn't look his mother in the eye as he was slouched over, looking down at the floor below, trying to block out the images he saw in the mirror from his mind.

"I know…you've every right to be…" Victoria acknowledged sincerely. In the corner of his eye, Nathan spotted that she was also holding Ranjit's black locket.

"And not just the aura…but you know of Chimera too…" Nathan remembered.

"Yes, I do. I knew about them from your father a long time ago…" Victoria confirmed.

Hearing this, Nathan finally raised his head and turned to meet his mom's gaze.

"I still have a *lot* of questions about the black aura…but they can wait. Because right now, I want you to tell me everything you know about Chimera…including how dad knew about them too…" Nathan insisted.

"That's what I'm here for," Victoria replied, looking down at the black dragon on the locket she was holding before turning back to Nathan. "It's about time you knew the full story – and I promise, no more lies!"

"No more lies," Nathan repeated in agreement, twisting his body into position so he could give his full focus to his mother's explanation.

"Okay, so to start with…if I were to summarise what Chimera was…" Victoria thought aloud as she began her account. "Richard said it best when he described them as a satanic cult that turned into a terrorist organisation led by its fanatics. They were based in Etracova…and as you know already, that's where Richard originally came from…"

"D-dad never…talked about his time in Etracova much – other than that one bedtime story about the dragon in the cave when I was a kid…" Nathan recalled. "S-so is Chimera the reason why?"

"Pretty much…" Victoria verified. "When you were young, I remember you once asked Richard about what happened to his family…and he told you that they had died in a freak accident which is why he ended up leaving Etracova for Entritica. Well…that's only half of the truth. In actuality, it was Chimera that killed his family…they attacked his village…and Richard was forced to evacuate for his own safety…"

"My god…that's horrible…" Nathan uttered in disbelief. "H-how old was dad when this happened…?"

"He was only fourteen," Victoria answered. "The assault on the village happened twenty…no, twenty-one years ago…"

"S-so about five years before I was born…" Nathan stated after calculating the difference of years in his own head, using his own age of sixteen to compare.

"Yes…and you can probably guess, but it affected Richard for a long time…" Victoria continued. "As you know, Clint and I were in an orphanage after our parents died in a car accident caused by a drunk driver…that place was where I met Richard who joined shortly after leaving Etracova. Because of the trauma, he was really reserved back then and didn't want to engage with anyone – completely different to the loving man and father he became. Then again, the same was true for me and Clint as we were also processing the loss of our parents at that time…

"It's not easy for troubled teenagers to get adopted it seems. Nobody seemed willing to take on the full responsibility of looking after me, Clint or Richard so the three of us were moved onto the foster care scheme, in the hopes that we could at least get temporary carers. Luckily, we found a couple – Hannah and Sarah Yates-Harris who were in their fifties and had many years of experience fostering kids like us – who were happy to look after me and Clint together. But after hearing of Richard's story from the care workers, they took pity on him and agreed to foster him too. They were good people – the best even…"

"I-I never got to know Hannah but I do miss Nanny Sarah…" Nathan commented forlornly – Sarah had died not long before he'd joined Silver Dawn Comp. Victoria nodded in mutual mournful agreement before carrying on with her venture down memory lane.

"After the first few weeks of living together and the quiet period had passed, Richard and I slowly started getting to know each other. We became friends to begin with, but he still didn't talk about his family for the first two months. Then, one day, I asked Richard about his gold locket – the one he gave to you. He told me that it was a symbol of hope, protection and purity that was used by freedom fighters who would oppose Chimera. It was the first time he'd mentioned that name so naturally, I asked him about it…

"That's when he opened up to me about who Chimera were and what they had put him through. He showed me their insignia– the black dragon on this locket…" she said, balling Ranjit's locket in her fist. "Richard told me that they specialised in destruction, brainwashing children into joining them and aimed to conquer the rest of Etracova so they could rule over it with an iron fist. He was in a dark place for a while because of them, but I think confiding in me helped to ease the pain for him as time passed.

"From there, our feelings for each other slowly grew, though due to living in close quarters with each other like family, we didn't act on them until Hannah passed away from cancer two years later…our shared grief was what ultimately brought us together and, as you know, the rest was history. Yet deep down, Richard never truly let go of his grudge against Chimera and he could never bring himself to revisit Etracova after they took over more areas of it – it was just too upsetting for him to face…"

"Wow…they really put dad through hell…" Nathan commented bitterly once Victoria had finished her story. "Despite all that, he made sure to avoid them and Etracova until they declared war on us…A-are Chimera really that dangerous? For dad to go so far as to join the army to fight them…he must have seen them as a threat…yet our government have kept their name anonymous throughout…"

Victoria stood up from Nathan's bed and pondered her son's words for a moment, all while looking out the window where the sun was now partly obscured by the clouds.

"You make a good point…" Victoria remarked thoughtfully before returning her gaze to Nathan. "I'm afraid I don't know myself…it may have been something only Richard knew. When he first told me that he was going to enrol in the army for the war, he claimed it was to provide a better standard of living for us – in fairness, there was a demand for more soldiers at the time with a cash incentive being offered for new recruits. I still questioned it though and when I pressured him enough, he blurted out that he couldn't lose his family again…I figured that he felt threatened by whoever the enemies were to come out with that, but I never would have guessed that it was Chimera again. It all adds up now though…"

"I hate to say it, but…" Nathan muttered, catching his mom's attention. "I think I understand how dad must have felt…I hate Chimera for taking him away from us just as he must have hated them for killing his parents. I want them to pay for making him suffer so much and he obviously felt the same way." He paused briefly, head lowered to gaze at the floor once more, to collate his thoughts before turning back to look at Victoria. "Mom, d-do you…do you think dad enlisted in the army so he could get revenge on them?" Nathan asked her yearningly. "I mean…I can't really judge him for doing that – after all, I risked my life yesterday in the hopes of *just* getting information about Chimera. It's just…now I can see how self-destructive it can be…" he rationalised, the influence of the black aura still lingering in his mind.

"For you to say that at such a young age…" Victoria quipped fondly. "In spite of his years, Richard was a wise man, probably because of all the pain that he endured through his life…but you might have already surpassed him in that area. He'd be proud of you for that – and it's a big reason why he bequeathed that locket to you," she said, her pupils focusing on the golden dragon around Nathan's neck. "Those values that it represents – hope, protection and purity – were something that Richard embodied and he had faith that you would inherit those same ideals." Hearing his mother say this, Nathan stroked the locket affectionately, feeling pride and reassurance at these words.

"As for whether Richard joined the army purely for revenge…I'll admit that yesterday, I had my doubts when I first found out that Chimera was our enemy," Victoria confessed. "But do you remember the last words he said to both of us before he departed for war?"

"Y-yeah I do…" Nathan replied, proceeding to recall Richard's message to them. *"You two are the purest lights in my life. I'll fight to the end to defend you both. Until I come back, please protect one another* – that's what he told us…"

"That's right, and it was your locket that reminded me of that," Victoria affirmed. "If your father was acting solely for revenge, he wouldn't have stayed away from Chimera for as long as he did. He only volunteered to stand against them once he believed our lives to be at risk – we meant the world to him.

"Honestly, while I do think that Richard's fear and hatred of Chimera did factor into his decision to enrol in the army, he was a family man through and through and his primary purpose in joining the fight was to protect us. Do you know why I'm telling you this?" she asked Nathan.

Confused, he shook his head in response.

"It's because I want you to understand that people aren't black and white," Victoria revealed. "Nobody is purely good or purely evil, that goes for Richard – and for you too. You've both had darkness in your hearts at some point in your lives from what you've experienced. But it's the choices that you both made to overcome that darkness that revealed the kinds of people you really are. It may have impacted Richard, but Chimera didn't define his life. He had us, his family to do that. And that malicious aura within you doesn't define you – unless you allow it to."

Nathan took a moment to comprehend the weight of his mother's words. He'd always held Richard on a pedestal, believing him to be the epitome of what a man should be. It was only recently that his father's shortcomings and errors in concealing the truth of Chimera and the black aura had come to light. Before that, Nathan had only ever seen the dad who'd reinvigorated his own faith in himself after he'd almost made a fatal decision four years ago on Seppuku Bridge. Having that heroic image of Richard shattered last night devastated Nathan more than anything else, even more than the near-death experience with Ranjit and the revelation of the aura inside him.

Yet, Victoria had just reminded him of something important – that his dad wasn't perfect and that was okay. Richard had his flaws but was still a good man who loved them both deeply and had his reasons for making the choices that he did, genuinely believing that he was protecting them. Now, living up to his father's legacy didn't seem so insurmountable for Nathan and with that realisation, a pressure seemed to subside within his psyche. All of a sudden, even with all of the darkness that still dwelled inside his heart after his dad's death and his unintentional attack on Ranjit, it still felt possible for Nathan to become a good man in the same vein as Richard. Of course, he was aware that he'd been walking a very fine line between rationality and impulse this last week – he could no longer risk veering down such a murky path, for it could corrupt him and turn him into another Ranjit. Slowly, it dawned on him that this was the lesson that Victoria wanted Nathan to take away with him today.

"I-I understand...I won't...I won't look for danger like that again mom..." Nathan promised earnestly. "I'll be honest...I still want to research Chimera...to know what we're up against...to find out what my dad feared so much about them...and to find out if they have a weakness. B-but I won't be so reckless next time!"

"I believe you," Victoria asserted to Nathan's surprise. "Seems you've been scared straight."

"You can say that again..." Nathan muttered. "I just want to do something that would be useful somehow – I hate feeling so powerless against them..."

"And I'm sure you can do that now without confronting thugs like Ranjit..." Victoria said, raising her eyebrow as she did so while Nathan shamefully lowered his head. "So...are *we* okay?" she asked him finally.

Nathan nodded in response. "Yeah...we will be," he whispered.

"Good..." Victoria replied with relief in her voice. "We need to be there for one another. It's what Richard would have wanted after all..."

Just as Victoria stood to leave the bedroom so that her son could have some time to digest everything, Nathan spoke up to ask one more question.

"This aura that I have in me...is there a reason why I have it? Like...is there supposed to be some sort of purpose behind it?" he questioned, trying to find meaning to it.

Victoria turned her head to glance at Nathan, grasping the yearning look in his eyes to hear something hopeful. She took a moment to consider her answer before giving him one.

"Truthfully, I don't know for certain why you have that power," Victoria responded sincerely. "I can't say whether or not there is some grand purpose behind you having it. But even if there wasn't, that doesn't mean you can't find one. Even though it's caused you a lot of grief up until now, I still believe you can make something positive out of it."

Victoria could sense a renewed brightness from Nathan as her words resonated with him, the sun poking out again from behind the clouds and illuminating him. She smiled reassuringly at him as she exited and closed the door behind her, allowing him space to rest from the experiences and bombshells he'd processed in such a short time.

Exhausted, Nathan lay down on his bed, staring up at his ceiling as he felt his eyes struggle to stay open. He decided to listen to his body – which was now feeling the effects of the painkillers – and succumb to the fatigue, falling into a peaceful slumber.

When he had the energy to prise his eyes open again, Nathan gazed out the window to see that the sun was higher in the sky compared to earlier when he had his heart to heart with his mother. Realising that he'd napped for about three hours and that it was nearly 11am, Nathan surged out of his bed and dashed into the bathroom to shower, keen to not waste any more of the day.

Half an hour later, once dressed, Nathan hurried down the stairs to find Victoria answering the front door. He heard her thank the formally dressed deliveryman as she accepted something from him before he departed. Victoria turned around, carefully holding an urn in her hands and Nathan realised what this was about.

"Dad's ashes..." he uttered, mournfully examining the urn.

"I requested them last week at the funeral..." Victoria remarked, instinctively holding it close to her heart.

"Last week...feels like it's been so much longer than that..." Nathan quipped as he pondered how much had happened at school since then.

"So...what do you think we should do with him?" Victoria asked her son. "Do you think he'd want to be scattered somewhere?"

Nathan observed how his mother tightly hugged the urn, remembering Richard's last words about them being the purest lights of his life, as well as the impact that his mother had on him during his adolescent years.

"He'd want to be wherever you are..." Nathan answered. "You were the one who changed his life and his heart for the better..." Victoria smiled and nodded in approval.

"*We* did that..." Victoria reassured him, embracing him with one arm before making her way into the living room to place the urn on the fireplace while Nathan watched.

In that moment, Nathan felt a vibration in his trouser pocket. He reached inside to pull out his mobile phone. Upon unlocking the screen, Nathan discovered that he had received a few messages from Thomas and Abbie to check that he was okay after yesterday's events. He opened them up to respond to them but paused when he saw Thomas' most recent text, the one sent seconds ago.

Nath, did you hear about the tsunami last night?! It's just been on the radio and more of our soldiers have died!

As soon as he read this, Nathan dashed through the living room towards the kitchen to turn the radio on, something that didn't go unnoticed by Victoria who followed him to see what the fuss was about. She entered the kitchen behind Nathan where they each heard the news bulletin.

"...1.48am last night, a freak tsunami occurred on the shores of Entritica. It is believed that over 20 vessels were destroyed and that 400 naval officers perished. Eyewitnesses have stated that they then saw enemy forces step onto Entritican land and proceed to..."

Almost instantly, the broadcast completely cut out to Nathan's irritation. Frustrated and wanting to know more, he tried to calibrate the frequency of the radio in the hopes of finding the signal again, but it was to no avail. Nathan and Victoria stood in silence for a moment as they digested what they'd just heard.

"I don't think they lost the signal..." Victoria speculated. "It was done too abruptly...but what does this mean...?"

Nathan contemplated the announcement, particularly what had been said about the tsunami and how many of the naval fleets had died. It felt eerily alike to what had happened to his dad...

Suddenly, Nathan recalled what he couldn't previously from his confrontation with Ranjit – he'd claimed that his father had been killed in a hurricane in the Zalhara Timberlands! Not just that, but the disaster was somehow brought about by the leader of Chimera, Maris, the name finally coming to the forefront of his mind. Finally, Ranjit had declared that she and Chimera would set foot onto Entritica and that another disaster would happen – this prediction had seemingly come true! As the memories of their conversation flowed back, a trembling Nathan glanced at Victoria, aware that he couldn't ignore this.

"Mom, I need to investigate this!" he insisted. "Can I invite Thomas and Abbie around? I could really do with having them here..."

"Yes, o-of course..." Victoria agreed.

While Victoria sat down at the dining table, still reeling from the broadcast, Nathan hurriedly dialled Thomas' number and then Abbie's to ask if they were available. After they both said they'd be round to his shortly, he put his phone away and waited in anticipation for their arrival. Bit by bit, it seemed for Nathan like the pieces of the puzzle were falling into place, although after the news of the ominous tsunami, he himself was now growing concerned with where completing it would lead him to…

Chapter 11

Half an hour later, Thomas was dropped off in his mom's car outside Nathan's house. There, he found Abbie standing at the edge of the driveway, awkwardly shuffling about with her hand on a nervous young fair-haired boy's shoulder. He quickly realised that this was Ben.

"You brought your brother with you?" Thomas hissed under his breath.

"I know, it's not ideal!" Abbie muttered, strategically placing her hands over Ben's ears so that he couldn't hear her. "My parents are at it again…I didn't want him to be around all that yelling and fighting…" she explained regretfully.

"Oh…right, sorry…" Thomas remarked, his voice softening once again. "Wait, how long have you been out here?"

"A-about five minutes…" Abbie stammered. "Honestly…I-I'm a bit scared to go in…"

"Because of what happened yesterday?" Thomas asked, the incident at the bridge still fresh in his own mind.

"No…I'm scared his mom will hate me…" Abbie confessed. "I'm just turning up, not even announcing that my little brother's with me…and she must know about me throwing Nathan's locket away by now – hardly a glowing first impression, is it?"

"A lot has happened since that day…probably too much…" Thomas reminded Abbie, trying to reassure her. "But we're both here now, so let's go in together…"

Comforted by his words, Abbie smiled and nodded at Thomas. However, before they could move towards the door, it opened up and Victoria was there to greet them.

"You've been there a while, I was wondering when you were finally going to come in," Victoria chuckled, having already seen Abbie waiting outside. "Don't worry, I don't bite" she joked playfully as she beckoned them inside. Ben hid behind Abbie as she and Thomas strode down the driveway until they met Victoria in the doorway.

"M-Mrs Bennett…" Abbie squeaked. "I-is it okay if my little brother Ben stays here too…? S-sorry it's so short notice, it's just a bit chaotic at the house at the moment…" she requested, her face glowing red from embarrassment as she explained the situation.

"Yeah absolutely!" Victoria agreed with a smile on her face to Abbie's relief. "I can keep him entertained while you both talk with Nathan."

"Thank you," Abbie replied gratefully as Ben stepped from behind his sister, seemingly more relaxed from being around Victoria's welcoming demeanour.

"How is Nathan…?" Thomas asked Victoria. "Is he okay after yesterday…?"

Before she could answer, Nathan's voice could be clearly heard from further up in the house as he angrily cried out the words, *"God damn it!!"* to Thomas and Abbie's surprise.

"He's…been a bit preoccupied this morning since he heard the news about the tsunami," Victoria explained, however she was unable to mask the concern in her voice. "Rather than hear it from me though, you'd best see how he is for yourselves…" she suggested as she closed the front door after Thomas, Abbie and Ben had stepped into the hallway.

Once Abbie had finished telling Ben to be a good boy for Victoria, she and Thomas made their way up the stairs towards Nathan's room while Victoria led Ben into the living room. Seeing that the bedroom door was shut, Thomas politely knocked until a flustered Nathan opened it.

"Good, you're both here!" Nathan acknowledged as he cradled his laptop in his arm.

"Nath, how are you?" Abbie asked him carefully.

"Frustrated!" Nathan retorted bluntly as he paced around his room. "Any articles about the tsunami are being taken down again – I can't find anything!"

"Nath…" Abbie tried to interrupt but to no avail as Nathan continued to focus on the tsunami.

"The government are hiding something!" Nathan ranted. "There's no other way that radio broadcast would have been cut off just as Chimera were ment-"

Before he could complete his sentence, Thomas snatched the laptop away from Nathan to his and Abbie's shock, forcing his attention back onto them.

"Nathan, we *will* get back to this," Thomas insisted. "But first, we need to talk about what happened yesterday with Ranjit. Particularly about that black energy that was surrounding you…"

As he heard this, Nathan automatically looked down to the floor, averting his gaze from his friends – he didn't intend to for he knew he had to reveal the truth eventually, yet he still felt a sense of shame for what it had caused him to do.

"I hate to say it, mate…" Thomas sighed having seen Nathan's reaction. "But that level of rage was *not* normal. I've never seen anything like it and it's like you were being controlled by it. For your sake, I think we need to investigate it…"

"Thanks, but we might not need to do that…Mom told me yesterday that I've had that aura since birth…" Nathan replied as he raised his head again to see Thomas and Abbie's faces, their eyes widened in response to what he'd told them.

"Are you serious?! Since birth?!" Abbie exclaimed.

Nathan nodded and although he was unable to explain why this mysterious aura dwelled within him, he told Thomas and Abbie everything that he had heard from Victoria the day prior. He described how Richard had seen the energy manifest when his life was in danger as a baby. He then confirmed that the sensation that Richard had felt that day was comparable to how Thomas and Abbie had depicted their own experience when they saw the dark energy emanating from him at the bridge yesterday.

"My god…" Abbie uttered as she reeled from Nathan's account of what he'd been through. "Th-that…must have been a lot for you to take in…" she recognised sympathetically.

"Yeah…it still is…" Nathan agreed, deflated at having to relive the discussion. "Was hoping that…you guys could help me make sense of it all…" he proposed hopefully.

"Well, I'll admit that it's beyond my understanding Nath," Thomas conceded. "But you've got my support regardless – after all, that power did save my life from Tobias," he added without hesitation.

"And mine from Ranjit yesterday," Abbie mentioned encouragingly, highlighting the good that the aura had done. Having his friends' backing with this helped to raise Nathan's spirits once more.

"Thanks, you guys," Nathan said appreciatively to them. "And I know...I need to try and get a better understanding of this power myself... including why I have it..."

"Well, no better time than the present!" Abbie chirped cheerfully hoping to maintain Nathan's morale. "We might be able to find a clue behind it if we compare each instance where the black aura emerged. We could find a common theme."

"I think I've already found one," Thomas remarked. "Each time I remember sensing the energy, Nathan was filled with rage to the point that he blacked out..." he thought aloud, recalling the incidents with Tobias, Abbie and Ranjit. "Could be that the aura is linked to your emotions?"

Looking back at the past events, Nathan did see merit to what Thomas just speculated. However, he realised that there was one event that Thomas' theory wasn't true for.

"What about the first time that the aura emerged? When I was a baby?" Nathan countered. "I can't imagine feeling anger at only a few days old..."

Hearing Nathan's argument, Thomas and Abbie quietly searched for a logical explanation as to why the aura would materialise at that stage.

"Ooh, I know!" Abbie blurted out. "Danger! You could have activated the black aura due to your life being at risk!"

"You could be onto something there Abbie," Thomas commented thoughtfully. "We were in dangerous situations with Tobias and Ranjit after all..."

"But what about the time *with* Abbie?" Nathan argued sceptically. "Sure, I lost my dad's locket, but it wasn't exactly a life-risking event..."

"Wait! Nath, you said 'lost', right?!" Thomas called out abruptly.

"Um, yeah...why?" Nathan questioned, confused as Thomas started to pace around the room.

"That time with Abbie, you lost your locket..." Thomas thought aloud while Nathan and Abbie watched him, his eye twitching as his mind ticked along. "And then the time when you were a baby, you could have lost your life...and for the Tobias and Ranjit incidents, me and Abbie were in harm's way so you could have lost us!"

"That might be it!" Abbie agreed. "For each of those times, you were in danger of losing something that was important to you!"

Nathan silently mulled this prospect over in his head before realising that he couldn't find any holes in their theory.

"You might have hit the nail on the head…" Nathan accepted. "Like you say, maybe it really is an event of loss that triggers it. The only thing I don't understand is, why didn't the aura go berserk when I found out that my dad died…?"

"Actually, I have an idea on that too and it's to do with both the danger aspect and your emotions," Thomas said, drawing Nathan and Abbie's attention. "The sensation from the aura yesterday was the strongest I'd ever felt. But compared with Abbie throwing the locket, although I did feel a sinister chill from you, it was the weakest one by far. It seems that the aura has had different intensities depending on the situation…"

"And you think that's influenced by dangerous situations and Nathan's emotions?" Abbie deduced.

"Exactly," Thomas confirmed. "I think the gravity of the situation and the strength of Nathan's rage significantly affects how powerful the black aura is."

Nathan nodded at Thomas' suggestion, now fully convinced. "That makes sense…it wasn't like my own life was threatened when I heard about dad's death," he rationalised. "And as for rage…well when I heard that news from mom…I think I just put all my energy into helping *her* grieve. Truth is, I didn't even feel angry when I found out…I just felt…empty…" he sighed deeply.

After these words left his mouth, Abbie sat down beside Nathan on his bed and put her arm around him to try and comfort him. Seeing this, Thomas shuffled over and awkwardly tried to pat Nathan on the shoulder to try and replicate the support, only to miss and catch Abbie's hand instead. At the sight of a baffled Abbie and Thomas' bright red face upon doing this, unsure whether to keep it there or retract it, Nathan let out the slightest snicker and placed his own hand on top of the two of theirs, rubbing gently to assure them that he'd be okay.

"Look," Nathan began. "I think we've covered a lot of ground with whatever this black aura inside me is, but let's put a pin in it for now because I wanted to discuss the tsunami with you both. I've remembered the conversation I had with Ranjit before he revealed the gun. He told me that my dad and many other soldiers were killed in a hurricane…"

"What?!!" Thomas and Abbie responded in shocked unison.

"That's not all," Nathan continued. "Ranjit told me that the leader of Chimera is called Maris and she's behind the natural disasters. After this tsunami report – which he predicted would happen – and how quickly it's being covered up, I think he was telling the truth…" Nathan paused to observe Thomas and Abbie's reactions to the unpleasant news, watching their eyes blink repeatedly in bewilderment as they tried to digest the revelation.

"H-how…h-how is that possible?!" Abbie stammered as she rose from the bed to pace around the room, while Thomas just stood where he was, his head in a daze. "H-how can one person be behind catastrophes of that scale?!"

"I don't know either," Nathan conceded. "But for any articles about the war to be struck down all this time – I think our government has known about Chimera and Maris for a while. And they've wanted to cover it up for as long as they could to prevent panic…"

After another moment of silence while Abbie considered Nathan's words and Thomas uncharacteristically continued to stare vacantly into space, Abbie's head bobbed up and down in agreement.

"Yeah, I think you're right Nath," she concurred. "I remember Joshua's reaction to hearing Chimera's name yesterday. Then he was very quick to escort Ranjit away before we could get any more information out of him," she mentioned, recalling the fright on Joshua's face. "He wants to join the army after all, so surely he'd have some idea of what's happening on the battlefield?"

Upon realising this, Nathan's eyes widened and he grabbed his phone, furiously scrolling through his contacts until he found Joshua's phone number. He dialled it three times, however he failed to get a response back much to the disgust of Abbie.

"Has he not even messaged you to check that you're okay after yesterday?!" she yelled in outrage. "I know he's your cousin but that's borderline heartless!"

It hurt for Nathan to be reminded of how distant Joshua had been with him of late, however he knew Abbie was right about his cousin's strange behaviour. If he knew about Chimera and Maris all along, it would go a long way to explaining it. While he contemplated this, Abbie had noticed that Thomas seemed trapped in a trance.

"Tom? Thomas?!" she called out, snapping him back to reality as he staggered back in surprise.

"Ah…! S-sorry…I…um…" Thomas babbled agitatedly.

"Are you alright?" Abbie asked him. "You've not said one word since Nathan brought up Maris and Chimera..."

As soon as Abbie uttered those last few words, it triggered another memory from yesterday for Nathan who abruptly raised his head up and twisted his body round to face Thomas.

"Wait! Thomas, you knew who Chimera was!" he cried out in realisation as the look on Thomas' face hinted at a sense of shame. "You were the one who recognised their amulet and even said you knew them *well enough*. How though?! How do you know of Chimera?!"

Thomas sighed before answering. "Well, I did say I'd discuss it with you. Truthfully though, I'd hoped you guys would never have to find this out... The reason why I know about Chimera is because one of their founding members...is my father..."

"No way...!" Abbie uttered, stunned by this revelation.

"Your father...?! The same one who...? My god..." Nathan replied as he processed this news.

"Y-yeah...that *man*..." Thomas remarked venomously. "I-I'm not sure where my mind's at right now. Part of me never wanted to hear of or risk crossing paths with Chimera again. And yet, I think I'd relish in the chance to pay that man back for how he treated my mom..."

"That must have been really difficult for you..." Abbie commented compassionately.

"Tom, from what you've just told me about Chimera, it sounds like we have a common enemy," Nathan insisted.

"Because they killed your dad?" Thomas remarked.

"Not just that, but for what they put my dad through when he was younger. Turns out that when my dad was still living in Etracova, they killed his family and forced him to flee here," Nathan explained to their disbelief.

"Seriously?!" an alarmed Abbie reacted. "To think both of your dads would be connected to Chimera..."

"I know, right?!" Nathan agreed. "I want to avenge my dad and Thomas wants to get revenge on his...I think this is a sign that we're meant to achieve this together..."

"Achieve?" Thomas questioned curiously. "Achieve what...?"

"Taking down Chimera!" Nathan proclaimed determinedly. "Or at least researching them to find out how they can be taken down! I know it sounds like Maris and Chimera are untouchable, but I don't buy it. They must have some sort of weakness that can be struck at and if it got discovered, it could help our army win the war…"

"Nathan, you do realise that the army will already have soldiers and officers in their ranks, trained for researching Chimera's vulnerabilities, right?" Abbie pointed out to him, trying to calm him down. "They'll surely find something if it's there. I know you feel you owe it to your dad to take action but remember that they're experts trained for this while we haven't even left school yet. What makes you think that we can achieve more than what they're already doing…?"

Before he answered, Nathan spun his locket around in his hand. As he did that, he thought back to Victoria's response to his question about why he may have the black aura, her words echoing in his mind:

I can't say whether or not there is some grand purpose behind you having it. But even if there wasn't, that doesn't mean you can't find one.

"I get what you're saying Abbie, I do," Nathan reassured her. "But I just can't get rid of this gut feeling that it's something that I'm *meant* to do – not just for my dad but for me as well. If I could just find any bit of information about Chimera or Maris that could contribute to defeating them, I think it might help me to feel at peace. Plus, I promise I won't run into danger like I did yesterday. Not again." Once he was certain that Abbie had accepted his answer, Nathan turned back to Thomas. "So how about it, mate? Will you help me look into this?" he requested.

Upon being asked this, Thomas clammed up and couldn't bring himself to give a response. This didn't escape Abbie's notice and she decided to pacify the situation once more.

"Nath, that's a big thing to ask someone just out the blue…" she reasoned as she tried to assist Thomas. "Don't forget, we're all still shook up after everything that happened yesterday with Ranjit. We just need some time to think…"

"Oh…yeah…of course, sorry. I didn't mean to put anyone on the spot…" Nathan apologised, recognising that he had been acting a bit coercively. As he said this, Thomas' body and shoulders instinctively relaxed again.

"It's okay," Abbie reassured. "It's been a tense twenty-four hours and we have discussed some heavy stuff. I think it would be good for our sanity to just take a break from it for a bit. In fact, I have an idea – what if we all have a sleepover here tonight?" Abbie suggested to Nathan's and Thomas' surprise.

"A sleepover?" Thomas echoed curiously. "We've never done one of those before – I wouldn't know where to start with that. Besides, are you really sure you feel comfortable having a sleepover with two boys?"

"I always wanted to do one when I was younger, but I never had any real friends before you guys," Abbie confessed as Nathan flashed her a considerate smile. "So, I'm game if you both are." Thomas looked back towards Nathan who was still seated on the bed to see if he approved of the idea.

"Well, I'd need to get mom's permission first-" Nathan explained until he and the others heard another voice on the side of the door.

"I think it's a great idea, Abbie," they heard Victoria call out. Nathan stood up to open the door to find his mom standing there. "Sorry, I'd only just come up here myself, I didn't mean to pry," she stated bashfully. "But I do think some company would do you the world of good Nath, so you've got my blessing."

"Okay, thanks, mom," Nathan replied brightly before turning back to Thomas and Abbie, the latter of whom had a gleeful expression on her face. "In that case, let's do it then! Let's have a sleepover."

"Fair enough, I'll call my mom to let her know," Thomas decided as he pulled his phone out of his pocket.

"I can get some food from the shops for you all," Victoria told them before she headed back downstairs.

While Thomas was calling his mother, Abbie left him and Nathan in the bedroom as she followed Victoria, passing through the living room where Ben was watching some cartoons until she caught up with her in the kitchen.

"M-Mrs Bennett," Abbie cried out as Victoria turned to face her. "Sorry if I spoke out of turn with suggesting the sleepover. I just thought of it in the heat of the moment, but I should have got your approval first before saying it…"

"Oh, Abbie dear, don't worry about it," Victoria maintained. "Like I said, I thought it would be good for Nathan so I'm glad you came up with the idea. And please, just call me Victoria – Vic even."

"That's great, thank you…Vic," Abbie said relieved. "Also, I'm really sorry to ask this, but is it okay if Ben were to stop over tonight too…?" she added nervously, hoping that she wasn't asking for too much.

"Yeah, of course," Victoria agreed, to Abbie's delight. "He's been as good as gold by the way. It's really brought back memories of when Nathan was a child, so it's been nice to have him around."

"I really can't thank you enough for this! If you need me to help with anything for the sleepover, please just let me know," Abbie stated gratefully, hoping to repay the kindness that Victoria had shown her.

"I'm sure I'll be fine but thank you," Victoria insisted. "Before you go back up though, I do just want to say that Nathan did tell me about the time you took Richard's locket from him…"

Abbie gulped anxiously as Victoria brought this up for it had been the moment she had been dreading since she first stepped foot in the house. However, she couldn't have predicted what Victoria would say next.

"He also told me you went as far as to go into the drain to get it back for him. On top of that, you even followed him to the bridge to try and save him from his own rash decisions yesterday. As far as I'm concerned, you've more than redeemed yourself for your mistake so you really don't have to tread on eggshells around me. I'm glad that Nathan has friends like you and Thomas."

In stunned silence, Abbie bit her lip and nodded to show her appreciation for Victoria's acceptance of her. As Victoria left the kitchen behind to go out and do some food shopping, Abbie wiped a few tears away from her eyes, genuinely moved to have been welcomed by Nathan's mother so quickly, before she re-joined Nathan and Thomas.

****

Throughout the rest of the day, Nathan, Thomas and Abbie spent time together talking about things other than the war, ate snacks that Victoria had bought from the supermarket for them and played a mix of racing and fighting video games long after the sun had set. During this time, Abbie could hear her brother Ben laughing downstairs while Victoria kept him entertained. Eventually, once it got late enough, Nathan switched off his console.

"Abbie, are you *sure* this is your first-time playing video games?" Nathan chuckled sceptically as he removed the disc from the tray.

"Are you asking that 'cause I kept beating you both?" Abbie laughed.

"You must have played before! There's no way one person can have that much beginner's luck!" Thomas accused.

"Maybe you two just really suck?" Abbie taunted with a smug grin.

"Seriously though, I still find it hard to believe you've never played video games before," Nathan reiterated. "You looked like you were having a blast."

"Well, I would have liked to but any money that we could have used to buy the consoles, my parents just spent it on alcohol," Abbie pointed out bluntly. "I wish my parents could be more like your mom, Nath. She's amazing! Especially with how she's looked after Ben today."

"Yeah she is…I suppose I've been really lucky to have had her and dad…" Nathan remarked affectionately as he reflected on happy memories with them from his childhood.

"Hey Thomas…" Abbie addressed him, drawing his attention to her. "We've heard about your terrorist dad now, but what is your mom like?"

"Mom? Yeah, she's great. To have raised me by herself the way she has done – she's a woman to be reckoned with," Thomas answered proudly.

"Wow, by herself?" Abbie quipped impressed. "So you've never had a father figure in your life?"

"Not really," Thomas replied. "I guess mom was too busy with work and looking after me to find time to meet someone else…"

"Not even a grandparent?" Abbie wondered inquisitively.

At being asked this, Thomas automatically looked away, his pupils darting uneasily around him. After a few awkward moments of silence, Abbie turned to Nathan.

"Have I asked something I shouldn't have?" she asked him.

"Tom…doesn't exactly have a good relationship with his granddad…" Nathan explained, trying to cover for his friend. "I-it's a bit difficult for him to talk abo-"

"My granddad bullied me…" Thomas interrupted abruptly, shocking Abbie with the revelation. With their full attention back in his direction, Thomas pushed himself to continue. "He hated me…for being my father's son. He only ever saw me as that and he'd berate me for it constantly. Hell, half the voices I heard in my head when I was younger were his…telling me that I was a monster that should never have been born…"

"He actually said that?! That's awful!" Abbie yelled, appalled by what Thomas had told her. "I'm so sorry. Did your mom ever know?"

"My granddad tormented me whenever she wasn't around – he knew what he was doing," Thomas reflected agonisingly. "Of course, I felt I couldn't say anything when I was younger. I was in such a dark place and…I felt somehow that I deserved what was happening…"

"You didn't," Nathan reinforced sternly yet spoke the words softly.

"Yeah, I know that now," Thomas acknowledged. "When mom did catch him out though, she disowned him for how he'd harassed me. It happened four years ago and we've not seen him since…"

"Well good riddance in that case!" Abbie declared. "How did your mom even meet your dad if he was a terrorist?" As Abbie continued to ask questions, Thomas started to fidget anxiously. "And what did he do to her for your granddad to take his hatred out on you? Did he physically abuse her or something?"

"I-I'm sorry…" Thomas stuttered as his body started to tremble. "Th-this is a bit too much for me…I-I can't…"

"No, don't be, it's my fault! I have been bombarding you," Abbie realised, the guilt creeping up on her. "If it's too uncomfortable, you don't have to tell us…"

"If you don't mind, I'd prefer that right now…" Thomas confirmed as he got up from the bed.

From there, he stared out pensively at the night sky through Nathan's window, trying to take his mind away from his toxic granddad. High above the outlines of the buildings and surrounding mountains in the distance, the sky was dotted with clusters of stars which illuminated the encompassing darkness. After a few minutes of eerie silence, Abbie tried to break the tension again.

"Hey, it's great that you and Nathan have had each other to get through things. I wish I'd met friends like you sooner…" Abbie said optimistically, drawing a smile from Nathan and causing Thomas' body to relax a bit. Still eager to disrupt the silence, Abbie carried on. "Thomas…you mentioned earlier how you used to hear voices in your head until Nathan came into your life. I was wondering…just because I want to understand it a bit more…how did you manage to cope with it before Nathan?" she asked carefully but interestedly.

"Well…" Thomas thought aloud. "It was a real struggle back then…but I suppose the one thing that did bring me peace was writing and drawing.

I used to draw a comic for myself about a hero I created – I called him Gandora…"

"Oh yeah, I remember that!" Nathan recalled. "He was like an antihero that punished criminals, wasn't he?"

"Yeah, he was," Thomas corroborated. "I guess it was a bit of an outlet for me to vent my frustrations and put my feelings to paper. My character, Gandora, represented all that – what I desired to be at that time…before Nathan came along of course…" he rationalised as he drifted back into his trail of thought.

"Seems like you were pretty creative to come up with something like that," Abbie remarked admiringly.

Thomas took another moment to reflect before he spoke again, this time turning to face Nathan.

"Hey, Nath," Thomas said. "You asked me earlier to help you investigate Chimera, remember?"

Nathan's eyes lit up as he heard these words. "Wait, you mean…?!" he deduced.

"Yeah, I'm in," Thomas confirmed confidently. "Let's take those bastards down!"

"Woah, are you sure about this Tom?" Abbie questioned with concern.

"I am," Thomas repeated determined. "Talking about Chimera, my granddad, even my creation, Gandora – it brought it all back for me. How I was tormented for the sins of my so-called father. As well as my goal of seeing them get brought to justice," he rationalised, thinking of how that ambition manifested itself in the concept of Gandora. "Nath, we've both suffered at Chimera's hands and just like you said, we both want the same thing. So, let's do what we can to achieve it – together!"

"Thanks Tom! I knew I could count on you…" Nathan exclaimed gratefully, stepping up to bump fists with Thomas in a sign of unity. In the corner of his eye, he caught a worried expression from Abbie. "Abbie, I just want to investigate what Chimera's weaknesses are. I swear I won't be running into danger again – I already promised my mom this yesterday!" Nathan insisted. "Plus, I don't ever want to put you both at risk again. I've already lost my dad, I don't want to lose you guys too! Please believe me…"

Abbie took his plea into consideration, also reflecting on Victoria's words earlier that day about her being glad Nathan had her and Thomas as friends, before finally replying, "I already know you won't be doing anything dangerous again. Because I'll be making sure of it," Abbie boldly declared, Nathan's eyes widening in shock as she uttered the words.

"You'll really help us?!" Nathan asked hopefully.

"Yeah, 'fraid you two are stuck with me now," Abbie joked. "We survived a shootout yesterday so I think we're all in deep enough as it is – might as well see it through. Got to make Chimera pay somehow for putting you two through hell, right?" she finished, offering out her fist to Nathan and Thomas having seen their exchange seconds ago.

Without hesitation, both boys brought their fists into contact with Abbie's, each silently agreeing to work together to investigate Chimera in the hopes of finding a vulnerability or a means to defeat them for good. Then, Nathan abruptly let out a huge yawn.

"Way to ruin the moment Nath!" Abbie chuckled. "You bored of us already?"

"Didn't exactly get a lot of sleep last night. Being held at gunpoint will do that to you..." Nathan commented bleakly.

"Yeah true...we should all probably get some sleep then. We can make a plan of how to get intel about Chimera tomorrow," Abbie suggested.

"I'll go ask my mom to get the sleeping bags ready," Nathan decided as he headed towards the bedroom door.

"Hey Abbie..." Thomas called quietly, catching Nathan's attention as well as hers. "What you said about me and Nathan being there for each other...you were right. I am lucky to have him as a friend. One silver lining about my experiences with Chimera and the voices I used to hear in my head is that it makes me appreciate having Nathan in my life more," he elaborated, drawing a bashful smile from Nathan. "So thanks for reminding me of that..."

"Heh, I've never known friendship like the one you two have," Abbie noted almost enviously. "It's rock solid. I can't even imagine the pair of you arguing."

"Well, if it ever happened, I'm sure we'd resolve it in our own way," Nathan determined resolutely, prompting Thomas to nod in agreement.

As Nathan left his room, he paused at the top of stairs to value the loyalty that Thomas and Abbie had demonstrated to him yesterday and today. Despite what he'd gone through these last few weeks, he reflected on each of the sentiments they'd conveyed and realised that he too felt blessed to have them in his life. Once the moment had passed, he continued down the stairs to help Victoria bring up any of the new sleeping bags she'd bought from the supermarket. With his loved ones around to provide comfort, he was ready to get some proper sleep to prepare him for his upcoming investigation into Chimera and Maris, the goal of uncovering their mysteries at the forefront of his mind...

⊷⊶◅◆▻⊷⊶

Chapter 12

The next morning, Nathan was woken up as he felt the warmth of the sunlight shine down on him through his window once again. Nathan struggled to open his eyes but he could feel something pressing down on his chest while he stirred. He pulled his right arm free to groggily rub his eyes, only to find a blurry figure standing over his bed. His vision started to clear and as he heard a giggling followed by the clicking sound of a camera, he could make out the shape of Abbie looming over him.

"Abbie?" Nathan groaned wearily. "What are you doing...?"

"Aw, I could ask you two the same thing," Abbie sniggered. "You look so cute together!"

Nathan stared up at her bewildered until his eyes glanced downwards to see that the mass across his torso was another arm draped over him. Instantly, his eyes widened and his head slowly turned to his left to find Thomas' head centimetres away from his.

"Uh Tom?" Nathan called out, shaking him to try and wake him up gently. Instead, Thomas squirmed and ended up inching even closer to Nathan. At this stage, he'd realised that Thomas' side of the bed was almost empty because he'd subtly encroached into his own half like an infestation. Losing patience and now feeling claustrophobic, Nathan started to get more assertive with his efforts to shift Thomas. "Tom..." he cried as he pressed his hand into his friend's shoulder to no avail. "Have you...ever heard..." he continued as he pushed the sleeping Thomas' body with more force, yet it was as if the body was acting of its own accord, defiantly backing Nathan to the edge of his own bed. "Of...*personal space?!*" Nathan finally yelled out, freeing one of his legs and kicking Thomas away, sending him tumbling out of the bed and onto the floor. As Abbie howled with laughter at the scene, Nathan clasped his hand over his mouth at what he'd done while Thomas, now awake, picked himself up off the floor.

"Well, I'd call that a rude awakening!" Thomas snapped grouchily while he dusted himself off.

"Sorry," Nathan said sincerely. "But you were *right* up in my face! And Abbie was taking pictures of us! *Please* don't post them online!"

"I promise I won't," Abbie reassured. "It's just for my own personal amusement – as well as a bit of payback for making me sleep on the floor," she chuckled.

"Hey, you're the one who lost rock, paper, scissors!" Thomas reminded her.

"Well, at least you beat me at something…" Abbie retorted, remembering how easily she'd won against them on the video games the night prior.

Before the three of them could create any more ruckus, they all heard Victoria's voice calling them from the bottom of the stairs.

"Since it *sounds* like you're all awake" Victoria commented sarcastically. "I should let you know that breakfast will be ready in ten minutes so hurry up and get ready!"

Upon hearing this, Abbie who had already got dressed due to waking up earlier than Nathan and Thomas, turned away from the two boys while they changed out of their pyjamas and into their clothes.

"Right, we need to make a plan for gathering intel on Chimera! Where do you guys think we should look next?" Nathan asked as he tugged his shirt over his head, a lot more energetic compared to the previous morning.

"I mean we could keep looking through website articles, but they keep getting removed," Abbie pointed out as she faced the wall, still with her back to Nathan and Thomas out of respect for their privacy.

"Hey Abs," Thomas addressed her as he pulled his trousers up his legs. "Didn't you say yesterday that you thought Joshua might know something from how he reacted to Chimera's name?"

"Oh yeah, that's right!" Abbie realised. "He was definitely acting shifty with how quickly he escorted Ranjit away, plus he's training to join the army so he must have surely heard some news about the war."

Nathan thought back to his dad's funeral where Joshua was talking with the headmaster, Mr Jones, who also had army contacts. Then, he checked his phone again to see that his cousin still hadn't returned his calls from yesterday.

"In that case, Joshua might be our best lead," Nathan determined. "We're both dressed now Abs," he confirmed once he saw that Thomas was fully clothed, prompting Abbie to pivot around to face them again. "I think we need to interrogate him to find out what he knows. Shall we corner him before school tomorrow?" he went on to suggest.

"Works for me!" Abbie concurred while Thomas gave a brief nod indicating agreement.

"I'd also like to know how it's possible for someone to *create* natural disasters," Thomas voiced sceptically, remembering Ranjit's claim that Maris was capable of this.

"We can research that today for a change. Hopefully we'll find something useful," Nathan decided, eager himself to find out the cause of yesterday's tsunami and the supposed hurricane that killed his dad.

"Sounds like a plan!" Thomas agreed.

As the strategizing ended, Nathan, Thomas and Abbie headed downstairs for breakfast. Afterwards, Thomas, Abbie and Ben each left for their homes, thanking Victoria for her hospitality on their way out. From that point, they continued to read up on anything throughout the day that could explain the recent catastrophes. Sadly, they were unable to find anything concrete that day and after enough time had passed, they mutually agreed via text messages to call it a day. They concluded that it would be better to focus on resting to be ready for the encounter with Joshua tomorrow, thus bringing the weekend to a close.

****

Monday morning came around quickly and after leaving their homes and meeting in front of the school gates earlier than normal, Nathan, Thomas and Abbie found separate hiding places so that they could keep watch for Joshua, ready to ambush him. They observed from afar as more students started to flock through the gates, some being dropped off by their families while others had walked or taken the bus. Time passed by and frustrations grew for the three as there was still no sign of the typically punctual Joshua. When the students began to thin out with ten minutes remaining before the school bell, Nathan and the others were close to abandoning the plan for the time being.

Just before they lost hope though, Thomas caught sight of Joshua arriving in the distance and signalled this to Nathan and Abbie. From there, they bided their time as Joshua got closer and closer to the school gates.

Once he'd gotten near enough to the entrance, Nathan stepped out from behind the wall to confront his cousin.

"N-Nathan..." Joshua stuttered, taken aback at seeing him there and fully aware that he'd last seen him at the bridge with Ranjit with no further communication on his end since then. "H-how are you holding up?" he asked Nathan nervously.

"Asking that a bit late, aren't you? By about three days as I count it," Nathan retorted coolly, drawing a guilt-ridden expression from his older cousin. "But never mind all that, we need to talk," he insisted.

"Nath, I know you must have a lot of questions about Ranjit, Drew and the others," Joshua acknowledged. "But I'm really short on time so we'll have to talk about this later..." he added dismissively, stepping one foot forward with the intent to bypass his younger cousin. Defiantly though, Nathan mirrored his movement and stomped his own foot in front of Joshua's.

"You're not fobbing me off again..." Nathan stated seriously, glaring Joshua in the eyes as he spoke. Meanwhile, Thomas and Abbie emerged from their own hiding places, the former standing shoulder to shoulder with Nathan while the latter positioned herself behind Joshua, ensuring that there was no escape for him.

"We weren't asking your permission to talk..." Abbie reinforced, the sound of her voice causing Joshua to glance over his shoulder at her. Nathan detected a change in Joshua's body language once he'd realised that he was enclosed amid the three of them. He seemed strangely calm and calculated yet he gripped his backpack tightly in his arms. "What're you hiding in there?" Abbie interrogated, also noticing how vigilantly he'd started to shield his backpack from them.

"That's none of your concern," Joshua claimed.

"Oh, is that so?" Abbie barked sarcastically. "Then how about something that *is* our concern, seeing as we were there – what happened to Drew after he was shot?! Is he okay?!"

"Keep your voice down!" Joshua hissed, his eyes darting around to make sure that no other students were around to hear.

"Why the secrecy?" Thomas questioned, confused. "A teenager was shot – what happened to him, how do people not know and how has nothing been in the news about it?!"

"Okay, calm down…" Joshua urged a frantic Thomas. "Drew survived – but he's in a coma…" he revealed, to the horror of Nathan, Thomas and Abbie. "I-I don't know when or if he'll recover…and Dan and Denzel are still in shock so I wouldn't expect to see them in school today…"

"I see…" Nathan commented morosely. For all the grief he'd had from Dan, Denzel and Drew in the past, he wouldn't have wished this on them – especially after discovering that Ranjit had been abusing them too. "But what happened after Ranjit got arrested? How did that incident not even get mentioned in the news?" he wondered aloud.

Joshua hesitated to answer this and Nathan noticed him anxiously bite his lip.

"H-he *did* get arrested…right?" Nathan reiterated tensely.

Joshua's pupils shifted away from Nathan, unable to look him in the eye as he let out a deep sigh. This reaction was enough for Nathan to deduce what had happened before Joshua could explain himself.

"You let him go?!" Nathan yelled incredulously, too angry to even give his cousin a chance to deny this, though the truth was already evident to him. "He could have killed us! What were you thinking?! You were supposed to take him to the police! How could you let that psychopath get away?!"

"Because Ranjit threatened to frame you for the crime…" Joshua snapped at Nathan who fell silent along with Thomas and Abbie as they heard this revelation. "You'd already given him a beating…he said it wouldn't be a stretch to convince everyone else that you'd attacked Drew and the others, especially with your history…" Joshua recounted regretfully while Nathan mulled over what he was being told. "He claimed he still has sway over Dan and Denzel, even after what he'd done to them, and that they'd corroborate his version of events…unless I let him go." Nathan's head lowered to the floor, as if by the weight of his unwarranted reputation and how people would perceive him if this were to happen. "I'm sorry Nath, but I couldn't let you go through something like that again – being interrogated by the police and risking you being labelled a murderer because of that scumbag's lies…" Joshua insisted.

"So what, this is your way of *protecting* me?!" Nathan responded, raising his head to face his cousin once more. "By letting a potential terrorist roam free?! You could have called Ranjit's bluff about pinning the blame on me! We have enough to prove he did it!"

"No, we don't!" Joshua argued impatiently. "We still have no idea if Dan and Denzel will attest against Ranjit – he could have easily threatened their lives. The one thing that would have been concrete was the gun itself. But it got swept away in the river! Even if we found it now, his fingerprints will have been washed away..."

"Then what about the locket he dropped?" Nathan pointed out to Joshua's surprise. "Yeah, we know that it's the emblem of Chimera. It proves that Ranjit's aligned with the enemy!"

"R-right..." Joshua uttered feebly. "I-I'm afraid I can't use that for evidence..."

"Why not?!" Abbie shouted, pushing for an answer. "It shows that Ranjit's a traitor!"

"Because if anything were to come out about Chimera, there could be widespread panic across the country!" Joshua blurted out.

"Hmm, interesting! *Why* would there be so much commotion from just knowing who the enemies are?" Thomas speculated aloud rhetorically. "Could it be because...they're the ones behind the tsunami?" Hearing Thomas say this, Joshua shuffled his body and tightened the grip on his backpack as he tried to keep his poker face on. However, Nathan caught a bead of sweat drip down his brow along with the way his eyes betrayed how worried he really was.

"T-the tsunami?" Joshua stuttered, starting to get flustered. "You mean the one from Friday night? Th-that was just a freak accident!"

"A freak accident that Ranjit predicted!" Nathan retorted. "Hard as it is to believe, he wasn't lying about that. So, it begs the question as to what *else* he was telling the truth about. For example...Maris?" Nathan caught Joshua's pupils fearfully dilate at the mention of Maris' name. "Seems like you've heard of her..." he concluded assertively. "In that case, since we're discussing the catastrophes...what might you know about my dad being killed in a hurricane?!"

Joshua's lip trembled as he seemed on the edge of wavering at being probed with this question. Nathan observed him expectantly, aware that he'd got him on the ropes and may finally learn the secrets behind Maris and Chimera...

In that instant though, the school bell started to ring, momentarily distracting the four students. Its reverberating chime snapped Joshua out of his daze since he realised it was only minutes before the start of registration.

"Now I really am late!" Joshua stressed, eager to evade Nathan's demand to know about the hurricane. "Sorry but I really have to-" he went on to say but before he could finish, Abbie had already rushed past him to position herself between Nathan and Thomas, blocking Joshua's path to the gates.

"Not until you tell us what you know! You're not getting past the three of us!" Abbie contended, defiantly standing her ground. This caused Joshua to raise an eyebrow at her.

"Is that a challenge…?" he queried in a low, cautionary tone, something that left Nathan feeling wary. He could feel his handle on the situation start to slip while Joshua had seemingly relaxed from his earlier standoffish demeanour.

"If we have to beat the truth out of you, then so be it," Abbie confirmed, shocking Nathan and Thomas with this proclamation. They exchanged nervous glances, clearly not sharing her confidence of achieving that – after all, Joshua had been training to join the army as well as martial arts and had previously dispatched Dan effortlessly.

"You actually think you can…?" Joshua quizzed her doubtfully. "Last time we fought, I remember it didn't turn out very well for you, did it?"

"Shut up!!" Abbie barked furiously.

"Wait, the last time you fought?" Thomas echoed, confused by Joshua and Abbie's interaction.

"That's right, we fought in the finals of a martial arts tournament two years ago, didn't she tell you?" Joshua revealed mockingly, astonishing Nathan and Thomas and attracting the ire of Abbie even further. "Of course, only *one* of us actually continued with it, didn't they?"

"I said shut up!! You don't know anything about it!" Abbie protested, her body trembling as the words left her mouth.

"Abbie, calm down…" Nathan advised, sensing that the plan was spiralling out of control.

"Well, one thing I do know is that my skills have doubled since that day – because I *kept* training," Joshua taunted Abbie, knowingly pushing her buttons. "There's no way I'll lose to someone who *quit* over one loss!"

The next few seconds were a blur for Nathan and Thomas as an incensed Abbie threw a punch towards Joshua's face. In one swift motion, Joshua dropped his backpack, intercepted her fist by grabbing hold of her wrist and yanked her arm downwards, dragging her around his body in a circular motion. Before Nathan and Thomas could even react, Joshua used Abbie's momentum to hurl her into the pair of them, knocking all three of them onto the ground. Seeing his opportunity, Joshua sped past them and made his escape through the school gates but left his backpack behind in the process. A frustrated Nathan slowly stood up and hobbled towards the gateway to find that Joshua had disappeared from view by now.

"Damn it, he got away!" he vented irately. "Abbie, how could you let him get inside your head like that?!"

Abbie picked herself up from the pavement without saying anything. She silently stormed past Nathan who caught a glimpse of her face, one bright red from humiliation and anger. He called out to her, hoping to apologise for scolding her, however Abbie's mind was too busy lingering on her own blunder while she marched off towards the school for her to hear Nathan.

"Leave her...she's probably beating herself up over it – we'll catch up with her later," Thomas recommended as he scrambled over to Joshua's backpack. "At least Joshua left this behind. What do you think? Maybe he really was hiding something in here?"

"We can have a look, but I doubt it," Nathan sighed as he helped pull Thomas back to his feet. "He's probably been trained in the army to protect important information. If it was that crucial, he wouldn't have left it here to risk us getting our hands on it. I think he knew we'd be distracted by it if he shielded it enough, so he used it as a decoy..."

"Well, guess there's only one way to find out," Thomas murmured lethargically as he heaved Joshua's backpack onto his shoulder. "We should go else we'll get done for being late..." he said, realising how much time had passed before he saw the disappointment written on Nathan's face. "We can come up with another plan later..." Thomas encouraged, trying to lift Nathan's spirits.

The two boys ambled their way down the path leading to the school, Nathan's frustration over losing his best potential lead not showing signs of subsiding.

Elsewhere, inside the school, an anxious Joshua knocked on one of the office doors. He was greeted by the headmaster, Mr Jones who invited him in.

"Did you get my message, sir?" Joshua enquired fervently as he stepped into the office.

"I did," Mr Jones confirmed as he closed the door behind him. "Before we discuss that though, have you heard anything more about Drew's condition?" he asked considerately, having already been made aware over the weekend by Joshua of the bridge incident that happened last Friday.

"I'm afraid he's still comatose…and his condition is critical…" Joshua answered.

"That's awful…Ranjit had always been troubled…but I truly hoped that he'd never be capable of something like this…" Mr Jones remarked regretfully. "And what about Nathan? Do you know how he's coping after what happened?"

"He's fine," Joshua claimed. "About that, he's actually the reason I'm later getting here than I wanted to. You need to try and stay away from Nathan," he warned the headmaster. "He's been really digging into what's happening with the war since Richard died and he's not letting it go. He knows too much now – he knows about Chimera and Maris, plus he even learned about the hurricane from Ranjit! I was close to cracking when he revealed that to me. If people find out the truth about how powerful Maris really is, it would be disastrous!"

"Pardon me for interrupting Joshua…" Mr Jones interjected. "I will actually be outside of school anyway for most of the day. I'll be visiting Dan and Denzel – I'm hoping to encourage them to come forward as witnesses to the attack on Drew instead of corroborating Ranjit's version of events. That way, nothing will come back on Nathan and there'll be sufficient evidence to convict Ranjit," he explained to Joshua's relief. "But as for keeping Nathan away from the truth, instead I really think you should be honest with him about what's going on with the war. If he's this determined to get to the bottom of all this, he will find out sooner rather than later. So surely it would be better for him to hear it from you over a stranger?"

Joshua contemplated Mr Jones' advice for a moment before responding. "I heard on the radio about the tsunami…and also about Chimera arriving in Entritica. I-is it…is it really true?" Joshua asked him fearfully, already expecting the answer.

"I'm afraid so…" Mr Jones verified. "And from the reports I heard from my contacts over the weekend, they're approaching farther inland. It'll be a week before they reach the capital – and there's not much our armies can do to protect His Majesty from Maris' power," he revealed as Joshua pursed his lips and nodded his head in reluctant understanding.

"Then I can't tell him…" Joshua decided, his eyes close to watering. "The truth would break him…I couldn't do that to him…"

Mr Jones sighed upon hearing Joshua's choice. Naturally, he didn't approve but he couldn't force his will either.

"I'm sorry Joshua but you won't be able to protect Nathan forever. The government won't be able to hide Chimera's existence much longer…"

"Speaking of Chimera, that's why I wanted to see you," Joshua spoke abruptly, eager to move past discussing Nathan. "I have some more information about them." He pulled out a small black device from his blazer pocket.

"A voice recorder…" Mr Jones noted. "Joshua, what have you been doing?" he asked his student, concerned.

"You need to listen to this…" Joshua instructed as he hit the play button. Both men fell quiet while they listened to static silence until a desperate raspy voice could be heard:

"Just please tell me that you'll protect my son…If this comes out about what he did, he'll surely be arrested…Yes I know, you gave me your word that you would…You're certain that it won't be long, then?…I see…Yes that's a relief to hear…Of course, our agreement is still on, I'll keep supplying to Chimera…And you'll keep your end of the deal regarding the favour you owe me?…Excellent, I'll let you know when that time comes…I look forward to seeing you soon…Maris…"

Joshua stopped the recording as Mr Jones processed what he had just heard, turning pale as he did so.

"That voice…that was Ranjit's father, Anil wasn't it?" the headmaster deduced, recognising it from past discussions he'd had with him.

"Yeah, it is…" Joshua acknowledged. "You heard him say it at the end of his call, he was talking to Maris…Not only does it suggest that he's protecting Ranjit from prison, but it proves that he and Ali Ammunitions are in cahoots with Chimera after all! This news could be game-changing for the war!"

"How did you even get this information…?" Mr Jones asked him, still reeling from the recording.

"I infiltrated his house yesterday to spy on him. I hit the jackpot when he made that call," Joshua divulged proudly.

"You shouldn't have done that!" Mr Jones reprimanded him. "That was far too risky! I know you want to join the army, but I don't want you putting yourself in danger needlessly!"

"I wasn't spotted if that's what you're worried about. This is what I've been training for, remember? To be able to make a difference and it's paid off!" Joshua protested, waving the voice recorder in front of him to validate his point. "If this news comes out, the authorities could potentially halt any weapons production at Ali Ammunitions which would cut Chimera's artillery at the knees!"

"Well, I can't say that's a guarantee...what concerns me is that it could also place the school as a target of Chimera if our anonymity was uncovered..." Mr Jones muttered uneasily.

"Either way, we'd be exposing one of Chimera's main allies!" Joshua countered optimistically. "So, what do you think? Will you take it to the authorities? This evidence will have more weight if it comes from you..."

The headmaster breathed deeply and thought carefully about what Joshua was proposing.

"Let me...meditate on it," Mr Jones requested. "As I said earlier, my priority is talking to Dan and Denzel to see how they are after Friday's events. I'll have a better idea of what to do once I've attended to them. Nevertheless, I will take it off your hands and deliberate on how best to use this knowledge..." he finished before receiving the device from Joshua.

"Okay sir, I'll leave the decision with you..." Joshua accepted. He turned to leave the room but before he could exit, Mr Jones called out to him one more time.

"Joshua...I didn't mean to scold you, you demonstrated exceptional courage and stealth in being able to gather this intel..." the headmaster stated, praising his student's skills and development to which Joshua beamed with delight. "I just...I just don't want you risking your life for all this – you're still one of my students after all. Ranjit and Anil are dangerous and I wouldn't forgive myself if you got killed on my account, before you could reach your potential as a soldier...So please, let me handle the rest from here..."

Joshua quietly nodded as he closed the door behind him. While he appreciated the headmaster's compliments, he couldn't help the conflicting sensation that he felt deep down about being effectively told to stay out of whatever was to come next. In his mind, he was no longer the student, the child that Mr Jones still saw him as. It was a thought that persisted in his mind as he departed.

On the other side of the door, Mr Jones wistfully eyed the voice recorder that contained the treasonous evidence he'd heard. Much like Joshua, he also experienced an inner turmoil of what to do with this information, knowing he had to determine whether the benefits of dealing a blow to Chimera were outweighed by the risks of possibly incurring their wrath…

Chapter 13

Later that afternoon, five minutes into the lunch hour, Abbie sheepishly made her way to the usual meeting spot, the courtyard bench, where she expectedly found Nathan and Thomas waiting for her. As the clouds loomed over her, Abbie sighed before approaching the two boys from behind.

"Hey guys..." she greeted them dejectedly, catching their attention as they turned to face her.

"There you are. I was starting to think you were ignoring our messages..." Nathan commented with relief in his voice. "Are you okay? We've not seen you since this morning..."

"Yeah, have you calmed down now after earlier...?" Thomas asked gently.

"I'm fine..." Abbie insisted, remaining on her feet while Nathan and Thomas were sat on the bench. She heaved another deep sigh before speaking again. "I'm sorry I ruined the plan...You were right before, I shouldn't have let Joshua get to me like that..." she conceded regretfully. "Did you at least find anything in his bag?" she wondered, her eyes flitting towards Joshua's backpack that was resting at Thomas' feet.

"We were just discussing that. I checked through it during first period..." Thomas answered. "Nothing in there but textbooks and notepads and there's nothing in any of them referring to the war," he disclosed penitently to Abbie's disappointment. "It's just like Nathan said, Joshua left it there as a decoy..."

"He's never cared much about his studies – only the stuff he was good at like sport and joining the army..." Nathan remarked, taking the backpack from Thomas. "He won't be in a rush to get that back, so I'll hold on to it."

"Right, I see..." Abbie uttered. "I-I don't know what to say..."

"First time for everything," Thomas snickered, trying to lighten the mood, though he quickly shut up as Abbie scowled back at him. "Sorry, I'll think twice about teasing you now – you've done martial arts after all..."

"Speaking of," Nathan interjected, looking directly at Abbie. "You were really triggered when Joshua brought that up and we didn't even know you'd done martial arts before. Was it really that important to you?"

Abbie bit her lip and shuffled awkwardly, gazing up at the grey sky while she hesitated to answer Nathan's question. Eventually, she relented.

"I took it up about two and a half years ago," Abbie revealed. "I'd bugged mom and dad about letting me do it for ages – I'd always had the passion for it from kung fu movies and thought I'd be able to use it to defend Ben if I ever needed to. They finally let me do it once mom got a job so they could pay for the classes. It was fun learning the techniques and it gave me something to focus on when things were bad at home and school."

"But after I'd done it for a year and became an orange belt, mom lost her job and dad said they couldn't keep paying for the classes, even branding it a waste of time unless I was some sort of prodigy. A few days later, I saw an advertisement in the newspaper for a local martial arts tournament that offered £500 to whoever came in first place. I told my parents about it and they said that if I actually won and got the prize money, they'd let me continue with the classes."

"So, I entered the tournament and trained hard for it. When the day came, despite only having learned it for a year, I managed to make it all the way through, even beating a brown and a black belt in the quarter and semi-finals. I really started to believe that I could win the whole thing and I was elated – I'd finally found something that I had a talent in and actually loved doing…"

"Woah, that's really impressive…" Nathan praised Abbie, awestruck by her accomplishment. "But…what happened after that…?"

"You've guessed this already, haven't you?" Abbie inferred. "I met and fought Joshua in the finals…and it was a disaster! He completely outclassed me and I couldn't even get a single hit on him. I lost…" she spat bitterly. "Worst of all, he rubbed salt in the wounds by offering to give me the prize money afterwards…"

"Wait…*worst?*" Thomas echoed. "Am I missing something? I thought winning the money was a good thing. It'd have helped you pay for the classes, right?"

"Yeah, but I wanted to *earn* it! Not have it handed to me out of pity!" Abbie exclaimed angrily. "It was the most insulting thing he could have done!"

"I see...so you didn't take the money in the end..." Thomas gathered.

"It wouldn't have made a difference if I did take it," Abbie stated. "I failed to win the tournament so as far as my parents were concerned, their minds were made up and nothing was going to change that."

"Gee, sorry to hear that Abs..." Nathan expressed gently. "You did sound passionate about it; it'd be a shame to quit something you loved so much. Did you at least try and continue it in your spare time?"

"No, I didn't see the point..." Abbie muttered. "Like I said, my parents branded it a waste of time if I couldn't do it professionally."

"Well even if they say that, it doesn't mean that they're right," Nathan assured.

The three fell silent for a few moments, a sudden chill shooting through the air as Nathan's words resonated with Abbie.

"D-do you...really think that?" Abbie squeaked meekly.

"Of course!" Nathan confirmed. "It doesn't matter how hard they try; no parent is perfect. Take my parents for example; even though my mom and dad always did their best to protect me, they got things wrong and made mistakes along the way..." he added, thinking of how they'd kept the truth of the black aura from him for so long. "But at the end of the day, they're only human and nobody's given a manual on how to be a mom or dad."

"And some don't even make the effort – you already know about my granddad now," Thomas reminded her. "I used to believe all the horrible things he'd say about me until my mom finally caught wind and cut him out. Don't let your family kill your passion if it's what you really want to do," he implored.

"Huh..." Abbie uttered while her mind processed their advice. "Never really talked about this with anyone but my parents before – and they made me feel embarrassed by it," she disclosed. "I appreciate it guys, but it's not like I can convince my parents of that. There's no way they'd fund the classes again, even if they were earning more than benefits..."

"You said earlier that you wanted to earn the prize money rather than be given it – perhaps you could apply the same principle here. Maybe try getting a part-time job outside of school hours?" Nathan recommended.

His idea took Abbie by surprise. "Y-you really think somebody would hire me...? Even with my background?" she asked doubtfully. "My parents always used to say that people like us wouldn't get jobs..."

"Well, they won't if they don't even try to improve themselves..." Thomas chimed disapprovingly. "If you really want to take the classes, it's worth a shot. What have you got to lose?"

Abbie carefully considered Nathan's and Thomas' suggestions, the merit behind it becoming more apparent as the thought lingered in her head, no longer obstructed by the demoralising viewpoints of her parents.

"I'll definitely bear that in mind..." Abbie agreed, a hopeful glint flickering in her eyes.

"Oh, one last thing," Nathan said. "My cousin's got a lot of flaws, that's for sure. But I guarantee that Joshua didn't offer you that money out of pity. Like you, he threw himself into martial arts training and other sports as a distraction. For him, they were a way of coping after his mom died four years ago..." he revealed to a stunned Abbie. "And yeah, he ended up excelling at all of them, picking up trophy after trophy along the way. But he has a real thing about greed which is also linked to his mom. It's not my place to delve any further into that though, I just thought you should know that he wasn't looking down on you or anything like that..."

Abbie quietly nodded at Nathan's description of Joshua, this new knowledge giving her even more food for consideration.

"Okay so Nath, now that we're all back on the same page, what's our next move?" Thomas questioned, finally addressing their failed mission to get any further information about Chimera from Joshua this morning.

"I've been thinking about that all day," Nathan sighed. "After Joshua, I was planning to try and get answers from Mr Jones, but I haven't seen him at all today. He wasn't even at the morning assembly. Other than him and Joshua, we don't have any solid leads..."

"Do you think Joshua already warned Mr Jones about our skirmish?" Abbie speculated. "Could be why he's suddenly gone MIA..."

"Makes sense," Thomas concurred. "So how do we even get to *see* Mr Jones to try and get the truth out of him now?"

"I have one idea, but Mr Jones has to actually be in the building for it to work..." Abbie mentioned.

"Well, there's not many other people we can ask now until the headmaster's back. It's annoying but we're gonna have to wait until he returns to get anything substantial," Nathan concluded begrudgingly. "For now, I'll keep looking online for any more news and see if I can do more research into Chimera and whatever this *Maris* is..."

"We could try the library computers," Thomas proposed. "She's allegedly capable of causing calamities...maybe there's a book that might shed some light onto that?"

Nathan pondered Thomas' suggestion before turning to Abbie for her input. "Might as well try it," Abbie muttered, shrugging her shoulders apathetically at the notion. "It's the only option we have at the moment..."

Silently agreeing, Nathan rose from the bench along with Thomas and the three of them headed in the direction of the school library, hoping to find new clues there. Just as they reached the bottom of the stairs that led to the library, Nathan and the others were stopped in their tracks by the presence of Lucy who boldly approached them as she descended.

"I was just on my way to see you two..." Lucy declared, addressing Nathan and Thomas. "Did something happen last Friday with you and Ranjit?" she queried sternly.

The two boys exchanged nervous glances, aware that the last time they had seen Lucy, she'd tried to dissuade them from confronting Ranjit. Before they could respond, Lucy had already gaged their uneasy reaction and elaborated.

"Kamran's been unusually secretive this weekend. His whole family too. Plus, there's no sign of the headmaster, Ranjit, Dan, Denzel or Drew today. All of that can't be a coincidence and Nath, you were planning to face Ranjit. Something's happened and you know what it was, don't you?"

After a moment of silence and sensing that Lucy wasn't going to back down from this, Abbie stepped forward, believing Nathan and Thomas had clammed up.

"Well...the thing is..." she started to say until, to her surprise, Nathan interrupted her.

"Ranjit shot Drew...and tried to kill me too," Nathan told Lucy bluntly, her eyes widening in horror from the revelation. She had expected something bad, but nothing of that magnitude. However, Nathan wasn't finished there as he continued, shocking Thomas and Abbie as he held nothing back from her. "That's not all. Ranjit's betrayed Entritica and sided with our enemies – a terrorist organisation called Chimera..."

Lucy's eyes blinked rapidly in disbelief and her lips trembled at the mention of Chimera's name.

"W-w-what...d-did you just say...Ch-Chime...ra?" she stuttered uncontrollably, reeling from the news.

"I'm afraid so," Nathan affirmed sadly.

"D-do you know them?" Thomas asked Lucy, concerned. Then, a disturbing thought crossed Nathan's mind as he recalled her words about Kamran's family acting cagey. Though it could have been down to Ranjit's heinous act alone, he feared there could be more to their behaviour.

"Y-you should know that...if Ranjit's aligned with Chimera...there could be a chance that the rest of his family has too. You need to be careful..." Nathan warned her.

Rendered speechless and unable to protest these claims, Lucy slinked away from the group, barely able to look them in the eyes as she left.

"Wow, I didn't think you'd be so upfront with her," Abbie told Nathan as they climbed up the stairs. "Are you sure you did the right thing, telling her all that?"

"She was seeking answers – she needed to hear the truth from someone," Nathan asserted sympathetically. "The government may want to keep everyone in the dark, but I don't. Once I know the truth, I'll make sure as many people hear it as possible..." he vowed as they reached the top of the stairs where the library was.

Nathan, Thomas and Abbie entered the school library where they spent the remainder of their lunch break searching for any new information on the Internet. Unable to find anything significant during that time, they were forced to call it a day and see through the last few lessons of the day. After returning to their homes, they each racked their brains as they continued to vainly research Chimera and the war, long after the sun had set. Though he didn't want to stop, Nathan eventually heeded Victoria's advice to get some rest, knowing he needed to remain fresh to make any progress.

****

Tuesday arrived and to Nathan's frustration, Mr Jones was still nowhere to be seen during the morning assembly, meaning they could only continue the same research from yesterday in the library. The hours passed without any new information cropping up so Nathan, Thomas and Abbie were forced to regroup in the library during their lunch break, the same place they were at twenty-four hours ago.

While Nathan was still having no luck with finding news articles relating to the war, Thomas decided to change tactics. He felt it was a long shot, but he typed the following phrase into the search engine:

Can humans cause natural disasters?

Once the results were generated, Thomas scrolled down the page, skimming past a few old headlines about catastrophes that resulted from manmade weapons of mass destruction. Suddenly, he excitedly clicked onto a link to an encyclopaedia website that caught his interest.

"Nath! Abs! You might want to see this!" Thomas whispered enthusiastically at them.

Nathan and Abbie hurried over towards his computer screen to find a webpage titled 'Mages'. They followed Thomas' finger and read the description he was pointing out:

Though believed by many to be folklore, mages were supposedly still prevalent seventy years ago before dying out in civil wars against one another. They were humans that inherited or gained the ability to manipulate elements associated with nature such as wind, water, earth, fire and lightning...

"Manipulate elements associated with nature...where have I heard that before?" Nathan mumbled aloud to himself curiously.

"Do you think this is the answer we've been looking for?" Abbie asked Thomas doubtfully.

"I don't know..." Thomas responded, second guessing himself. "It even states at the beginning that they could just be myths..."

"That's it, I remember!" Nathan exclaimed abruptly, drawing the focus of Thomas and Abbie. "Tom, does it mention anything about dragons on that page?"

Thomas turned back to look at the screen, tapping the down button on the keyboard to browse through the page. "Yeah, I can see it here," he confirmed, stopping to read an excerpt, with Nathan and Abbie leaning in for a closer look, that stated the following:

It was thought that there was a strong link between mages and dragons for both are associated with being capable of controlling nature. As a result, dragons were hunted to the brink of extinction by humans...

"Hm, I wonder..." Nathan muttered contemplatively upon digesting this information.

"Wonder what?" Abbie quizzed, confused

"I've heard about dragons before," Nathan explained to the others. "When I was a kid, my dad used to tell me about them. Dragons were popular in Etracovan lore – it was one of the few things he'd talk about from his own childhood. I remember one story he'd tell about a dragon in a cave underneath his village."

"Okay, but what does that have to do with-" Thomas was about to ask until Nathan pre-emptively answered his question.

"Dad had also mentioned that dragons were elemental beings. Plus, I know that they seemingly originated in Etracova – where Chimera were based. If there really is a link between dragons and mages, it's not that far-fetched to think a mage would be present in Etracova and be leading Chimera..."

"Are you really sure about this, Nath?" Thomas challenged. "Mages and dragons are only urban legends. Even if they did exist, they died out seventy years ago."

"Ranjit said it himself – he called Maris a god," Nathan retorted. "Who knows how long she's been alive for. And being able to conjure natural disasters? Sounds pretty godlike to me..."

"Not just that" Abbie interjected. "But there's been a hurricane and a tsunami – catastrophes associated with wind and water, two of the elements on that webpage."

"I was thinking that too. I think we've cracked this..." Nathan agreed, knowing the evidence to support the notion of Maris being a mage was piling up. Thomas also nodded in approval, finally convinced as well. Nathan couldn't help but feel an apprehensive excitement as the pieces of the puzzle seemingly began to fall into place. Instinctively, he knew what steps he needed to take next. "Now we just need to get someone to confirm it as the truth..."

"So that leads us back to Mr Jones," Thomas deduced accurately. "The question is, how do we get to see him to have the chance to interrogate him?"

"Well, as I was trying to say yesterday, I have an idea of how we can do this..." Abbie propositioned, attracting Nathan and Thomas' attention as they turned their heads to face her. "Not sure how you'll both feel about it though..."

"What is it? Tell us," Nathan asked interestedly, his eyes lighting up.

"Speaking from experience, there's one sure-fire way to get yourself in the headmaster's office...and that's getting yourself in trouble. Not just any trouble – *big* trouble," Abbie asserted bluntly.

Nathan and Thomas fell silent for a moment at the suggestion of doing this, exchanging uncomfortable glances in the knowledge that they shared the same thoughts.

"W-what were you thinking of?" Nathan stuttered nervously.

"To get the attention of the headmaster, even to the point of forcing him to come back to school, it'd have to be a fight of some kind...maybe something like a food fight to cause a lot of chaos..." Abbie suggested.

"A fight...i-is doing that really our b-best option?" Thomas wondered, not thrilled with the idea.

"We could risk expulsion doing that," Nathan lamented grimly. "After all, I'm the boy who almost killed someone four years ago and Thomas is still known as the kid who heard voices in his head. We've had to keep our heads low ever since. Because if we got in trouble again, not many teachers would fight our corner..."

"Yeah, I get it," Abbie acknowledged. "So instead, what if you two were the victims and I was the aggressor?" she offered, startling the two boys.

"Abbie, no! We can't ask you to do that!" Nathan hissed in protest. "Your standing isn't much better than ours! I wouldn't want you to get suspended or worse!"

"Guys, it's okay," Abbie insisted. "Even if that did happen, it's not as if I'm likely to move into sixth form anyway – I just don't have the grades for it. I can afford to take the hit more than you guys."

"You shouldn't have to take *any* hit!" Thomas retorted.

"Well do you have any better options? Either of you?" Abbie questioned.

Once again, Nathan and Thomas went quiet with neither one being able to provide an answer. They ended up being saved by the bell figuratively and literally as it chimed to signal the close of the lunch period.

"Look, we have to do something tomorrow one way or another, else we'll get nowhere. I know you don't want that, Nath," Abbie rationalised as students around them departed from the library for their last classes of the day. "If you guys can't come up with something better by tomorrow, we're going with this plan and that's final," she determined before walking out of the library herself, leaving Nathan and Thomas to dwell on her ultimatum.

****

Hours later, as the school day concluded, Nathan and Thomas walked together amongst the hordes of students leaving through the school gates. With Abbie's words to them still on their minds, there was a tension in the air between them that lingered until they were no longer on the school grounds. At that point, Nathan finally spoke.

"Do you have any better ideas?" he asked, getting straight to the point.

"Afraid I'm coming up empty, mate..." Thomas confessed gloomily to Nathan's unsurprised dismay.

"Okay, well I'll try and think of something tonight," Nathan tried to reassure. "We can't let Abbie risk her future like that, even if she is okay with it."

"I know..." Thomas uttered defeatedly. "Right now, I'm just praying that Mr Jones shows up tomorrow so we don't have to go through some half-baked scheme to lure him here."

"Same here," Nathan agreed. "Something big would be needed to make that happen though. Something really major..."

The two boys bid farewell on that worrying note and headed towards their homes, each hoping that the answer would come to them before the next morning.

Meanwhile, Lucy was leaving the school building long after many of the other students had left. As she exited through the doors and the sky darkened, she was distracted by the sound of her phone. She pulled it out of her bag to find that the caller was Denzel and she quickly answered it.

"Denzel!" Lucy blurted. "I've been worried about you guys! Are you, Dan and Drew okay? I heard something happened with you three and Ranjit last Friday!"

"L-Lucy..." she heard Denzel's voice quiver over the phone. "I...I needed to call you before you went round to see Kamran. Y-you should... stay away today..."

"Denzel, what's happening?!" a flustered Lucy cried out. "I heard from Nathan that Drew got shot by Ranjit! Is that really true?!"

"Yeah...it is..." Denzel admitted morosely. "A-and you should stay away...because me and Dan have just r-reported Ranjit to the police. They should be going around to arrest him shortly..."

"My god..." Lucy uttered in shock. "But why now?! And how is Drew?!" she reiterated.

Denzel didn't answer but Lucy could just about pick up an audible gasp from him through the phone. In that instant, she began to infer what Denzel couldn't say rather than what he could.

"D-don't t-tell me that…" Lucy stammered, prompting Denzel to break the news.

"D-Drew…h-he died this morning…in hospital…" Denzel sobbed, trying to hold it together.

Lucy's blood ran cold as she heard these words. Though she didn't have any special connection to Drew or any of Ranjit's former cronies, they were still fellow students that were the same age as her. To know that Drew was dead before he could even become an adult was a haunting revelation. What made it even worse though was comprehending that his murderer, Ranjit, was not only capable of a heartless act at such a young age but was the kin of her boyfriend. She remained silent as Denzel pushed himself to keep speaking.

"Ranjit killed him…y-yet if we'd only listened to Drew and broke away from him sooner, I feel like n-none of this would have happened…" Denzel proclaimed, ridden with guilt. "Th-that's why we've reported Ranjit. It may be playing with fire, but we owe it to Drew…Mr Jones made me and Dan realise that…"

Lucy's lips had turned dry, as though all the saliva had evaporated from her body upon being informed of this devastating news.

"I-I'm so s-sorry…" Lucy sympathised, tears starting to well in her eyes.

"I-I thought you should know…before you got caught up in the drama too…" Denzel squeaked shakily. It was then that Lucy summoned the strength to ask one final question that she needed to know the answer to.

"Denzel…I know that Ranjit has aligned with Chimera too," Lucy disclosed as he listened carefully to her words. "Please tell me…has his dad, Anil, sided with them as well?" she requested desperately. Denzel didn't say anything straight away, prompting Lucy to beg one more time. "Please…I need to know…" she pleaded. After a moment of hesitation, Denzel finally responded.

"He has…" he confirmed, rain beginning to pour down from the black clouds above as the two words resonated in Lucy's mind continuously, far louder than the thunder that followed.

Unconsciously, she ended the call with Denzel as she succumbed to a stupor, burdened with the knowledge that the family her boyfriend was part of were now war traitors. Lucy stumbled along her path home, her ignorant innocence forever tainted by this information as the realisation sunk in that she would need to decide her own allegiances in light of this – whether that be the side that guaranteed security or the side that preserved morality…

━━◆◆▷◆◆━━

Chapter 14

After a fretful night's sleep, a groggy Nathan struggled to pull himself out of bed. He shuffled his way to the bathroom where he washed his face in an effort to try and stimulate his eyes. Once he'd dabbed the water from his cheeks using a towel, Nathan looked up at the mirror above the sink, staring into his reflection in one last desperate attempt to conjure up an epiphany.

However, even this failed to generate any more ideas that could pose a better way of ensuring a meeting with Mr Jones than what Abbie had suggested. He had agonised over this all of yesterday evening, including during his dreams. Yet all roads led back to the same option of Abbie staging a fight to cause trouble and warrant the headmaster's attention – essentially using her as a scapegoat. Despite her insistence that she would be fine no matter what happened, this plan still didn't sit well with Nathan. He hated the idea of her potentially compromising her future for his goals and he was clutching to the hope that he could talk her out of taking that risk.

Nathan spent the next hour getting ready for the school day, showering, getting dressed and eating his breakfast. With each passing minute, the moment of truth of whether or not they'd need to lure Mr Jones to the school loomed ever closer. Just as he'd finished his cereal, he heard his mother call him from the living room.

"Nathan! Come quick! You need to see this!" Victoria shouted.

He got up from the dining table and made a beeline for the living room. There, he found Victoria standing feet away from the television monitor instead of sitting down on the sofa. Nathan looked past her to see the morning news being broadcast on the screen, just in time to see the mugshot of a familiar face flash up – Ranjit Ali.

"Some tragic news, today," the reporter on the television announced. "As one of the heirs to the Ali Ammunitions empire has been arrested for the murder of a fellow Silver Dawn Comprehensive School classmate, Drew Baker yesterday."

"Dr-Drew's dead...?" Nathan uttered in horror.

While an image of a smiling Drew was presented on the screen, a paralysing sensation washed over Nathan as the terrible reality of the situation slowly sunk in. Before he could even begin to process it though, the broadcast continued, showing footage of the woodlands surrounding Seppuku Bridge being cordoned off by police.

"According to an anonymous source, the incident occurred last Friday at the infamous Seppuku Bridge with Ranjit brutally shooting Drew in cold blood," the reporter detailed. "Drew was admitted to hospital that evening where he spent his final days in a coma. He passed away in his sleep yesterday morning after succumbing to his wounds..."

As the report transitioned to brief interviews with Drew's devastated family, who were mourning his loss and expressing their desire to see Ranjit brought to justice, Victoria looked over her shoulder at Nathan.

"That could have been you..." she whispered sadly in a hushed, relieved voice, yet the message was heard loud and clear. Nathan reflected on how fortunate he had been to survive that encounter and a nauseating pang of guilt struck his chest as he did so. He distressed over whether Drew would still be alive if he had just stayed away from Ranjit that day. However, the report had not finished yet as the newsperson carried on covering the story.

"This awful development has come out amidst theories that Ranjit's father and the CEO of Ali Ammunitions, Anil Ali has stopped supplying weapons to our armies," the reporter explained. "The family have complained about unwarranted hate campaigns and slander against them from trolls in recent weeks, but it seems that this has now been taken a step further as evidenced by scenes this morning."

Nathan and Victoria watched on as the screen displayed a recording of the Ali household which was taken in the early hours of the day. To their surprise, they saw that the front of the house had been vandalised, spray-painted in red graffiti that spelled out the word, '*Traitors!*' for all to see.

"What on earth..." Nathan commented in disbelief upon seeing the scene of the crime.

"Whether there is any truth to the claims of the Ali dynasty betraying Entritica remains to be seen, though these new developments will do little to quell speculation..." the reporter concluded before shifting along to the next news story, leaving Nathan and Victoria to digest the bulletin.

"Wh-who would do something like this? And why?" Victoria questioned rhetorically about the defacement of the Ali family property.

"Well, it sounds like they weren't short of enemies if they were the targets of hate campaigns. It could literally be anyone," Nathan remarked.

"M-maybe someone from school who knew Drew – Dan or Denzel?" Victoria wondered. "I mean, it couldn't have been Thomas or Abbie, right?"

As he heard his mom say this, Nathan answered on impulse. "N-no, of course not!" he insisted hurriedly.

However, upon the utterance of Abbie's name, Nathan couldn't help but recall their debate from yesterday – namely, her belief that *big* trouble was needed to reel Mr Jones back to school, along with his and Thomas' reluctance to agree to a staged fight. When taking these facts into account, a dreadful thought crossed his mind; could Abbie have taken drastic measures by assaulting the Ali household in a misguided effort to keep Nathan and Thomas out of trouble?

"Nathan…Nathan!" Victoria called out to him, snapping him out of his trail of thought. "Are you okay? That can't have been easy for you to hear about Drew," she added compassionately, presuming his death to be the reason for his abrupt trance.

"N-no, it wasn't…" Nathan acknowledged sorrowfully. "I mean, like you say, I was there…I saw Ranjit shoot him…but I still didn't want to believe that he could die. I just…convinced myself that he'd recover…"

"I'm sure a lot of people felt the same," Victoria noted. "Listen, it's up to you, but are you sure you feel up for going to school today?" she asked carefully, fretting for her son's state of mind.

"Yeah, I need to see how Thomas and Abbie are too," Nathan asserted with Victoria nodding in acceptance.

"Okay but be alert. I'm not sure how the school will react to the news about Drew but the headmaster's going to have to address it…" Victoria warned.

It occurred to Nathan that Victoria was correct. Unfortunate as it was, this was precisely the *big* event that they'd needed for Mr Jones to return to the school. Confronting him was now an option and it no longer required him, Thomas or Abbie to risk getting in trouble to achieve it. It was not lost on him though that this minor victory was at the expense of someone's life, so any relief that he may have felt was now sullied with shame. Nevertheless, he could not let this opportunity slip through his fingers for it could shed light on the path needed to avenge his father, Drew and anybody else who had died at Chimera's hands.

With this resolve in mind, Nathan left his house for school, watching Victoria wave goodbye to him from the door. Before he vanished around the corner though, he couldn't help but stop in his tracks and think once again about Drew – more notably about Drew's family whom he'd seen being interviewed, and how that Friday was the last time they may have seen their son before he was shot. Not that he needed it after losing Richard, but the tragedy was another reminder to cherish his loved ones while they were around. Thus, he ran back to his mother and embraced her, Victoria being all too happy to return the sentiment and hug him back. Having got that out of his system, Nathan was able to bid adieu to Victoria and carry on towards school without any regrets.

Twenty minutes later, Nathan had reached the street of Silver Dawn Comprehensive School. It was Wednesday, the middle of the week, and this usually meant that the moods of both teachers and students were brighter due to the weekend drawing closer. This wouldn't be the case today because even from a distance, Nathan detected a heavy atmosphere with each step he took in the direction of the school. He wasn't the only one who felt it though for once he was halfway down the road, Nathan spotted more students heading for the same destination, their heads drooping downwards as the memory of Drew weighed on their thoughts.

Once Nathan reached the school gates, he saw that there were already bouquets of flowers being placed there to honour Drew. There were a few students and parents gathered around the makeshift shrine to pay their respects. Initially, Nathan felt conflicted about doing the same for he'd had a chequered history with Drew, as well as Dan and Denzel due to their affiliation with Ranjit. However, it was Drew's courage in finally standing up to Ranjit, even acknowledging that they'd also been his victims just like Nathan, that left the lasting impression. Choosing to remember him in that light, one that inspired him, Nathan joined the crowd in silently honouring their fallen classmate.

The civil quiet was then rudely disrupted by the noise of heckles and jeers coming from afar. As these commotions crept closer and got louder, they became more impossible to ignore. Nathan along with a few other bystanders stepped away from the memorial to see what the fuss was all about.

Nathan observed as a black limousine slowly crawled along the road towards the school. Behind it, his attention was grabbed by a group of onlookers who were being restrained by some security guards, trying to prevent the civilians from following the elongated car. From a distance, he could vaguely hear the slurs and abuse that the citizens were hurling in the vehicle's direction.

Nathan turned his head back towards the limo just as it was turning into the driveway to the school. He saw that egg yolks were dripping down the car doors – obviously the work of the unruly mob – but also noticed that the windows were blotted out, preventing anyone from seeing who was inside the car. His curiosity regarding the mystery passengers had already been aroused by the sight of this, however it peaked when he heard one of the protestors blurt something out as the guards held him back.

"Traitor scum!" they angrily bellowed while the limo was halfway down the school path.

Seeing an opportunity to break away from the crowd whose attention had also been diverted by the hecklers, Nathan headed through the school gates to pursue the limo. He hid behind one of the nearby trees, giving the car a wide berth so as not to alert the passengers to his presence. Nathan carefully watched as the limo parked right in front of the school, ignoring any designated spaces.

Once the limo's engine had been switched off, the driver stepped out of the vehicle before proceeding to open the passenger door. From there, Nathan could just about spot a hooded figure exit the car, shiftily looking around as they did so. He saw that the person was draped in a black coat and wearing sunglasses – they clearly didn't want to be recognised. The only discernible aspect that Nathan could identify was that the individual had a complexion that resembled Ranjit's.

The shady man was then followed by two more people. One was a cocksure younger man, about a couple years older than Joshua, dressed in a garish green suit. Judging by his appearance, he looked to be the son of the man he was tailing. The second person was a young schoolgirl with black hair that Nathan instantly recognised – Lucy.

Nathan witnessed Lucy slinking her way into the building while the suited young man impatiently waited for her with his arms folded and an irritated expression. Seeing this, Nathan quickly realised that this brash businessman was Lucy's boyfriend, Kamran Ali. With that in mind, as well as the angry mob that had chased down the limo, there was only one possible conclusion as to who the cloaked figure would be – it was surely the director of Ali Ammunitions and suspected defector himself, Anil Ali.

After the three had disappeared inside, Nathan hurried over to the courtyard where he hoped to find Thomas and Abbie. He approached it to find there were more students gathered there than normal, talking with their friends yet all looking sombre and in a state of shock over what had happened to Drew. Nathan stumbled amongst the crowd for about a minute until he felt a hand grab his shoulder from behind. He turned around and came face to face with Abbie, also seeing Thomas over her shoulder.

"You've heard what's happened, right? About Drew?" Abbie tested Nathan, already suspecting that he had anyway.

"Yeah, I saw it on the news. It's awful…" Nathan confirmed glumly. "Are the others out here to mourn too?" he queried, noting the number of students surrounding them since they would usually be spread out around the school, whether that be in the corridors, the library or near the field.

"Partly, but they're also out here to hear what's going to happen today. Apparently, there's been word from some of the teachers that Mr Jones is going to send everyone home in light of Drew's passing…" Thomas explained.

"I see…" Nathan responded, remembering Victoria saying that the school would have to address the news somehow. "So…that means Mr Jones is here today?" he asked.

"I saw him enter the school today. He's definitely here," Thomas clarified.

"Okay good, but he's not the only one. I've just seen Lucy arrive at school in a limo – with Anil and Kamran Ali!" Nathan revealed in a hushed tone so as not to cause a stir.

"Are you serious?!" Abbie hissed in disbelief. "After what Ranjit did, they should be keeping their heads low if they had any sense! What on earth are they doing here?!"

"They were all over the news this morning! They're taking a massive risk journeying out in public right now!" Thomas noted.

"Well it could be to do with Ranjit…" Nathan considered thoughtfully. "Or it could be to do with their house being defaced last night…"

"Oh yeah, that was on the news too, the house had graffiti all over!" Abbie recalled from the broadcast. "Do they think it was someone from the school? Like Dan or Denzel?"

"Hold on…it wasn't you?!" Nathan questioned her, surprised.

"No, of course not," Abbie replied before she slowly registered Nathan's gentle accusation, her eyes widening in the process. "Wait, you seriously thought I did that?!" she exclaimed, almost affronted by the allegation with Thomas wincing in the background at the prospective quarrel.

"Sorry," Nathan squeaked guiltily. "I should have known you wouldn't. I was just worried you'd resorted to it as an alternative to acting out a fight at school…"

Abbie huffed an exasperated sigh. "It's fine. I suppose I might have considered the idea…if I'd even thought of it, of course," she relented. "But I promise, it wasn't me."

"I believe you," Nathan declared with relief. "Besides, at least we don't have to resort to some dodgy plan to lure Mr Jones here now."

"Are you sure we should be confronting him today?" Thomas mused, his eyebrows furrowing in concern. "He might have his hands full with dealing with the fallout from Drew's death…"

"I know," Nathan acknowledged. "But we're also trying to find the truth out for people like Drew – to see if we can limit the amount of victims that there has to be. With the Ali family in the same building, we may never get another chance like this."

"Yeah, true…" Thomas conceded. "So what's the plan then? If the rumours are true that we're gonna be sent home, we haven't got much time to play about with…"

"Right," Nathan agreed. "So what are we waiting for? We should go now…" he decided.

Despite Nathan's determination, he detected from their expressions that Thomas and Abbie remained conflicted about interrogating the headmaster with the very recent news of Drew's death. While he too was uneasy about the situation, he knew that overthinking would only deter him from taking action. So, choosing to take the proverbial first step, he turned towards the school building and marched through the crowds of students with his friends tailing him.

However, before they could enter, they soon stopped in their tracks upon crossing paths with a familiar face.

"You!" Nathan gasped as he came face to face with his cousin Joshua again.

"I've been asked to find you three…" Joshua prefaced. As a prefect, he stood ahead of them with an air of authority, though with the fresh memory of their last standoffish encounter, there was an awkwardness in the way he spoke to his cousin.

"Finally had to come out of hiding then, huh?" Nathan taunted, playing on Joshua's shame.

"If you've come for another round, I won't be making the same mistake again!" Abbie warned while Thomas held her back from causing a commotion.

"No, that's not it," Joshua refuted wearily. "You've probably guessed already, but Mr Jones will be holding an assembly soon to pay homage to Drew and he'll be sending everyone home afterwards. Before that though, he's asked me to bring you three to his office…"

Nathan's eyes lit up at this revelation. "Seriously?!" he blurted out incredulously as the prospect of questioning the headmaster about the war was seemingly being handed to him on a silver platter.

"What's it about?" Thomas questioned curiously.

"Not here, there's too many students about," Joshua stated sternly. "I'll tell you once we're inside…"

Thomas and Abbie looked at Nathan who nodded his approval at Joshua's proposition. With all four in agreement, they followed Joshua into the building as it seemed that their patience and efforts would at last be rewarded, finally feeling on the cusp of discovering the definitive truth about what they were really up against in this war…

—◅◈▻—

Chapter 15

Once Joshua had led the group inside the school and away from earshot of any other students and teachers, Nathan wasted no time in demanding answers from his cousin.

"So, what does Mr Jones want to see us about?" he queried as he, Thomas and Abbie tailed Joshua through the empty corridors, their footsteps echoing loudly in the void around them. "You did say you were going to tell us…"

"You've all been accused of a crime – vandalising property…" Joshua replied bluntly, not even turning his head back to face them.

Upon hearing this, Nathan quickly deduced who was making such a claim. Quietly hiding his delight at the chance to grill the headmaster and Anil Ali about the war, he kept his composure and continued to press Joshua for more information.

"It's Ranjit's dad, isn't it?" he stated, wanting to test whether his cousin would be honest with him this time. After Joshua didn't respond, Nathan was forced to elaborate. "I've already seen him arrive earlier, as well as the news this morning," he emphasised. This drew a deep exhale from Joshua.

"Yes, it's him…" Joshua finally admitted before falling silent again. This didn't deter Nathan from quizzing him though.

"A lot of people are saying that he's aligned with the enemy. What would you say? Is it true?" Nathan asked while Thomas and Abbie observed patiently, not uttering a word. Joshua took the same approach however as he did not react to the question. Determined, Nathan persisted. "I mean, there must be some truth to it if people are driven to spray-paint his house and egg his limo. Now that everyone knows what Ranjit did, he'll only be under more scrutiny – eventually, he'll slip up and something will come out about Chimera…"

Again, Joshua gave no answer as all four turned a corner and were within feet of the headmaster's office. Just as his cousin made the last steps towards the office door, his hand outstretched ready to knock, Nathan seized the opportunity to get one last comment in.

"So, guess we're relying on Anil to tell us about Maris being a mage then?" he remarked nonchalantly.

Joshua's hand stopped short of making contact with the door and Nathan, Thomas and Abbie watched as he seemed to freeze completely at the mention of the word 'mage'. Just like two days ago when they had Joshua on the ropes, Nathan took his lapse in calmness to mean that he was near the bullseye.

It wasn't even Joshua that opened the door as it swung open, taking the prefect aback, and the four students were greeted by the headmaster himself.

"Ah, Nathan, Thomas, Abbie," Mr Jones addressed them, looking past Joshua to focus on the younger pupils. "Thank you for coming, this won't take long," he elucidated apologetically as he invited them into the office.

Although reluctant after his cousin's claim of being aware of the mage, Joshua stepped aside to allow Nathan, Thomas and Abbie passage through the door. One by one, they treaded warily inside the office where they immediately found three empty chairs ahead. A few more footsteps in and the three students saw that they were not alone in the room. Seated across the room from them was Anil who scowled wrathfully in their direction with arms folded, Kamran who played idly on his phone, barely noticing their arrival and Lucy who fidgeted awkwardly in her chair and averted her gaze as they entered. Holding their ground, Nathan, Thomas and Abbie sat in the empty seats and defiantly stared down Anil to show that they wouldn't be intimidated while Mr Jones closed the door behind him.

Leaving Joshua to act the role of gatekeeper, the headmaster strode to the centre of the room, commanding the attention of his students and the Ali family as he placed himself between the firing lines. In particular, Anil glared disdainfully at the back of Mr Jones' head while the principal turned to focus on Nathan, Thomas and Abbie.

"Right, I've asked you three here because you've each been accused of a serious crime," Mr Jones explained to them, cutting to the chase. "I'm going to ask each of you in turn and I'll start with you, Thomas," he declared, moving to the wall adjacent to the door and directing his gaze at Thomas who was sitting on the chair closest to Joshua, opposite Lucy. "Did you have anything to do with defacing the Ali family's property last night?" he probed.

"No, I didn't," Thomas answered calmly, keeping his eyes locked on the headmaster. After letting his response register for a few seconds, Mr Jones glanced over to Abbie who sat between her friends with Kamran directly across the room from her.

"Abbie, I'll ask you next. Where were you last night during the time the Ali household was vandalised?" the headmaster asked.

"I was at home, either looking after my brother or fast asleep," Abbie stated frankly as Anil sneered in the background. Mr Jones appeared to accept her answer before finally turning to Nathan, the one unfortunate enough to be seated opposite the judgmental glare of Anil.

"You're the last one then, Nathan. Would you happen to know anything about Anil's house being graffitied?" Mr Jones quizzed.

"We all only heard about it on the news this morning," Nathan replied sincerely to the headmaster. However, his head turned slightly towards Anil and Kamran for the next words that he uttered. "Along with the news about Drew…" he hissed icily. Though his inference didn't faze either of the two Alis, Lucy's head drooped down at the chilling reminder. At the door, Joshua also recoiled when Nathan brought up Drew.

"Yes, I'm aware that the three of you have had a…tumultuous history with Ranjit," Mr Jones acknowledged grimly. "It was for that reason that you were each suspected to have a motive for committing the vandalism. Naturally, that *alone* isn't substantial enough to warrant charging you with the crime," he rationalised, yet while his attention was directed at Nathan, Thomas and Abbie, it felt to the three of them that the words were being aimed at the Alis instead. "Nevertheless, *if* you were responsible, I wanted to give you the chance to own up to it so that we could address it without involving the police. So, I'll ask one more time – did any of you three spray-paint Anil Ali's house?" Mr Jones enquired.

"No, it wasn't any of us. I don't know who did it either, but you've definitely got the wrong people," Nathan reinforced straightforwardly. Thomas and Abbie quietly nodded in agreement.

Mr Jones regarded the three students once more, his eyes skimming over their faces before concluding that they were telling the truth.

"Very well, I believe you. The three of you are free to leave," he decided, much to Joshua's relief. Unfortunately, this did not satisfy Anil in the slightest who scoffed derisively at Mr Jones.

"Is this a joke?!" Anil howled. "You've barely even questioned them and you're just going to let them go scot-free?! I want a full investigation into their actions!"

"With all due *respect*, Mr Ali," Mr Jones said through gritted teeth. "There's no concrete evidence to suggest that any of them has defaced your property, and they've given me no reason to doubt their integrity."

"No reason?!" Anil exclaimed incredulously as he stood up from his chair which fell over from the force of his rapid movement. "If I didn't think you were covering up for your students before, I certainly do now!" Nathan, Thomas, Abbie, Joshua, Lucy and Kamran could all feel the tension in the air between the two adults as their tempers flared. "It's already clear that you give special treatment to your golden boy here," Anil accused, pointing wildly at Joshua who stoically remained at the door. "But to claim that *these* three have integrity goes beyond stretching the truth! You've got the lunatic who hears voices in his head," he branded Thomas who was appalled at being reminded of this. "Then there's this trailer park trash who's already been expelled from her last school and who'll probably turn into an alky like her parents," he labelled Abbie who stared daggers at him while trying to keep herself calm.

"Mr Ali, do not speak about my students like that!" Mr Jones warned, raising his voice for the first time, meanwhile Lucy cowered quietly in the corner as the situation threatened to intensify further. In a frenzy though, Anil ignored the headmaster's caution and turned his attention to Nathan.

"And last but certainly not least, we have the infamous *'Dragon Boy'* of the school who almost killed someone at eleven years old!" he spat venomously.

Fed up with Anil's hypocrisy and unable to hold his tongue any longer, Nathan finally bit back.

"It's a shame Ranjit didn't stop at *'almost'*," he retorted to the shock of Mr Jones, Lucy and Joshua who had all been so used to the mild-mannered personality of Nathan. "Else Drew would still be alive!"

"Wh-who do you think you are, talking to me like that, boy?!" a startled Anil demanded.

"Who am I?" Nathan uttered rhetorically as he slowly rose from his chair, leaving Anil rattled upon meeting him eye to eye. Before Joshua could move to stop his cousin, Mr Jones stretched his arm outwards in front of him to signal that they should let things play out, much to the prefect's bewilderment. "I'm someone who's sick to death of hearing you chuck dirt at others with your 'holier than thou' rubbish when I've been tormented by *your* son for years. I'm someone that was almost pushed into taking my life by *your* son. And I really wish I could say the same for Drew, but I'm someone who was lucky enough to survive against *your* psycho son – the same one that's been arrested for shooting a defenceless schoolboy, remember?" Nathan unleashed in a blistering tirade against Anil that impressed Thomas and Abbie and rendered everyone else in the room speechless.

"Y-you…" Anil gasped, taken aback by Nathan's brazenness which concerned even Kamran, who had put his phone down for the first time since Nathan and the others entered the office.

"That's right. I was there. I actually saw Ranjit do it and I know who he's aligned with…" Nathan revealed to Joshua's horror, for he had wanted to keep his cousin's name out of the incident. On the other hand, Mr Jones continued to quietly observe Anil succumb to panic. Aware that Kamran was watching now, Anil's mind whirred as he desperately tried to take back the power in the room, afraid of appearing inferior in front his son.

"H-ha, I get it now!" Anil tried to laugh off. "Y-you're the one who reported my son – after framing him! That's it! You must be the one who shot Drew really and tried to shift the blame to Ranjit! I mean, you've already bashed an innocent bystander's head in with a rock, you've got form for it! You're clearly unhinged!" the ammunitions director accused, leaving Lucy aghast since she was a victim of the so-called 'innocent' bystander. Likewise, Mr Jones' expression betrayed a feeling of disgust towards Anil's outlandish comments. Fortunately, Anil's attempts to chip away at Nathan's psyche were for nought as the student would not be deterred here.

"It's funny, your mouth is moving, but all I hear are Ranjit's words," Nathan remarked sarcastically. "He really has got you wrapped round his little finger, hasn't he? Maybe *you're* why he's been allowed to become what he is? I don't know what concerns me more – the idea of you turning your son into a murdering monster or him making you his brainwashed puppet!" he spat out, feeling no remorse for the narcissistic man before him. Anil had no retort this time as the sting of Nathan's words, alleging that he'd failed his son left him completely flustered and stumbling over his own words. Seeing this, his son Kamran ultimately came to his father's defence.

"Hey, you have no right to criticise my dad just because you've lost yours!" Kamran snapped unsympathetically.

To everyone's surprise though, it wasn't Nathan who reacted to Kamran's comment first but rather his girlfriend, Lucy, who slapped his arm, eyeballing him with a frosty glare. Kamran scowled back at her but did go quiet, almost as though he wasn't accustomed to Lucy condemning him. Glossing over this, Nathan pivoted his focus to Kamran.

"Yes, that's right. My dad's no longer with us," Nathan acknowledged calmly, demonstrating a reluctant maturity that alarmed Joshua but inspired respect from his headmaster. "And, for the record, I wasn't the one who reported Ranjit to the police but I sure as hell wish I did. Because your brother is now part of that terrorist group that killed my dad – Chimera," he stated, the citing of the organisation's name causing Anil and Kamran to instinctively stiffen up as the tension in the office thickened. "I saw the proof of it myself when he dropped their emblem," Nathan continued before turning his head back to Anil. "Now it's just a question of whether the same can be said for you…"

"You'd better be careful what you say next, boy," Anil growled, his voice now much lower and more intimidating than earlier when he was frantically raving. "I could have you sued for slander…"

"Those sound like the words of a guilty man…" Nathan insinuated fearlessly.

Upon hearing this, Anil slowly stepped towards the boy until their noses were almost touching, something that compelled Abbie and Thomas to rise from their seats to support their friend. Again, Mr Jones held Joshua back from intervening, though he covertly pulled a device from his pocket as he did so.

"How about you *prove* it?" Anil challenged, believing he had regained the upper hand. However, Mr Jones re-entered the conversation to show Anil that he was very much mistaken.

"He can't…" Mr Jones interrupted, directing the focus of Nathan, Anil and everyone else back to him. "But I can…" he declared, revealing the voice recorder to the room. Realising what it was, Joshua anxiously tried to stop the headmaster.

"Sir, don't!" he called out in desperation.

But he was too late as Mr Jones pressed the button that played the audio for all to hear, with everyone falling taciturn.

"Just please tell me that you'll protect my son…If this comes out about what he did, he'll surely be arrested…" Anil's voice could be heard saying on the recording. The Ali figurehead went white as a sheet, his blood running cold as he felt the piercing gazes of Nathan, Thomas, Abbie and Lucy directed at him, especially after blatantly accusing the former of

framing his son for the murder. Anil's body was unable to move, paralysed from shock and powerless to do anything other than unwillingly listen as the incriminating audio continued. *"Yes I know, you gave me your word that you would...You're certain that it won't be long, then?... I see...Yes that's a relief to hear..."* Joshua closed his eyes and shook his head, already knowing what would come next. *"Of course, our agreement is still on, I'll keep supplying to Chimera..."* Before Nathan could process his catharsis for having his suspicions of the Ali family being in cahoots with the enemies confirmed, he and Thomas were briefly distracted as Lucy shot up from her chair at hearing Chimera's name being mentioned. When Kamran stood up to try and calm her, she recoiled away from him. Though curious about her reaction, Nathan couldn't concentrate on it now as the final part of the recording played. *"And you'll keep your end of the deal regarding the favour you owe me?... Excellent, I'll let you know when that time comes...I look forward to seeing you soon...Maris..."*

The name 'Maris' hauntingly echoed through the silent office for what felt like an eternity as the audio ended. Anil blinked in disbelief over what the headmaster had just revealed and with the disdainful scowls of the students bearing down on him, it slowly dawned on him that he couldn't fib his way out of this. While everyone's attention was on him, his pupils darted towards his son and he raised his eyebrows. Understanding the signal, Kamran sneakily tried to snatch the voice recorder away from the headmaster. To their dismay though, Mr Jones had already anticipated this and evaded Kamran's hand as he made a grab for it.

"Nice try, but even if you'd managed to get this from me, I've got back up copies saved," Mr Jones informed them, passing the device to Joshua who thrusted it into his blazer pocket.

"So, they really were working with Maris and Chimera all along..." Nathan summarised, still comprehending what he'd heard from the voice recording.

"I'm afraid so Nathan," the headmaster affirmed regretfully.

"How?!" Anil quizzed, still reeling. "The only way you could have caught me saying that was by-"

"Yes, I'd been suspicious of Ranjit ever since I caught wind of his scaremongering social media posts. So, as a former commander myself, I took it upon myself to spy on him," Mr Jones confessed. "And in order to find any evidence that your son had actually joined Chimera, I infiltrated your house this past weekend." Nathan noticed Joshua try to interrupt the principal with a horrified expression on his face, only to be waved off as Mr Jones continued. "That's when I conveniently caught you having that intriguing chat with the very person who's leading the charge against Entritica…"

"Well then, I think the police will be *very* interested to hear about a school headmaster breaking and entering onto my property!" Anil seethed furiously.

"I agree, they likely would be," Mr Jones conceded. "But they'd be even *more* interested to hear proof of you betraying our country to the enemy…I wonder which one is more severe: trespass or treason – what do you think?" he probed Anil who provided no response to the question because he could not find the words, aware that he was now over a barrel. However, he realised that he had one more card to play.

"You tell anyone about this…and I *will* send Maris after you!" Anil threatened. "You heard it yourself – she owes me a favour!"

Seeing an opportunity to get the final answer that he'd been seeking, Nathan jumped into the conversation before the headmaster could reply back.

"Maris is a mage, isn't she?" Nathan asked of Anil, Joshua contritely closing his eyes behind his cousin's back as soon as the question had left his lips. "I've heard the rumours about the natural disasters and I've connected the dots. That's why Entritica is struggling against Chimera, isn't it?"

"So, the *Dragon Boy* really has done his homework…" Anil praised albeit mockingly.

"Just answer me!" Nathan snapped impatiently.

Kamran stepped forward like a guard-dog trying to warn Nathan away from his dad, but Anil held him back with his outstretched arm. Prior to his response, the two adults, Mr Jones and Anil exchanged a brief but knowing look. It was as though, even with all their bad blood, they had managed to reach a mutual agreement about revealing the truth to Nathan.

"Yes, you are right. Maris is a mage," Anil confirmed to Nathan and the astonishment of Thomas, Abbie and Lucy for having heard the theory finally corroborated as fact.

Nathan couldn't help but beam slightly, knowing that he had proved his suspicions to be correct. He was optimistic that this information could be the key to finding a way to avenge his dad. However, Anil noticed how the corners of Nathan's mouth curled upwards and, as if he'd read the boy's mind, promptly chastised his naivety.

"If you think this knowledge is going to make a difference against Maris, you're *sorely* mistaken!" the director reprimanded, wiping the smile from Nathan's face because he sensed that his tone was much more serious this time and absent of any condescension. "With the amount of power that she wields, she's untouchable! Anyone who goes against her is a dead man walking!"

"I-I'd read that mages had died out seventy years ago," Thomas cited, trying to make sense of the revelation. "H-how could one still be alive?"

"Who knows..." Anil remarked, admitting to not knowing himself.

"R-Ranjit claimed that she was a god..." Nathan recalled aloud, curious of Anil's opinion.

"It's not a far-fetched claim..." Anil acknowledged. "Hurricanes, tsunamis, earthquakes, wildfires, even manipulating lightning – she can do all of those like it's nothing. How on earth can *anyone* expect to stand up to a force of nature like that?" he sighed hopelessly.

"So that's why you've sided with Maris? Self-preservation?" Nathan deduced, detecting the genuine fear in Anil's body language as his shoulders slumped in defeat.

"Not for *myself*..." Anil corrected. "Brand me a terrible father all you want, but I'm doing this to protect my sons and if that means siding with whoever the strongest is, so be it! I will do whatever it takes to guarantee their safety!" he asserted, something that caused Kamran's snooty exterior to soften upon hearing it.

"Even lie about a murder he's clearly caused..." Abbie spat unsympathetically, not forgetting about Drew. Anil flashed her a dirty look but bit his tongue since he knew he had no leg to stand on after they'd all heard his incriminating conversation. Instead, he kept his attention on Nathan.

"If you had any sense, you'd do the same boy..." he cautioned to which Nathan shook his head in disapproval.

"Well, I just hope you've kept the receipt for your soul..." Nathan muttered icily. "Because I think you'll live to regret it..."

"I just want to keep my sons alive. That's all that matters – I can't lose them too..." Anil reinforced.

This time, the room fell silent again as Nathan didn't have a retort. Even with Anil's track record of distorting the truth as demonstrated this morning alone, he could hear the sincerity in the Ali figurehead's words and knew there was nothing more he could say to convince him otherwise. For the first time that day, Nathan wasn't looking at Anil as an enemy and a traitor but rather, despite his many flaws, another man with a family to save, just like his own dad. With no words left for Nathan to say, the headmaster retook control of the conversation, backtracking to before he and Anil were interrupted.

"So, now that this is all out in the open, I have a proposition for you Mr Ali," Mr Jones stated. "You came here today wanting to press charges against my students for vandalism with no evidence that they've even committed the crime. We've also discussed their presence during the incident with Ranjit and Drew." Thomas and Abbie looked at each other nervously as this was mentioned. "However, you now know that you have a lot to lose if this recording was to be made public," the headmaster continued as Anil and everyone in the room listened intently. "Thus, this is what I propose: if you agree to drop any unwarranted charges regarding the damage done to your property, as well as to keep Nathan's, Thomas' and Abbie's names out of any police investigations involving Ranjit, I'll give you my word that I will not leak this audio to the authorities. I will even destroy any copies of the recording that I have."

"What?!" Joshua exclaimed in disbelief at what he'd just heard. Nathan, Thomas, Abbie, Lucy and Kamran were also surprised about the headmaster's suggestion. Anil's eyes lit up at the offer though.

"D-do you really mean that?" Anil questioned warily.

"I do," Mr Jones reassured. "You want to limit the impact that these 'rumours' will have on your family's lives. I want to protect my students from going through any needless stress that would only incriminate your son further. This way, we both get what we want."

Anil mulled over the headmaster's persuasive bargain, fully aware that he didn't have many better options. After his eyes skimmed over the worried faces of Nathan, Thomas, Abbie and Joshua, he glanced at Kamran once more which gave him the resolve to make his decision.

"Fine, you have a deal..." Anil settled to the relief of the other students and the satisfaction of Mr Jones. "But if you go back on your word, I swear that I will make sure you pay!" he threatened ominously.

"I know, I promise I'll stick to my word," Mr Jones acknowledged bluntly.

Anil looked over his shoulder towards Kamran. "We're done here. Let's go..." he determined before exiting the office, pulling the hood over his head to avoid being seen by any more onlookers. Kamran followed until he stopped in the doorway, realising that Lucy was still rooted to the spot, her eyes drawn to the ground and her body shaking uncontrollably.

"You coming or not?" he barked sternly, snapping Lucy out of her daze.

She stalled for a bit, turning to stare at Nathan and Thomas, almost like she was silently calling for help. A few more awkward seconds later, the boys watched as Lucy slowly walked towards the doorway with her head hung low while Kamran waited impatiently. She peeked back at them as Joshua closed the door behind her. However, they were still able to briefly hear Kamran's voice through the walls.

"It's because of *you* that we were dragged here in the first place!" he accused angrily from behind the walls before the sounds of their footsteps died down as they left through the corridor. Instinctively, Nathan stepped forward, wanting to pull Lucy away from the Alis, but he stopped in his tracks as the headmaster raised his hand, directing him to halt.

"I need to speak with you three before you leave," Mr Jones addressed Nathan, Thomas and Abbie while Joshua stood with his arms folded in front of the door. "I'm sorry you all got caught up in this. You shouldn't have had to find out the truth this way..."

"Frankly, we were planning to get answers from you today regardless. Doing this just saved us a lot of trouble," Abbie retorted.

"Right," Mr Jones uttered. "Still, it must have been difficult for you all to hear. I have to ask...how are you all feeling now that you know the truth?"

"None of that matters now," Nathan dismissed flippantly. "Ranjit's family can try and scare us all they want, Maris will have a weakness and I will find it!"

Mr Jones closed his eyes and sighed deeply at hearing this response. "I see. Then you haven't grasped the severity of the situation..." the headmaster commented regrettably.

"What do you mean by that?" Thomas wondered inquisitively.

"I'm afraid there's no easy way for me to say this..." Mr Jones said, opening his eyes again to give the three students his full attention, the muscles in his face straining to ensure that he didn't blink so that his next words couldn't be misconstrued as more lies. "Entritica are going to lose the war..." he disclosed.

Nathan felt his entire body go numb as this revelation pierced through his ears. Thomas and Abbie also fell eerily silent as they heard this, yet Joshua had a perplexed expression at what the principal had just told them. After pausing to let the news sink in, Mr Jones continued, "Anil is right about Maris – she is far too powerful. Our forces have gotten slaughtered by her magic, we have no way of countering her, and she and her followers have already set foot in Entritica," he informed them as Nathan and the others shook themselves out of their daze.

"N-n-no..." Nathan stammered. "Th-there has to be a way to stop her..."

"Even if there is one, it wouldn't be found in time. From the reports I've had from the army generals, at this rate, Maris will have taken over Entritica by next week..." Mr Jones lamented, alarming everyone in the room.

"How is this possible?!" Thomas gasped incredulously. "Shouldn't the government have warned us this could happen rather than plying the public with false propaganda?!"

"The government wanted to prevent the masses from panicking while they made efforts to come up with a solution. Strict instructions were given out, including to me, to go along with the façade of the war going in our favour to buy time in the hopes of turning those delusions into reality. But they failed and *yes,* I agree – the government have failed *us* by lying..." Mr Jones muttered bitterly, sympathising with Thomas' outburst. "We should have been informed sooner so that we could have time to take measures to protect our families. Instead, they buried their own heads in the sand. They'll be held accountable for their deceit – that is if Maris doesn't get to them first..."

"Y-you just mentioned 'measures to protect our families'. If what you're saying is true," Abbie cried out, still not wanting to believe what they were hearing. "What on earth could we possibly do to achieve that?!"

"Unfortunately, there is only one option available at this stage – and it is a drastic one..." Mr Jones advised.

"And that is...?" Nathan queried impatiently, but even he wasn't prepared for what the headmaster would answer back with.

"Evacuating Entritica – fleeing the country," Mr Jones confirmed bluntly, stunning Nathan, Thomas, Abbie and even Joshua.

"Y-you can't be serious!" Joshua protested, appalled by the notion and contesting the principal for the first time. "Just abandon our homes?! The lives we've all built here?! There *has* to be another way!"

"I'm deadly serious Joshua," Mr Jones insisted firmly. "I'm not just telling this to you four either. This morning's assembly – as well as using it to pay tribute to Drew's life, I'm going to announce that the school will be closed for the next two days out of respect for his memory. I will also tell everyone about the war now being unwinnable and strongly encourage *every* student to take those days to consider evacuation for their safety as well as their families. Meanwhile, I will use that time to decide the fate of the school which I will then reveal to all of you on Friday – whether I re-open it for anybody who is still determined to stay in Entritica, or close it indefinitely…"

Nathan could see in the stern and sombre gaze on the principal's face that this was no joke. Slowly but surely, it became apparent to him that this nightmare was real and he felt sickened to dwell on the fact that his dad may have died fighting in this war for nothing. Yet, as if able to sense his dejection, Mr Jones called out to him.

"Nathan, I'm sorry that things have turned out this way, especially after Richard's passing. This really is a last resort and I wouldn't be suggesting it if I didn't think it was necessary for your survival. That's what you all need to focus on doing right now – surviving so you can have a chance to live life to the fullest again someday. Because doing that will be the best way to keep your dad's memory alive…" Mr Jones professed.

For a moment, it seemed as though his words hadn't reached Nathan for he was still staring off into space, shell-shocked. Seconds later though, Nathan slowly nodded, showing that he understood the principal's attempts to remind him what was important, but he could not muster the energy to say anything back. Knowing this, Mr Jones didn't push his message any further, however he did have one more request for the students.

"Before you three go, there's one last thing. I hate to ask this of you, but for your safety, it's crucial that you don't leak any information about Anil's involvement with Chimera to anyone else," Mr Jones beseeched, something that Joshua disapprovingly raised an eyebrow to. "As you've no doubt experienced with Ranjit, the Ali family are dangerous and if word were to get out about their treachery, they'd know it was one of us. Anil would seek revenge – you heard his threats yourself. Plus, I am concerned about Lucy's proximity to them. She's safe as long as she doesn't double-cross them, however her protection can't be guaranteed if Anil believes that we've informed the police…"

To the headmaster's relief, Nathan, Thomas and Abbie each silently agreed to keep quiet about what they knew, feeling too drained to argue otherwise.

"Okay then," Mr Jones uttered. "I will be starting the assembly shortly to fill in the other students about what will be happening with the school. As you've heard everything already, all three of you may be excused to go home, talk with your families and reflect on what I've shared with you – I owe you three that much at least…as well as a thank you for your time today…and your understanding…about everything…" he finished gracelessly due to being riddled with remorse.

Joshua opened the office door to allow Nathan, Thomas and Abbie to leave. The three of them slinked towards the doorway, their heads hung low and still not uttering any words as they struggled to come to terms with what they'd have to do next. As Nathan passed Joshua, his head tilted slightly in an attempt to look him in the eye, but in the end, he couldn't find the strength to do even that as his head just drooped back downwards. Seeing his cousin look so defeated after losing his dad cut through Joshua's heart like a knife. Once he was certain that they had all disappeared down the corridor, the prefect closed the door behind him and glared back at Mr Jones.

"Why on earth did you play that recording to them?!" Joshua demanded angrily through gritted teeth. "That was our trump card against the Alis and you just revealed it to them on a silver platter!"

"Once I'd persuaded Dan and Denzel to give witness statements against Ranjit, I knew that Anil would try to shift the blame towards Nathan to protect his son from prison. So, in order to keep Nathan away from any more unnecessary encounters with the police, I needed a bargaining chip," Mr Jones explained candidly.

"Why would you go that far?! Even taking the blame for trespassing when we both know it was me who did it?!" Joshua questioned.

"Because I remember how deeply it affected him after the incident with those two crooks who tried to kidnap Lucy – he nearly took his own life because of the bullying and Mr Nelson's despicable behaviour. I didn't want him to have to go through that again when we know full well that he's innocent!" Mr Jones justified forcefully. "And I covered for you because, even though I didn't instruct you to investigate the Alis, I still feel responsible for you feeling the need to do that. Besides, as a headmaster, I have a duty to try and protect my students, whether that be from bullies like Anil or their own impulses. But I can't protect them from the truth, and neither can you."

"Yet, it still seems like you're trying to hide the truth to me!" Joshua accused. "I mean, dangling Lucy's life like a carrot to blackmail them into keeping Anil's betrayal a secret?! If the government heard about Anil supplying weapons to Chimera, evacuation wouldn't even be necessary – they could cut them off and it could change the tide of the war!"

"No Joshua… it wouldn't…" Mr Jones maintained. "Anil was right about Maris' power. I've heard it from other soldiers out on the battlefield. She doesn't even need an army to crush our forces, she can do it by herself. We can't stop her – Entritica *will* lose the war. The risk is not worth the reward; people being aware of Anil's defection to Chimera won't make a difference to the war…but breaking our agreement with Anil will stir the hornet's nest…"

"Just because he claimed to be owed a favour from Maris?!" Joshua scoffed sceptically. "He could have been bluffing…"

"He wasn't bluffing," Mr Jones assured bluntly. "He is dangerous and I know he would seek revenge for turning him and his family in…and he would use Maris to do it. It would put our students in harm's way and I will *not* risk that!"

"Then you're as bad as Anil!" Joshua harshly slated his mentor. "You were in the military! You've cooperated with them during this war! You should know that your first duty should be to your country, but you've already thrown in the towel!"

"Yes Joshua, I *was* a soldier!" Mr Jones snapped, losing his cool with his prize student for the first time. "But that was my past! Now, my first and foremost duty is to my pupils and my school! I will do what I feel is right in order to protect that before anything else!"

As the two scowled at each other while at loggerheads, a moment of clarity washed over the pair, both of them realising that they'd let their tempers get the better of them. They took a few deep breaths to calm down before Mr Jones shuffled over to the microphone that was connected to the school speaker system.

"Can all students please make their way to assembly?" the headmaster ordered politely as Joshua observed. Mr Jones switched off the microphone and turned back towards the prefect. "Joshua, I know this has all been a lot to take in this morning and your help is always appreciated. I have to run the assembly now but if you want to discuss this after I get back, you're welcome to stay in this office and think over what we've spoken about," he suggested, trying to establish his authority once more through professionalism. "If not though, you may go home whenever you are ready and we'll pick things up again on Friday."

Joshua quietly stood and watched as Mr Jones exited the office, leaving him alone to mull the events of this morning over in his mind. At a loss for what to think, he sighed deeply, leaned against the headmaster's desk and, in the middle of concentrating, automatically folded his arms.

However, in that moment, he felt an object squished between his arm and his chest, wrapped within the material of his jacket. He reached into his blazer pocket and to his surprise, pulled out the voice recorder – the original one documenting Anil's confession – that Mr Jones had passed to him earlier after Kamran had failed to snatch it away. He'd completely forgotten about it because of the drama that had ensued before him.

Seeing this device in his left hand though, a thought crossed his mind and to him, it felt like a sign of what he *had* to do. Without hesitating to consider the alternatives, Joshua departed from the office, pulling his mobile phone out of his trouser pocket with his right hand. He scrolled through it until he found the contact number for one of the commanders of the Entritican army. He tapped on the screen to dial the number and was satisfied to hear a voice quickly respond.

"Hello, my name's Joshua and my headmaster Mr Jones introduced me to you previously. I'm calling because I have some game-changing evidence that you need to see…" Joshua established, marching resolutely through the corridors, confident that he was doing the right thing.

The conversation between the two continued as Joshua exited the school, rain now pouring down heavily from fierce black clouds at this point. Yet the boy was almost giddily oblivious to the foreboding storm that was about to occur…

Chapter 16

Days off from school would normally fly by far too quickly for students. Yet for every student at Silver Dawn Comprehensive School, the next two days crawled along at a snail's pace as they were forced to come to terms with, not only the possibility of their responsibility-free school days being brought to an abrupt end, but the necessity of uprooting their lives and leaving their homeland. These thoughts weighed heavily on the students' minds as they divulged to their families the truth of what Entritica's fate would be in the war. For the majority, two days wasn't enough for the gravity of the situation to sink in, especially when all the pupils could do nothing but wait for Friday morning to come around to see what Mr Jones would opt to do with the school. It wasn't long before some of the students fittingly branded it on social media as 'Judgment Day'.

Eventually, Friday morning arrived as Thomas lethargically shuffled through the school gates, mixing in with the other students who ambled down the driveway. Amongst the crowd, he bumped into Abbie and they walked together between the listless murmurs of students asking one another how their parents reacted to the suggestion to evacuate. Though they were silent for the first few moments, barely having the energy to greet each other, Thomas and Abbie soon followed suit and discussed the subject on everyone else's lips.

"H-how did your mom take the news...?" Abbie asked Thomas anxiously.

"She's been packing supplies almost non-stop since I mentioned that Chimera were our enemies..." Thomas stated glumly.

"I see," Abbie uttered. "I-I guess hearing their name again must have brought back some bad memories-"

"Of my dad...yeah..." Thomas acknowledged, finishing Abbie's sentence before her.

"D-does that mean...y-you're going to be leaving even if the school stays open?" Abbie guessed, unable to hide the apprehension in her voice.

"It seems that way…" Thomas admitted bluntly.

Abbie gulped at the prospect of Thomas not being around in her life. Despite only being friends with him and Nathan for the last two weeks, she'd felt a kinship with the two boys that she hadn't experienced before. Being around them had made her feel more at peace with herself and the thought of losing those connections felt like a dagger slicing through her heart. Picking up on the abrupt silence, Thomas consciously tried to kick-start the discussion.

"What about your parents? How did they react?" Thomas queried.

"I don't think they're taking it seriously…" Abbie griped wearily. "I told them the news but they just think it's all rubbish. They're too pig-headed to see sense…"

"Dealing with them must be a real headache for you…" Thomas sympathised.

"Pretty used to it at this point…" Abbie grumbled.

Thomas and Abbie set foot in the courtyard, looking past the masses of students towards the school building itself and taking in its finer details such as the intricate brickwork and the sturdy steel supports that kept it upright. It was the structure that they'd spent a sizable portion of their days in, that had accommodated their education and helped them to grow as adolescents. While they certainly had plenty of unpleasant memories of their time here, the fact that this could be their last day here caused them to regard the school with a sentimental fondness that felt foreign to them.

"Even though people saw me as a lost cause here…" Abbie reflected bitterly on her reputation as a troubled outcast. "This place still gave me a chance after I was kicked out of Northwood County…"

"Just think though – if you hadn't got expelled, Nathan and I probably wouldn't have got to know you like we do now…" Thomas pointed out in an attempt to brighten her mood. It proved effective as it brought a smile to Abbie's face.

"Well, when you put it like that…" Abbie snickered, unable to mask her joy at hearing Thomas say that. "If coming here led me to you guys, getting expelled was worth it," she affirmed positively.

"I had my hardships when I came here too," Thomas remarked. "But without this place, I wouldn't have met Nathan. I'll always be grateful for that…"

"Yeah, same here. I just hope he'll be okay – hearing that we're going to lose the war really knocked him for six..." Abbie recalled aloud, the memory of how quiet he went in response to the revelation still fresh in her mind.

Thomas and Abbie turned away from the building and back towards the school gates, expecting Nathan to arrive soon. They could still see a swarm of students slowly seeping in through the gateway. However, from a distance, they noticed a distortion that split through the horde, a single anomalous figure powering its way through the gathering. Upon first glance, both Thomas and Abbie assumed that it was the headmaster himself. The closer the person got to the courtyard though, they realised that whoever this was, they weren't tall enough to be Mr Jones.

To their surprise, they saw that it was Nathan – finally able to see his face as he broke away from the despondent flock and stormed purposefully, not in their direction but towards the school. Thomas and Abbie rushed over to intercept him, but they could see from the determination in the way that Nathan marched and his focused impression, that this was a different version of their friend than the one who crumbled at hearing what the outcome of the war would be.

"Nathan...yo, Nathan!" Abbie called out to Nathan, catching his attention though he seemed a tad irked about his flow being disrupted. "Are you okay? We've been worried about you since Wednesday..." she added affectionately.

"I'm fine – no need for concern," Nathan insisted bluntly. "I've had time to think about everything Mr Jones told us."

"W-what did you tell your mom?" Thomas asked curiously.

"Everything," Nathan reiterated quickly. "I told her about Maris, the Alis' betrayal, the fact that we're going to lose the war...and yeah, I told her that we need to consider evacuating the country..."

"Okay then..." Thomas mumbled, relieved to see that Nathan wasn't in denial at least. "How did she react?"

"Obviously neither of us *want* to leave Entritica..." Nathan reinforced through gritted teeth. "But we'll do what it takes to survive so she's been packing any essentials for if the worst-case scenario happens..." He then took a few steps towards the building, trying to exit the conversation but Abbie blocked his path, frustrating Nathan which didn't escape her notice.

"Why are you in such a rush to get away?" Abbie questioned, almost hurt by his standoffish manner. "Are you sure you're okay?"

"I'm fine, I just need to get to the library!" Nathan blurted out impatiently.

"The library? Why there?" a confused Thomas wondered.

"Because there's some old books about dragons and mages in there! I saw them online on the school library listing yesterday evening!" Nathan explained frantically. "They might have crucial information and I need to grab them today while I still have the chance!"

"Wait, you're still going on about this?!" Abbie exclaimed in disbelief. "Even after everything we've heard about Maris being unstoppable?!"

"Yes, I am!!" Nathan asserted rebelliously, startling his friends with the proclamation while his face turned red. "The rest of Entritica may be ready to give up all hope, but I'm not! If there's a way to stop her, I swear I'll find it!"

With that, Nathan stomped past Abbie and made a beeline towards the library. Thomas and Abbie exchanged a brief look, one mixed with astonishment and apprehension, but mostly mutual agreement before dashing off in pursuit of their friend. They repeatedly called out Nathan's name, but alas, he showed no signs of slowing down.

That was until he reached the doors to the back end of the school, only for them to be pushed ajar in front of him. Two students emerged from behind the doors and Nathan came to a screeching halt upon seeing them. Thomas and Abbie also followed suit by stopping in their tracks beside Nathan once they saw who the recognisable, yet forlorn faces were – Dan and Denzel.

"Hey…it's you guys…" Dan greeted meekly. "W-we were actually… hoping to bump into you…"

There was an uncomfortable silence between the five pupils as they stared each other down. Although the air of hostility that previously existed whenever the two sides clashed was now absent, they were each unsure of what to say after the years of antagonising that Dan and Denzel had subjected them to under Ranjit's influence. However, having experienced the same life-threatening scenario that Dan and Denzel did one week ago, Nathan put the past aside and cautiously made the first move.

"H-how are you both holding up...? After Drew I mean..." Nathan asked gently, noting from the lack of colour in their faces that they were still grieving for their friend.

"I-it's still hard to...to believe he's gone..." Denzel answered sincerely, nearly choking up with emotion. "A-and all I could think these last few days is...that if we didn't go ahead with Ranjit's plan...h-he might still be here..."

Nathan bit his lip upon hearing Denzel say this, straining his eyes as though he was holding something back. "I hate to say it but...I'd wondered the same thing about myself. Like whether he'd still be alive if I'd stayed away from Ranjit's trap...just ignored his bait..." he lamented bleakly.

"Guys...neither of you were the ones who pulled the trigger..." Abbie reminded them, not forgetting how Ranjit had shot in her direction when she arrived to save Nathan.

"Well said," Dan agreed. "Regardless, we should have listened to Drew sooner. He'd seen what Ranjit was doing to us long before we even accepted what was happening and had been trying to get us away from his influence for a while. Him standing up to Ranjit the way he did that day..." he recalled, his eyes close to watering at the thought of Drew's last act of defiant courage. "He deserves justice. That's why we finally did the right thing and shopped Ranjit to the police..." Dan revealed to the surprise of Nathan, Thomas and Abbie.

"Y-you were the ones who did that?!" Thomas gasped, astounded by this.

"And you're both okay with this? What if Ranjit or his family discover that you ratted him out?" Nathan queried with concern.

"None of that matters now," Denzel declared resolutely with Dan nodding in concurrence. "If we let Ranjit just get away with killing our friend in front of us, we'd never forgive ourselves. We owe it to Drew..."

"It's not the only thing we owe though," Dan prefaced, now putting his focus squarely on Nathan. "Even if you were Ranjit's target, he was baying for blood that day and would have sacrificed *anyone* for Chimera's cause. So if you hadn't shown up when you did and beaten up Ranjit, he would have probably killed us too. You saved our lives...so, thank you..." he expressed, something that left Nathan stunned.

"Not just that, but we also owe apologies to you guys," Denzel interjected before turning to face Abbie. "I'm sorry for pushing Ben. It was inexcusable and I deserved the black eye for doing it..." he apologised, taking Abbie aback. "As for you two..." Denzel continued, directing his attention to Nathan and Thomas. "I-I know we've been awful to you over the years. There's probably nothing we could say that...that could make up for the horrible names we called you...and for helping Ranjit...b-bully you guys. So, we're not asking you to forgive us. Just know that we're sorry for everything we ever did and that we don't want to be those people anymore. We need to be better...for Drew's sake..."

Having poured their hearts out to the group, Dan and Denzel lingered for a few moments to see if Nathan, Thomas and Abbie had anything to say back, fully ready to accept any backlash that came their way. Instead, the three remained silent, still at a loss for words over how different Dan and Denzel seemed now, apparently shaken straight by the betrayal of Ranjit and the loss of Drew. With nothing left to say and not wanting to make the situation more uncomfortable, Dan and Denzel bade farewell to the group, wishing them the best before clearing out of their way and giving them a wide berth as they made their departure. However, Nathan called out to them just as they were about to vanish from view, both Dan and Denzel looking back over their shoulders at him.

"Take care of yourselves...and stay alive for Drew's sake," Nathan cautioned considerately while Thomas and Abbie watched on. Though he didn't directly say it, they could guess from how at peace he sounded that this was his way of forgiving Dan and Denzel. The two former foes also interpreted Nathan's words in this manner, amicably mouthing the words 'You too' to them before leaving the three behind, out of respect.

"Do you really think those two have changed?" Thomas quizzed sceptically, still unsure of whether he himself could pardon them for their past actions.

"Ranjit was always the instigator," Nathan stated. "Dan, Denzel, Drew – they were all as scared of him as we were. It's a shame that it took Drew's death to get here but now that Ranjit's hold over them is gone, they'll have the chance to redeem themselves..."

"You know, I was talking with a shopkeeper yesterday," Abbie interposed, something that Thomas raised an eyebrow to. "I'd mentioned that I was a student at Silver Dawn Comp and she brought up Drew. Apparently, he was a regular at the shop and she even said that he was such a lovely and helpful young man to her. She was really devastated when she heard that he'd been killed…"

"Wow…" Thomas uttered in shock. "It's…a very different picture to the Drew we got to see. I just wish we got to know that side of him…"

"He acted differently at school because of the crowd he was with. That so easily could have been me…" Abbie lamented, regretfully reflecting on her brief affiliation with Ranjit's crew.

"It's like Nath said, Ranjit was a parasite, dragging others down to his level – right, Nath?" Thomas commented, glancing over to where he thought Nathan was.

To both his and Abbie's alarm, Nathan had disappeared as they saw the school door swinging back and forth from the momentum until it clicked shut. They'd both been so engrossed in the conversation about Drew that they hadn't noticed that Nathan had left. That's when they realised that he'd taken his opportunity to escape to the library while they were distracted.

"Should we go after him?" Abbie posed the question to Thomas.

"We should probably leave him to it…" Thomas decided. "When he has his mind set on a goal, nothing's gonna stop him…"

"Yeah, I don't think I've ever known someone so determined…" Abbie sang her praise for Nathan.

"By the way, what were you doing at the shop?" Thomas asked curiously, keen to change the subject. "Were you looking for supplies or were you getting Ben out of the house for a bit?"

"Oh, it was actually for a different reason," Abbie corrected excitedly. "I decided to take your and Nathan's advice on Tuesday and try to get a job. I asked the lady there if she needed help or had any weekend shifts going and she agreed to give me a trial run tomorrow."

"Ah that's brilliant news, well done Abs!" Thomas celebrated jovially.

"Hey, I've got to actually pass it first," Abbie pointed out, though she did let out a chuckle at seeing Thomas' enthusiasm for her.

"Either way, you'll still gain something whether it's experience or the job itself! It's a step forward no matter how you spin it!" Thomas professed positively. "Oh, I'm so happy you're getting the chance to show what you can do Abs!"

"Thanks Tom," Abbie expressed with a proud smile. "Not just for this, but for believing in me in the first place – you and Nath…" she added, remembering their previous encouragement three days ago.

"Where is the shop anyway?" Thomas enquired interestedly. "If you get the job and me and Nathan stick around, we could visit you on shift."

"I'd love that!" Abbie beamed eagerly. "Here, I can find it for you," she said, pulling her phone from her blazer pocket. Thomas watched as she brought up the Internet to find the shop location using the online maps.

Before Abbie could even type the shop's name into the search engine, she and Thomas spotted a breaking news story on her website's home page – one that included Anil Ali's name in the headline along with the words, 'Treachery Exposed!" Both looked nervously at one another, wary about what they could be about to see. Abbie clicked into the broadcast link and played the video:

"This just in, director of Ali Ammunitions, Anil Ali, has been conclusively proven to be a war traitor after new evidence has come to light," the reporter informed while the time of 8:27am was displayed in the bottom right corner of the screen. *"Speculation had already been rife that Anil had aligned with Etracova and further fuel was added to that fire two days ago when his own son Ranjit Ali was arrested for the murder of a fellow student of Silver Dawn Comprehensive School, Drew Baker. During the investigation, several social media posts that were linked back to Ranjit over recent weeks were discovered through his own admission, ones that were scathing in nature towards Entritica,"* she detailed as these comments were displayed in the video for all to view. Thomas and Abbie each recognised them from a week ago, the ones that claimed *'Entritica will burn', 'A new order is coming'* and *'Death to the King'*…

"As a result, rumours began to circulate regarding his father, Anil's involvement in all of this. However, what was previously conjecture has now been found to be fact after the following audio of Anil himself was submitted."

Thomas and Abbie listened in silent horror as they heard the same voice recording that they'd heard two days ago from Mr Jones. *"Of course, our agreement is still on, I'll keep supplying to Chimera…and you'll keep your end of the deal regarding the favour you owe me?...Excellent, I'll let you know when that time comes…I look forward to seeing you soon…Maris…"* In the background, Thomas could hear gasps of shock from other students who had also caught wind of the broadcast on their own phones. There was no hiding for Anil now. Everybody would know now – exactly what Mr Jones had wanted to prevent…

"On orders from the army commander, the chief of police has put a warrant out for Anil's arrest in the early hours of this morning and has urged anybody with any news of his whereabouts or activities to come forward. Only time will tell if Anil is found but one thing is for certain, his capture and interrogation could provide an opportunity to turn the tides of the war in Entritica's favour. Thus, we strongly beseech anyone with information about Anil to alert the authorities as soon as possible..." the reporter concluded as the video came to an unsettling end.

Despite the hope that the broadcast had tried to instil into the public, Thomas and Abbie were there when Anil threatened revenge on Mr Jones if this audio was ever leaked, claiming that he'd enlist Maris' help to do it. The headmaster had not taken this warning lightly, even pleading with them to not breathe a word to anyone. For this recording to have been aired on the news could only mean one thing – only somebody from that summit could have presented it to the authorities. Thomas and Abbie, now robbed of their previous delight over the latter's job possibility, could feel a rumbling, one that seemed to shudder the earth beneath them. As the sky turned black above them, they couldn't help but fear what consequences this development could bring about...

Meanwhile, Nathan entered the library and wasted no time in finding the library books that he was seeking, darting straight towards the history, folklore and myth section. He yanked a few books down from their shelves, cleared the dust off and turned over the first few pages to find the contents. If they didn't list anything related to mages or dragons, Nathan disregarded them and moved on to the next book. He repeated this process several times, slamming the hardback covers against the table more ferociously with each undesired result.

Eventually, Nathan came across a book that piqued his interest. It was titled *'Demons, Dragons and other Servants of the Devil'* and it seemed to be a study guide of the occult. Seeing this brought a glimmer of hope to Nathan that it may contain a chapter on mages which could reveal a weakness of Maris that had eluded the rest of Entritica up until now. He turned to the contents page and while he didn't see 'mages' explicitly stated, there were other terms that could be tied to the concept such as 'warlocks' and 'witches'. Deciding to have a brief gander through the book, Nathan pinched a slither of pages between his fingers and flicked them across, estimating that he'd open up to the section about witches.

In actuality, he'd overshot the distance and gone a bit further ahead to the chapter about demons. Realising this, Nathan began turning the pages backwards one by one, skimming through each one as he did so on his way to the witches' portion of the book.

However, in his haste, a certain page caught his eye. As he leaned over the table, his shadow cast over the book, Nathan backtracked until he located the page that piqued his interest – one that contained a sub-heading called *'The Devil's Spirit'* where he read the following extract…

Thought to have originated from the first dragons to have existed, the Devil's Spirit is considered to be a power born from the darkest desires of the heart. It is exceptionally rare for any mortal to possess this ability, potentially only being inherent in less than 0.01% of the population. The defining feature of the Devil's Spirit is a black aura that emanates from the body of the wielder…

Nathan's eyes widened in disbelief as he read that last sentence. The words 'black aura' rang alarm bells in his head as this had been a recurring theme mentioned by Thomas, Abbie and his mother during his past incidents. Although he had never seen this for himself, their accounts of what they experienced from Nathan lined up. His heart sank at the very idea of such a power being linked to an evil entity like the Devil, but fuelled by apprehensive intrigue, he continued to read on:

For anyone ill-fated to be a vessel for the Devil's Spirit, it is unleashed in instances of great peril that provoke an intense emotional reaction. The drawbacks of succumbing to this awakening are that the power is uncontrollable and the subject will retain no memory of his typically violent actions during the possession. However, in exchange, the spirit will ensure that for a limited amount of time, the possessee is invulnerable, even able to absorb the elemental magic associated with dragons, hence its dreaded infamy amongst the like. Plus, the spirit grants the user limitless power that can escalate based on the situation in question. Usually, this will only be a slither to enhance the vessel's power and/or durability in a crisis. Yet, there have been claims, though unsubstantiated, from long ago where the user's passions have been excessive enough for the Devil's Spirit to form the shape of a monstrous dragon – one with the ability to wipe out the life force of anyone who comes into contact with it and powerful enough to wipe out populations with ease…

"Nathan!" someone called out at him.

Nathan loudly gasped out in shock as the abrupt voice distracted him. Breathing rapidly after what he had just studied, he looked to his right to see Lucy looking at him with concern. He also heard the librarian disapprovingly order him to shush for the noise he had unwittingly caused.

"Are you okay?" Lucy whispered to him, observing how pale and panicked he looked.

"Um…yeah…yeah, I-I'm fine…" Nathan responded as he caught his breath, the extract about the Devil's Spirit still playing on his mind. "Wh-what are… are you…" he muttered as he hurriedly seized the book and shoved it into his bag, something that Lucy also noticed until Nathan zipped it shut and gave her his full focus. "What are you doing here…? C-can you even risk talking to me?" he asked, remembering that the last time he saw her was when she left the office with the Ali family after they learned of Anil's betrayal of Entritica.

"W-well, there's something that I have to tell you Nathan…" Lucy stuttered.

"Sorry Lucy, but can it wait? I've got to get back to the others-" Nathan was about to say, keen to brush her off so he could get some space to digest the rest of the book. To his surprise though, the usually timid Lucy wasn't backing down, blurting out her next words so that he had no choice but to listen:

"The person who spray-painted Anil's house – was me!"

It took a few moments for Nathan to comprehend what Lucy had just told him. His eyes blinked as the words resonated in his mind, slowly at first until they gradually pushed out his curious thoughts about the Devil's Spirit. Once he was finally able to concentrate on the girl in front of him, Nathan let his opinion on her actions be known.

"A-are you serious?! What were you thinking?!" he exclaimed, frantic with worry for the risk she'd taken. After being hushed again by the librarian, Nathan continued but muttered under his breath this time. "You could have been arrested if Anil caught you! Hell, how would your boyfriend have reacted?!"

"Kamran already knows…" Lucy revealed with a heavy sigh. "I-I did it while it was still night-time, but I regretted it the next morning when Kamran told me that Anil wanted to get the police involved. I didn't want anybody innocent to get blamed so I told him the truth…"

"Hold on…you both knew it was you when Anil was accusing us?!" Nathan hissed irately.

"I-I know, I'm sorry!" Lucy apologised. "You guys shouldn't have had to be put through that – hearing the horrible things he was saying about you all made me feel sick!"

"B-but why?! Why even vandalise their house in the first place?!" Nathan questioned, trying to understand what would possess her to do that. He recalled seeing the footage of the graffiti on the television, remembering that it said *'Traitors!'*. Upon this recollection, something dawned on him. "W-wait a minute…you spray-painted the word *Traitors…*" he murmured to himself as Lucy pursed her lips together nervously. "F-for you to have used that word…d-did you know that the Alis had aligned with Chimera… before we even heard that audio…?" Nathan deduced.

"I-I heard it…from Denzel…the day before…" Lucy confessed glumly. "W-when he told me…I just didn't even know how to react – I just felt numb…" she told Nathan who attentively listened to her account. "I don't even remember the walk home…I just got in and…saw some of my mom's gin on the kitchen counter. I just wanted to try and block it all out…so I had a drink…"

"Right, because all good ideas start with 'I had a drink'…" Nathan remarked sarcastically. "So you were drunk when you did it?"

"No…I only had a couple of swigs…but it gave me enough liquid courage to go and deface their house. I remember doing all of it…" Lucy explained, startling Nathan with her admission. "But I still panicked when I heard that Anil wanted to press charges…"

"And Kamran still covered for you…I suppose someone from that family had to have a conscience…" Nathan stated.

"Ha…I'm not so sure about that…" Lucy scoffed acrimoniously.

"W-why do you say that? Has something happened?" Nathan asked her apprehensively.

"Well, after the meeting with Mr Jones on Wednesday, we got into an argument," Lucy clarified, reminding Nathan that he'd overheard Kamran chastising her as they left the office. "On the way to school that morning, after I was having doubts about their loyalties to Entritica, he'd tried to reassure me that they weren't working for Chimera. So naturally, once I found out he was lying from that recording, I was livid and could barely stand to be around him. Then he accused me of being ungrateful to him for keeping my 'crime' a secret – yeah, 'crime', that's how he said it…" she said in response to Nathan's appalled expression. "When he said that, I called out how he was implying that I owed him for it," Lucy continued while Nathan heeded her story intently, almost as though their past friendship was being rekindled. "But that's when he said the worst thing of all – he 'joked' that I was lucky because he could have easily asked for sex in return for keeping the secret…"

There was a short but deadly silence between the two as Nathan processed Lucy's last sentence.

"He said *what*…?" Nathan reacted bluntly, though the revulsion in his voice at what he'd just heard cut through the air like a scythe.

"Glad you're as disgusted as I was…" Lucy acknowledged. "And when I pulled a face, he had the nerve to accuse *me* of being too sensitive! I've given him the cold shoulder for the last two days and he's not even *tried* to apologise for crossing the line…"

"There's not even one good apple among that family – they're all rotten to the core!" Nathan bemoaned, shaking his head in anger. "S-so what does that mean for you and Kamran? I-is there any chance of you guys fixing things?" he wondered aloud.

"I'm not sure we can come back from all this…" Lucy affirmed. "His sex comment and lack of remorse was bad enough – but them lot being affiliated with Chimera? I could *never* sink low enough to associate myself with those bastards!" she spat venomously.

"Strong words…" he commented about Lucy's hostile language about Chimera. It was very similar to Thomas' attitude when the organisation's name was first discovered which led him to make an assumption. "H-have you heard of Chimera before?" Nathan queried.

"I told you before how my dad was a soldier in the army six years ago, remember?" Lucy replied.

"Yeah, y-you told me that he was never found…that's awful…" Nathan recollected. Prior to Lucy saying anything, Nathan's eyes widened as he had an epiphany as to what she was alluding to. "Hang on…you're saying that your dad disappeared because of-"

"Chimera. That's right," Lucy interrupted. "He was fighting in Etracova against them to try and help underprivileged villages that were under siege from them. They're the reason he went missing – I'm sure of it!"

"Wow…I'm so sorry to hear that. No wonder you can't bear to be around them then…" Nathan sympathised. "But what will you do now?"

"When I was looking for you this morning, I heard a lot of whispers about fleeing Entritica. Is that true?" Lucy quizzed, causing Nathan to remember that she wouldn't have heard Mr Jones' announcement due to leaving with the Alis before the assembly.

"Y-yeah it is," Nathan confirmed dejectedly. "I-I'm not sure what we're going to do yet…"

"Well, if you guys do decide to evacuate, please let me come with you!" Lucy pleaded.

Nathan was left stunned by Lucy's proposal, at a loss for what to even say in response. While it felt relieving to know that she hadn't been sucked into the Alis' treacherous scheme, he was still conflicted due to fearing for her safety and whether there would be any repercussions for her if she blatantly sided against them. He didn't want her to share the same fate as Drew.

Elsewhere, as Nathan was faced with this dilemma, Mr Jones was in his office, sat at his desk and watching his laptop with hands clasped over his mouth. Like Thomas and Abbie minutes ago, he had just seen the breaking news video containing the voice recording of Anil's conversation with Maris. His immediate reaction was to frantically search through his office cabinets and desk drawers, trying to remember where he'd placed the voice recorder that he received from Joshua – until he recalled that he'd passed the device back *to* Joshua after Kamran had tried to snatch it away!

Mr Jones sighed sadly as it struck him what must have happened – instead of returning the recording to the headmaster, Joshua had secretly kept it and submitted it as evidence to the army general and authorities. With Anil's threat of revenge looming over him, Mr Jones paced around the office, fretting over what to do next now that this information was out.

Suddenly, his mobile phone that was sitting on his desk began to ring. Mr Jones walked over to it and saw from the screen that the number was withheld. He gingerly picked the phone up and answered the call.

"Hello…?" the headmaster spoke. There was an unsettling pause before the caller replied.

"I warned you, didn't I? That there'd be consequences for breaking our promise…" the raspy voice chillingly proclaimed, one that Mr Jones instantly recognised – Anil!

"Anil, I swear that I didn't leak that recording!" Mr Jones insisted in a desperate attempt to try and appease him, but it fell on deaf ears.

"My family's l-l-lives could be in jeopardy! We could have to go on the run! I'm not interested in your e-e-excuses!" Anil furiously stuttered, almost as if he was either shivering or trembling with rage. "Even if I was willing to listen, it's far too late at this point!"

"S-so why even call? What's your motive?!" Mr Jones questioned.

"This is a courtesy call..." Anil claimed ominously. "To tell you that you have fifteen minutes to get everyone to evacuate the school..."

"F-fifteen minutes?! Why?! What have you done?!!" Mr Jones demanded.

In that moment, the headmaster stumbled for it felt like the room around him was moving. However, seconds later, he became very aware that this wasn't just his imagination because the shaking sensation showed no signs of subsiding – in fact, its strength was escalating as books started to fall from the shelves in his office and the walls around him started to creak and groan.

Simultaneously, Nathan and Lucy experienced the same thing in the library, their conversation disrupted as they were forced to use the tables to support themselves, yet could feel the legs vibrating wildly against the floor. At the same time, Thomas, Abbie and the other students staggered around as the ground seemed to shudder around them.

These ripples could also be felt throughout the rest of the building. Joshua had been patrolling the corridors, proudly hearing students and teachers talking about how the Ali family's betrayal had been exposed, knowing that he'd made it happen. But the smile was soon wiped from his face when he wobbled from feeling the effects of the mysterious shockwaves rocking through the hallways. Concerned, he placed the palm of his hand onto the floor and detected that something was rumbling beneath the earth, the sheer force of the tremor causing his hand to quiver uncontrollably. As he felt the vibrations intensify beneath him, his pride crumbled once he remembered Anil's threats, realising what calamity was about to happen. Without hesitation he sprinted in the direction of the headmaster's office, where coincidentally, Mr Jones had also figured out what Anil must have done...

"A-Anil...please tell me you didn't..." Mr Jones uttered, his trembling voice barely more than a whisper now.

"I did…I cashed in my favour with Maris…and requested her to destroy the school!" Anil revealed callously.

"H-how could you…? There are children in here you, sick son of a-!" Mr Jones was about to lambast, his voice cracking from contempt for the coward he was speaking to, but Anil cut him off.

"That's the reason I'm forewarning you. I suggest you take what l-l-little time you have to get them out of there!" Anil asserted. "Heed my words because I tried to warn you about crossing me and you didn't listen… that mistake will cost you your beloved school…because Maris cannot be stopped…"

On that note, Anil hung up – leaving the headmaster, along with the school full of students, to contend with the catastrophe that Anil had indirectly, yet maliciously, unleashed on them via Maris as the school and the very earth around them threatened to collapse…

Chapter 17

Back in the courtyard, several students tumbled down to the ground as the earth heaved them off their feet. Thomas was almost one of them had it not been for Abbie catching him in time. Meanwhile, Nathan and Lucy were still in the library, clinging desperately onto the table to balance themselves whilst the accelerating vibrations violently shook the walls around them, threatening to tear them apart.

"What the hell is going on?!!" Nathan yelled out in panic, his arms trembling from the force of the shockwaves.

"I don't know!!" Lucy screamed back, her legs wobbling like jelly in response to the tremors.

Suddenly, the headmaster's voice could be heard over the school's sound system, both by the students inside the library corridors and those outside in the courtyard.

"Everyone, this is an urgent announcement! You all need to leave the school grounds effective immediately!" Mr Jones broadcasted, his voice stern and commanding but still unable to hide a fearful quiver in his intonation. "Most of you will have seen the news broadcast this morning – that the director of Ali Ammunitions, Anil Ali, has been exposed as a war traitor!"

Nathan and Lucy's eyes widened in shock at hearing this. This was then followed by a sinking feeling in the pit of their stomachs as they realised, even without Mr Jones' explanation, who was responsible for these abrupt quakes.

"Well, the voice recording that was played during that bulletin…" he gulped before carrying on with his message. "The person who submitted it was me…" Mr Jones claimed, unaware that Joshua had just reached the office and was standing outside, appalled to have overheard the headmaster accepting responsibility for what he had done. In their respective locations, Nathan, Lucy, Thomas and Abbie were all astounded to hear Mr Jones say this, remembering how seriously he was taking Anil's threats and even begging them not to say anything to the authorities.

"After overhearing his admission, I…I knew that he was dangerous and believed that putting him behind bars and taking away an ally of Chimera would help Entritica's chances in the war," Mr Jones explained carefully, however when he felt the force of the tremors strengthen, he knew he had to rush through his speech for the students' sakes. "But in an act of vindictive spite, Anil has informed me that he has ordered Maris to destroy our school!" the headmaster declared, generating an audible and haunting gasp from almost every pupil in the courtyard. "We don't have much time left so that's why I'm telling you all – you have to get away from here right *now*!!" he ultimately warned before turning off the microphone and ending his proclamation.

Thomas' and Abbie's ears were pierced by the screams and wails of the other students who fled in terror, scrambling over one another to try and get closer to the school gates and off the grounds. Likewise, the teachers struggled to calm the situation for they too were gripped by fear as the shuddering earth caused even the sturdy steel supports to creak and groan from their impact.

Concurrently, the librarian hurried the remaining students out of the library, supervising them while they crept cautiously across the floor as the bookshelves began to collapse and topple over. Amidst this chaos, Nathan placed his hand on Lucy's shoulder to shake her out of her trance.

"Lucy, come on, we have to go!" he urged unyieldingly. She wordlessly nodded in agreement and the two leaned on one another to prevent themselves stumbling over on their way towards the library doorway.

At that same time, Joshua stepped out into the doorway to confront Mr Jones, the latter astonished to see him there.

"J-Joshua! W-why did you come here?!" Mr Jones blurted out, taken aback by his presence.

"S-sir, I-I'm so sorry…I-I never thought all this could happen…" Joshua clumsily apologised for allowing the audio confession of Anil to be made public.

"Joshua, we can discuss this later, but bigger things are happening right now!" Mr Jones insisted.

But just as he said this, the entire office trembled violently, damaging the doorway enough that a chunk of the above wall dislodged and fell directly onto Joshua's head before the headmaster could alert him. As Joshua slumped down to his knees in a daze, Mr Jones rushed to his side to check that he wasn't wounded.

Outside, Thomas and Abbie remained outside the school doors, observing the bedlam that was happening where some students were getting knocked over and even trampled on by the disorderly ramble flocking fearfully towards the gates.

"Sh-shouldn't we be getting out of here too?!" Thomas yelled out, wondering why Abbie hadn't made any movements.

"Nathan's still inside!" Abbie reminded him. "I'm not leaving until he's with us!"

Though concerned, Thomas didn't argue back – until he glanced in the direction of the school fence and spotted something that horrified him.

"We may want to reconsider that…" he squeaked feebly.

Hearing this, Abbie looked over her shoulder and saw Thomas' pale lips quivering. She slowly turned to follow where his eyes were focused and quickly realised what he was referring to.

The two of them observed as the Earth's surface opened up, the crack rapidly spreading from the school outskirts toward the building itself, creating the most tumultuous earthquakes that they had felt yet. Thomas and Abbie each withdrew themselves away from the fissure until their backs were against the wall. Though they used it to keep their balance, the shockwaves that they felt pulsating through the bricks and cement were enough to tell them that the structure wouldn't hold for much longer – especially when they watched in terror as the opening reached the school building, splitting apart the terrain beneath it…

Their worries shifted to Nathan who was still inside the school with Lucy, the pair of them finally having treaded their way out of the library. However, just as they thought they'd got past the worst of it, an abrupt but almighty shudder rocked the building, causing the floor they were standing on to sway to one side as if the ground was slumping downwards.

"What was that…?" Lucy gasped anxiously.

Instead of answering her, Nathan looked out the window behind him and what they saw rendered them both speechless. Outside, an enormous fissure was forming at the centre of the school and it was widening, ravaging the foundations around it and swallowing up anything within its range – including the courtyard bench, their favourite meeting point, which left

Nathan and Lucy feeling crushed to watch the site of those memories vanish into the nothingness.

They knew they didn't have the luxury of mourning for it though for they observed the building slowly start to collapse in on itself, the debris disappearing into the expanding void. Within seconds, the library they had just conversed in, caved in as the supporting pillars subsided underneath the crumbling foundations. From the uncontrollable vibrations that were oscillating through the corridor, Nathan and Lucy could tell that it was only a matter of time before the entire school building was distorted beyond repair.

"We can't stay here any longer!!" Nathan asserted after grasping the reality of the situation. He grabbed hold of Lucy's hand and tried his hardest to run through the now empty corridor and as far away from the fissure as possible, aiming to get them to a safer area. But as the aperture grew ever larger, it affected more areas of the school and started to pull the structure downwards, meaning that the level corridor they were running through began to slope against them. Nathan and Lucy strenuously stumbled their way towards the end of the hallway, hoping they could make it before they too were swallowed by the fissure.

Elsewhere, Mr Jones was trying to lift a woozy Joshua to his feet but the latter's legs were trembling while he tried to regain his awareness. The headmaster knew he had to be gentle in case Joshua had suffered a concussion – unfortunately the situation wasn't allowing for that as Mr Jones felt small pieces of plaster and dust drop down on him. It concerned the principal enough to raise his head upwards to look at the ceiling.

To his dismay, he saw that the roof was cracking apart above them, unable to withstand the sheer force of the continuous earthquakes. With the looming danger of the ceiling collapsing on top of them, Mr Jones heaved the sluggish body of Joshua towards the doorway, a difficult feat considering the teenager's muscular frame was essentially serving as an anchor for the headmaster.

Just before they could get out of the office, the intensifying tremors caused by the spreading fissure ultimately led to the upper floor giving way and caving in. Out of instinct, Mr Jones carefully hurled Joshua through the doorway in a way that he wouldn't knock his head again, saving him from the wreckage that then plummeted down, consuming the office and the principal along with it.

Similarly, the floor beneath Nathan and Lucy started to crumble away as the building began to break down from the pressure of the vibrations. Lucy almost fell through to the bottom storey had it not been for Nathan pulling her to safety in the nick of time. As he looked back to do this however, he noticed how rapidly the fissure had extended from the sight of the chasm it had created in its wake threatening to catch up to them. The corridor continued to sink further towards the gaping hole and if they didn't act quick, the incline would be so steep that there would be no scaling it and they'd just slide down into the abyss. With that impending peril lying before them, Nathan dragged Lucy with him as they both trudged onwards, the end of the hallway being a few more yards away.

Alas, before they could reach it, the foundations of the school deteriorated even further, causing the corridor ahead of them to fall apart, bringing their run to a halt as they were faced with yet another chasm. Behind them, the rest of the hallway was rapidly collapsing, reduced to nothing more than rubble that got swallowed up by the fissure bit by bit. Lucy, sensing that the floor beneath them was also weakening under the strain of the shockwaves, realised how dire their chances were.

"Nath, I don't think we're gonna make it!" she stated, knowing that they couldn't outrun the avalanche of debris that was coming. Hearing this and seeing that there was a ground floor across the gap, Nathan had one option left.

"Then we're just gonna have to jump for it..." Nathan reluctantly decided to Lucy's shock.

"Are you serious?! What if we fall down there?!" Lucy shrieked fearfully, looking down the seemingly bottomless crevice below them.

"Lucy, there's no time! It's our one chance!" Nathan reminded as the corridor continued to subside and dwindle.

Realising that Nathan was right, Lucy resigned herself to the plan and, with a deep sigh, braced herself for the jump, her heart beating swiftly at the sight of the rift.

"Together, on three..." Nathan prompted Lucy before he counted down. "One, two...three!"

Nathan and Lucy both leapt across the gulf, just in time to avoid the total collapse of the corridor they were in, and their arms just managed to catch the rim of the ledge while their legs still dangled over the void.

Unfortunately, Lucy lost her grip and despite clambering to regain her hold, it seemed to her despair that she was going to drop down into the dark nothingness underneath her. Thankfully, Nathan noticed and used his left hand to grab Lucy's wrist before it was too late.

However, it soon became apparent that their position was now even more precarious because he didn't have the strength to pull himself or lift Lucy back up onto the ground. Ultimately, Nathan was now the only thing keeping himself and Lucy from certain death as his right hand desperately gripped onto the edge while he essentially carried the weight of two people, his strength sapping with each second that passed by. With no other choices remaining, Nathan used whatever energy he could to scream out at the top of his lungs.

"HELP!! HEEELLLPPPPP!!!" he loudly bellowed over and over again with Lucy also following his lead once she'd gathered what he was doing, both of them hoping that someone would still be around to rescue them.

Several corridors away, the echo of Nathan's cries resonated far enough for them to stir Joshua. The sounds distracted him enough to rouse him from his haze, his vision finally clearing. He coughed heavily as the dust from the rubble continued to settle around him. Slowly, Joshua got to his feet, using his fingers to feel for his surroundings through the particles that formed a thick, dirty fog.

Regaining his wits, Joshua grew flustered once he realised that Mr Jones was nowhere in sight.

"Sir...? Sir?!" he called out repeatedly, silently praying that he was okay. Once the dust clouds dispelled, Joshua was horrified to see that the headmaster's office was now in ruins and unrecognisable, having been crushed by the floor above it. Just as it sickeningly dawned on him as to what fate befell Mr Jones, he heard someone feebly address him.

"J-Joshua..." the voice spluttered. Joshua felt a wave of relief engulf him as he recognised the speaker as the headmaster himself. He rushed over to where the voice had come from and found Mr Jones, half of his body being pinned down by the rubble.

"Sir! Thank god you're alive!" Joshua exclaimed before plucking pieces of debris away to try and free him. "I'm so sorry, this is all my fault! If I knew Anil could orchestrate all this, I-I'd have never...!" he reflected remorsefully, unable to bring himself to finish his sentence. "Just hang in there, I'm going to get you out!" he reassured, knowing he needed to focus on the task at hand.

"N-no...y-you have to g-get out..." Mr Jones groaned, with Joshua temporarily freezing in shock upon hearing this.

"D-don't talk nonsense!" Joshua retorted, disregarding the headmaster's advice as he continued to prise the wreckage away. "I'm not leaving you here! I've already messed up once, I'm not doing that again!"

"Y-you didn't...I was the one w-who messed up..." Mr Jones uttered, taking Joshua aback again. "I-I should have seen the s-signs with Ranjit sooner...If I had, m-maybe I could have s-stopped Anil...b-before he got too involved with Maris..." the headmaster lamented, the regret evident in his voice. "I-instead, I was prepared to let him get away with committing treason...while y-you were just trying to d-do the right thing...and make sure he got retribution, no matter what c-came of it. I-it takes a brave man to do that...and you're a b-braver man than this old c-coward..." Mr Jones acknowledged modestly, a sentiment that touched the heart of his young student. "I-I'm proud of the man you've become...and a s-splendid soldier, y-you will be..."

Joshua rubbed at his eyes with his palms, repressing the urge to succumb to his emotions – his mentor had just recognised him as a future soldier so in his mind, he had to prove him right.

"T-that's enough talking..." Joshua suggested. "You need to save your strength so let me handle the rest..." he insisted as he resumed uncovering the rubble from around Mr Jones' body. Unbeknownst to his student though, the headmaster could not only sense that more shockwaves were coming, but that the ground behind him was starting to loosen along with the foundations – and it was only a matter of time before it collapsed completely...

During this time, Thomas and Abbie were still waiting for Nathan outside the school building – or at least the part of it that was still intact. For each second that passed without him turning up, their hearts sank further and further. They silently exchanged a pale-faced, dejected look that let the other knew they had the same dreadful thought – the soul-crushing fear that their friend wasn't coming back...

As this was happening and while Joshua was preoccupied with saving Mr Jones, Nathan and Lucy were still in peril, dangling over the pit and hollering themselves hoarse until they could shout no more. Nathan struggled to maintain his grip on both the ledge and Lucy but could feel that the power in his arms was waning. Understanding the dire straits that they were both in, Lucy urged him to make an unthinkable decision.

"Nath, you have to let me go…" she stated, much to his distress.

"What?! No way! I'm not letting that happen!" Nathan argued vehemently.

"You're not gonna be able to pull us both up!" Lucy pointed out. "At this rate, we're both gonna die! This way, at least you can survive – I'll just weigh you down!"

"Lucy, listen to what you're saying!" Nathan pleaded with her, hoping to make her see sense. "If you fall down there, you'll be dead!"

"Yes, I know – and I've accepted that…" Lucy insisted, causing Nathan to look down at her. As well as the endless abyss below, he stared directly into Lucy's eyes and could almost see her pupils wobbling, clearly fighting back tears. Yet, he could see the resolve in them – she was gravely serious about this. "It's okay…" she uttered, reinforcing her choice once more while also trying to absolve him of any guilt that he was no doubt feeling.

Nathan could feel his heart pounding wildly in his chest, as if to pump the blood into his arms to revive his fading strength. His fingers were trembling, threatening to release their grip on Lucy at any moment. Yet despite all this, there was something deep within him that refused to let go of her, even more than the fact that he still considered her a friend. Even though she had given her blessing to save himself over her, it was the hopelessness in her voice that he could not be content with. He'd recognised that same bleakness before – in himself, four years ago when he believed that death was the only option for him. Upon having that epiphany, Nathan realised that he'd never forgive himself if he allowed Lucy to die believing that. With that, he tightened his grip on Lucy's wrist to her surprise, he took a deep breath and, in a last-ditch effort, shrieked the loudest he possibly could.

"HEEEEEEEEEEEELLLLLLLLLPPPPPPPPPPPPPP!!!" Nathan howled deafeningly, the gaping chasm amplifying the volume even higher so that it carried through the remaining hallways once more.

Miraculously, Nathan's cries for help travelled far enough that even from outside the remaining walls, Abbie could just about hear them, surging up at the sound.

"Thomas! Did you hear that?! It was Nathan! He's still in there, I'm sure of it!" Abbie professed hopefully.

"W-…a-are you sure?" Thomas questioned sceptically, having not heard anything.

"Yes, I am! He needs help! I heard him!" Abbie repeated eagerly.

"Y-you're certain you're not just clutching at straws…?" Thomas wondered, still doubtful that Nathan could have survived up to this point and worried that Abbie would be needlessly running into such a dangerous environment.

"I *didn't* imagine it!" Abbie asserted impatiently. "He's in there and we *need* to save him!"

Before they could debate this further, their attention was diverted by the jarring sounds of screams coming from behind the school gates. In the distance, they witnessed as another fracture in the Earth's surface began to form, generating more earthquakes in the process. To their horror, they even powerlessly watched several students, the ones who had been at the back of the crowd frantically trying to escape the school grounds, wail out in anguish as they fell into the widening crevice towards certain doom. Having seen this along with observing the fissure splitting the ground apart en route to the school building, it only made Abbie fret even more for Nathan's safety. She was about to rush in for the rescue but Thomas grabbed her arm, having read from her body language what she was going to do.

"Abbie, don't! It's too dangerous!" Thomas warned, filled with worry for what could happen to her too. However, Abbie wasn't in the mood to listen.

"Don't try and stop me!" she snapped back, even resorting to elbowing him in the ribs – Thomas doubling over in pain and sinking to his knees in response to this – before disappearing into the school. After taking a moment to recover, Thomas struggled against the juddering tremors to get back to his feet so he could pursue Abbie.

The earth rumbled violently as the cleft inched closer to the remains of the school, the integrity of the land deteriorating underneath it. In the destroyed office, Joshua was still too engrossed in plying the wreckage that was crushing the headmaster to notice the impending threat. On the other hand, Mr Jones could sense the ground behind him was giving way bit by bit, finally yielding to the strain imposed on it by the quakes.

Just as Joshua was heaving a huge pillar away from the pile though, Mr Jones noticed that the floor beneath his student was starting to break up. He knew that fragile surface would not hold up under the incoming shockwaves. So, when Joshua, after successfully removing the pillar and easing the pressure on Mr Jones' upper body, held his hand out to try and jerk him free from the remaining debris, the headmaster made his mind up, smiled and extended his own arm.

But instead of grabbing Joshua's hand, he grasped his wrist to gently pull him forward before placing his palm on his abdomen and pushing him backwards, sending him out of the office as the ground and surrounding walls spasmed uncontrollably.

In a matter of seconds, Joshua, his face contorting into a silent scream of despair, watched the remnants of the headmaster's office plummet down into the endless chasm, Mr Jones vanishing along with it, having sacrificed himself to save his pupil in his final moments...

This fact wasn't lost on Joshua, yet it didn't make his mentor's demise hurt any less. Though his mind was in disarray after failing to save him, he knew he had to get out of the rapidly crumbling building now or else Mr Jones' last act would have been for nothing. Thus, he hobbled his way out of the corridor, powering through against the churning convulsions of the earthquakes as well as his own overwhelming grief...

Like with Mr Jones, the gulf caused by the fissure threatened to consume Nathan and Lucy with the former close to releasing his grip in the wake of the fiercest tremors yet. He could feel his fingers on the cusp of slipping against the vibrations, still trying his best to fight that urge. Seeing his struggle, Lucy pleaded with Nathan once more to save himself.

"Nath, this is your last chance! If you don't let me go now, you're gonna die too!" she cried out, hoping that he'd finally listen but he still refused.

"And I already told you that I am *not* letting you go!" Nathan shouted back, unrelenting despite these impossible odds.

"Nathan, you *can't* save us both, just accept it!" Lucy asserted, aware of his limited strength and watching mounds of soil plummet downwards with each ferocious shudder. Instead of submitting to his fatigue though, Lucy's words seemed to motivate Nathan more.

"Don't tell me..." Nathan grunted as his arms ostensibly reinvigorated themselves, his waning clutch on Lucy and the ledge inexplicably restored. "What I can...and *can't*...DO!!!!" he expressed defiantly.

In one swift motion, Nathan's abrupt surge of adrenaline helped him to heave himself up to the ledge with one arm, a feat that left Lucy wide-eyed and flabbergasted. Once there, he had the momentum to pull Lucy upwards until she could grab the edge of the jutted earth herself. With that, both Nathan and Lucy rolled themselves onto the flat surface, huffing and puffing heavily as they processed the hazard that they had narrowly escaped.

"Nathan…t-that was…" Lucy wheezed breathlessly, unable to get the words out to convey her praise while Nathan wriggled up from the floor until he was on his hands and knees, still in disbelief at what he'd just accomplished and the fact that they were still alive. "H-how…how did… how did you…" she panted, lifting her head up to look at Nathan.

She then let out an audible gasp which caught Nathan's attention and when he raised his head, he soon realised why. To his shock, his hand was radiating with a flickering black aura – his first time seeing it with his own eyes. It was only for a few seconds before it dissipated, leaving Nathan and Lucy to exchange an expression of bewilderment and tentative awe.

Their brief silence was interrupted by the arrival of Abbie who came charging down the corridor, side-stepping any debris in her path.

"Nathan!!" she blurted out upon seeing him, attracting the attention of Nathan and Lucy. "You had us worried sick! Thank god, you're alive!" she shouted with relief, embracing him as he scrambled up to his feet.

"Yeah, just about…" Lucy remarked, picking herself up without any support due to Abbie concentrating on Nathan who remained quiet. Before Abbie could even acknowledge Lucy, the surrounding walls started to crack and crumble as earth started to shift once more, the fissure threatening to expand outwards and swallow up the ruins of the school.

"This place is falling apart! We have to get out *now*!" Abbie ordered the pair of them.

Without hesitation, the three of them dashed as fast as they could through the remaining corridors, Abbie taking the lead as she guided Nathan and Lucy to the exit among the wreckage.

At the same time, Thomas shuffled his way down the first corridor from the entrance, still clutching his ribs. He was about to turn the corner but was stopped when he came across a dejected Joshua who had emerged from the passageway that had once led to the headmaster's office.

"Joshua…? W-what are you still doing here?!" Thomas exclaimed upon seeing him.

"I-I was…t-trying to save Mr Jones…b-but…h-he's gone…" Joshua revealed, trying his hardest to keep his composure, however Thomas could see the anguish written all over his face.

"Oh…oh god, I'm so sorry…" Thomas consoled to the best of his ability, though he was at a loss for what to say due to having difficulty digesting the information himself. It just seemed so unthinkable to him that Mr Jones, a former soldier in his own right, was no longer with them. An awkward silence descended upon the two young men which got disrupted as the shockwaves rippled throughout the hallway, causing pieces of the ceiling to dislodge and crash to the floor around them.

In that moment, Nathan, Abbie and Lucy appeared from around the corner and found Thomas and Joshua. Once he saw that his cousin was still inside the school, exposed to the danger of the calamity that was befalling them, Joshua concealed his surprise and instinctively snapped out of his stupor. On the other hand, Nathan was certainly alarmed to see Joshua here.

"W-why the hell are you still here?!" Nathan blurted out without thinking.

"He was with the headmaster…" Thomas answered on behalf of Joshua before he could get a word in, the latter biting his lips in regret. "H-he couldn't save him though…" he added, wincing from pain.

"Are you okay?" Abbie asked Thomas.

"M-Mr Jones is…d-dead?" Nathan uttered, seeking clarity from his cousin.

"No! You flaming elbowed me in the ribs!" Thomas angrily reminded Abbie.

"Yes…he is…" Joshua confirmed forlornly to Nathan. "I-I failed him…a-and I failed you…"

"I-I'm sorry, I didn't think I hit you *that* hard!" Abbie rebutted defensively, irking Thomas.

"J-Josh…I-" Nathan stammered, trying to find the words to comfort his cousin.

However, between Thomas and Abbie's petty squabble and Nathan and Joshua's making the first steps towards a heart-to-heart, Lucy could hear an almighty rumbling followed by what sounded like a landslide. She quickly realised that the section of the corridor that they were just running from was caving in, being consumed by the expanding crater that she and Nathan had barely avoided.

"Guys, can we address this later?" Lucy interrupted, forcing the group's attention back to her. "You know, maybe at a time where everything's not *literally falling apart!!*" she reinforced, screaming the last three words to underline her point.

Having had that reality check, the five students hurried their way to the exit, Nathan in the centre with Thomas and Abbie on his right while Lucy and Joshua were to the left of him. They picked up the pace when a thunderous noise deafened their ears as the hallway floor behind them began to collapse along with the deteriorating earth. With Nathan and Lucy physically and emotionally drained from their near-death experience and Thomas having a deficiency of stamina, Joshua and Abbie, as the more athletically capable students, grabbed their arms and pulled them along with them to prevent the risk of them lagging behind.

Just before they reached the doorway, Nathan couldn't help but feel a bittersweet nostalgia about being in this part of the school with Thomas, Abbie, Lucy and Joshua. It was only a month ago, on the day he learned about his dad's death, that they were all in this same passageway at near enough the same time. At that point in time though, the group couldn't be more divided. And now, in the most unimaginable and tragic of circumstances, the five of them were united in this corridor, about to leave the school that tied them all together – but with the knowledge that any return to their old lives would now be forever impossible…

Nathan, Thomas, Abbie, Lucy and Joshua managed to escape through the doorway while the school collapsed inwards. They looked over in the distance towards the gateway but Thomas and Abbie remembered that one of the cracks had originated from there, blocking that pathway on its trajectory to the school building. Just when it seemed that they were trapped with the sinking school, Joshua found the solution.

"The fence!" he called out, pointing in the direction once he'd seen that there were no cracks obstructing their route to safety. Joshua led the other four over to the railings, everyone having to steady themselves at one point when another earthquake rocked the ground beneath them.

Once at the railings, Joshua and Abbie put their differences aside and worked together to provide a footing for the other three. Thomas used it to climb over the fence first, followed by Lucy and then Nathan. As soon as all three were safely on the other side, Joshua and Abbie jumped up, grabbed the top of the railings and pulled themselves over the edge to join the other three.

The five of them were relieved to have survived, but when they turned back to look through the railings, they could see for the first time what the other students and teachers in the distance had witnessed. They watched as the last area of Silver Dawn Comp crumbled into pieces and vanished into the crevice with not even a brick left behind.

"The school…i-it's all gone…" Lucy murmured despondently.

There was nothing that Nathan or anyone else there could add to make the sentiment hurt any less. What was once their school had been reduced to a vast empty chasm, a scar on the very earth itself and it only served as an example of the all-powerful threat that they were up against – and the destruction that she was capable of…

Chapter 18

Below the sky overcast with thick black clouds, time seemingly came to a standstill for Nathan as he stared out through the railings at the haunting abyss that was once his school. It was a perception that his fellow survivors shared. On the one hand, his best mates Thomas and Abbie were standing to his left with their stomachs churning from what they were seeing. On the other, his estranged friend and cousin, Lucy and Joshua respectively, stood on his right, their faces white as sheets from their brushes with death.

Their ears were deafened by the blaring ringing of multiple fire alarms that had been triggered by the earthquakes which had finally settled. It overpowered their senses until their attention was diverted by a damp, cold sensation that stemmed from the soles of their feet. Nathan and the others looked down to see that there was a shallow, dirty pool of water at the base of their shoes, leading them to turn around and find that the road had become flooded – no doubt from the damage that the tremors had inflicted on the drains beneath them. Across the road, the houses on the opposite side of the road had also been tarnished from the calamity's impact, though not to the extent of the school which had clearly been the intended target.

In the distance, the group could see that there was still a mass gathering of students near the gates, many of whom were trembling in a state of shock and being consoled by the teachers. Although faint, Thomas and Abbie could just about spot several students kneeled on the ground, sobbing uncontrollably. It was a chilling reminder to them that they'd witnessed a cluster of pupils plunge into the cavernous pit, meaning that these students were most likely mourning for their classmates. As a few distressing wails broke out from the crowd and fleetingly powered through the echoing sirens, Nathan, Joshua and everyone else thought solemnly about all who had died in this dreadful disaster, including Mr Jones…

"This is a nightmare…" Thomas stated feebly, barely able to articulate the words as he observed the scenes happening around him.

"H-how…how does one person…e-even have the power to do all this…?" Abbie added, now seeing first-hand the power that Maris wielded.

A brief and uncomfortable silence descended upon the group, the five of them faced with the monstrous crater, a blemish on the very terrain where their school previously stood. When considering it alongside Maris, both the depths to the fissure and her power seemed limitless…

"G-guys, I don't want to be the bearer of more bad news…" Joshua spoke up, Abbie, Thomas, Nathan and Lucy each turning their heads to the right to listen to him. "But for a disaster to occur here of all places…this far inland…"

"It means that Maris is close…doesn't it?" Nathan deduced which his cousin confirmed with a meek nod to everyone else's dismay.

"And we've been told that Maris is a god…so if that really is true…" Abbie muttered, again taking in the devastation around her. "Then Entritica truly is finished…" she accepted reluctantly, the dejection seeping through in her voice.

"S-so…what are we supposed to do now…?" Lucy questioned, feeling utterly lost as her head drooped down to the ground.

It was a question that neither Thomas, Abbie nor Joshua could answer for they were all still processing the horrific events that had unfolded. However, Nathan kept his head held high, defiantly glaring a hole through the foreboding dark clouds, refusing to lose his resolve.

"The plan hasn't changed. We do what Mr Jones suggested…we go back to our families and evacuate Entritica!" Nathan declared, commanding the attention of his comrades as he reminded them of their late headmaster's announcement to them two days ago.

"Nathan's right…it may be our best chance of survival," Joshua approved, raising his head to look at the sky, his own motivation renewed slightly by Nathan's determination. "Many others will do the same once this becomes public knowledge…which I'm guessing won't be long now…" he noted, spotting two helicopters in the air, hovering over the fissure.

"Abandoning the country…we'll be leaving our homes behind…" Abbie lamented sadly.

"But we'll be doing it to protect the thing that makes our houses a home – our families…" Thomas remarked with Nathan being in total solidarity with him.

"I'll do whatever it takes to keep my mom safe…" Nathan asserted resolutely.

"Me too," Thomas agreed, his mind made up about fleeing. Their tenacity and devotion to their loved ones swayed Abbie towards the same conclusion.

"Ben's too young to have to be around all this. I have to get him away from here – it's time I made my parents see sense!" Abbie decided.

Despite the tragedy that had befallen them all, Lucy sensed the bleak atmosphere change around Thomas, Abbie and Joshua. It was as if their fighting spirits had been rekindled by Nathan's energy, even in the face of these overwhelming circumstances – it was a foreign feeling for her, yet one that she found both inspiring and uplifting.

"I-I'll tell my mom too…about the plan to leave Entritica…" Lucy informed them. "Hopefully I can persuade her to come with us…"

"Wait…us?" Abbie echoed, her eyebrows furrowing in confusion.

"Yeah…I mean, a-aren't we all going together?" Lucy queried, taking the others aback.

"Um…we hadn't actually discussed that yet…" Nathan responded awkwardly, the thought having not even entered his mind previously. However, now that Lucy had planted the seeds there, it was clear from the glints in Nathan's and Abbie's eyes that the more the idea lingered, the more they liked the sound of it.

"O-okay…well, do let me know what you decide to do," Lucy requested earnestly.

During this exchange, Joshua's ears picked up the approaching sounds of ambulance and police sirens, becoming aware that the emergency services were about to arrive.

"Look, we need to act now and get back to our homes! I need to make sure dad's okay…" Joshua predicated, taking charge of the situation as the eldest of the five.

"Right, I'd better call mom too…" Thomas said, pulling his phone out from his pocket with Abbie following suit and searching through her bag for her own phone.

"Nath, if you still have your phone, you should do the same. Victoria will be worried sick about you…" Joshua advised.

"Yeah, I know…" Nathan replied before noticing that Lucy was still understandably spooked from the catastrophe, her arms quivering and her legs appearing far from sturdy. "Will you be okay getting back home?" he attentively asked her.

Lucy struggled to get her words out, her own mind clouded with doubt after she was almost killed. Joshua butted in before she could answer.

"I'll escort Lucy home. I'll make sure she gets back safely," he reassured both Nathan and Lucy. "Nathan, you just focus on getting back to Victoria," Joshua ordered his younger cousin.

In spite of their earlier tension, which had yet to be fully resolved after Joshua's knowledge of the cause of Richard's death had been discovered, Nathan didn't argue back for he knew letting his mom know he'd survived was more important. He reached inside his blazer pocket where his phone was resting against his breast, just underneath the strap of his backpack.

It was at this moment that Nathan became conscious, for the first time since escaping the school, of the fact that his backpack was still draped over his shoulders – he hadn't lost it, even when he and Lucy were dangling over the fissure. This meant that he still had the book that he'd taken from the library, one that was now impossible to return due to the school's obliteration.

Before he could dwell on this thought for a moment longer, he was distracted by Joshua angrily calling out to Abbie who was using her phone to take a photograph of the crater.

"Are you serious?!" Joshua shouted at her. "People have died and you're taking pictures to post on the Internet?!" Upon hearing this, Abbie furiously stomped over to Joshua until her face was inches away from his.

"You really think that little of me, don't you?!!" she snarled bitterly as Nathan, Thomas and Lucy watched their discussion. "F.Y.I, my parents thought all these disasters were just a government conspiracy! I took a photo so I can prove to them beyond a shadow of a doubt that it's real and pull their heads out the sand!"

"O-oh…S-sorry…" Joshua mumbled, backing down on this occasion compared to their last confrontation when he'd antagonised her further. Abbie turned her back to him in disgust, not in the mood to accept his apology.

As Nathan, Thomas and Lucy tried to diffuse the situation, an ambulance and a police car drove past them on their path to the school gates, cutting through the flood and splashing the group. While they wrung the water out of their clothes, Joshua observed as the medics and police officers exited their vehicles to tend to the traumatised students and take statements from any teachers who were in a fit enough state to provide one.

"Guys, you should hurry home now!" Joshua suggested, predicting that things were going to get more chaotic now that emergency relief had arrived. "I'll stay behind – I-I need to tell them about Mr Jones' death... and how Anil ordered the attack on the school. After that, I'll take Lucy home..." he explained, remembering his promise to do the latter for Nathan.

When his cousin nodded in agreement, Joshua rushed off towards the crowd of survivors to grab the attention of a police sergeant. Meanwhile, Lucy remained rooted to the spot, reluctant to leave Nathan and Thomas' side. The choice was taken out of her hands however once their phones started to ring, the two boys glancing down at their screens to see that their mothers were calling them.

"Right, I'd better get moving!" Nathan proclaimed, both him and Thomas stepping backwards in their respective directions, creating distance between them and the two girls. "Lucy, stick with Joshua! We'll all talk later!" he blurted out swiftly before he and Thomas dashed away, leaving Abbie and Lucy behind.

Seconds later, as he was running down the pavement and getting further away from the disaster site, Nathan answered the phone to Victoria.

"Mom, I'm alive! I'm alive! I'm alive!" Nathan emphasised hurriedly, hoping to calm his mom whom he could hear sobbing and gasping over the phone.

"Oh, thank god, thank god!!" Victoria cried out gratefully. "I just saw the breaking news...I really feared the worst..."

"I-it's been on the news already...?" Nathan uttered out of surprise.

"It has..." Victoria confirmed. "A-all those people...i-it's just too horrible..."

"I know..." Nathan replied, having to pause not only for breath but to even find the words to convey the terror that he and the others had faced minutes ago. After falling silent for a few seconds, the only way that Nathan and Victoria could find to properly express their mutual dismay, the former tried his best to move on from that painful reminder. "I-I'll be home shortly Mom, just hang in there..." he told her reassuringly.

"Please, please be careful Nathan...I love you..." Victoria begged, still fretful that there could be further tremors.

"I love you too, Mom…" Nathan echoed before ending the call so he could focus on making it home safely, his legs still wobbly from the experience.

On his journey home, Nathan came across several streets that had also been affected by the earthquakes. Though the roads were free of floods and the houses were intact, the wounds to the landscape were still apparent. Huge potholes had opened up in roads due to the strain of the calamity. Car alarms were blaring loudly throughout the streets after being triggered by the constant shockwaves. Trees had toppled over, crushing fence panels and even demolishing garden sheds. Some of the more derelict buildings had slates which had dropped from roofs, glass that had shattered, and pipework which had dislodged and dangled hideously from the outer walls. All Nathan could do was pray that the disaster had occurred far enough away from his house for it to not be impacted too severely.

Thankfully, the further Nathan travelled out of range from his ravaged school and the closer he got to his home, the less prevalent the effects of the catastrophe became. Several minutes later, he'd reached his street and used his remaining stamina to propel his legs through those final few steps until his house came into view.

Victoria was waiting in the doorway to greet her son and as soon as Nathan appeared from around the corner, she darted over to embrace him. Weary from all that he'd been through, Nathan returned her hug, nearly collapsing into her arms from exhaustion and burying his head into her shoulder. They clutched at each other tightly, both using the other for support while breathing heavily from relief and fatigue.

"I really thought I'd lost you…" Victoria whispered tenderly into Nathan's ear, her heart thumping in her chest as she said it.

"It was terrifying…" Nathan opened up, reliving the moment that he and Lucy were hanging over the edge of the fissure. "But I'm here now…" he reminded his mom reassuringly.

Eventually, once she found the courage to relinquish her grip on her son, Victoria guided Nathan into the house and sat him down on the sofa in the living room to rest. Meanwhile, the television continued to broadcast the calamity that had swallowed up Silver Dawn Comprehensive School. Thanks to the cameramen in the helicopters, Nathan was now able to see a bird's eye view of the chasm and appreciate the sheer scale of what he'd just survived…

"Maris did this…" Nathan relayed to Victoria, confirming what she had already suspected. "Mr Jones told us so…before he died…" he squeaked sadly, his eyes fixed to the screen the whole time.

"Oh Nathan…I'm so sorry…and Joshua must be devastated too…" Victoria remarked empathetically. There was a moment of silence between the two as the news cut to footage of paramedics interacting with the students and teachers that had managed to escape the attack. They were treating them both physically and mentally while the survivors grieved for those who weren't so fortunate. "She's capable of causing all this…" Victoria uttered as she observed the broadcast.

"Joshua said she's getting close…" Nathan added.

"Which means we aren't safe here…" Victoria concluded, both realising that they were on the same page. Victoria took a deep sigh before continuing. "Nathan, this might be difficult for you to hear, but-"

"Mom, we need to evacuate," Nathan declared, beating his mother to the punch.

"Well, that certainly speeds things up…" Victoria acknowledged, having already anticipated from Nathan's tone and body language that persuading him wouldn't be too challenging. "Are you sure you're ready to do this though?" she asked him, needing to know if he appreciated the magnitude of what they'd be doing by fleeing the country.

"It's okay mom, I know the score," Nathan insisted. "Dad would want us to do this – he loved Entritica, but he wouldn't want us to be in danger. It's why he fought in this war in the first place…against that monster," he commented bitterly about Maris. "For his sake, we have to survive…even if we have to leave Entritica behind…"

"Good, looks like that's decided then," Victoria stated, approving of her son's resolve. "Do you have any objections about leaving today?"

Nathan considered her question carefully. While it felt sudden to leave their home behind and it hurt to do so, he knew that the dire situation called for it, so he shook his head to indicate that there were no misgivings on his part.

"Okay," Victoria responded. "Then I should tell you that while you were making your way home, I was on the phone to Clint. We discussed travelling together so we could go with him and Joshua…if that was okay with you too, of course…"

"Fine with me," Nathan consented, remembering again how Lucy had brought up the possibility of fleeing as a group with their families. "How would we get out of the country though? If Maris can create disasters like hurricanes, I'm not sure flying on a plane would be safe..." he contemplated.

"I agree," Victoria established. "Clint suggested that we take a boat to Lyrasia – now that Chimera are actually in Entritica, I doubt we'll see another tsunami since they're inland now," she explained as Nathan listened intently. "The downside is we'd have to cross a mountain to get to a port..." she highlighted, knowing that their province was surrounded by a range of them.

"Which one?" Nathan questioned curiously.

"The one that's closest to the sea – Mount Tamara..." Victoria revealed. "It'll be a trek to cross, but after that, we could reach the port in about two or three days..."

Although anxious about traversing over a mountain, Nathan knew it would be a necessity for escape so accepted the decision. "So the plan's to go to Lyrasia?" he wondered.

"If it's safe, yes," Victoria confirmed. "From there, we can play it by ear. If we wanted, we could even visit Richard's birthplace, Etracova. It would be nice to know more about the culture he grew up around..."

The news bulletin about the destruction of Silver Dawn Comprehensive School finally came to an end as Nathan and Victoria settled on their plan of escape. After the announcement from Wednesday, Victoria had already packed most of the essentials over the last two days in preparation for this inevitability. All that remained was for Nathan to search through his bedroom to see if there was anything crucial that he wanted to bring with him. With that, Nathan headed up the stairs to his room while Victoria called her brother Clint to fill him in on what their arrangements were.

Once in his bedroom, Nathan finally pulled his backpack from his shoulders, relieving them of the load for the first time since arriving at school that morning, and chucked it onto his bed. Then, he reached into his pocket for his phone and began to message Thomas and Abbie in their group chat as follows:

Hey guys, hope you both got back home okay – please let me know. I've spoken to my mom and our plan is to cross Mount Tamara and then get a boat out of Entritica. We'll be travelling with Joshua and my uncle.

Nathan didn't have to wait long for a reply as two minutes later, Thomas responded back to his text:

All okay over here, thanks. Just told my mom now. There's a village at the foot of Mount Tamara. We could meet you there if you'd like and go together?

Nathan felt quietly joyful reading Thomas' message. Ever since Lucy had first mentioned the idea earlier, he held out hope that in these dire circumstances, he could at least travel with his friends beside him, the ones who had consistently been there with him after the death of his father, other than his mom of course. That desired vision came a step closer to reality as Abbie's message flashed up on his screen:

Sounds good to me. I'll give you a bell once me and the family get there. Be careful guys. Xx

Just like that, the strategy to evacuate was truly taking shape which Nathan found remarkable considering the fissure had occurred less than an hour ago. It was a clear sign that everyone now knew the urgency of the situation and was acting accordingly, even Abbie's parents if her message was anything to go by. Satisfied, Nathan dropped one more text into the chat:

Brill! I'll see you all there then. Take care. X

With the plan set in stone, Nathan placed his phone on the bed so that he could get changed out of his school uniform. As he removed his tie and unbuttoned his shirt though, he realised that he'd almost forgotten to inform Lucy of where they'd be meeting. He unlocked his phone and scrolled through his contacts to find her number.

However, once Nathan found it, it served as a painful reminder that he only had Lucy's old number because she had changed it shortly after she started dating Kamran – around the time she started to distance herself from him and Thomas. It was something that had slipped his mind after his heart to heart with Lucy prior to the school's collapse, almost as if the gap between them these last eight months had never existed.

Forced to come to terms with this, Nathan returned his focus to undressing, removing his shirt and trousers before placing them on coat hangers. He then wasted little time in changing into some black jeans and pulling a thick red jumper over his head, aware that he would need to wear warm clothes if he was to climb a mountain. His next priority was to pack several different garments for wherever they'd be travelling to, whether that be Lyrasia, Etracova or someplace else. Before Nathan did that though, he picked up the coat hangers suspending his school attire, ready to put them inside his wardrobe.

But he took a few moments to examine the uniform and another pang of sorrow struck his heart – he would not get the chance to wear this outfit again. While it hurt to abandon his family home, Nathan knew the option to return here one day still remained. On the other hand, the same could not be said for his school. The place that had facilitated much of his childhood development along with the forging of his bonds with Thomas and Abbie had been reduced to a crater, yet another thing that had been annihilated and stolen away from him by Maris and Chimera. The uniform only served as another reminder of the innocence that was forever lost to him now…

Nathan knew he didn't have much time to dwell on this though, so morosely packed the uniform away in the corner of his wardrobe before choosing various items of clothing that he wanted to take with him. It took several minutes but once he'd made his selections, he removed the coat hangers so that they were ready to be placed into his backpack.

Just as he was about to empty his backpack however, Nathan was distracted by the faint sound of a vibration which unnerved him after the earthquakes from this morning. To his relief, he soon realised that his phone was pulsating and when he picked it up, he discovered that he was getting a call from an unrecognised number. He was hesitant to answer it but after it had rung for half a minute, Nathan ultimately relented.

"Hello…?" Nathan spoke cautiously, unsure what to expect.

"Nathan! It's me, Lucy!" the caller replied, Nathan's tension eased by the sound of his friend's voice.

"Oh Lucy, it's good to hear from you!" Nathan responded back to her. "I'd wanted to call but I forgot that I never got your new number. Did you get mine from Joshua?"

"Actually…I always kept your and Thomas' numbers…" Lucy revealed to Nathan's surprise. "Yes, Ranjit made me delete them from my phone, saying he'd hurt you guys if I didn't. But before I did that, I wrote them down on a secret note that I hid under my bed…"

"Oh my god…that's awful…" Nathan commented sympathetically, appalled to hear about the lengths that Lucy had to go to on account of Ranjit.

"I know..." Lucy agreed. "Anyway, the reason I'm calling...I-I never got the chance earlier...t-to thank you for saving my life..."

"Hey, it's okay...besides, I'm not sure I can take much credit for it anyway..." Nathan remarked automatically, the words leaving his mouth before he could stop them.

"T-that reminds me...for you to say that...it means you saw it too, didn't you?" Lucy uttered, something that initially left Nathan confused which she picked up on from his silence. "The black aura...?" she elaborated.

Her words sparked a recollection in Nathan's mind. Lucy was correct. He had seen the black aura radiating from his hand – moments after he'd pulled them to safety!

"Yeah, I did..." Nathan confirmed uneasily.

"I thought so...I saw it from your reaction..." Lucy recalled. "You-you haven't seen it before, have you?"

"No...no I haven't..." Nathan acknowledged. "L-Lucy...d-did the aura look the same as...t-that time you were almost...k-kidnapped by Otis and Tobias...?" he stuttered, reluctant to bring up yet another unpleasant event from her past.

"It was definitely the same energy as before...just calmer and less intense," Lucy described. "And about that, I was wondering...when you were holding onto that ledge...did you black out at any point?"

Nathan forced himself to re-visit every second of that frightening experience to try and find any gap in his memories. That's when he came to a startling epiphany.

"No...I was conscious the entire time..." he realised. "Even when I... the black aura...pulled us out of that chasm...I-I remember everything..."

"I see...that's what I'd suspected too..." Lucy admitted. "You didn't seem consumed by it like the time before. In fact, it felt like you were in control of it this time. It might explain how you were able to see the aura with your own eyes...and why it wasn't so erratic either..."

Hearing this possibility was music to Nathan's ears. For the first time since discovering the truth about this power one week ago, he didn't feel like some helpless vessel that could succumb to its influence at a moment's notice. Instead, it was as if he was closer to uncovering its secrets and perhaps finding a way to gain mastery over it. Though the theory had merit, it was still conjecture at this stage, so Nathan tried to contain his excitement as he continued to talk to Lucy.

"I-I really hope you're right on that one, but I guess time will tell..." Nathan pondered.

"Either way Nathan, if it weren't for you, I'd be dead. That's twice I owe you my life now and I can't even begin to fathom how I could ever repay you..." Lucy added. This time, she was the one who fell quiet, as though she didn't know what to say next which didn't escape Nathan's notice. Realising how heavy the conversation had been to this point, he tried to lighten the mood.

"Well, I give you my word that I *won't* ask for sex in return..." Nathan nervously joked, recalling their earlier discussion about Kamran before the earthquakes started. There was silence for a few seconds which made Nathan worry that he'd crossed a line. "Sorry, was that too soon...? I-I didn't mean to offend, I swear!" he blurted out anxiously, hoping that he hadn't made things awkward between them when they were building bridges again.

Instead, Lucy started to giggle from hearing his abrupt apology before breaking out into full-blown laughter down the phone, something that left Nathan feeling relieved.

"Oh Nath, you're so cute!" Lucy chuckled jovially. "I've missed you so much, nobody makes me laugh like you and Thomas did," she divulged to him. "I just want things to go back to the way they were...when Ranjit and my mom weren't getting in our way..."

"Aw Luce..." Nathan replied compassionately. "H-have you talked to your mom about evacuating...?" he asked her.

"That's the other thing I wanted to call you about..." Lucy stated. "I told her about it...but she's adamant on us staying. Apparently, she's made some arrangement with the Alis that, in her words, will guarantee our safety against Maris and Chimera...she isn't budging at all."

"I see..." Nathan reacted, being sure to take the time to allow Lucy's words to sink in. As he did this, Lucy continued to speak.

"Nath, even if my mom stays in Entritica, I still want to come with you guys!" Lucy professed. "She might be able to sell her soul but I can't bear the thought of siding with Chimera and I want to find out what happened to my dad – if he's still alive somewhere, I want to find him. So if I join you guys, then I can-" she was about to finish, however Nathan suddenly interrupted her by saying something that she did not foresee.

"Lucy, I think you need to do as your mom says and stay here with her..." Nathan declared reluctantly, leaving her stunned.

"W-what?! Why?!" Lucy questioned in protest. "After what happened to the school, surely it would be safer to be as far away from Maris as possible, right?!"

"I'd like to think so but truthfully, we'll be heading into the unknown," Nathan rationalised. "If your mom really has arranged a deal with the Alis that'll keep you both protected, then I'd argue that *that's* the safer option. They clearly have clout with Maris for them to orchestrate the fissure," he explained, his mind still fixating on the incident and the danger that they'd contended with. "I know it's frustrating – I really do – but you need to prioritise your safety right now. Besides, even though you have a strained relationship with her, would you really be okay with leaving your mom here by herself?"

Lucy paused before answering, mulling over Nathan's advice, trying to find a flaw in his reasoning. Yet no matter how hard she tried given their history, she couldn't quite harden her heart enough towards her mom to reject Nathan's argument.

"N-no...I guess I wouldn't..." Lucy mumbled. "S-so that means if I'm staying here...and you're leaving...then this is us saying goodbye..." she realised glumly.

"Yeah...yeah, I guess we are..." Nathan acknowledged, saddened to think that he had been so close to rekindling his friendship with Lucy only for him to lose her again. Despite this, he believed that this was the right thing to do for her sake. He was about to say something to try and soften the parting, however Lucy beat him to the punch.

"I want to see you again one day. So, you better stay alive!" she avowed firmly, which initially surprised Nathan, but left him smiling seconds later.

"I will..." he asserted reassuringly. "Don't you get dying either!"

On that sombre, yet hopeful note, Nathan and Lucy bid farewell to one another before ending the call. He stared down at his phone longingly for several moments until he heard his mother addressing him from the bottom of the staircase.

"Nathan, are you nearly ready? We need to get moving soon!" Victoria called up to him.

"I'm nearly done! I just need ten more minutes!" Nathan answered back.

"Okay, just don't be too long now!" Victoria instructed.

With the time ticking away, Nathan refocused his attention to his backpack, lifting it up and emptying the contents onto his bed. His school textbooks tumbled down onto the covers and he gathered them up one by one so that he could store them away in his wardrobe. He did this until there was one book remaining – the one he'd taken from the library.

The library book had landed on his bed, pages open and facing downwards, while the hardcover displaying the title *'Demons, Dragons and other Servants of the Devil'* was visible to Nathan's eyes. When he turned the book over, he saw that it had conveniently opened to the same page that he was previously reading, the one sub-headed *'The Devil's Spirit'*. Nathan briefly skimmed through the pages again, but after his discussion with Lucy, the phrase that currently stole his focus was the one that read:

The drawbacks of succumbing to this awakening are that the power is uncontrollable and the subject will retain no memory of his typically violent actions during the possession.

Yet as Lucy had pointed out, this wasn't the case during the fissure. Nathan could recall the entire experience and had seen the aura himself, breaking the pattern of his past incidents. If Lucy's theory was true, that he was in control of the Devil's Spirit, this meant that Nathan had achieved a feat that defied the very literature he was researching.

This possibility piqued his interest more than ever, so he promptly closed the book and carefully placed it into his backpack, even using some of his clothes to further protect the hardback from being damaged. Nathan kept going until his bag was full and there were no further garments remaining on his bare bed.

With his packing finished, Nathan draped the backpack over his shoulder and looked around his bedroom, knowing that it would be the last time that he would be in this room until the day came when he could safely return. He pursed his lips together as he reminisced on fonder times when he was younger, such as when his father would read him bedtime stories or when his mother would kiss him goodnight. The memories kept flooding back to him, ending with two moments from six days ago. The penultimate was Victoria opening up to him about Richard's past and Chimera, along with giving him hope that he could do something positive with what he now knew as *'The Devil's Spirit'*. The final one was his sleepover with Thomas and Abbie, when they'd spent time together laughing and playing as teenagers should do, while also vowing to work together against Chimera. Nathan clenched his eyes shut, repressing any tears due to his determination to 'stay strong for his mom', before departing his bedroom and leaving the last remnant of his childhood behind…

⋯◄►⋯

Chapter 19

Nathan made his way down the stairs until he was in the hall, standing before the doorway where Victoria was waiting for him. Like her son, she had a rucksack draped over her shoulders, but she also carried an additional luggage bag in her hand, one filled with the supplies that she'd packed over the last two days.

"Mom, are you really going to be alright carrying all that stuff?" Nathan asked her, conscious of the journey they were about to make.

"Yeah, this is nothing," Victoria reassured, raising her arm to demonstrate that while the bag was bulky, it was still light. Nathan accepted her answer and noticed that she was wearing a thick parka, no doubt in anticipation of Mt Tamara. Following her example, he grabbed a jacket of his own from the coat stand in the hallway.

"Um…I should let you know, mom," Nathan began as he shrouded his body with the coat. "I told Thomas and Abbie where we're going. They've said they're going to join us with their families. Y-you don't mind, do you?" he wondered anxiously.

"No, of course not," Victoria consented to Nathan's relief as they both stepped outside. "Clint told me that he and Joshua will wait for us in The Raging Dragon Tavern. If you let Thomas and Abbie know, it'll make it easier for them to find us."

Nathan nodded and texted his friends to update them of the rendezvous point as his mom focused on locking the door. Once he was finished, Nathan looked back up at the house and immediately felt another wave of overwhelming sadness wash over him, aware that returning here would not be possible for quite some time. He tried to hold it together but Victoria spotted his hands trembling.

"Nath, you've been through a lot already. Are you really sure you want to do this today?" Victoria queried, worried for how much her son was taking on. "I mean, we could postpone until tomorrow if you wanted…" she offered as a suggestion.

Instead of saying anything in response, Nathan quietly grabbed his mother's hand and held it tightly. Victoria understood instinctively what was happening and they both gazed at their home, appreciating what they were leaving behind one more time in silent solidarity. As they ruminated about their time with Richard and the happy memories that they had made with him, Victoria's soothing touch and motherly warmth helped Nathan to settle until his arms ceased shuddering.

"Okay I'm ready," he confirmed after enough time had passed. "Time to go…" Nathan decided, to which Victoria concurred. With that, they both turned away from their home and ambled down the street, commencing their excursion towards Mount Tamara.

Once they were several roads away and could no longer see any cracks in the tarmac, suggesting that they were far enough away from the area impacted by the earthquakes, Nathan and Victoria started to catch a few buses that would take them to the mountain. During each ride, they could both see various other households also preparing to evacuate, family members standing outside their homes with suitcases and travel bags. When they were passing through nearby towns, Nathan noticed that there were shops and businesses that had been shuttered down, adorned with signs that stated they were '*Closed until further notice*', no doubt a consequence of this morning's developments. This belief was supported by the articles that he was seeing online from his phone, ones that speculated whether this was the end of Entritica as everybody knew it. He could only look through so many of them before putting his phone away, needing space from the pessimism.

****

A few hours later, the final bus arrived at the foot of Mount Tamara which cast a massive shadow over the village that Nathan and Victoria entered. The clock in the centre of town displayed the time as 3pm, and the drop in temperature could certainly be felt due to the proximity to the mountain. Along with his mom, Nathan searched around for the Raging Dragon Tavern, hoping to be able to ask someone for directions but they soon detected that the village was rather desolate with hardly anyone out and about.

Despite this, Nathan and Victoria soon found the tavern after a few minutes of wandering around the area thanks to the sign above it. The building was quite old and derelict with moss growing on the brickwork, though the wooden doors and stained-glass windows were kept in good repair.

Victoria pushed the doors open and stepped into the pub with Nathan tailing her. The interior felt quite spacious but that may have been down to how empty it was, apart from the bartender and two men who were seated on bar stools – Clint and Joshua, the former immediately standing up to welcome his sister upon seeing her.

"So glad you're both okay!" Clint greeted gladly, hugging Victoria closely out of relief – so tightly that he felt her stomach rumble against him.

"Yeah we're alive – just really hungry now," Victoria replied warmly, weary from travelling on various buses for the last few hours. During the siblings' exchange, Nathan noticed that Joshua had remained sat at the bar, despondently staring off in the distance.

"Then we'd best get something to eat, we'll need as much strength as we can get for what comes next," Clint acknowledged, already looking ahead to the mountain expedition. "Nath, you mind holding the booth for us?" he asked of his nephew.

However, Nathan didn't respond. Victoria and Clint soon realised that he and Joshua had their attention caught by the same thing – a television in the corner of the tavern that was broadcasting some breaking news. On the monitor, they could all see a report that Anil Ali had been captured for treason, having been found hiding in his walk-in freezer. Footage of the arrest aired shortly after which showed Anil drunk and shouting obscenities at the authorities that had to be censored while they bundled him into the police car.

As amusing and satisfying as it was to watch Anil's downfall, it was then followed by a haunting reminder of what he was being apprehended for. Videos played of some of the teachers at Silver Dawn Comprehensive getting interviewed, though their faces and voices were being disguised to keep them anonymous. They opened up about what Mr Jones had announced to them about Anil ordering Maris to destroy the school, each providing the same testimony that would incriminate the traitor. The final interviewee spoke about how much he'd admired Mr Jones and seemed to choke up when they brought up how the headmaster had sacrificed himself to save their life. Though his vocals had been altered thanks to editing, the disclosure of those details was enough for Nathan to deduce that this was

Joshua talking. Any doubts of this were erased when his cousin lowered his head mournfully as his blurred visage appeared on the screen.

Once the bulletin had ended, Nathan made his way to the booth as Clint gently dragged a dejected Joshua away from the television so that the cousins could sit together while he and Victoria could order the food and drinks to the table. When it was just the two of them, Nathan saw how gloomy Joshua was and awkwardly tried to snap him out of his funk.

"Hey, they got him…" Nathan whispered, referring to Anil's arrest. "He'll pay for what he did…" he tried to reassure Joshua, but he remained dejected. Nathan sighed as he tried to find the right words. "I'm sorry about Mr Jones. I know how much he meant to you…" he sympathised which finally drew a surprising reaction from his elder cousin.

"Mr Jones wasn't the one who leaked that recording – I was…" Joshua confessed, shocking Nathan as he reminded him of the audio of Anil's conversation with Maris that the headmaster had claimed responsibility for. "I-if I hadn't have done that, he might still be here…along with everyone else who died…t-their blood's on my hands…" Joshua stated, his head still lowered with his gaze fixed on his trembling palms.

Nathan was taken aback by this revelation, realising that this was what Joshua was on the cusp of telling him when they were back in the collapsing school. There was about half a minute of silence between the two of them as Nathan digested this information, comprehending the mixture of emotions that he was experiencing. Their friction was detected by Victoria and Clint who, unbeknownst to their sons, started to concoct a plan to get them to mend fences. Meanwhile, Nathan saw that his cousin was punishing himself and instinctively uttered something to Joshua in the hopes that it would put his mind at rest.

"Josh…just remember that…you weren't the one who ordered the attack…and you weren't the one who made the fissure happen…" Nathan insisted. He couldn't bring himself to say anything more than that because he still felt anger, even a sense of betrayal towards his cousin for keeping so many secrets about the war from him.

Instead, while Joshua quietly mulled over his words, Nathan pulled out his phone to see if there had been any notifications from Thomas and Abbie. To his delight, they had both messaged to say they were expecting to get to the Raging Dragon Tavern in just under an hour.

"By the way, Thomas, Abbie and their families are coming with us too," Nathan bluntly told his cousin, realising that Joshua and Clint likely didn't know that previously.

"Oh…yeah, the more the merrier I guess…" Joshua remarked listlessly, still hung up on his failure to save Mr Jones. Another awkward pause followed until Joshua thought to ask a further question. "I-I managed to get Lucy home…is she not joining as well?" he wondered.

"I already know that Lucy's safe," Nathan affirmed brusquely. "We spoke on the phone before we left the house. And no, she's not coming. She told me her mom had made a deal to keep them both protected with the Alis so I told her she should stay with her…"

"Right, I see…" Joshua responded with nothing else to add.

As the two young men fell silent once again, they were mercifully joined by Victoria and Clint who tried to overcompensate for the tension between them by exchanging stories of their times as children. It did little to smooth relations though with Nathan still feeling resentful towards Joshua who remained consumed by guilt. The atmosphere was temporarily broken when the drinks and later, the food arrived which had all been placed on Clint's tab at his insistence. Everyone ravenously consumed each morsel of food on their plates, famished from the travelling they had done thus far today, but also to fortify themselves for the mountain-climbing that was soon to come.

The minutes passed by until Thomas arrived at the tavern with his mom, Melissa Cartwright, two faces that Nathan was happy to see. The two friends immediately began to catch up with Nathan filling Thomas in about his conversations with Lucy, both before and after the calamity. Similarly, Victoria and Melissa each shared their concerns over the mutual hatred that their sons had for Chimera, both agreeing that they wanted to get them far away from the invading terrorists.

A quarter of an hour later, Victoria, Clint and Melissa were trying to motivate a morose Joshua, telling him that there was nothing more that he could have done to save Mr Jones. However, their attempts were disrupted when a coarse, unkempt man abruptly entered the pub followed by a short, impatient woman, the pair of them bickering as the former stomped his way to the bar and demanded a beer. Nathan's and Thomas' attention was caught when the tavern doors swung open again and they saw an embarrassed Abbie shuffle her way in, holding her tired younger brother Ben in her arms.

"Dad! Do you really have to drink now?!" Abbie hissed.

"We're uprooting our lives! I think the occasion calls for it, you snobby cow!" her father retorted.

"Frank! Don't talk to her like that in public!" the mother snapped at him.

"Oh, give it a rest Linda, you're doing my head in already!" Frank grumbled before picking up the beer glass that had been placed on the counter and greedily guzzling from it. Linda sighed defeatedly as she pulled a stool out and took a seat, still keeping a distance from her husband.

"Fine! Whatever! One for me too barkeep!" she requested loudly. While the money was passed to the bartender in exchange for the beverages, Abbie's eyes met with Nathan's and Thomas', her friends flashing her a sad, sympathetic smile in return for her mortified visage.

More meals were soon ordered to the table for Thomas' and Abbie's families, everyone knowing the importance of conserving their energy. With ten people now in the party, it became necessary to occupy multiple tables. Seeing that Abbie needed to have a break from her parents, Nathan and Thomas offered to sit with her and Ben on a smaller table. That left Victoria, Clint, Joshua, Melissa, Frank and Linda to share a bigger one. Despite this, Victoria and Clint gave a wide berth to Abbie's parents, uncomfortable with their drinking which served as a painful reminder of how their own mom and dad were killed by someone driving over the limit.

There was a moment before the food arrived when the clock struck 4pm. This was noticed by Thomas who woefully pointed out to Nathan and Abbie that they would have normally finished school at this time. Because of the invaders, they knew those days were behind them now. The fissure had only happened around seven hours earlier, yet the time had crawled so much since then, it was as if the disaster had occurred days ago. It wasn't raining outside, but Nathan, Thomas and Abbie mutually agreed to follow recent traditions and have a minute of silence to pay respect to their lost school. Although he wasn't on their table, Joshua had observed what they were doing and copied their actions, respectfully closing his eyes and carrying thoughts of Mr Jones while the adults around him continued conversing.

Once the remaining meals arrived, Thomas, Abbie and their families set about to devouring everything that lay on their plates. Thirty minutes later, once all the food had been consumed and the dishes had been cleared, Clint suggested to everyone that they should start climbing Mount Tamara soon. Taking this as the signal to make final preparations, each person took it in turns to go to the toilets, the youngest ones going first. After Thomas, Abbie and Ben returned, Joshua, Victoria and Melissa ventured up to the bathroom while Clint went to the bar to pay the tab. With the parents out of earshot,

Nathan took the opportunity he'd been waiting for to broach a subject to Thomas and Abbie.

"Guys, I need to talk to you about the black aura…" he informed them.

Before they could continue, Abbie shushed the others because she could see that Ben was drifting off to sleep. As soon as she was convinced that he was settled, she nodded to Nathan, indicating that it was okay to talk.

"I was wondering *how* the hell you survived in that place…" Thomas whispered, remembering the fear that he and Abbie felt when Nathan was seemingly trapped in the centre of the fissure. "It activated again, didn't it?"

"I-is that true…?" Abbie questioned with concern.

"Yeah, it's true…" Nathan confirmed. "Except this time, I saw it with my own eyes…"

"What?!" Thomas gasped as Abbie's eyes widened, both startled to hear this. "Are you certain?!"

"There's no doubt," Nathan reinforced firmly. "Lucy and I nearly fell to our doom in that chasm – we were hanging by a thread. I pulled us up to safety by what I thought was sheer willpower at first. Until we both saw my hand glowing with that black aura…"

"I thought you two looked spooked when I found you…" Abbie recalled. "I mean, almost dying would do that too but it seemed like there was more to it somehow – now it all makes sense…"

"It wasn't just that though. Unlike the times before, I didn't lose consciousness. I remember everything that happened," Nathan explained. "Which means…"

"That you weren't possessed by it like last time…" Abbie deduced, the memory of Ranjit being beaten up by a Nathan influenced by the black aura only a week prior still fresh in her mind.

"Well, that's great news!" Thomas asserted excitedly. "It shows that the power can be controlled!"

"There's more as well," Nathan stated. "Before the earthquakes struck the school, I was in the library and managed to take a book with me. I've got it in my bag now. It's called *'Demons, Dragons and other Servants of the Devil'* and there's a section in there about the black aura…"

"Are you serious?! What did it say?!" Thomas remarked, trying to keep his voice lowered for Ben's sake, though he was struggling to contain his enthusiastic curiosity.

"The book referred to it as *'The Devil's Spirit',*" Nathan detailed, thinking carefully about specific lines that he could remember from the tome. "It's all wrapped up in my clothes right now, but I can show it to you properly once we've crossed the sea. Off the top of my head though, it basically said that the power awakens when the vessel – which I guess is me – is triggered by an intense emotional reaction related to being in danger…"

"That does check out with the other occasions," Abbie acknowledged thoughtfully.

"Anything else?" Thomas probed.

"Um…" Nathan uttered, focused on evoking any memories within the chapter that stood out to him. "Well, it did say that the power *should* be uncontrollable with the possessee having no memory of using the aura. Although that does seem to be contradicted now…" he pondered, with Thomas and Abbie listening intently. "Oh, and it also stated that for a short period of time, the Devil's Spirit grants the user invincibility and an unlimited amount of power, the amount being dependent on the circumstances…"

Thomas and Abbie were astounded at what they were hearing and needed to take a moment to comprehend all the information that Nathan had given them. Unbeknownst to them, Joshua had emerged from the bathroom, passing his dad who had paid the bar tab, and had seemingly been drawn to the nearby slot machine. However, his attention was quickly diverted when he overheard their discussion. Curious, he stood at the machine with his back to them, secretly eavesdropping on the three. Thomas was the first to offer his thoughts to Nathan.

"Nath…this could be huge!" he claimed eagerly, something that surprised Abbie.

"Y-you think so…?" Nathan asked interestedly.

"Absolutely! Invincibility *and* limitless power?! If that's true, this could even be the key to stopping Maris!" Thomas declared.

It was a proclamation that caused Nathan's eyes to sparkle with hope. The same notion had been quietly forming in the back of his mind since Lucy had highlighted that he'd essentially *controlled* the Devil's Spirit during the fissure. If he could find out the secret to mastering the power, it seemed feasible to him that he could get revenge on Maris for his dad. Behind him, Joshua wrinkled his forehead out of inquisitive trepidation for what his younger cousin might be getting himself involved in. To his relief though, Abbie chimed in on the debate.

"Guys, I think we're getting ahead of ourselves," she muttered to the pair. "Something called 'the Devil's Spirit' doesn't exactly *sound* like a good thing. Plus, we don't even know *how much* of that book is true yet. Part of it has already been disproved when Nathan retained his memories of using the power. What if the other parts are false too?" Abbie argued.

Nathan and Thomas didn't have a counterargument to this as demonstrated by their lack of immediate response. "Ugh...I guess that's possible..." Thomas conceded, unable to hide the deflation in his voice. This threatened to puncture the hope of the three friends until Nathan realised that there was currently no concrete proof to suggest that Abbie was completely correct either. Thus, he knew what needed to be done next.

"Well, if we don't have an answer right now, we'll just need to do some research into it," Nathan decided rationally, something that caused Joshua to raise his eyebrows, pleasantly surprised by his solution and maturity. "You're right Abbie, we shouldn't be rushing into things – not like I did with Ranjit anyway. But we can't lose hope either..." he continued, conveying a sentiment that seemed to raise Thomas' and Abbie's spirits again. "I have a good feeling that the answer is in that book somewhere. No matter how long it takes, I'll get to the bottom of it myself..." Nathan vowed resolutely. He shuffled in his chair, about to grab his backpack that he'd left on the other table, however Thomas grabbed his arm before he could stand up.

"Nath, I'm not letting you do this alone mate. You're like a brother to me after all..." he told him firmly, taking Nathan aback.

"T-Tom...y-you..." he stammered, visibly getting choked up by his friend's declaration.

"Like we said before, it's going against Chimera, so we're in this together!" Thomas asserted.

"The three of us," Abbie echoed, voicing her support too. "We'll find a way..."

Feeling touched by their offers, Nathan hesitated for a moment before nodding to accept their cooperation. He then stood up from his chair to retrieve his belongings and finally noticed that Joshua was positioned at the slot machine with his back to them. It crossed his mind that his cousin had sneakily listened into their conversation, however Victoria, Clint and Melissa returned from the bathrooms before Nathan could confront him about it.

"Okay, if we're all ready, we should start making our move now before sunset..." Clint announced, seeing that the party were all present.

Immediately, everybody got up from their seats and made sure they had everything they needed for the climb. Nathan and Victoria grabbed their luggage bags and rucksacks, along with Clint, Thomas and Melissa. The latter also picked up a tourist pamphlet that caught her eye, one that detailed some of the history and facts about Mount Tamara.

Meanwhile, Frank and Linda were starting to bicker over who should carry what during the trek up the mountain. This prompted Abbie to head over to diffuse the situation, all the while holding a sleeping Ben in her arms and carrying both their backpacks on her shoulders. This was spotted by a distant Joshua, briefly distracting his mind from dwelling on Nathan's refusal to give up hope, even in the face of Maris' godlike might. He held a newfound admiration for Abbie, his lips curling up into a small, appreciative smile while watching her care for her little brother.

"Josh, are you okay son?" Clint called out to Joshua, placing a hand on his shoulder and snapping him out of his trance.

The young man turned to find his dad, Victoria and Nathan looking at him, having detected that his mind was elsewhere, though assuming it was due to Mr Jones. His eyes met with Nathan's for a moment and it was as if he could see a fierce fire burning in them, so brightly that he almost winced. Yet in that instant, there was a reassuring quality about it that reignited his own passion, one that almost died along with his mentor hours earlier.

"Yeah…I will be…" Joshua replied to Clint, unwavering in his answer.

"In that case, we'd better get going. Time's a-wastin'!" Nathan insisted in an upbeat tone, almost automatically as he and Victoria headed towards the exit first with Clint tailing them.

"I'll be right behind you…" Joshua spoke under his breath, quietly blown away by his younger cousin's resilience.

With that, he made his way out of the tavern doors followed by Thomas, Abbie and their families to join Nathan, Victoria and Clint. Once they were outside, the next phase of their journey towered over them. Everyone knew that it was going to be arduous, but it was their best option of escaping the country right now and they were determined to traverse it for the sakes of keeping one another safe from Chimera. As that sentiment stuck within the minds of Nathan and the others, they all marched purposefully towards Mount Tamara…

Chapter 20

As the minutes of the day passed by, the sun slowly began to disappear from view behind Mount Tamara as Nathan, Thomas, Abbie, Joshua and their parents ascended their way up the slope. Very little conversation was had in the early stages because at Clint's instruction, everybody placed all their effort into the hike, huffing and puffing with each stride taken. The further up they all scaled, the more obscure the town beneath them became until the buildings were barely specks to them.

Treading up the rough and rocky surface certainly took its toll on everyone, especially after the exhausting events that had transpired today. There were a few breaks that needed to be taken between walking, mainly by those who lacked the stamina like Nathan, Thomas, Frank and Linda, their leg muscles throbbing as they panted for breath.

The sky started to darken, the final rays of sunlight fading whilst the group continued their trek upwards. Seeing this and knowing that the higher they travelled, the colder it would get, each person slowed their pace, choosing to take a more leisurely stroll to reduce the chances of setting up camp at an altitude with freezing temperatures during midnight. Clint and Joshua continued to lead the rabble with Victoria and Nathan closely behind them, the latter limping lethargically on his aching feet. A few feet away from them were Melissa and Thomas, the former supporting her weary son who had his arm draped over her shoulder. While she was doing this, Melissa was also taking the opportunity to read through the pamphlet that she'd picked up from the Raging Dragon Tavern.

"Ugh…mom, do we really have to climb the whole thing…?" Thomas grunted, wheezing with each word that he spoke.

"Well, according to this," Melissa replied as her eyes scanned over the brochure. "There's a large tunnel a third of the way up Mount Tamara that goes all the way through to the other side. It should be a suitable shortcut for us…much to your relief, I bet?" she disclosed, knowing how exhausted he felt.

"Th-that's putting it mildly…" Thomas gasped. "So the mountain just formed with a cavern already inside it? That's handy…"

"There's actually some interesting folklore written about this mountain here," Melissa added, continuing to read from the pamphlet. "It says that Mount Tamara was speculated to have been forged during a battle between two dragons a very long time ago. Some believe that to be the reason for certain areas of the mountain appearing quite refined and sculpted – particularly the tunnel within the centre and the summit being completely flat…"

"Wow…y-you're pretty into that leaflet…" Thomas remarked, detecting the enthusiasm in Melissa's voice and seeing how wide-eyed she was when browsing through it. "Then again, you always loved when you came across those kinds of legends…"

"Yeah, I did," Melissa acknowledged. "Speaking of which, when we get to Lyrasia, I've been thinking that I may try and make some money as a freelance journalist, just until we come up with a plan of where to go next…"

"Really?" Thomas uttered in surprise. "You've not done that since Etraco-…s-since I was born…" he reflected pensively.

"Hey, I helped Nathan before, didn't I?" Melissa replied, reminding her son of how she helped clear his best friend's name after the Tobias incident.

"Oh yeah…" Thomas uttered in realisation. "Still, it's been a long time since you've done it on a regular basis…"

"I know. But with things the way they are, it might be time for me to take that risk again…" Melissa stated resolutely.

"I see…" Thomas responded, almost unsure of what to think of it at first. After a few seconds had passed though, he followed up with some words of encouragement. "Well, if that's what you want to do, then I believe in you, mom!" he urged supportively.

In response, Melissa with her arm already around Thomas' waist to keep him propped upright, gripped him lovingly near the ribs in silent appreciation as they plodded along the craggy mountain terrain.

Meanwhile, Frank and Linda were tailing behind them, grumbling about the aches and discomfort they were suffering before bickering with one another over who was in more pain. They were so engrossed in their petulant squabbles that they'd failed to realise that their children, Abbie and Ben, the last members of the group were lagging as the older sibling felt the fatigue from carrying her brother throughout the majority of the hike.

This did however get observed by Joshua who had instinctively looked back to see how everyone else was coping with the walk. Not wanting anyone to get left in the dust, he told his dad that he was going to fall back to help the others before leaving him with Nathan and Victoria. On his way to Abbie's and Ben's location, Joshua passed Frank and Linda who didn't even acknowledge him because they were still mid-argument. He did everything to disguise his dissatisfaction at their behaviour, instead choosing to focus his attention on Abbie as he approached her.

"Hey, you doing okay back here?" Joshua asked, something that a bewildered Abbie automatically tensed up to upon hearing.

"Why do you care?" Abbie retorted cynically. "I thought I was just some quitter that you wanted to keep away from your cousin, afraid I'd be a bad influence on him!"

"Look, for what it's worth, I was wrong to say that..." Joshua confessed with a reluctant sigh. "And you were right before – about you being there for Nathan when I wasn't..."

This declaration left Abbie speechless for a few moments, never expecting him to actually admit fault. Eventually though, she broke her silence.

"He and Thomas have been there for me too...and after what I did to them in the past, they had every right to turn me away. Yet, they still accepted me when I was alone..." Abbie accepted, reflecting on her brief but regrettable period being affiliated with Ranjit. "I-I even got a job to pay my way towards martial arts lessons again – well, until we had to evacuate, that is – but it was thanks to them encouraging me..."

"Oh...wow, I-I didn't know...t-that's really commendable..." Joshua babbled awkwardly. He then glanced back up the mountain to see that the others were still walking ahead of them, the distance between them widening. "W-we need to catch up with the rest of the group," he told her. "I-If you like, I can carry Ben for you..." Joshua proposed, addressing the sleeping child in her arms. Though appreciative of his offer, Abbie initially frowned and wrinkled her nose, hesitant to put Ben in the care of someone who was still only an acquaintance to her. Understanding this though, Joshua reassured her. "You've been carrying him almost the entire trip, you need some rest. I promise I won't drop him – I'll be careful not to."

"Well...okay then..." Abbie finally relented. "But break your promise and all your karate and army training won't stop me from breaking *you*..." she added with a stony stare, though her face cracked into a smirk.

Abbie gently transferred Ben from her arms to Joshua's, being careful not to disturb his slumber. As they started to move, Clint toddled alongside Victoria and Nathan at the front of the pack, the two adults looking to address the schism between their sons.

"Hey Nath..." Clint called out to his nephew, drawing his attention. "Victoria and I...w-we know that things have been frosty between you and Joshua for a while now."

"Uncle Clint, I get it's difficult for you both, but you can't just force us to mend bridges like that. We're not exactly little kids anymore..." Nathan pointed out.

"Actually, I want to hear things from your perspective," Clint insisted, alarming Nathan who hadn't anticipated such a response. "I mean, I'm his dad but I know my son isn't perfect – he's certainly been tunnel-visioned about joining the army, I can see how he'd lose sight of other things around him. It's only fair I hear your side of things..." he explained with Victoria nodding approvingly of what he was saying, confident that all was going according to their plan.

Knowing that Clint was prepared to listen to him, Nathan relaxed and opened up to him about his grievances with Joshua, starting with his cousin's earlier revelation about leaking the voice recording of Anil's confession without consulting anyone first.

Simultaneously, Joshua and Abbie stomped their way across the uneven ground, taking big strides in their efforts to close the gap between them and the others. The two plodded along quietly, still unsure of what to say to one another given their tenuous history. A few minutes later however, Abbie opted to break the tension.

"Josh...c-can I ask you something personal?" she asked coyly.

"Depends what it is," Joshua answered frankly.

"Okay, well...don't feel you have to answer if it's still raw, but...Mr Jones seemed to mean a lot to you. W-why was that...?" Abbie quizzed, hesitant to broach the question.

Joshua was also taken aback at first. He was still processing the headmaster's death but after a brief pause, he decided that talking about it might help him to come to terms with the loss.

"M-my third year at Silver Dawn...was a really difficult time for me... for a number of reasons," Joshua recounted. "To start with...around the time the school year started...my mom died from an overdose..."

"O-oh yeah, I-I remember Nathan telling me this a few days ago…" Abbie murmured. "You said an overdose – w-was it medication…?"

"Not exactly the *prescribed* kind…" Joshua commented bitterly. "She left my dad for a rich wheeler-dealer called Pierce two years prior. I could have forgiven that if he was decent, but I got bad vibes from him right away. Once their honeymoon phase was over, apparently Pierce's debts began to mount up and he took cocaine to try and get by. He dragged mom down with him and got her hooked on the stuff too…" he grumbled, the disgust seeping out in his voice. "I even remember her coming round to the house wanting to see me while high as a kite. Dad didn't want me being around that so he turned her away and told her not to come back until she'd sorted herself out. T-that was the last time I saw her…before she…"

"That's awful…" Abbie empathised. "It really is the worst – addiction…"

"Addiction? More like greed…mom was always like that…only thinking of herself…" Joshua scoffed.

"Hmph, who does that remind me of…?" Abbie replied, looking ahead at her parents who were still rowing, completely oblivious to their children trailing behind them.

"Anyway," Joshua continued, keen to move away from painful memories of his mother. "I'd struggled with my grades the last two years – I know I'm not exactly smart, but my family situation didn't help much so you can imagine how much they suffered after mom died. I did some tests later that year though and I got diagnosed with dyslexia which was a lot to take in. And then to top it off, Nathan started getting bullied because of the incident where Lucy almost got kidnapped…"

"Yeah, you really had a lot to contend with…" Abbie recognised. "The school should have understood that though, surely?"

"Have Nathan and Thomas told you about the previous headmaster, Mr Nelson?" Joshua questioned.

"The name rings a bell, but it was only mentioned in passing…" Abbie confirmed as she thought back to previous conversations.

"Well, the school's public image was in the toilet around that time due to a high number of failing grades. As a result, Mr Nelson wanted to improve its profile – by any means necessary…" Joshua explained.

"That wasn't done by getting the students more engaged with their studies, was it…?" Abbie guessed.

"No, it wasn't," Joshua verified. "Instead, he was more focused on trying to remove any underperforming students that he saw as a hindrance to the school's image."

"And how did he go about doing that?" Abbie quizzed anxiously.

"By making the school environment as hostile as he could for us," Joshua answered coldly. "He'd go out of his way to humiliate me whenever he had the chance, chip away at my confidence, play on my insecurities in front of other students – it got so bad that I wanted to switch schools which is exactly what Mr Nelson was hoping for..."

"That's despicable!!" Abbie exclaimed, appalled. "B-but you didn't leave..."

"All thanks to Mr Jones..." Joshua praised proudly. "He was the deputy head at the time and the only teacher willing to give me a chance, who actually helped me believe in myself again when I was at my lowest. It was because of him that I discovered my strength in sports and he helped me to find my calling...joining the army..."

"So that's why," Abbie remarked, finally understanding the impact that Mr Jones had on Joshua. "I'm glad he was there for you then...but man, what a scumbag Mr Nelson was!"

"It wasn't just me whom he targeted. He also had it out for any students that he deemed problematic...and after rumours spread about Nathan almost killing one of those thugs with a brick, he became a marked man too...Mr Nelson was the one who pushed Nathan to...to attempt suicide..." Joshua revealed gloomily.

"No..." Abbie uttered in barely a whisper out of a mix of disbelief and disgust.

"I heard it all myself," Joshua stated. "I snuck into Mr Nelson's office to try and find some evidence that would incriminate him. I'd previously spied on him while he was on the phone to Anil and was convinced that he'd been bribed to allow Ranjit to join the school after being expelled from his last one. That's when I heard the door handle turning, so I quickly hid in the cupboard. Once I saw Nathan in the room, I started recording everything, all the vile things that Mr Nelson was filling his head with – saying how it might be better if he wasn't around..."

"H-how could someone be so evil?!" Abbie spat furiously.

"I sent the audio to Mr Jones as proof of Mr Nelson's corruption. Long story short, it led to him getting struck off from his position and jailed with

Mr Jones taking over as headmaster. Still, I'll never forgive Mr Nelson for that…" Joshua said as he finished his anecdote, Abbie nodding in agreement with his final statement on the matter.

"Someone in that role abusing the trust of the students he's meant to protect – no kid should have to go through that…" Abbie commented solemnly.

For a brief moment, Joshua and Abbie got distracted as Ben seemed to squirm in the former's arms before settling again.

"Well, nobody this young should have to experience all of this…life really can be cruel…" Joshua lamented, looking down at the young lad with a soft expression.

"True, but take it from me, my brother's a lot tougher than he looks," Abbie declared. "With our parents, he's already seen and endured more than most kids his age should. Besides, even in times where Ben doesn't feel so strong, I'll be there to support him."

Hearing Abbie assert this, Joshua couldn't help but think about his cousin. He gazed off into the distance past Frank, Linda, Thomas and Melissa to Nathan's location where he was talking with Clint and Victoria, just about done recapping the events that had led to the tension between them.

"In short, I just can't believe that he kept so much about the war hidden from me," Nathan summarised to his uncle. "I mean, him knowing about Maris, Chimera, Anil's betrayal and reporting him to the police – I can get past all that. But hiding the truth about how dad was killed? That's the one thing I can't forgive…"

"Yeah, I understand. I'd have felt the same way if I was in your shoes…" Clint conceded. "Although I can't speak on Joshua's behalf, I'm certain that he wouldn't have done that to hurt you. If anything, I think he knew that hearing how futile the war really was would have been more painful for you and wanted to spare you from that," he clarified while Nathan listened carefully.

"And it wasn't just Joshua. After what happened today, we've all only just learned the real truth on the news about what we're up against. The government probably issued strict instructions to the soldiers not to leak the truth to try and prevent widespread panic," Victoria added.

When his mother brought this up, Nathan reflected on his encounter with Bradley at the memorial two weeks ago. He remembered how cagey the soldier was and considering what they now knew about him being the sole survivor of the hurricane, his evasive demeanour now made complete sense to him.

"I know…I get how heavy the burden must have been for him to carry…" Nathan acknowledged. "I just wish he trusted me enough to be honest with me. And yeah, I know, he's only worrying about my mental health but this isn't like four years ago. I've been forced to grow a lot since then and I wish he could see that…" he rationalised, thinking about the development he'd undergone in the last few weeks alone.

Clint and Victoria heeded what Nathan was telling them, ensuring that his feelings were not dismissed. Meanwhile, as Joshua continued to carry Ben and walk alongside Abbie, her words about supporting her brother resonated with him, making him realise that she'd been doing the same with Nathan. He remembered his cousin's conversation with Thomas and Abbie from the bar, hearing his pragmatic yet optimistic attitude in such dire circumstances.

"Abbie…" Joshua called out to her, catching her attention. "You know earlier in the pub…when you and Thomas were talking with Nathan about something called the… 'Devil's Spirit' was it?" he asked coyly.

"Ha, I knew it! You were eavesdropping earlier!" Abbie accused triumphantly, causing Joshua to blush and guiltily bite his lip. "Nathan and Thomas may have had their backs to you but I saw you lurking at the bar! So what, is this you trying to get me to spill the beans?"

"While I *am* curious about that, I didn't bring it up for that reason," Joshua admitted. "During that talk you guys had, it made me realise how mature Nathan's gotten, especially considering all that's happened. I was afraid that if he knew the truth about Richard's death, he'd be ruled by revenge and do something reckless. But hearing him earlier – he was hopeful, yet not naïve with it; calculated rather than impulsive – I guess what I'm saying is, I've not given him enough credit," he explained before pausing for breath, while Abbie listened intently, nodding in agreement with his appraisal of Nathan. "He's come a long way from the boy I used to play guardian angel to…and not to downplay his willpower because I can see he has that in spades now, but I think your and Thomas' influence has helped him grow too. S-so…I guess I should say thank you…for being his friend…" Joshua finished gratefully.

"Am I hearing things, or did you *actually* just compliment me?" Abbie retorted mockingly with a smug grin on her face.

"I know, I know, I'm eating humble pie here!" Joshua chuckled. "But seriously, you guys looked out for him when I didn't, so I owe you one…"

"Well, all I have to say on that is this – you can always have too *little* support, but you can never have too *much* support," Abbie advised. "I'm still going to be there for Nath, but that doesn't have to stop you from doing the same. Now that we're leaving Entritica, maybe now's the time for you two bridge the gap…?"

"Hmm, I'll give it some thought…" Joshua replied, the sincerity apparent in his tone. "You know Abbie, you are pretty wise for your age… Ben's lucky to have you…"

"I'm blessed to have him," Abbie claimed, gazing affectionately at her little brother as Joshua carried him. "Thanks for being so gentle with him."

"No problem. Also, don't think I forgot about you keeping your eye on me at the bar. Anything I should know about that?" Joshua teased playfully, Abbie's influence drawing this side out of him, making him think of something other than dwelling on the war for the first time in a while, even if just briefly.

"Ha, get over yourself!" Abbie chuckled, struggling to contain her beaming smile.

They both continued with their hike, picking up the pace until they caught up to their parents. During this time, Joshua gave meticulous consideration to Abbie's suggestion, quietly impressed with how smoothly she'd swayed him to her way of thinking. Deep down though, he knew that the time had come to make amends with his cousin.

****

Half an hour later, Clint noticed that most of the party were running on fumes and with night now upon them, made the decision to call it a day. It wasn't long before everyone was setting up camp, unfurling their sleeping bags and searching for the smoothest patch of ground to rest on. They also made sure to eat some of the food that the parents had brought with them to restore their strength.

More time passed by until one by one, the group started to fall asleep, succumbing to exhaustion. Although Abbie had woken him to make sure he ate something, Ben quickly drifted back into a slumber. While his sister tucked him into his sleeping bag, their parents, Frank and Linda started to snore their heads off. This left Abbie with the task of getting them into something padded to shield them from the icy mountain temperatures. Thankfully, Joshua came to assist her with the task, knowing the struggles that she'd had with them.

After Thomas began to crawl into his sleeping bag, Nathan ambled over to his own makeshift bed. Joshua watched him from afar as his cousin smoothed out any lumps in the material. Once he was done helping Abbie wrap her parents in multiple blankets, he decided to bite the bullet and confront Nathan. Joshua approached him just as he was knelt down on the ground, beating the creases out of the sleeping bag.

"Hey Nath…" Joshua addressed him, drawing his cousin to gaze up at him. "Y-you got a sec?" he asked gently. Nathan automatically glanced over to where Victoria was with the corner of his eye before giving an answer.

"Yeah sure, what's up?" he wondered.

"I-I just wanted to say…I'm sorry for shutting you out these last few months…" Joshua apologised. "With the war…with Richard…with everything…"

Nathan didn't say anything immediately, wanting to let his cousin get his words out so he could process them, the advice from Clint and Victoria still playing on his mind.

"I-I should have looked out for you more…a-and I can see now that I should have been straight with you from the beginning…" Joshua stuttered nervously as Nathan remained mute. A bead of sweat dripped down his forehead as he ran out of things to say, so he chose not to drag the moment out any longer. "Look, I-I don't expect you to forgive me after what I've done, but…just know that if you ever need my help with anything, I'll be there for you…" he proclaimed.

Joshua then turned away with his head lowered, about to leave his cousin in peace. Just as he made the first step forward however, Nathan finally broke his silence.

"Having to keep all of that stuff bottled up…that must have been really hard for you…" Nathan recognised sympathetically, taking his cousin by surprise. Joshua twisted his body around to look at Nathan, his body relaxing upon seeing his soft, forgiving expression.

"Yeah…it was…" Joshua responded listlessly. "And now…I can't help but think that if I had just opened up to you…I could have made better decisions than the ones I did…" he added, still harbouring guilt for the role he believed he played in indirectly causing the school's destruction.

"Josh…you should know that…I talked to Clint about you reporting Anil to the police…" Nathan confessed, to which Joshua took no exception. "We both agreed the same thing – that for all we know, Anil could have easily ordered Maris to attack the school anyway. At least this way, the public knows what a traitor he is and he can be brought to justice. You had the courage to make that possible…" he insisted, reminding Joshua of Mr Jones' final words to him about being a braver man than the headmaster. "And like I told you at the pub, you didn't create the fissure or call for it to happen. So please stop blaming yourself because Maris is the one who's at fault, not you!" Nathan asserted to his older cousin.

Joshua averted his gaze for a moment, taking time to contemplate Nathan's argument. Once it began to make sense to him, his feeling that he needed to punish himself began to diminish slightly. With that, he meekly nodded at his cousin, indicating that he would try to heed his suggestion. Sensing that Joshua was still shaken, Nathan sought to address this.

"How are you feeling…you know, after what happened with Mr Jones?" Nathan quizzed kindly. "I know how important he was to you…"

"I-I really miss him…I s-still can't believe he's really gone…all of it…" Joshua admitted earnestly as he mourned his mentor's death.

Hearing him express this gave Nathan a sense of deja vu as he recalled these very feelings when he learned of Richard's demise. With this shared pain between them, he instinctively felt a renewed connection to Joshua that had previously seemed unreachable. It was as though his older cousin felt the same way because the next question he asked Nathan was about his dad.

"How did you do it? How did you keep going after losing Richard? I'm really trying to stay strong with everything that's going on…but I-"

"Josh, it hasn't even been a day yet since the fissure…when I found out that dad died, I was just as lost as you feel right now…and I've missed him every day since…" Nathan explained. "But I keep going because I don't want to let his and Mr Jones' sacrifices be for nothing – so being strong is the only choice I have…"

Joshua nodded in understanding, a spark igniting within his eyes in response to Nathan's fiery spirit. In the background, Clint and Victoria, the only two adults still awake after Melissa had fallen asleep along with Thomas, watched on proudly as their sons reconciled. Similarly, Abbie was getting comfortable in her sleeping bag, also keeping a curious eye to see what become of the interaction between the two cousins.

"Y-you're trying to find a way of bringing down Maris aren't you…? I-I overheard you talking with Thomas and Abbie back in the bar…something about the 'Devil's Spirit'?" Joshua brought up.

"Yeah, that's right," Nathan confirmed unabashedly.

"D-do you…really believe that Maris has a weakness…?" Joshua queried, the tone of his voice mired by a conflicting mix of doubt and hope.

"I managed to grab a library book from the school before it collapsed. It's called *'Demons, Dragons and other Servants of the Devil'.*" Nathan informed him. "We already have some theories from it but we're going to keep researching it until we find something concrete."

"I see," Joshua replied. "In that case, count me in too. The more of us working together on this, the better our chances are of uncovering her secrets – how she can even create natural disasters and whether we can counter her power," he stated, pledging himself to aiding with their plan. Without hesitation, Nathan accepted the offer.

"Thanks Josh, once we're out of Entritica, I'll fill you in on all the details," he established, to which his cousin agreed.

"No more secrets from me, I can promise you that. You've got my full cooperation," Joshua reinforced.

"Good, because we're gonna need it – for dad's and Mr Jones' sake…" Nathan professed, the two cousins finally making amends.

On that note, Joshua left Nathan to settle down for the night, knowing that the group still had the rest of Mount Tamara to traverse in the morning. Having watched her friends get on the same page, Abbie drifted off to sleep, satisfied that their alliance and prospects were stronger than ever.

Though they'd been motivated to travel this far by sheer adrenaline, it wasn't long before Nathan, Victoria, Joshua and Clint also yielded to their fatigue and fell asleep. What had seemed like perhaps the longest day of their lives had mercifully drawn to an end. Tomorrow would be a new day and a step closer towards achieving their shared goal of exiting Entritica and crossing the sea to Lyrasia. Tonight though, they would rest as best as they could – both with the horrors of the morning's events and the hopes that the situation couldn't worsen any more than it already had…

Chapter 21

The next morning arrived with everybody waking up at the crack of dawn. The group spent just over the first hour of the day, warming themselves up after a night spent sleeping on the freezing cold mountain. Once ready, they were soon traversing their way back up Mount Tamara which was getting steeper and more difficult to scale the further up they climbed. It wouldn't be long before they would be unable to simply walk their way up the hill. With each strenuous stride that was taken over the stony surface, everyone was silently praying that it wouldn't be much farther until they found the tunnel that would take them through to the other side of the mountain.

To their delight, they reached this point one hour later as the opening of the passageway came into view, exactly as it was described in the pamphlet that Melissa had brought along. When Nathan gazed upwards in the direction of the summit submersed in clouds and glanced back to see how high they had actually climbed, he suspected that they had cleared half of the entire mountain. Everybody took time to appreciate the magnitude of this feat that they'd accomplished, letting the moment sink in for them. Feeling motivated by this achievement, it felt as though nothing could deter the group now.

Realising that the party should take a rest after hearing the exhausted wheezing of Nathan, Thomas, Frank and Linda, Clint and Joshua volunteered to venture into the tunnel so that they could scope out how safe it would be to journey through. While they were occupied with this, the other members of their troop took the opportunity to fuel themselves with food and replenish their stamina.

A few minutes passed by and as Nathan was munching into an apple, he received a text message from Lucy who, knowing that he was heading towards the outskirts of Entritica, asked him to let her know that he was okay. He typed out a brief response to reassure her before catching a glimpse of Abbie, a perplexed expression painted on her visage. He didn't have chance to question her about it though because Clint and Joshua returned from their reconnaissance mission, commanding everyone's attention.

"We've checked it out and nothing looks untoward in there," Clint relayed to the group. "Seems sturdy and wide enough for all of us to walk through."

"Also, some of you may be glad to hear this," Joshua chimed in. "But the path's all downhill from here."

Thomas breathed a loud sigh of relief, his body aching from the consistent exercise he'd been forced to endure yesterday. The other parents, Victoria, Melissa, Frank and Linda also appeared visibly thankful upon receiving this news, already fighting through fatigue. However, Abbie continued to stare off into space, having seemingly not heard what Clint or Joshua had told her which got noticed by the latter.

"Abbie? Abbie, are you okay...?" Joshua called out to her, snapping her out of her trance. "If you're feeling tired, the next leg of the journey will be a lot easier," he reiterated in an attempt to reassure her.

"S-sorry," Abbie replied hurriedly. "I was trying to concentrate...I swear I heard some noises just now..." she explained to the bewilderment of the others.

"N-noises? What kind of noises?" Melissa asked her curiously.

"Like rumbling noises," Abbie elaborated. "It's faint...but I'm sure I heard it..."

After hearing her vague description, everyone else quietened down to try and listen out for the sounds that Abbie was referring to.

"You must be imagining it!" Frank snapped dismissively, losing his patience with the exercise seconds later. Despite this claim though, Nathan was able to detect what sounded like a deep yet distant growl that occasionally oscillated in volume, escalating into a boom when it did so.

"No, I-I think I hear it too..." he cried, still carefully listening while the others watched him. "It sounds like it's coming from outside..." he guessed because he believed that the noises were echoing around them in the open air, rather than emanating from the tunnel. "I just can't tell *where* it's coming from..."

"M-maybe it's t-thunder...?" Ben squeaked timidly from behind Abbie.

"Thunder?! All the more reason to get in the tunnel then!" Linda exclaimed in a panic.

"True, we need to get moving. Everyone inside!" Clint instructed, keen to make some progress ahead of noon's arrival. As the group shuffled their way into the passageway, Thomas did take his chance to mumble something to Nathan and Abbie before they entered.

"Just a thought, is it possible that you're having PTSD from yesterday? It's understandable if so, yesterday was traumatic for all of us..." Thomas theorised.

Nathan and Abbie briefly contemplated this, realising that it wasn't out of the question. While the former decided to accept this after seeing that there were no dark clouds in the sky, making the chance of thunder unlikely, the latter was not so convinced. Nevertheless, with Clint lighting up the path with his flashlight, they followed suit and made their way inside.

The tunnel was wide enough for two people to travel side by side with Clint and Melissa leading the way, closely followed by Joshua with Thomas, Nathan with Victoria, Frank with Linda, and Abbie with Ben in that order. Upon travelling further into the passageway, Joshua, Victoria and Frank used their phones to provide more sources of light. Once the area was illuminated, the group could see for themselves that Joshua's and Clint's assessment of the passageway seemed to be correct. Not only were there some steel beams being used to prop up the earth above them, but the surrounding rock walls had also been delicately carved out, erasing any protruding imperfections that could be hazardous to hikers.

Joshua and Thomas could hear their parents discussing this in front of them as Melissa explained the efforts that explorers had taken to ensure that the tunnel was maintained, having read this information from the pamphlet. Clint seemed quite engrossed by what she was saying, his ears falling on each word she uttered, something that surprised Joshua.

"Didn't know my dad was so into history – I'd be bored silly if this was taught in class," he whispered to Thomas, baffled to watch the pair of them cracking jokes about what he deemed to be a dull topic.

"Seems like mom's enjoying herself too," Thomas commented in a hushed voice, watching how relaxed her body language was. "Never really seen her laugh like that around a man before. It's quite nice actually...she went through enough with my dad..."

"Ah...I-I see..." Joshua replied, not fully sure of what to say to Thomas' statement. "Well, while I'm thinking about it, I should tell you that when we get to Lyrasia, I'm gonna help you guys find a way to defeat Maris and Chimera," he informed him.

"Oh wow, Nath filled you in then?" Thomas deduced, shocked to hear this. "Are you sure about this? Abbie would be joining us you know…" he highlighted, still under the impression that they hated each other. Realising this, Joshua quickly corrected him.

"We made peace yesterday. I admit, I really misjudged her. Sounds like she's really kept you and Nath in line," he chuckled.

"I wouldn't go *that* far," Thomas laughed off. "Well, I suppose it will be handy having someone who's army-trained in the group. If the time ever came, maybe you could teach us how to fight against Chimera?" he wondered inquisitively.

"Y-you mean defend yourself against Chimera?" Joshua guessed, thinking this was what Thomas meant to say.

"Y-yeah, sure!" Thomas blurted out hastily, oblivious to the fact that his mother had overheard him, even though she was talking with Clint. Aware of her son's resentment towards Chimera and his terrorist father, Melissa discreetly frowned at the idea of him wanting to learn how to fight. She did hide this worry from Clint though when he asked her if anything was wrong after picking up on her perturbed expression.

Meanwhile, Abbie and Ben were at the end of the queue, closely behind their parents. The former was holding her brother's hand while they walked, her eyes focusing on the glow from Frank's phone. Each time the light flickered, she couldn't help but feel more uneasy and it felt to her as if the ground beneath her was starting to wobble.

"Abbie, a-are you okay…?" Ben quietly asked his sister.

"Hmm? Yeah, I'm fine bud. W-why do you ask?" Abbie replied, trying to sound upbeat through frantic breaths.

"Because you're hurting my hand…" Ben answered.

Hearing this, Abbie glanced downwards to see how tightly she was squeezing her little brother's hand, almost crushing it. She relinquished her hold immediately, mortified to see the discomfort etched on his face.

"Oh Ben, I'm so sorry, mate!" Abbie apologised profusely as he nursed his hand. "I-I don't know what came over me…"

A few seconds later, once the aching had subsided Ben tenderly grabbed Abbie's arm to her alarm, as though he sensed her distress. She felt his thumb stroke against her, his reassuring touch instantly calming her down.

"I got you sis…" Ben uttered softly.

"Thanks bro…" Abbie responded appreciatively. Although she felt comforted by Ben's presence, she couldn't fully rid her mind of the perception that the earth was shaking again like yesterday. She recalled Thomas' previous words about PTSD and started to believe that his theory was valid – that her mind was playing tricks on her, tormenting her with reminders of the fissure. Thus, Abbie tried to convince her brain that the mild shudders that she was experiencing weren't real as she continued down the declining path before her.

An hour elapsed with the group making much quicker progress through the tunnel than when they were struggling uphill the day prior. By midday, they had passed the centre of Mount Tamara which also happened to be the halfway point of the tunnel. To preserve the batteries of their phones, it was agreed that Thomas, Nathan and Linda would take over the duty of acting as torches from Joshua, Victoria and Frank respectively. From the lights of their phones and Clint's flashlight, the path was visible to all, remaining as smooth and devoid of any hazardously uneven terrain as the first half of the descent did. It was a testament to the hikers who had maintained the tunnel in such suitable condition for so long.

Having witnessed how Victoria and Joshua had extended and manoeuvred their arms to ensure that their phones were in the optimum positions to brighten the dark passageway, Nathan and Thomas tried to mimic their movements in order to best guide the others. Watching her son take charge in this manner, Victoria took the opportunity to heap praise on him.

"Nath, I just want to say that I'm so proud of how you've coped with all this," she said, beaming with delight. "Nobody would have blamed you if you'd crumbled from this much chaos, yet you've stepped up big time and been so brave."

"I-I'm just trying to do what dad would have wanted of me…he asked me to protect you after all…" Nathan claimed bashfully.

"And your father would be proud of the man you've become. Coming to terms with his passing, making peace with your cousin, leaving our home behind…" Victoria detailed, listing the ways that Nathan had showcased his growth over the last few weeks. "You've handled everything that's come at you without losing your way – as someone who went through that himself as a young man, Richard would have had all the respect in the world for you…"

"Yeah…well he knew it wasn't easy either. But there's a reason we were both able to keep going through hard times – because we both had you…" Nathan acknowledged, regarding his mother with love and gratitude for all that she had done for him. "Well, I'm lucky to *still* have you anyway," he added as Victoria did her best to not clam up.

"Y-you saying that reminds me…" she stuttered, wiping her eye as she spoke. "I-I meant to tell you this when we left the house yesterday, b-but there was just so much happening that it slipped my mind. We still have Richard too because I've brought him with us…"

"Brought him with us…?" Nathan echoed, not understanding what his mom was referring to. However, it dawned on him seconds later. "H-his ashes?!" he mouthed, startled by this.

"That's right," Victoria confirmed. "You said it yourself, he would have wanted to stay with me. And this way, the three of us can still be together."

"Oh…right, yeah of course!" Nathan replied, a little flustered by the revelation. "Sorry, I-I just never imagined that it would be under these circumstances…b-but yeah, I agree, it'll be comforting to have him nearby…"

"Don't worry, I've made sure that the urn is secure too," Victoria reassured.

She continued to talk however Nathan's mind began to drift elsewhere. His eyes were drawn to the ground, believing there to be a slight sensation in the soles of his feet, stemming from beneath the earth. While it was troublingly reminiscent of yesterday's earthquake, Nathan tried to assure himself that this was only in his head, searching around for any signs of a tremor in the hopes that he wouldn't find one.

To his dismay however, Nathan was able to make out from the glare of his phone light that the ground was shuddering, seeing the specks of dirt shift and dislodge from the hardened soil. Not just that, but from his recent experience, he could sense that the vibrations were slowly getting stronger. This wasn't just his imagination after all.

"Nath…Nathan! Is everything okay?!" Victoria called out to him softly after realising that he was distracted by something.

"Y-yeah I'm fine!" Nathan answered, putting on the best brave face that he could so as not to worry his mom. "I-I was just thinking about…a-about everything that you've done for me," he said, thinking on the fly. "L-listen mom, I never really took the chance to tell dad this…so I want you to know that…I-I'm really glad that I'm your son."

Victoria reached out for Nathan's hand, holding it affectionately to comfort him.

"I'm thankful to be your mom ever since the day you were born," she established firmly. "And as your mom, I'm going to keep you alive no matter what happens. So, let's hurry through this mountain and out of Entritica – what do you say?"

Nathan nodded vigorously, eager to get his mother and friends out of the passageway as the rumbling below began to escalate. "I love you mom," he uttered.

"I love you too, Nath," Victoria responded back.

The pair of them picked up the pace, taking bigger strides through the cavernous tunnel. Behind them, Abbie had noticed this through the darkness, looking past her parents to just about catch Nathan's legs abruptly moving twice as fast as they were moments ago. She quietly wondered where he'd got this urgency from, but her attention was diverted by her brother as he gripped her tightly, applying more pressure to her wrist.

"Ben? What is it?" Abbie whispered to him.

"T-the ground…I-I can feel it s-shaking…" Ben stammered nervously.

Abbie's eyes widened fearfully upon hearing him say this and realising that the earlier tremors were intensifying. It meant that the previous mild judders that she'd detected underneath the earth were not merely harrowing illusions after all, despite wanting to believe that they were. Sweat started to drip down from under her hair at the prospect of enduring such an ordeal again, yet Abbie's priority was still to reassure her brother, even if that meant temporarily lying to him until she'd alerted the others.

"I-I'm sure it's nothing mate…" Abbie claimed, keeping her voice calm for Ben's sake while she thought frantically to come up with a plan. She searched ahead through the gap between her parents, seeking help or an answer and spotted Nathan again. In that moment, she deduced from his agitated demeanour and the furious rapid pace that his legs were marching at that he was sensing the same pulsations beneath them. With this knowledge, Abbie knew that she could work with Nathan to make everyone else aware, but she needed to discuss this away from Ben so as not to upset him until necessary. "Ben, w-why don't you walk with mom and dad for a bit?" she suggested. "They seem pretty tired; I think you could cheer them up the same way you did with me."

"O-okay…if you say so sis…" Ben remarked reluctantly.

Once encouraged by Abbie, he walked in the middle of Frank and Linda before holding both of their hands. Though they were both initially taken aback by this, Abbie noticed that they did relax a bit more to have their youngest walking alongside them. Satisfied with this, she hurried past her parents so that she could catch up with Nathan. For a few seconds, she wandered ahead in the dimly lit cave with her arm outstretched, the force of the tremors below accelerating bit by bit with each step, until she was within reach of her friend and the light from his phone. Abbie placed her hand on Nathan's shoulder, startling him and Victoria, before spinning him around until he was face to face with her.

"H-hey, what's going on?" Victoria cried out upon seeing Abbie lock eyes with Nathan.

"You're feeling it too, aren't you…?" Abbie asserted, her pupils wavering along with the oscillations underneath them. Hearing the dread in her voice, Nathan instantly knew what she was referring to.

"It's happening again…more earthquakes…" he confirmed glumly, hating having to verify her worst fears – and his. Seeing that the others had come to a halt, Joshua, Thomas, Clint and Melissa backtracked their steps to find out what the commotion was about.

"What's happening?" Melissa questioned inquisitively.

"We need to start running, it's not safe in here!" Nathan warned them with Abbie nodding in agreement.

"I thought so. It's just like what happened yesterday…" Joshua stated, revealing that he'd also felt the shockwaves.

"Wait, you sensed them too?!" Thomas blurted, implying that just like his friends, he was aware of the tremors. "We've been walking together the whole way! Why didn't you say anything?!"

"I-I thought it was just my imagination…" Joshua muttered meekly.

"Can someone explain what's *actually* happening already?!" Frank yelled, annoyed by how obscure the teenagers were being.

"It's earthquakes, dad! Just like the ones we *barely* survived yesterday!" Abbie summarised bluntly, emphasising the gravity of their situation. "We have to get out of here now!"

"Well, I've not felt anything!" Frank disputed stubbornly.

"Dad, *we* were the ones who witnessed our school get destroyed…!" Abbie snarled through gritted teeth, quickly losing patience with her pig-headed father while Linda tried to keep Ben calm. "Don't try and tell me that I don't know what the signs of an earthquake are!"

"How do you know it's not just the trauma tricking you all?!" Frank argued arrogantly. "For all I know, you could just be hallucinating it!"

In that moment, the previously light tremors strengthened suddenly until they were violently rocking the walls of the tunnel, Ben clutching Linda's leg as the ceiling of rubble started to loosen with dust dropping down onto them.

"You convinced *now*?!" Abbie snapped, satisfied to see her dad silenced with no response now that the presence of the quakes could no longer be denied.

"Enough talking!! Let's move! NOW!!" Clint ordered decisively.

Heeding his instruction, Nathan and the others wasted no more time in vamoosing their way through the rest of the passageway. The earth above them continued to split apart as the falling dirt soon progressed to pebbles followed by bigger rocks. Everybody sprinted as hard as they could with as much energy as they could muster. Sweat poured from their foreheads, drawn out by a blend of fatigue and fear. Though the desperate descent downhill proved easier on the feet, even as the blood pumped vigorously to their thighs, Thomas still showed signs of wavering. Thankfully, he had Melissa and Joshua to act as supports to prevent him from tripping as they held him as upright as they could. With their speed and endurance, Clint and Abbie had little difficulty with evading the debris, whilst Nathan was also able to keep up, seemingly spurred on by Victoria's presence.

Unfortunately, the same could not be said for Frank, Linda and Ben who were trailing behind everyone else, neither parent having the stamina to keep up whereas the little lad's legs were not strong enough for the dash that this dangerous situation demanded. Nathan and the rest of the group, even Abbie, were so panicked that they were oblivious to this. That was until Ben stumbled over a stray rock, letting out a wail of pain upon collapsing to the ground. This alerted Abbie to her family's predicament and without hesitation, she leapt over to her brother's side, scooping him up off the floor into her arms.

Suddenly, the ground shook with an almighty force, sending the most powerful shockwave coursing throughout Mount Tamara yet, the group left perturbed by the rippling effects resonating within the tunnel walls. Abbie clung to Ben, sheltering his head in her shoulders while Nathan, Thomas, Joshua and the adults staggered around, trying to maintain their balance.

And then, inexplicably, the tremors subsided. Everyone steadied themselves as they detected the distortions in the earth fading away before the soil settled again. After a few seconds had passed, Victoria, Clint, Melissa, Frank and Linda began to relax, quietly grateful for the reprieve.

"I-is it over…?" Linda asked, almost pleadingly.

Encumbered with the memories of their life-threatening experience barely over twenty-four hours ago, Nathan, Thomas, Abbie and Joshua remained vigilant, using their phone lights to timorously survey the tunnel. As he was moving his phone around, Joshua had an epiphany, recalling what happened during his last moments with Mr Jones. Remembering how the roof above them had collapsed in his office, he raised his arm into the air towards the ceiling of the cave. He felt his heart sink by what he observed.

"No…it's not…" Joshua mumbled dejectedly in response to Linda's question. He then reached for Clint's flashlight, snatching it from his hand and shining it in the direction of the vault of the passageway. The beam revealed to the horror of everyone that the rocks above were breaking apart rapidly. Joshua guided the light further back into the tunnel behind them which demonstrated that the cracks had worsened, threatening to collapse…

Sure enough, it wasn't long before the group heard the reverberating ruckus of rubble tumbling down from deeper in the passageway. A quick flash of the torch showed that the tunnel was caving in – and it was approaching them fast!

"RUN!!!" Nathan instinctively screamed out upon seeing this.

With the threat of being crushed underneath the debris looming, everyone bolted away, throwing every ounce of energy they could into their legs. Abbie carried a tearful Ben while ushering her parents ahead, the two of them now motivated to avoid dying in the confines of a tomb, even if that meant having to run to do it. Nathan clasped Victoria's hand with his own, both of them propelling themselves forward for the sake of the other just as Joshua and Clint were tugging Thomas and Melissa along with them respectively, their ears deafened by the impending landslide.

To the relief of all, the opening of the tunnel finally came into view, brightening up the pathway and providing motivation to the group to make one last push towards the exit and outside to safety. As they got closer however, Abbie detected a familiar sound coming from beyond the hole leading out of the cave. It was the same repetitive booming noise that she'd heard before entering the passageway, only this time it sounded much louder and more violent, almost like explosions.

"Guys, I'm hearing a lot of noise coming from out there!" Abbie notified everybody.

"It is pretty loud!" Joshua acknowledged, able to hear it clearer being near the head of the party.

"Whatever it is, it can't be as bad as what's happening in here!!" Linda shrieked hysterically, preoccupied with outrunning the rockfall.

Not even Frank could argue with that statement. With that, everyone promptly ceased talking and hurtled towards the finish line as the tunnel they were just traversing through was reduced to ruins behind them. They kept running until they were feet away from the exit, at which point, the landslide closed in on them, seconds away from burying them. While Clint, Joshua, Melissa, Thomas, Victoria and Nathan were lucky enough to comfortably make it out with moments to spare, Abbie was forced to shove her parents out through the opening. She then followed this up by leaping with Ben in the nick of time to save their skins from certain doom as the last pieces of rubble collapsed and closed off the tunnel permanently.

Drained of energy after their distressing dash out of the cave, Nathan, Thomas, Abbie, Ben, Linda and Frank dropped down onto the rock-strewn terrain. Victoria and Melissa tended to their sons as Joshua helped Abbie and Ben to their feet with Clint doing the same for Frank and Linda – even though they were assisting the others, they still staggered around, their hearing distorted with the echoes of crashing rocks ringing in their ears.

Eventually, Nathan regained his senses, his vision clearing and his mother's face becoming less blurry. He was able to see that her mouth was moving, saying words to him that he was unable to hear until a few seconds later, when the resonances of the landslide finally died down.

"W-'re ok-y N-than…we g-t out of th-re…w-we're out of the woods now…" Victoria mouthed to her son before embracing him tightly. Nathan patted her on the back as a signal of reassurance that he'd recovered from the experience.

While his mother checked on Clint and Joshua after they'd helped Abbie's family, Nathan's focus was diverted by the noises he could hear as his hearing returned. Despite the sounds of heavy rock collisions now gone from his ears, this had now been replaced by loud booming clatters that resembled thunder, just as Abbie and Ben had described earlier.

Realising that these deafening rackets were coming from behind him, Nathan turned around to investigate – but his face immediately fell at what he saw.

"G-guys…" he uttered to everyone, drawing their attention. "We're not out of the woods…we're not out of the woods *at all*…" Nathan informed them dejectedly.

Victoria and the others cautiously stepped forward to see what Nathan was referring to. They were all rendered wide-eyed and horror-stricken when they gazed upon the scene ahead of them.

The ear-rattling turbulences they'd heard weren't thunderstorms – it was gunfire.

Before their eyes, everyone watched powerlessly as a platoon of their soldiers were engaging with hundreds of terrorists all wearing the mask of Chimera. On the one hand, the clashing of swords, the roar of firearms and the wails of agony were carried upwards into the air by the winds that amplified the unsettling sounds. Conversely, bodies slumped downwards onto the ground, blood splattering and soaking into the soil where they once stood.

Worst of all, the group slowly realised that their only means of turning back had been closed off to them.

They had unwittingly stumbled into, what the Entritican armies would label, no man's land…

⟶⊶⊷⟨◇⟩⊶⊷⟵

Chapter 22

Under the foreboding grey sky, Nathan and the others were frozen in fear at the sight of the warzone that lay before them. Ben started to weep as he witnessed the many corpses strewn across the wasteland, the soldiers often forced to step over their own fallen comrades so that they could continue battling the enemy. Abbie tried to comfort her brother, shielding him from the scene, however she too was shaken by what they were confronted with. Although a teenager, she was still a kid – it was impossible not to feel overwhelmed by such a despairing visual.

It was a sentiment shared by her friends, Nathan and Thomas, as well as her parents who all stared despondently at the fighting and bloodshed. Victoria and Melissa were left speechless, only able to provide reassurance to their sons by squeezing their hands tightly. Even Joshua, the one who had been trained for the army was rattled, his lips trembling and his arms shaking when faced with the true realities of war. As for his father, Clint, the expression that he wore was one of remorse.

"T-this is my fault…" Clint mumbled listlessly. "I brought us here…I never thought that Chimera would ever come this way…" he continued, feeling responsible for having suggested to cross the mountain in the first place.

"Clint, you can't think like that," Victoria told him, unwilling to let her brother shoulder that blame. "Chimera's invading Entritica, they probably have platoons covering all routes out of the country by now," she rationalised thoughtfully.

"Well, knowing that doesn't do us any good *now*, does it?!" Frank snapped out of both anger and panic.

"Alright, enough of that! The situation's dire enough without us all bickering!" Melissa declared, trying to restore order between the adults. "There's no other way around it – we're going to have to climb back up the mountain, but properly this time!" she determined.

"How are we going to do that?! We're all spent!" Linda wheezed, nursing her abdomen.

"What *other* choice do we have?! We can't risk staying here!" Melissa retorted.

Thomas raised his head, sizing up the mountain and although he hated to disagree with his mother, he could see where Linda was coming from. Everyone was exhausted, still reeling and panting for breath after their narrow escape from the collapsing tunnel, plus this side of Mount Tamara was much steeper than the one they'd traversed yesterday evening. It was practically vertical which made the prospect of clearing it by foot alone unfeasible. Thomas looked to his left and saw that Joshua was also assessing the cliff face, stepping towards it to place his hand on the craggy surface. After examining the integrity of the rock for a few seconds, he glanced back at his dad.

"Let me try climbing it first. I need to make sure it's safe..." Joshua proposed.

Clint gave an approving nod to his son who started to scale the colossal mound that towered over the group. Joshua pulled himself further up, carefully selecting protrusions in the rock that seemed the most stable while Nathan, Abbie and the others nervously watched him. There were a couple of anxiety inducing moments where Joshua almost lost his footing as pieces of earth broke away from Mount Tamara and dropped down to the ground below. It took a few minutes of climbing for Joshua to conclude that the sturdiness of the mountain had deteriorated because of the landslides. Unbeknownst to him however, a couple of Chimera soldiers had spotted him high up on the mountain in the distance, also alerting them to the presence of Nathan and the rest of the party intruding on the battle.

"I'll have to try another area...the rock around here is too weak now..." Joshua called down to them.

"Okay but come back down first," Clint advised. "We need to try and stay hidden..."

As soon as he heard this, Nathan realised that everyone had been so focused on observing Joshua that nobody had kept an eye on the soldiers fighting. He glanced over his shoulder and was greeted by a very unwelcome sight.

"Too late for that – we've got incoming!" Nathan warned the others.

Thomas, Abbie and their parents turned around and to their horror, found two of the terrorists charging in their direction, shrouded in black and menacingly brandishing their weapons at them. Clint instinctively jumped ahead, placing himself in front of the others to intercept the aggressors while Joshua, once he became aware of the impending danger, clambered down from the mountain to join his father's side.

As the threats got closer to them, even with Joshua and Clint ready to go on the offence, the friends and family that they were protecting braced themselves for the worst. Abbie embraced Ben, bravely preparing to use herself as a shield. Contrariwise, Frank self-interestedly cowered behind his wife Linda. Melissa automatically placed a protective arm in front of Thomas. Yet, when Victoria motioned to do the same, Nathan refused to be seen as helpless again and instead stepped forward to stand side-by-side with her, just as his cousin was defiantly doing against their foes alongside Clint.

Suddenly, just as the terrorists were feet away from engaging Joshua and Clint, they were struck down when two bullets pierced through them, the blistering racket of the gunshots reverberating in the air around them. The masked men slumped onto the ground while Abbie tried to cover Ben's eyes to prevent him from seeing the disturbing display.

The group didn't even have time to process their relief, for their attention was diverted by the sounds of plodding boots approaching nearby. Thankfully, these weren't enemies but rather allies, distinguishable by their camouflaged clothes and the fact that their faces were exposed, rather than concealed behind masks.

"You all shouldn't be here! It's far too dangerous!!" one of the men shouted out to them.

Nathan's eyes widened upon hearing the voice, one he recognised immediately. He turned away from the two bodies to find a familiar face in front of him.

"Bradley?" he uttered, surprised to see him again after their last encounter at the memorial service. Similarly, the weary young soldier, now dressed in uniform, couldn't contain his shock at crossing paths with Nathan once more.

"N-Nathan? I-is that you?!" Bradley blurted out in disbelief.

"Sir, you know this kid?" one of his comrades queried.

"Y-yeah, he's Richard's son…" Bradley responded, a tinge of sorrow seeping out in his words. It was telling how much he valued Richard by the way he neglected to mention that he even went to the same school as Nathan, viewing the former as the more significant tie that he had to the boy. Bradley's head tilted so that he could regard the rest of Nathan's accomplices, his focus first shifting to his mother next to him. "Then, you must be Richard's wife, Victoria…" the soldier deduced. "Y-you should know that he thought the world of you two…"

"The feeling was – *is* mutual," Victoria acknowledged, filled with mournful pride. Meanwhile, artillery thundered and swords clattered in the background behind Bradley whose eyes now lingered on Joshua.

"A-and you're Richard's nephew, a-aren't you…? I-I know you from somewhere else, don't I…?" he addressed Joshua, the teenager's visage now jogging his memory slowly.

"T-that's right. It's me, Joshua – from the year below you and Gill, remember?" Joshua affirmed. "You've both been together four years now, haven't you?"

"Huh, oh yeah, w-we did only leave Silver Dawn last year…" Bradley reminisced fondly. "So much has happened since then…" This was the second time since the memorial that Nathan had seen the soldier soften as he dwelled on memories of simpler times. But with the battle raging on ahead, the boy knew that now wasn't the time for carefree reflection.

"Silver Dawn's gone, Bradley," Nathan disclosed to him, snapping him back to reality. "It was destroyed by Maris…in another disaster…"

The reflective smile vanished from Bradley's face as he quietly digested this revelation, the cogs in his mind whirring over another thing that Maris had taken from him. Once the news had sunk in, the cries of comrades from his platoon reaching his ears again, he turned his head to address the two soldiers accompanying him.

"Men, stand guard. I need to talk with these civilians…" Bradley commanded firmly while disguising his devastation. The two companions followed his instruction without hesitation, turning around to assess the battle and keep watch for any more interlopers. With that concern tackled, Bradley returned his focus to Nathan and everyone else. "So, you all know about Maris and what she's capable of…?" he queried the group rhetorically.

"*Know* doesn't do it justice – we experienced the fissure with our own eyes! We barely escaped with our lives!" Abbie interrupted, almost spitting with passion as she spoke.

"It's true…Mr Jones was killed too…" Joshua verified to which Bradley breathed a regretful sigh in response, having also seen him like a mentor. "The news went public yesterday. Soon everyone in Entritica will know the truth of what we're up against…"

"It's not just the earthquake," Nathan stated while Bradley listened intently. "We also know about the tsunami…and the hurricane that killed my dad…"

"I-I see…" Bradley reacted, his eyes now wavering at the presence of Nathan and Victoria. "I-I'm sorry for lying to you both…a-about his death…" he apologised, feeling remorse for having concealed the truth of Richard's fate from Nathan at the funeral.

"I understand why you did it," Nathan relented, surprising Bradley. By now, he'd let go of any grudges that he may have previously held about this after making peace with Joshua. Having developed sympathy for the difficult choices that his cousin had faced, he recognised that Bradley was no different. "Besides, there are bigger things at stake right now," he noted, not losing sight of the dire situation that they had found themselves in.

"Y-you're all trying to evacuate Entritica…aren't you?" Bradley deduced sadly.

"Yes," Victoria confirmed. "I'm sorry, we can't possibly thank you all enough for fighting as hard as you have for our country," she expressed, grateful for the many sacrifices that their armies had made, her husband's ashes representing that. "But this is our best chance to protect our families and we have to take it!" she determined resolutely.

Bradley pursed his lips as he heard Victoria's rationale, feeling remorseful responsibility for failing to reward the country's faith in the army. He concealed these thoughts from the others though, aware that there was nothing he could say or do to convince them otherwise.

"There's no need to explain, honestly," Bradley assured them. "It's just unfortunate that you came this way…we used explosives to destroy the tunnel…as a failsafe to stop Chimera from advancing if they defeated us here…" he confessed, revealing this to be the cause of the tremors that the group had experienced moments ago. "I'm sorry for getting you all caught up in this mess…"

Everybody went quiet for a few seconds, having dissenting opinions on how they felt about this information. Melissa and Linda were peeved about having their and their families' lives put at risk by the army. Victoria and Clint were more sympathetic to the dilemma of the soldiers, appreciating that they needed to do what was necessary to prevent Chimera from invading the rest of Entritica past Mount Tamara. Nathan, Thomas and Abbie were just relieved to hear that the shudders of the earth were triggered by the detonations manually set by the platoon, rather than the signs of another quake.

"Hmph, well you can make it up to us by keeping us alive..." Frank muttered bluntly, shattering the silence and leaving Abbie embarrassed by his brazenness. Despite the unrealistic nature of the request, Bradley obliged with a nod without hesitation.

"I can't guarantee anything, but I'll do my best to protect you and get you all away from here – I owe that much to Richard..." he determined before glancing over his shoulder past the battlefield where there were two bridges stretching over the valley that lay beyond the plateau the soldiers were all fighting on. Bradley pointed out the one that was farthest from the warzone. "Use that bridge," he instructed the group. "It'll take longer for you to reach the coast but it's your safest bet right now. Me and the rest of the soldiers will try to keep Chimera distracted long enough so that you can escape from here."

"Bradley, are you sure about this? You have your own fight to worry about," Nathan queried, concerned about potentially detracting from the warriors' ability to fend off Chimera if they were preoccupied with protecting them.

"Yes, I am," Bradley reinforced. "We may be soldiers but we're also protectors, just like any policeman or firefighter. It's our duty so let us worry about that. You just need to focus on yourselves – it's what Richard would want after all..."

Nathan accepted Bradley's answer, confidently placing his trust in the young man and seeing the influence that his father had on him. Victoria also voiced her gratitude for Bradley's bravery.

"Thank you so much. For this and for being at my husband's side throughout this awful war..." she expressed appreciatively.

"It was a pleasure to have known him," Bradley replied with a smile. He turned towards the two soldiers still standing as sentries, letting them know what needed to be done. When he did this though, Thomas noticed that he had an arm missing, only seeing it now for the first time after having his view obscured by Joshua and Clint who were positioned in front of him. With this playing on his mind, he called out to Bradley which attracted his attention.

"Y-you only have one arm…a-are you really okay to fight?" Thomas questioned, perturbed about the former student's wellbeing. To his surprise though, Bradley let out a hearty laugh in response to this.

"No offence kid, but you're a million years too young to be worrying about me!" Bradley insisted, channelling the positive, calming vigour of Richard and instantly alleviating any concerns that Thomas had for him. "Besides, to combat Maris, we'll need all the help we can get," he added before continuing to relay the plan to his comrades.

It was this last statement that resonated with Joshua. He looked out at the battlefield, watching Chimera and the Entritican army collide with one another as gunfire blared out into the air and more bodies were strewn across the ground. Thinking of all the training that he'd undergone to become a soldier, something bubbled up in his heart, telling him that he couldn't simply spectate or run away while others were fighting. Thus, he stepped forward to stand with Bradley and his brethren.

"Bradley, I'll help you guys fight!" Joshua declared, startling his family and the soldiers with his proclamation. In particular, Clint and Nathan's eyes widened in horror while the colour faded from the faces of Victoria and Abbie.

"Son, what are you doing?!" a flustered Clint gasped, interrupting Bradley before he could speak. "You aren't ready for something like this!"

"Yes, I am dad!" Joshua argued, turning back to face his father. "This is what Mr Jones has prepared me for – I have a duty to do this too!"

"But Josh, look what's happening out there. You could get *killed*…" Nathan stressed, clearly terrified for his cousin's life.

"Nathan's right. Please Josh, you need to think carefully about this!" Clint beseeched. Unfortunately for him, his son's resolve wouldn't be swayed.

"Dad, I *have* thought and I've already made up my mind!" Joshua reiterated. "I'm fit, I'm able, I've trained for this my whole life! If I did nothing now and any of you got hurt or killed…I couldn't live with myself…" he professed earnestly. "At least this way, I can help the army keep Chimera distracted while the rest of you escape. That's what matters most, right?!" he blurted with neither Clint, Nathan nor anyone else able to refute his logic. Satisfied with their silence, Joshua returned his focus to Bradley. "So please, let me fight with you!" he urged once more.

Bradley considered Joshua's plea, aware that the young man had technically left school now which was when he himself had joined the army a year ago. Yet he was still instinctively wary about letting someone younger than him walk into such danger.

"How comfortable are you using a gun?" Bradley quizzed, recalling questions that he had been asked upon enlisting.

"Had plenty of practice in CCF – Pistols, rifles, shotguns, you name it!" Joshua rattled off without missing a beat. "And before you can ask, I've also trained with swords in fencing for years and I'm well versed in a variety of martial arts! You were only one year above me in school, so you know about my achievements well enough," he reminded Bradley, subtly accusing him of playing dumb. "Any other questions?! Because unless you've forgotten, there's a battle going on over there!" Joshua finished, oozing with confidence, courage and defiance.

"You're the one who's bloody kept us here!" Bradley pointed out but cracking a smirk as he did so, amused by his assertiveness and finally relenting. "Very well, you're in…" he accepted. Bradley then proceeded to remove his protective vest and hand it over to Joshua. "You take this – it's tradition to give these to the youngest soldiers to make sure their safety is prioritised," he explained. "Plus, I can just grab another vest from one of the bodies, not that they'll need it now…"

Joshua poked his arms through the holes and zipped up the jacket. He could feel the thick padding against his flesh, specially designed to reduce the damage from blades and bullets. Clint watched him wear the vest and beamed with bittersweet pride at seeing his son achieve his dream. Joshua caught the expression on his dad's visage, sensing his emotions and feeling guilt for having inflicted it on him.

"I'm sorry dad…this is just something that I have to do…" Joshua acknowledged.

"I know son…" Clint replied understandingly. "So, I'll do what I must too. If you're going to fight, then so am I!" he decided, astounding Victoria and leaving Joshua at a loss for words.

"Clint, no!" Victoria exclaimed. "Don't be stupid, this is way too much! I've already lost Richard; I can't risk losing you too!"

"Vic, what kind of father would I be if I let my son put his life on the line for my sake?" Clint retorted. "That's backwards – if he's going to step into danger, I'm walking right in there with him! You'd do the same if it was Nathan!" he added, knowing that was one truth his sister couldn't argue against, something that was confirmed by her relenting body language.

"D-dad, you need to lead Nathan and the others to safety…!" Joshua barked in a vain effort to keep his father out of peril. As he suspected, Clint would not back down.

"I can entrust Vic with that – she's *my* sister after all," he claimed, conveying his faith in Victoria. "Look Josh, argue all you want but you won't win this quarrel! I'm the one you got your stubbornness from after all! We're fighting this together! End of story!"

Joshua paused for a few moments, his mouth agape as he searched for the right words to say. Before he could speak though, Bradley interrupted, "Can you all hurry and make up your minds already?! People are dying out there!" he yelled at the group, showing his impatience for the first time.

Luckily, it was the only time he needed to display his annoyance because everyone respected the young commander enough to act on his input, conscious that time was of the essence. After getting Bradley's blessing to take a few moments to say some parting words, Clint turned back to the group to have one last interaction with Melissa and the others before embracing Victoria, the two siblings holding each other more tightly than usual. Nathan observed the exchange, his heart aching for his mother who could very well be saying goodbye to her brother for all she knew. His attention was diverted however when Bradley addressed him.

"Nathan," the soldier called out, causing Nathan's head to turn towards his location. "I know I didn't appreciate it at the time, b-but talking to you at the memorial that day…it gave me the strength to keep going…so thank you," Bradley expressed to the boy who remained silent this time, still processing the fact that his uncle and cousin were about to step into the warzone. "You said it yourself, I *was* there for your dad in his time of need. Now it's *your* turn to be there for your loved ones…because they're gonna need you now more than ever," he finished, echoing the words that Nathan had left him with back at the stone tablet.

Nathan hesitated before quietly nodding in response, just as Victoria and Clint relinquished their hold on one another.

"Guide the others – I'm counting on you, sis," Clint instructed, his forehead pressed lovingly against hers.

"You better not die out there…else I'll be really mad at you," Victoria whispered out of anxious affection, holding back her tears. As the two siblings finally broke away from one another, Abbie took her chance to wish Joshua luck.

"Josh, please be careful…" she urged him.

"Yeah, I will…" Joshua replied before turning his attention to his cousin. "Nath, I'm trusting you with the rest. Keep the others safe and we'll be right behind you. You understand?" he directed with a warming smile.

Once again, Nathan responded with a silent nod. In that moment, it dawned on him that not only was Victoria potentially bidding farewell to Clint – he was doing the same with Joshua, the cousin that he'd only mended bridges with yesterday. Instinctively, Nathan found himself slowly extending his arm towards Joshua, as if wanting to make one last attempt to persuade him to come with them. Before his mouth could even form the words though, Bradley gave the command to depart for battle.

"Men, it's time…" he informed his two comrades along with Joshua and Clint. "We're going in now!"

Bradley charged ahead towards the frontline with Joshua, Clint and the other two soldiers tailing him. Nathan watched despondently as his uncle and cousin disappeared into the distance, praying that they would be okay while simultaneously fearing the worst. Although he knew deep down that he wouldn't have been able to change Joshua's mind, Nathan regretted not saying something, *anything* meaningful to his cousin before he left. He didn't have time to dwell on this thought however, as he soon found out when Victoria placed a hand on his shoulder.

"Nath, I understand how you feel. But we can't stay here – we have to go…" she established firmly, masking her own anguish from her son out of necessity.

Despite his worry for Joshua's and Clint's safety, Nathan knew his mother was right. Like Bradley and Joshua had told him, the others needed him now and he had to try and keep them safe. The only way to do that was to escape so he knew the time for talking was over. Without further delay, he and Victoria led Thomas, Melissa, Abbie, Ben, Frank and Linda in the direction of the bridge, each of their feet carrying them across the terrain as fast as they could.

Once the five warriors entered the fray, Bradley and his two comrades intercepted a group of masked Chimera fanatics to allow Joshua and Clint to grab some weapons that were littered on the ground next to the fallen. Joshua pried a sword from a dead soldier's hand while Clint grabbed a gun before removing the bulletproof vest from another corpse. As more terrorists threatened to outnumber Bradley and the two soldiers, keeping them separate from the rest of their platoon, Joshua leapt into action. Using the blade he'd borrowed, he effortlessly deflected several strikes from their foes, his arms moving swiftly in sync with the sword and his feet stepping elegantly as he evaded enemy attacks. Bradley saw his expertise as a swordsman first-hand and was impressed and relieved to see that Joshua's self-confidence in his skills earlier wasn't unwarranted.

Joshua's inexperience as a soldier was evident though when he sliced down one of his adversaries. As he heard the man squeal out in pain before dropping stone dead onto the dirt, the young man recoiled, horrified at the thought that he'd just taken a life. This was noticed by another one of the masked men who lunged at Joshua, ready to deal an opportunistic killing blow.

Thankfully, Clint had his son covered when he shot the assailant down with the gun, the deafening sound snapping Joshua back to his senses. The parent and child looked at each other and gave a nod of mutual understanding. This was not the time to succumb to their emotions – that would have to wait until the fighting had subsided. That was the nature of war after all.

Having accepted that, Joshua and Clint fought off multiple enemies alongside Bradley, the latter still able to hold his own even with one arm as he fired his rifle with pinpoint accuracy into the vital spots of three terrorists in succession. The trio of heroes advanced until they were reunited with the rest of their army. With a fierce roar, Bradley rallied the troops to double down against their opponents, leading them into the final push.

Meanwhile, Nathan along with the rest of the party had crossed the halfway point between Mount Tamara and the bridge when the air filled once more with the ear-splitting screech of artillery being fired. Everyone cringed at hearing the unsettling racket, Nathan and Thomas cupping their ears in response whereas Abbie used her arms to shield Ben's ears as well as his eyes from the terrifying scenes as she carried him. The gunfire was enough to motivate even the wheezing Frank and Linda to power through their exhaustion on the path to the bridge. Each step they took towards it brought them all closer to safety, something that was not lost on Victoria and Melissa who guided their sons, their loving, maternal presence serving as encouragement for them to keep pressing on.

Simultaneously, now fuelled by Bradley's rousing battle cry, the soldiers started to force Chimera back towards the second bridge. With the Entritican defenders now all unified into one massive group, instead of being separated, they had the strength advantage in terms of quantity and quality. They outnumbered the remaining radicals of Chimera and they also had the superior weapons. As the masked terrorists retreated, several of them were incapacitated by the swords and bullets that pierced them. Joshua and Clint's hopes began to soar as they watched the opposing rabble crumble before the might and tactics of Bradley and the other soldiers. Their once uncertain triumph now seemed imminent.

Likewise, Nathan, Thomas, Abbie and their families were almost out of danger as they reached the last quarter of their sprint to the bridge. Their hearts were beating furiously and their legs were operating on pure adrenaline at this stage. Yet none of that felt relevant for it seemed that they were finally about to escape this hellish scene unscathed.

But before the relief could even set in for them, they learned that the nightmare had only just begun...

For in that moment, flames inauspiciously erupted from the earth before them, startling the group and drawing screams of terror from Melissa, Thomas, Abbie and Linda.

Worse still, Nathan, Victoria and the others, along with Joshua, Clint, Bradley and the soldiers watched helplessly as the blaze spread rapidly around the battlefield, surrounding the entire area in a perfect circle, cutting off any possible exit. It didn't take long for them all to realise that this was no ordinary fire – they were trapped by wildfire!

However, Nathan deduced that it was not natural for the flames to form in such a controlled manner. Similarly, Bradley and Joshua were left panicked by the cackling laughter emanating from behind the masks of some of the surviving followers of Chimera. They soon realised why as seconds later, everyone could detect a dark sinister energy approaching from the bridge nearest the warzone.

"N-no, please no..." Nathan uttered, praying that he was mistaken.

Sure enough though, a figure shrouded in a black cloak emerged from the blaze before the soldiers' very eyes, causing them to cower in awe. Joshua and Clint tried to stand their ground but were disheartened to see Bradley, the same man who had bravely led the soldiers' final assault moments ago, now shrinking back as he was held in the grip of fear. For the commander to lose his nerve to this extent could only mean one thing…

"I-i-it's…h-her…" Bradley squeaked timidly at the sight of the woman, confirming that the worst possible case scenario had come to pass.

Maris had arrived…

⫸⫷

Chapter 23

Even with smoke billowing from the inferno and filling out the area, Maris remained visible to everyone on the battlefield. For Nathan, Victoria and the rest of the group, she was little more than a distorted figure from their vantage point, yet her menacing presence separated her from that of her minions. They could sense the overwhelming power and authority that exuded from her, even at a distance.

As for Bradley, Joshua, Clint and the Entritican forces, they were faced with the undesirable image of Maris dispassionately staring them down, both the unstoppable force and immovable object that none of their platoons had been able to surmount. Bradley was still the only known soldier to have survived an encounter with the cult leader – albeit with one limb less – and from the way he was trembling, it was evident that he was reliving that trauma.

"S-sir? W-what do we do...?" one of the soldiers asked Bradley nervously.

Hearing his comrade's voice snapped the commander out of his daze, making him realise that they were in the heat of battle and he was no longer Richard's subordinate. Even with his position of leadership, Bradley was still a teenager whose head was clouded by both panic from his previous experience and the pressure to motivate the soldiers against the demonic entity that was Maris. Thus, it resulted in him making a hasty order.

"Fire! Everyone, fire at her now!!" Bradley blurted out.

Without hesitation, following Bradley's lead, Joshua, Clint and the other warriors opened fire on Maris, unleashing a barrage of bullets in her direction and roaring defiantly over the rattling of their guns. However, not a single shell found its target. Joshua was the first to deduce the reason why as he felt the winds intensify against their troops. Similarly, Bradley picked up on this same sensation seconds after, one frighteningly reminiscent of the Zalhara Timberlands, and ceased shooting to gage the situation.

As per their hunches, Joshua and Bradley observed Maris manipulating the wind around her, operating it as a protective shield to deflect the incoming bullets. Their instincts also told them that she wasn't just intending to use it for defence because they detected how the force of the gales was building up. Realising his folly, Bradley called out to the soldiers.

"She's about to attack! Everyone, run!" he signalled, trying to convey his abrupt change of tactics to try and limit the anticipated damage.

Regretfully, his warning came slightly too late as Maris directed the wind currents at the army, thrusting most of the soldiers, Bradley, Joshua and Clint included, towards the centre of the battlefield, sprawled out on the ground in a devastating display of dominance. Nathan witnessed this happen from afar, almost rooted to the spot while the flames continued to burn ahead of them, reminded of how he'd learned from Ranjit about Richard dying in a hurricane. His heart sunk, this sight of the winds being compressed into a concentrated assault on the freedom fighters serving as the final reinforcement to him that Maris really did kill his father…

There were a few soldiers who had managed to avoid the blast, stepping out of the way in time. Depleted of ammunition and armed only with knives and swords, they rushed at Maris. In response, the mage directed some of the flames from the wildfire towards the assailants who shrieked as they were engulfed by the blaze. As Bradley, Joshua and Clint plucked themselves up from the earth, they lifted their heads up to find Maris advancing in their direction. She started with a self-assured stride that picked up in speed until she was storming her way to her remaining enemies whilst her subordinates were content to let their master do the work as they stayed back, concealed by the smoke.

The threat of the spreading smoke did not go unrecognised by Victoria who heard the coughs of Nathan, Thomas, Frank, Linda and Ben nearby. While Maris engaged the soldiers, able to incapacitate many of them even without the use of magic, Victoria knew they had to find a way out of the ring of fire.

"Guys, we don't have any other choice! We have to jump over the flames!" Victoria stated, spluttering as she spoke.

"A-are you insane?! Look how high they are – we'll never be able to get over them!" Frank retorted, sweating from the intense heat. He had a point as the blaze burned at the same height as his chin, however Melissa came up with a solution.

"We can if some of us waft the flames away!" she suggested, unloading her backpack from her shoulders and pulling out a blanket and a towel. Quick on the uptake, Victoria grabbed hold of the towel and began to violently shake it in the direction of the inferno, using it as a makeshift fan. Melissa followed suit with the blanket, the combined efforts of both moms proving sufficient to create an opening in the wall of fire.

"Dad, let me go first and then throw Ben over to me!" Abbie instructed to Frank before carefully handing her brother over to him, the young lad gasping for breath as his little lungs fought to contend with the smoke.

Once it was safe to do so, Abbie vaulted over the wildfire thanks to Victoria's and Melissa's labours in diminishing the embers. Next, Frank heaved Ben above the flames and into Abbie's waiting arms just as planned before he and Linda joined their children on the other side, near the bridge. Then, Melissa threw the blanket to Abbie so that she and Frank could fan the flames for the other half of the party to cross the burning barrier.

After shaking off some of his anxiety, Thomas followed Abbie's family as he hopped over to safety – or at least to somewhere safer than where they currently were. Despite urging from Victoria and Melissa, Nathan was insistent that he wouldn't go through without his mom, so Melissa reluctantly went ahead of them, leaping through the blaze. With Abbie and Frank furiously shaking the blanket and Thomas and Melissa calling out to them, Nathan and Victoria held hands to brace themselves before finally making the jump as the fire flickered underneath them. Thankfully, they reunited with the group, relieved by the fact that they had all miraculously made it out of the inferno unscathed.

On the other hand, the same could not be said for the Entritican soldiers as Maris had dispatched half of their army single-handedly, all without sustaining any signs of damage on her person. She reached the middle of the ravaged arena, now enclosed by the spectating wildfire, where she found herself surrounded by Bradley and the remnants of his squad.

Unfazed by her foes, Maris made yet another demonstration of the difference in power between them by shifting the earth that they were all standing on. The soldiers staggered when the terrain directly beneath them protruded inexplicably up towards the sky, generating tremors as the chunks of ground grinded against each other. Quick to realise what was happening, Bradley instinctively pushed both Joshua and Clint off the rising platform, before it could ascend too high up from the soil, so that they disappeared from Maris' view. As for Nathan's perspective, he anxiously observed through the smoke and the flames as the massive mound of earth surged upwards, carrying Maris and multiple soldiers atop it.

Victoria placed her arm around her son's shoulder, keen to lead him away from the hazardous hellscape that they'd just escaped from. Their moment of relief did not last long however as while they shed their rucksacks from their shoulders, the silence was disrupted by a distressing call from Abbie.

"Guys! Ben's collapsed!!" she cried out in a panic.

Nathan, Victoria, Thomas and Melissa rushed over to find Frank trying to comfort a tearful Linda while Abbie cradled Ben, the boy's eyes closed, his skin pale and his arms limp – he was indeed unconscious. Victoria gently cupped her hand around Ben's, placing her thumb on his wrist.

"He has a pulse!" she exclaimed to his family before looking at his face and feeling gentle puffs of air expelling from his mouth. "And he's still breathing! He's inhaled too much smoke though! Does anyone know CPR?!"

"I do!" Melissa responded, stepping forward to assist. "Everyone, stand back, he needs space!"

With that, Melissa knelt down beside Ben and started to provide mouth to mouth resuscitation, making sure to clear her throat between administered breaths. Abbie remained close by to hold her brother's hand for reassurance. Victoria supported Linda by reminding her that Ben was alive and championed her faith in Melissa's abilities to save him. Frank also listened intently to Victoria's reinforcement and though he would never admit it, they were words that he needed to hear in that moment as he fretted for his son. Meanwhile, Nathan and Thomas did as Melissa instructed and kept their distance to allow Ben the best chance for survival, quietly wishing for the lad to come around. Seeing Ben in such a vulnerable state became a bit too much for Nathan to bear so he turned away from the rest of the group.

Unfortunately for him, the sight he was greeted with was even more distressing – his jaw dropped in dismay upon watching a torrent of water cascade downwards from the mound's summit. He spotted several figures being carried away within the deluge before crashing forcefully onto the ground.

As the liquid seeped into the earth, another frightening thought sunk in for Nathan – Joshua and Clint were still out there! Despite his cousin and uncle lingering in his mind since they parted ways on the warzone minutes ago, he had been preoccupied with Ben's life-threatening quandary along with their desperate escape from the inferno. But now, Nathan was haunted by the image of Joshua being out there, one of the casualties swept away in that dreadful downpour. He couldn't help but remember his cousin telling him that he'd be right behind him before marching into battle, his stomach churning at the idea that he may not be able to fulfil that promise. As far as he was concerned, they had just made amends and he couldn't stand the thought of things ending like this.

However, the voice of someone else rang in his head. It belonged to Bradley, serving as a reminder that his father's comrade was also in the firing line. Just like with Joshua, the parting words that Bradley had left him with echoed in his mind:

"You said it yourself, I was there for your dad in his time of need. Now it's your turn to be there for your loved ones...because they're gonna need you now more than ever."

Nathan ruminated on those words, allowing them to repeat over and over again like an incessant alarm bell. He wondered why he was fixating on this so much. After all, he'd helped get his mother and friends outside of the ring of fire, just as Joshua and Clint had wanted.

Suddenly, something clicked within Nathan. His loved ones *weren't* all out of danger because Joshua and Clint were still in the thick of it. The boy pondered as the flames settled and the fumes spread upwards. Was this the coded message behind Bradley's voice? That his cousin and uncle were still alive and needed him now more than ever?

Nathan glanced back at Victoria and the others, their attention still squarely on ensuring Ben's survival. Yet when he looked back towards the warzone, the voice grew louder, as if the soldiers were calling out to him for help, verifying what his gut instincts were already telling him. He couldn't ignore them any longer, not if there was something that he could do to rescue Joshua and Clint. So, seizing his opportunity while the others were distracted, Nathan took a deep breath to gather his courage, clear his lungs and harden his nerves before leaping over the subdued blaze and dashing towards the battlefield in the hopes of finding his cousin.

Moments later, Melissa lifted her head up and Ben coughed heavily upon regaining consciousness to the relief of his parents and sister. Abbie immediately hugged Ben while Frank and Linda thanked Melissa for saving their son along with Victoria for providing a calming voice throughout the ordeal.

"We're just glad he's still with us," Victoria humbly insisted in response to their gratitude. "But now he's awake, we have to get away from here," she stated, spluttering as the smoke persisted around them. "Nath, Thomas, it's time we got mov-" Victoria was about to say, turning her head to where she believed the two boys to be.

In that instant, she and the others realised that Nathan was missing. Thomas, Abbie and Victoria searched around frantically for any sign of him.

"Nathan...? Nathan, where are you?! Nathan!" Victoria cried out, her voice cracking under her anxiety and the distress becoming increasingly prevalent in each call she made.

"I-I don't understand...h-he was right next to me a moment ago..." Thomas blurted, feeling a blend of concern and guilt for letting him out of his sight.

Victoria looked around in all directions until she gazed over the wildfire – where she spotted her son running in the distance towards the giant slab of earth in the centre of the arena!

"NATHAN!!" she screamed automatically, disclosing his location to the rest of the party, their eyes all widening when they realised where he was and how far he'd gone.

"What the hell is he doing?!" Frank exclaimed in disbelief. "Is he *trying* to get himself killed?!"

"Nathan! Come back! You can't go in there alone!" Thomas hollered, hoping his friend would listen to him and see sense.

Sadly, Nathan was too far out of range to hear them by this point and Victoria's, Thomas' and Abbie's hearts sunk once he vanished past the thickening cloud of fumes that had formed from the fire. Without hesitation, Victoria began to charge towards the inferno.

"Vic, wait!" Melissa shouted but before she could get any more words out, Victoria told her in no uncertain terms to stay out of her way.

"I have to save my baby! *Don't* try and stop me!!" the flustered mother fiercely retorted.

On that note, she fearlessly vaulted over the flickering flames in pursuit of Nathan. Thomas wandered a few steps, as if about to follow after his best friend but Melissa grabbed his arm, firmly stopping him before he could even entertain the idea.

"I know how much Nathan means to you, but there's no way in hell that I'm letting you go out there!" she reinforced sternly. From the adamant tone in her voice, Thomas knew not to argue with his mom on this one.

"What is that idiot thinking?! How could he be so reckless?! I thought we were past this..." Abbie questioned desolately, fretting for his safety.

"I bet it's because Joshua's still out there..." Thomas rationalised. "Guess he just couldn't leave him behind after all..."

Melissa, Abbie, Frank and Linda had nothing further to add to this, only able to watch as Victoria wandered her way towards the sooty fog ahead. Her thoughts with Nathan and Joshua, Abbie quietly mumbled under her breath, praying that they would make it through this.

While his friends and their families heeded Joshua's and Clint's orders by remaining away from the battlefield, Nathan cautiously ambled his way through the smoke. With one arm, he shielded his nose and mouth to protect his breathing. He used the other to feel his way ahead of him, particularly when his vision was overwhelmed by the viscous haze that enshrouded the area.

Nathan continued blindly on this path until his foot caught something, causing him to stumble over. When he picked himself up from the ground, he found that his hands were covered in specks of dirt and dried blood.

He glanced back to see that he had tripped over a corpse. Out of shock, Nathan turned away only to find that there were numerous lifeless bodies strewn across the terrain around him, no matter where his pupils manically darted to. Unable to bear looking at them for long, he lifted his head upwards to gaze at the mound of earth that Maris had summoned, the sheer scale of it reminiscent of the memorial slab that paid tribute to fallen soldiers, like his dad. Now he'd had a despairing glimpse first-hand of what the site of his death may have resembled. These horrific scenes slowly brought Nathan crashing back down to reality, comprehending what he had dared to walk into – this was what war really was...

Nathan's eyes lowered all the way back down to the foot of the mound where he found another corpse in his line of sight. Though the front of the soldier's body was in contact with the ground, his head was tilted to the side, eyes staring vacantly back at Nathan. Alas, the face looking back at him was one that Nathan sadly recognised – it was Bradley...

He scrambled over on his hands and knees towards the body, detecting through his skin how damp the soil was following the torrent of water that had rained down earlier. Nathan placed his hand on Bradley's cheek before wincing at how stone-cold it was to touch. There was no response whatsoever from the commander. No matter how much Nathan wanted to deny it, it was unmistakable to him that Bradley was dead, another one of Maris' many victims. Albeit not to the same extent as with his father, Nathan felt a great sorrow at losing Bradley. Not only had he been a fellow student like Drew, but he'd also been a soldier that fought alongside Richard and had sacrificed his own life to protect them.

In that moment, Nathan became frightfully aware of the naïve risk he'd taken. He had ventured to a place where he was substantially out of his depth, putting himself in danger against Bradley's wishes, all for the slim chance of rescuing his cousin who had made the choice to fight. As he took another look at the destruction that surrounded him, being sure to properly process it this time, he regretfully grew more convinced that Joshua and Clint must have also perished at Maris' hands...

However, before he could dwell on that any further, his ears detected the sound of footsteps and coughing nearby. Initially believing this to be Maris, Nathan's blood ran cold as he instinctively froze up in the hopes that he could escape her notice. He could then make out an ambiguous figure moving from beyond the smoke clouds. Yet as the shape became clearer the closer it got, Nathan realised that there was a second person from the blurry outline – whoever this was, they were carrying or supporting somebody else. Then, he heard a voice speak.

"C'mon dad, stay with me!" one of the shadows uttered. Nathan's hopes soared upon hearing the very familiar voice. It was Joshua – he was still alive!

"Josh!" Nathan addressed him, rushing over to him as he emerged from the haze, much to his shocked cousin's chagrin.

"N-Nath?! Why in god's name did you come here?! You should have stayed with the others!" Joshua hissed, horrified to find Nathan in no man's land.

"And leave you out here?! Sorry cuz, I'm not abandoning you!" Nathan reiterated, the sight of Joshua in the flesh serving as vindication for returning to him. His attention then turned to the figure who had an arm draped over Joshua's shoulder – Clint. He was visibly conscious but could see that his eyes were glossy. "I-is he okay? W-what happened to him?!" Nathan asked out of concern for his uncle.

"When Maris raised that mound, Bradley saved us – he pushed me and dad off before it got too high off the ground. But dad still knocked his head when he landed. I think he's concussed..." Joshua explained.

"Josh...B-Bradley's dead..." Nathan broke the news to his cousin before tilting his head in the direction of his corpse, alerting Joshua to its presence.

"I-I figured..." Joshua remarked glumly, mourning the passing of his comrade. "Maris is on the other side of that slab right now, finishing off the rest of our forces. She's a monster like nothing I've ever seen before. We have to get away from here now while we still can!" he established.

Just as they were about to make a run for it, Clint spluttered violently and slumped downwards even more as Joshua struggled to support his body weight. It was apparent that he was starting to inhale too much smoke, something that the two cousins were also in grave danger of doing soon. While Joshua gently tried to shake some energy back into Clint, Nathan thought on his feet and searched around until he spotted the corpse of a Chimera soldier. Particularly, it was the mask that attracted Nathan's eye.

"I-I have an idea, we can use one of those masks to shield your dad's mouth from the smoke," Nathan suggested. He left Joshua's side and approached the body, kneeling beside it to remove the mask from the zealot's head.

But it was the face of the zealot that really defied Nathan's expectations. The boy was stunned to see how young the radical was – he was fresh-faced with no trace of stubble on his chin, just like Nathan. Though this foe could have been older, it was just as likely that he and Nathan were the same age only for his life to be tragically cut short. For Nathan, it put into perspective how impressionable some of Maris' followers could truly be – similar to Ranjit even – and in that instant, he experienced a surreal sense of sympathy for the people he once only viewed as pure evil. Nevertheless, it only served to fuel his hatred of Maris, thinking of how she could manipulate even teenagers into working for her.

After taking a few seconds to reflect on those feelings, Nathan stood up with the mask in his hand and swung his body round, taking a step forward to return to Joshua and Clint.

Suddenly though, a figure descended from the sky and landed directly between the two cousins, the impact from the descent generating a shockwave of air that swept Nathan back off his feet. Just as he was recovering, he heard the chilling sound of a woman's voice:

"Well, well, well, what have we here? You know, this isn't exactly a place for *children* to be playing..." the voice stated mockingly.

The words slithered their way into Nathan's ears as he slowly turned his head upwards, his eyes scanning the entity looming over him. Her body was draped in black clothes but unlike the rest of the terrorists, she was unmasked and Nathan could now see her face up close. The woman's complexion was extremely pale, further accentuated by the dark ensemble that she wore and the scarlet red hair that came down to her neck. But Nathan's limbs seized up and his blood ran cold upon locking eyes with her. There was an intense, fiery ferocity behind her eyes, though it was not one that imparted hope but rather instilled despair within his heart, sapping away his willpower. While Joshua winced in the background with Clint's arm around his shoulder, Nathan was left helpless and petrified as Maris stared him down with her deadly glare.

Despite her sunken eyes, Nathan was once again surprised by how youthful she appeared. After reading through the book he'd borrowed from the library, he'd built up an image of her being of an advanced age. Instead, judging from her smooth skin and high cheekbones, Maris looked as though she were only a few years older than Joshua with none of it looking artificial.

While Maris' attention was focused on Nathan, Joshua saw an opportunity to strike. He pulled out his gun, aimed it at the mage and fired three times in her direction. It was to no avail however as without even glancing at him, Maris created a forcefield of winds to repel the bullets, just like earlier.

"Seriously?" Maris laughed apathetically, her eyebrows furrowed as she looked over her shoulder at the trembling rookie soldier. "If that didn't work the first ten times, what made you think it would work now?"

Joshua fell silent, unable to respond. He was rattled by how eerily calm and jovial she was. She had complete control and she knew it, not even regarding him as a threat. Yet beneath Maris' stoic surface, Joshua could detect a sinister but familiar energy lurking in her. Seeing that neither boy was about to speak, Maris continued by offering an ultimatum.

"I've got no use for the old guy," she affirmed bluntly, disrespecting the middle-aged Clint. "But I'm always willing to welcome young blood.

So, if the two of you pledge your loyalty to me right now, I might just spare you…"

Nathan was appalled by Maris' proposal. Was this how she'd amassed so many followers – by coercing them into servitude? For him, there was no need for any internal debate – if this truly was his only option, he would rather die than work for his father's murderer. Before he could even reject it though, Clint stirred and surged back into action.

"L-leave my family alone, you *witch!*" he yelled, lunging towards the mage so suddenly that Joshua couldn't react quickly enough to stop his dad.

Maris snuffed Clint's burst of adrenaline as if he were a candle, dealing a brutal punch to his kidney and augmenting its impact with the force of the winds. Clint coughed up blood and slumped onto the ground in a heap while Maris looked down her nose at him with an expression of disdain, as though scorned from being branded a witch.

Witnessing his dad collapse at the mage's feet, an enraged Joshua yelled out and charged at Maris with his sword. He swung the blade at her multiple times with the enigmatic cult leader elegantly dodging each swipe without raising an arm at the soldier.

Elsewhere, Victoria was still wading through the dense haze, her vision and senses utterly overwhelmed by the toxic fumes. She tried to call out for Nathan but could barely shout because of the smoke compromising her voice. Even with her body and stamina weakening, Victoria's resolve to find her son remained strong, pushing her to struggle her way through the smog.

Meanwhile, Nathan remained frozen in fear, barely able to move as he watched Joshua's movements become more sluggish. His cousin may have trained to get an extraordinary amount of stamina however Nathan could tell that he had finally reached his limit, exhausted by today's events. Yet Maris hadn't broken a sweat against Joshua, even with the heat from the wildfire not far away. Nathan quickly deduced that this was her strategy – she wasn't taking Joshua seriously, she was toying with him, ensuring that he tired himself out. Before he had a chance to warn him, his cousin threw all his energy into one final slash only for Maris to intercept it effortlessly with her hand.

"When…will *you people* learn…" Maris snarled, snatching the sword from the startled Joshua's hands, having lost her patience. "*That you're not even close to being in my league!*" she finished before landing a vicious punch deep into his gut, forcing the wind out of him as he doubled over into the soil, just as Clint had done.

Nathan let out a gasp of terror as he witnessed Maris standing over Joshua. His older cousin had always been so dependable when they were kids, able to stand up to any hooligans, and now here he was, beaten and helpless before the mage. Joshua feebly raised his head to look in the direction of Nathan and Clint.

"D-dad...N-Nathan...I-I'm sorry...I-I am..." he murmured, just audibly enough for Nathan to hear, seemingly accepting his fate.

With these defeated words reaching his ears, something started to stir within Nathan, reminding him that he'd come out here for a reason – to save Joshua like he would have done for him. He knew that if he wanted any chance of achieving that, he had to act now and overcome the fear that was holding him back. Nathan mustered up the courage to move his body and after spotting a knife in the hand of the same deceased zealot that he'd taken the mask from, he reached out to grab it just as Maris was preparing the killing blow for Joshua.

"I'm through playing around. I gave you a chance to join me and you refused..." Maris spat at the soldier while forging a bolt of lightning in her right hand. "Now you pay the price – now you die!"

Before she could direct the electricity at Joshua, Nathan rocketed to his feet, dashed over towards Maris with knife in hand and seized her arm, intercepting it just in time.

"Nathan, run! Just save yourself!!" Joshua blurted out, not wanting his cousin to die for him.

However, Nathan's hold on Maris remained firm with the mage struggling to wrench her arm free. She was perplexed by the boy's abrupt increase in strength and after a few seconds, her annoyance reached its boiling point once again.

"Oh my god, get it through your head already!" she groaned, tired of her enemies' continued resistance. Once she realised that Nathan was not going to let go, Maris turned her head around to face him, ranting as she did so. "It's pointle-"

In that instant though, Maris detected a malicious energy emanating from Nathan, one so intense that she froze up on the spot upon catching sight of the boy's menacing visage. Her expression of surprise did not escape the angered Nathan's notice, realising that she'd lowered her guard.

Out of desperate instinct, he used the opportunity to slash the knife towards her head...

From her location, Victoria heard a woman scream out in pain nearby. She twisted her neck around immediately and beyond the clouds of smoke, she could feel a sinister presence flare up in the same direction that the wail came from. Thinking of her son, Victoria hurried off towards the energy without hesitation...

Maris staggered backwards, the lightning in her right hand diminishing but not fading away completely. She watched in shock as blood dripped from her forehead into the palm of her left hand before raising her head to look at Nathan again.

Nathan's eyes were fixated on Maris' pallid face as the blood from the scar trickled down, the crimson liquid painting over her nose and cheeks. Even while downed, Joshua caught sight of this, including the bloody knife in Nathan's hand.

"N-Nath...h-how did you...?!" he uttered, awestruck by what his cousin had just done.

Similarly, Nathan was left in a daze as he tried to comprehend his actions, while Maris silently stared at him in disbelief. The magnitude of Nathan's feat was apparent to all three of them. He'd accomplished something that no soldier had been able to achieve up until now – he had *wounded* Maris.

As Victoria raced towards their location, the smoke began to thin out, allowing her to distinguish Nathan's outline along with Maris'. Realising the danger her son was in, she sprinted as fast as she could to try and save him.

For Nathan, seeing the damage that he'd done to Maris reminded him of his encounter with Tobias years prior. It was an unpleasant memory that made his stomach churn and left him in a panicked state of unease to think that history was repeating itself. On the other hand, Maris eyed Nathan up and down, noting from his quivering stance that his abrupt burst of adrenaline had petered out. Yet, out of all the possible adversaries that she faced off against, the fact that an untrained child had caused her to bleed was something that had Maris experiencing a multitude of emotions: morbid amusement; reluctant humility; unbridled fury. She disguised all of this with a smirk, her attention squarely on Nathan while unbeknownst to her, Victoria was drawing closer to them.

"Not bad kid...not bad at all..." Maris commended Nathan.

Joshua tried to take advantage of the distracted mage and get back to his feet only for his body to fail him, still incapacitated from the mage's attack. However, he raised his head to see the spark of electricity reignite in her hand behind her back, his eyes widening with the realisation of what was about to happen.

"But unlike you, I'm willing to make the kill!" Maris established.

With the lightning crackling in her hand again, Maris thrusted her arm towards Nathan, ready to direct the bolt at the petrified, defenceless boy. At the last second though, Joshua tugged on her leg in one last ditch attempt to throw her concentration off. It proved effective, albeit only briefly, as Maris shook him off and angrily kicked Joshua away from her.

But in that small window where Joshua diverted Maris' focus to him, Nathan heard footsteps approaching to his left. He turned to see his mother arrive before pushing him aside to the ground. As he fell, Nathan's jaw opened in a shocked, silent scream, watching Victoria mouth the following words to him:

"I love you..."

Less than a second later, Maris pivoted her body around, still believing Nathan to be standing there, and blindly fired the lightning bolt which struck Victoria in the heart. Nathan stared in horror as the impact of the attack carried his mom off her feet and sent her crashing into the mound of earth.

There, her body limply fell back to the ground, lying motionless while the mound started to crack and crumble, unable to sustain the force of the collision. Seeing her unresponsive, Nathan could feel a heart-stopping numbness wash over him, as though experiencing what fate had just befallen his mother.

Despite not wanting to believe it, his own eyes could not deceive him.

Victoria was dead as soon as the lightning struck her...

And if witnessing this hadn't been cruel enough, before he could even process what had happened in those tragic moments, the mound collapsed in front of Nathan, breaking apart into chunks of rock that buried Victoria, Bradley and several other bodies that were in the vicinity.

Once the dust had settled, it started to hit Nathan that Victoria was gone. Joshua looked on, having also observed the events that had just occurred and felt wretched as his cousin inched closer to the rubble on his hands and knees. Nathan soon stopped as his head drooped down, his eyes physically staring at the ground but his vision blurry, unable to take in the clumps of dirt due to his mind being fixated on one notion – he was alone. He had lost his father…and now he'd lost his mother…

And as the earth below darkened around him, it slowly dawned on him that Maris was towering over him – the very person responsible for murdering them both.

"That was your mom, wasn't it?" Maris deduced in a soft whisper while Nathan had his back turned to her. "She must have come out here looking for you…"

A pang of guilt struck Nathan's chest as he heard this. He knew the mage was right and if he'd considered the possibility of this happening, he would have *never* journeyed out here. Before he could dwell on this thought however, Maris continued, "I'm sorry for your loss kid…really, I am," she conveyed in a tone that almost resembled sincerity. "But take solace in knowing that…you'll be reunited with her real soon…"

As Maris pointed two fingers towards Nathan's neck, lightning crackled from the tips, the glare reflecting on the ground for even the boy's dazed eyes to see.

The flickering lights stirred Nathan once more. Yes, he'd made a rash regrettable mistake in coming out here. But hearing the crackling chatter of the electricity inches away from him, reminded him that it was Maris who had done all this; Maris who had slaughtered all these soldiers; Maris who had taken his parents from this world – away from him. With these thoughts filling his mind, a bubbling rage began to swell within Nathan, fuelled by grief as the lightning that Maris was channelling surged in power.

"Nathan, no!!!" Joshua screamed out to his cousin, still debilitated from the pain. It seemed as though his words would fall on deaf ears though.

"Farewell…" Maris whispered to Nathan.

She shot the lightning at point blank-range…only for it to dissipate right in front of her eyes, much to the shock of her and Joshua.

Before Maris could comprehend what was transpiring, Nathan released a frenzied, blood-curdling wail. In that instant, an overwhelming, sinister energy exploded from him in the form of the black aura that consumed his body.

Taken aback by this, Maris jumped backwards and hastily fired another lightning bolt at Nathan only for the black aura to absorb it. As Nathan's body fell to the ground and his eyes rolled back until the pupils were no longer visible, the spirit gradually enlarged in size before looming over the battlefield above an awestruck Joshua and a quivering Maris.

"I-impossible...h-he has it too...?!" Maris stammered to herself in disbelief.

Her head raised upwards to take in the terrifying spectacle of the black aura taking the form of a massive, monstrous dragon staring down threateningly at her.

Submerged in sorrow and hatred, Nathan had lost himself and succumbed to the full, latent power of the Devil's Spirit.

And Maris was its target...

⊷⊶⋘◈⋙⊷⊶

Chapter 24

The Devil's Spirit announced its arrival onto the battlefield by unleashing a thunderous roar, one that sent shockwaves through the air and dispersed much of the smoke that had obscured the area. Maris instinctively raised her arms to her face, trying to shield herself from the worst of the impact. Joshua buried his head towards the earth, keeping his eyes protected as specks of dirt were blown along the landscape.

Within seconds, the ripple effects of the Devil's Spirit reached the two bridges, alerting the remnants of Maris' followers who had remained behind after obeying her orders as well as Thomas, Abbie and their families. Recognising the sinister chill that they felt, Thomas and Abbie turned around to behold the sight of the incorporeal black aura manifested in the form of a humungous dragon, high above the dwindling flames.

"N-Nathan…?!" Abbie uttered out of distress, identifying the energy as the same one Nathan had unwittingly fallen under the influence of against Ranjit. Only this time, the power being displayed was on a much grander scale.

Taken aback by this unexpected image, the shock of seeing it was too much for Melissa who fainted. Luckily, Thomas was quick to react, catching his mother before her head could hit the earth. While Frank and Linda watched what was happening in the centre of the arena, Abbie helped Thomas to lower Melissa until she was resting on the ground. Thomas was relieved to find that her breathing was normal and that she hadn't collapsed because of smoke inhalation. The teenagers' eyes met over Melissa's chest, knowing that they were thinking the same thing – for Nathan's black aura to have developed to this extent, something *really* bad must have happened out there.

Back on the frontlines, Maris unconsciously stepped backwards away from the dark dragon that glared menacingly down at her. Her disciples were not accustomed to seeing their master retreat from anyone, so naturally this was a concerning situation for them. Her eyes darted back towards the rubble where Nathan's prone body lay, the medium for the Devil's Spirit which continued to glow around him. Blinded by panic, Maris directed her fingers in the boy's direction, shooting several bursts of lightning despite having already tried this moments ago.

The results were exactly the same with the elemental attacks being swallowed up by the aura and leaving the catatonic Nathan unscathed. Maris unwittingly glanced back up at the sky, the dragon having kept its focus on her throughout. It was as though this phantom was trying to intimidate her and make her experience the same crippling powerlessness that she had inflicted on the people she had killed. Judging by the beads of sweat dripping down her bloodied face and the way her jaw automatically lowered, it was certainly working. Quickly running out of options, Maris glanced over her shoulder at her followers to address them.

"Soldiers! Hurry up and attack!" she called out to them, the desperation slipping out in spite of her commanding voice.

In that instant, Maris detected that the spirit dragon was on the offence. This was confirmed when she returned her attention to it, her head snapping around only to find the entity lunging towards her at rapid speed. Out of instinct, Maris used her magic to protect herself, conjuring up a barrier of wind and water around her body to repel the black aura, keeping it at bay. The dragon began to eat away at these supernatural shields, consuming them in the same manner that it did the lightning bolts. This forced Maris to expend more energy to strengthen her defences, although, by the way her legs wobbled, it was becoming apparent to her that her stamina wouldn't hold out forever.

A few of Maris' forces tried to seize their opportunity and flee from the battle only to be callously shot or cut down by some of her more devoted followers who outnumbered them. Once any potential deserters had been either dealt with or discouraged from leaving, the remaining zealots charged towards the heart of the frontlines to their master's aid. As soon as they were in range, they fired the few guns that they had collected from Entritica's soldiers and chucked daggers and swords in the direction of the dragon.

They then watched in despair as the bullets and blades simply passed through the vaporous apparition like sunlight piercing through clouds. Instead of hindering the Devil's Spirit, all that Chimera had managed to do was alert it to their presence. The head of the spirit turned its attention away from Maris and towards the terrified terrorists.

Coming to terms with how in over their head they truly were, the zealots of Chimera retreated back in the direction of the bridge, screeching as they scurried away. Alerted by their wails, Joshua lifted his head up and twisted his neck around in time to see the dragon dart after Maris' followers. Within a single blink of his eyes, the black aura had whizzed all the way over to their location and had begun to devastate them. All it took was the phantom phasing through their bodies for the zealots to crumple lifelessly to the floor one after another.

Joshua turned away from the dreadful scene, returning his focus to the source of the demonic aura – Nathan. He could sense the overwhelming hateful energy radiating from his body, recognising it from his encounter with Ranjit on Seppuku Bridge, and wondered to himself: was this the Devil's Spirit that he'd overheard Nathan discussing with Thomas and Abbie? He could think of no other explanation, yet if true, it astounded and saddened Joshua to think that something with the power to kill a fully grown man just by coming into contact with them resided within his younger cousin. Then again, it wasn't lost on Joshua that Nathan had just witnessed his mother get killed moments ago – if anything was going to push him over the edge to such an extent, this would be it…

While mourning Victoria, it was in that moment that Joshua was reminded of how Maris had also incapacitated *his* dad. Realising this, he turned to where the immobile Clint was and started frantically crawling over to him, praying that he hadn't shared the same fate as his sister.

Meanwhile, after she'd had chance to recuperate, Maris observed the Devil's Spirit polishing off her soldiers, using them as sacrificial pawns as she waited for an opening to strike. Once she felt confident that the dragon's attention was fully diverted, Maris began to gather energy into her right hand, moulding a mixture of fire and lightning into a sphere. With her left hand she used a gust of wind to launch herself high off the ground. As soon as she'd soared above the head of the spirit, she hurled the elemental orb in its direction.

Maris grinned manically as her attack found its target, spreading instantly and engulfing the phantom in flames. The incessant chattering of the crackling electricity captured the attention of Thomas, Abbie and Joshua who all looked on from their respective locations with concern at the blazing entity in the sky, wondering how this would affect Nathan.

The mage's joy was short-lived though, for both the fire and the lightning were devoured by the black aura in front of her eyes. As gravity pulled her back down to earth, it struck Maris that right now, she was defenceless while the dragon stared her down.

Before she could even react, the spirit retaliated, firing a concentrated burst of wind from its mouth. Thomas, Abbie, Frank and Linda observed in awe as the powerful gale sent Maris flying into the rubble of the same mound that she had previously raised from the ground. Joshua used his arm as cover once Maris' body crashed into the rocks, a sickening thud filling his ears as the impact of the collision left a huge opening in the wreckage.

While Joshua continued to inch his way closer to Clint, Thomas' and Abbie's eyes were fixed on the cloud of dust floating out of the crater. Seconds passed without any signs of movement from the hole, allowing their minds to whir. Maris was carried into the debris with a significant level of force, they both thought. Was it possible that she was dead…?

But there wasn't time for that notion to linger as the Devil's Spirit continued its onslaught, swooping back down on the few Chimera soldiers that were still showing signs of life. With her thoughts drifting back to Nathan upon observing this, Abbie made an impulsive decision.

"Nathan needs help – I'm going out there!" she established firmly.

"Are you nuts?!" Thomas replied incredulously while cradling Melissa's head in his hands.

"If it's anything like before, then that thing's possessing Nathan! We have to snap him out of it!" Abbie argued as Thomas frowned in response, clearly fretting for her safety which she picked up on. "Look, Maris and Chimera are either distracted or dead by now! If there was a safe time to go out there, it's *now*!" she insisted, hoping to reassure Thomas. His face twitched, suggesting to Abbie that he was coming around to the idea. However, his body language still indicated hesitance on his part. Aware that time was of the essence, Abbie called out to Frank and Linda who were crouched down by Ben's side. "Mom, Dad! Keep an eye on Ben!" she ordered hastily.

With that, before they could even talk her out of going, Abbie hurried off to find Nathan, hopping over the wavering wildfire in her haste. Watching her bravely charge towards the ravaged battlegrounds alone, Thomas sighed as he made his mind up.

"I'm going after her to make sure she's okay," he informed a bewildered Frank and Linda. "Sorry to ask but please keep an eye on my mom…"

Thomas begged them, entrusting her care to Linda before following Abbie into the warzone.

Thomas chased after her, struggling to keep up with Abbie's speed while trying to ignore the rampaging dragon in the distance. Despite his sluggish pace though, he was surprised to find that he was catching up to Abbie who had come to a standstill. Once Thomas reached her side, he soon found out why. She was rooted to the spot after finding the countless corpses of the soldiers spread out across the landscape. Thomas was naturally troubled by the sight of this, but he noted how the colour had faded from Abbie's face. Even with the courage she'd demonstrated in venturing onto the frontlines, she was not mentally or emotionally prepared to confront such a disheartening scene. Seeing her look so shaken, Thomas placed his hand reassuringly on her shoulder.

"C'mon. Nathan's waiting for us…" he whispered gently to Abbie, reminding her what was at stake. Abbie heard Thomas' words and nodded in agreement, steeling her nerves as they both pressed on, making their way over the fallen warriors to where their best friend was.

It wasn't long until Nathan's body became visually clearer to them on their approach to the pile of rubble. They soon realised that it wasn't just him there as they identified a figure on the ground making slight movements several feet away from Nathan. Thomas and Abbie approached carefully, unsure at this distance whether this was an enemy or an ally. After several cautious steps though, the soldier turned his head and Abbie instantly recognised the distressed face of Joshua.

"Josh! You're alive, thank god!" she exclaimed, rushing over to him with Thomas tailing her. The ex-prefect barely acknowledged them however and once Thomas and Abbie were close enough, they could see why. Joshua was kneeling over Clint, preoccupied with trying to revive his father. After he became aware of Thomas' and Abbie's presence, he instinctively glanced over at them, almost searching for their support.

"H-he's not responding…" Joshua squeaked meekly as tears rolled down his cheek whilst trying to press down firmly on his chest. Thomas and Abbie tried to assemble around him, concealing their anxiety at seeing the usually authoritative Joshua look so utterly vulnerable. They both knelt beside Joshua, Thomas cupping Clint's head in his hands as Abbie placed her fingers on his wrist to feel for a pulse.

"His breath is still warm…" Thomas stated upon sensing the mild heat coming from Clint's mouth.

"Th-there's a faint pulse…" Abbie added encouragingly. Although they were both trying to instil Joshua with hope, they couldn't bring themselves to say that both vital signs were weakening rapidly.

Elsewhere, the last of the Chimera radicals were finished off by the Devil's Spirit, their arms falling limply on the ground while their faces were painted with their, tortured, wide-eyed dying expressions. With nobody left to unleash its rage upon, the dragon wailed out with a fearsome yet pained howl towards the darkening sky which cast a gloomy shadow over Thomas, Abbie, Joshua and the rest of the devastated area.

"H-he's not waking up…" Joshua sobbed helplessly. "Dad, wake up… p-please wake up…"

"H-how did it all come to this…?" Abbie questioned as she succumbed to despair, never imagining that their attempted escape from Entritica could end up this way. Seeing Abbie's and Joshua's hopes crumble with the fear that they were too late seeping in, Thomas looked over his shoulder at where Nathan was, still unmoving and cloaked in the black aura. Using the thought of his best friend as motivation, wanting to do what he could to save his uncle, Thomas made one last-ditch attempt to try and rouse Clint from the brink of death.

"Clint, please wake up!" he chanted, repeating the words over and over at the top of his lungs, hoping that his voice would reach Clint, even in his unconscious state. It wasn't long until Abbie and Joshua were following his lead, silently praying for a miracle as their cries echoed throughout the wasteland.

Unbeknownst to them though, the slight breezes carried the sound of their voices towards Nathan – and despite his seemingly possessed state, his fingers twitched in response to the calls of his friends.

Simultaneously, the spirit dragon ceased roaring and turned its head towards the location of Thomas, Abbie, Joshua and the downed Clint. As if acting out of instinct, the phantom flew over in their direction.

Once directly above the group of four, the dragon descended, casting a shadow over them that grew larger the closer it got to the earth. This didn't go unnoticed by Joshua who raised his head upwards and upon seeing the beast soar at them, he promptly warned Thomas and Abbie.

"Guys, get back!!" Joshua shouted only to take the initiative himself and hastily pull both of them out of the black aura's path.

Joshua, Thomas and Abbie then observed in alarm as the spirit phased into Clint's body before re-emerging and replicating the action again. Joshua winced at the sight of his father's body convulsing each time the demonic aura engulfed him.

"Nathan, what are you doing?! Nathan, please *stop*!!" Joshua yelled out, pleading with the dragon that was lunging towards Clint for a fourth time. He placed a foot forward, almost ready to intervene, only to be held back by Abbie.

"Josh, wait! Look!" she exclaimed, pointing at Clint.

Joshua's and Thomas' eyes darted to follow her arm just as the Devil's Spirit prised itself away from Clint. To their shock, Clint let out a throaty cough, spluttering up soot particles that he'd previously inhaled. More importantly, he was alive!

"Dad!" Joshua blurted out of sheer relief, darting over to embrace his father.

"J-Josh...? W-where...where a-are...?" Clint murmured almost incoherently, disorientated after being plucked free from death's grip.

As the young man held his dad tightly, Thomas and Abbie realised that the dragon was suspended in the sky above them, having stopped now that Clint had been revived. Taking account of this, it suggested that the spirit's actions were no mistake.

"Y-you...you saved his life, didn't you?" Thomas addressed the entity looming over them. "Nathan, are you in there? Can you hear us?" he called out to it. The spirit didn't react though, it just stared back at Thomas and Abbie, albeit whether it was comprehending them as his friends was unclear.

"Oh Nath...what happened to turn you into this...?" Abbie wondered aloud in a sad tone, regarding the black aura with sympathy.

With Clint out of immediate danger, Thomas and Abbie returned their attention to Nathan. Thomas looked past the spirit emanating from his body and upon seeing the massive pile of debris behind him, he was reminded of a crucial detail.

"H-his mom came out here..." he gasped to Abbie in a moment of realisation, remembering how Victoria had jumped over the inferno in pursuit of him.

Thomas had already deduced the tragic events that had transpired, but in a state of denial, Abbie's head pivoted back and forth wildly, trying in vain to search for where Victoria was.

"W-where is she?!" Abbie questioned anxiously. When she found no success in locating her, she turned to Joshua who was still tending to Clint. "Josh! Where's Victoria?!!" she called out to him.

Joshua looked up at Abbie, a regretful expression on his face once he heard her mention Victoria's name. He opened his mouth as if to answer Abbie's question but, in the end, he couldn't bring himself to say the words, only able to lower his head in sorrow.

"No..." Abbie uttered, reluctantly accepting Victoria's death from Joshua's silent reaction. Once it had sunk in, she rushed over impulsively towards Nathan.

"Abbie, wait!" Thomas shouted after her. He wasn't quick enough to stop her though as she quickly reached Nathan's side. The look of concern spread across Abbie's face as she examined his visage, seeing only the bloodshot whites of his eyes and his mouth agape.

"Nath! Nath, it's Abbie! Can you hear me?! Please, you need to wake up!" Abbie pleaded with him. When he showed no signs of responding, she stretched out her hand towards Nathan's head.

"Abbie, don't!" Joshua hollered.

As soon as her fingers came into contact with the black aura, Abbie winced after experiencing a nasty zap shoot throughout her body, almost like she'd just touched a laser barrier.

"Ow! What the...?!" Abbie remarked. Despite the pain, she wasn't ready to let it stop her from trying to snap her friend out of his trance. She extended her arm again and tried to feel her way through the aura. Instead of passing through it though, the entity solidified, resisting her touch and shocking Abbie further as she pushed against it. "What the hell is this thing?!" she cried out with the Devil's Spirit seemingly having a mind of its own. "Nathan, please! We're trying to help you!" While she was struggling, Joshua gazed up at the dragon, sensing from its sinister energy that its hostility was growing as Abbie persisted in her attempts to reach Nathan.

"Abbie, you need to stop *now*!" Joshua warned, something that Abbie heeded after hearing the seriousness in his tone. "I want Nathan back to normal too! But we have no idea what touching him in this state might do to him – it might even *kill* him! Is that what you *want*?!" he reprimanded, his voice wavering with desperation.

Thomas and Abbie knew that Joshua had a point. After all, besides attacking Chimera's forces, the spirit had protected Nathan from Maris' attacks since its awakening and that could well be the reason why.

"So…then what do we do now?" Thomas asked, at a loss for how to proceed next. Joshua rose to his feet while Clint's arm was draped over his shoulder, the weary father groaning in discomfort, even with the gentle movements that his son was making.

"First things first, we have to get you two and dad away from here!" Joshua asserted.

"What?! We can't just leave Nathan here!" Abbie argued, shaking her head, aghast at the idea.

Their dispute was then interrupted by the spirit dragon who screeched at the three of them, however its glare was directed at Abbie. It was almost as if it was voicing its disapproval at her line of reasoning.

"Guys, call me crazy, but I think the dragon – I-I mean, Nathan – *wants* us to escape…" Thomas claimed.

"H-how can you tell?!" Abbie challenged with an expression of bewilderment.

"I-it's a gut feeling. And I don't think it's wrong…" Thomas answered honestly. The Devil's Spirit seemed to confirm this when it settled down.

"Look, once you three are safe at the bridge, I'll come back for Nathan myself. I promise!" Joshua insisted.

Abbie hesitated for a moment, still not liking the idea of leaving Nathan behind. She finally relented though after examining the black aura one more time, as though recognising the desires within Nathan's heart.

"Alright, fine! Let's make this quick then!" she accepted.

Their minds made up, Thomas and Abbie scrambled over to Joshua so they could help him carry Clint for ease. They worked it out in a way where Joshua and Abbie could do the bulk of the supporting while the physically weaker Thomas helped by holding one of Clint's legs.

Before they could move anywhere though, the trio heard the Devil's Spirit growl menacingly. Joshua looked up and noticed that it was staring at the pile of rocks from the mound. His own eyes darted towards the debris until they widened in fear.

"Ah crud…" Joshua cursed under his breath.

His words were still heard by Thomas and Abbie who turned their heads to follow his gaze. The three of them observed as two hands appeared atop the rubble, a figure pulling itself up from the crater to their horror – Maris was still alive.

"Hurry and run now!!" Joshua ordered sternly.

There were no arguments or signs of hesitation this time – Thomas and Abbie had seen the carnage that Maris had wrought. Without a second thought, the trio worked together to lift Clint off the ground and sprinted as fast as they could towards the bridge where Melissa, Frank, Linda and Ben were.

Meanwhile, Maris emerged from the wreckage, gritting her teeth while the spirit snarled as she made her presence felt. The blood on her face had dried up, resembling a crimson mask that was peeling away from her skin bit by bit. Sweat dripped down her brow as she huffed and puffed, fatigue finally setting in as she searched for a way to survive this encounter, any vulnerability of the Devil's Spirit that she could exploit.

Then, in the corner of her eye, Maris spotted Thomas, Abbie and Joshua scampering away with Clint in the distance. That's when a thought crossed her mind.

"I see…they're the ones you're protecting now…" Maris murmured to herself, sensing that the Devil's Spirit was more restrained than earlier. "They're the source of all that power – the ones keeping you going…so losing them should take the fight out of you…"

Just as Thomas, Abbie, Joshua and Clint were halfway between the bridge and the heap of boulders that they'd run from, Maris manipulated the waning wildfire. In a matter of seconds, she had reignited the flames, causing them to intensify and grow in size. The renewed heat was felt by Frank and Linda who winced at the blaze, distracting them from keeping an eye on Ben and Melissa. The frequently bickering parents shared a silent look of mutual concern, both fearing what this could mean for Abbie who had ventured out into that hellhole.

While Frank and Linda wished for their daughter's safe return, Maris directed the inferno towards Abbie, Thomas, Joshua and Clint. With a flick of her hand and the clenching of her fist, the wildfire spread inwards, a sight that made all three of the teenagers stop in their tracks. As the raging flames approached them, enclosing them in the area with no escape, the terror washed over them along with the belief that this was the end for them…

When all hope seemed lost though, the Devil's Spirit swooped down, placing itself between Nathan's friends and the firestorm. In an instant, the dragon turned into a blur that circled around the entire warzone at near enough the speed of light. Thomas, Abbie and Joshua watched in awe as the spirit effortlessly consumed the blaze, flame by flame. Contrarily, an expression of disbelief was plastered on Maris' face upon observing this feat, specks of dried blood flaking away as her arms dropped by her sides defeatedly.

Once the dragon had removed the rest of the blaze from the battlefield, it soared up towards the darkened sky with everyone raising their heads to follow it. The fire that the phantom had devoured was still burning within it, causing the dark enigma to intermittently glow with a golden hue. Thomas, Abbie and Joshua couldn't help but marvel at this spectacle, radiating like sunlight high above the ground whereas Maris instinctively stepped backwards, ready to retreat as the demon fixed its gaze upon her.

Seeing the mage place even one foot behind her was enough to provoke the dragon, compelling it to surge towards her at breakneck speed. In a panic and with her stamina on the verge of being depleted, Maris jumped down to the other side of the rock pile, running as fast as she possibly could to avoid the black aura. She soon realised however that she couldn't escape from the vicious velocity of the Devil's Spirit. With her abdomen racked with agony and her lungs gasping for air, Maris knew her options were running out.

"Two more...I can...manage...two more..." she mumbled aloud, assessing her situation. She conjured a small orb of wind in the palm of her hand whilst the black aura closed in on her. Maris waited until the spirit was a foot away and just as it was about to touch her, she chucked the sphere at the ground, launching herself up in the air and out of the path of the dragon.

Thomas, Abbie and Joshua were rooted to the spot as they witnessed Maris come into view, soaring high in the sky above the rubble. Thinking that she'd tricked the phantom, the cult leader had her attention drawn to Mount Tamara, plotting to use her remaining energy to propel her there so that she could seek refuge from the beast.

Before she could even prepare to carry out her plan though, Maris could feel the air beneath her heating up and her instincts warned her that she was in peril. Sure enough, she looked downwards to find that the dragon had altered its trajectory and was rocketing straight for her, its mouth widening to reveal a fireball to the shock of the mage.

With the three of them still supporting Clint, Thomas, Abbie and Joshua observed from afar as the dragon unleashed a torrent of flames at Maris, lighting up the gloomy sky with the orange glow of the embers. Out of desperation, the almighty leader of Chimera used her remaining stamina to try and boost her away from the attack.

However, the flames engulfed her neck and left arm before she could fully evade the blaze. Maris shrieked in pain, her clothes and flesh smouldering during her plummet back down to earth.

Thomas, Abbie and Joshua breathed a collective sigh of relief at seeing Maris' body crash to the ground with a heavy impact with no movement afterwards. Satisfied that the black aura would finish her off, the three took their chance to flee the battlefield, now devoid of wildfire.

Unbeknownst to them though, the dragon spotted them carrying Clint towards the bridge. Once they were a few yards from it, the spirit began to dissipate and lose its shape. The clouds darkened and the sky rumbled above as the black aura slowly faded away from the area, flowing back into Nathan's body.

While this was happening, Thomas, Abbie, Joshua and Clint were reunited with Melissa, Frank, Linda and Ben. Thomas had arrived just in time to see his mother awaken again after fainting.

"Oh mom! You're okay! Thank god, thank god..." he expressed gratefully, hugging Melissa tightly while Abbie did the same with Frank and Linda, the two teenagers still reeling from thinking how close they had come to being killed. Rain began to fall from the heavens as Joshua laid Clint on the ground and Abbie returned to Ben's side, each of them trying to wake up their unconscious loved ones.

Back at the rubble, with the Devil's Spirit returned to its vessel, the raindrops grew thicker and one of them splashed directly on Nathan's forehead. The sensation was enough to stir the boy, causing him to close his bloodshot eyes. When he reopened them, the pupils had returned just in time to catch a flash of lightning flare up above him.

In that instant, the scene gave Nathan a chilling reminder of what had happened just before he blacked out – how Victoria was shot down with lightning by Maris' hand.

The rain poured down around him, each drop that struck the terrain serving to cruelly hammer the reality of his predicament further. His father was dead. And now his mother was gone too. Grief slowly set in and overwhelmed him as he motionlessly lay on the ground, feeling helpless, empty and alone…

Suddenly, the pattering of the raindrops was disrupted by the sound of approaching footsteps. Even as they drew nearer, Nathan continued to listlessly stare up at the sky, no longer having the will to acknowledge the squelching noises that they made over the sodden terrain. It wasn't until the figure was directly standing over his body that he could see who it was – Maris.

The sight of his parents' killer was enough to rouse him out of his stupor but having been sapped of his energy by the Devil's Spirit, Nathan was still unable to move, no matter how hard he tried to channel his hatred as motivation. He did get a good view of Maris though – the scar that he'd scratched into her forehead remained visible, even if the blood that had gushed down onto her face had dried up now. This time however, Nathan could see that her neck and left arm had been burned, the odour of singed flesh penetrating his nostrils. As far as he knew, he'd only just woken up after falling unconscious so, oblivious to the carnage that the black aura had dealt to Maris and Chimera, he quietly questioned how she'd suffered those wounds. It seemed that he would get the answer to this as Maris addressed him.

"So…you have it too…the Devil's Spirit…" she muttered, huffing between breaths as she stared down at the defenceless boy. "To think that there's another like me after all…"

It was a revelation that stunned Nathan, even in his silent state – Maris not only knew of the Devil's Spirit too but by the sounds of it, she also possessed that same power. It would explain the malicious energy that he sensed from within her. Yet, he found it hard to fathom that he was capable of damaging her to this extent. Before he could dwell on this piece of information, Maris continued to talk.

"For me to be pushed this far…I hate to say it but it's commendable. You may be the only person in this wretched world besides my mentor who could pose a threat to me…" Maris conceded, her expression softening whilst showing respect to Nathan. "I just regret that we didn't meet sooner. We could have worked together as equals. Who knows, maybe we both could have avoided this fate…"

The mage looked away from Nathan for a second, her head facing the ground, almost showing a semblance of remorse as the downpour soaked the pair of them. Nathan's face and body were still numb from anguish and exhaustion, though his eyes expressed the disgust he felt at this monster trying to relate to him.

Unfortunately, while her head was lowered, Maris caught sight of her reflection in a puddle of rainwater that had formed beneath her. It was the first time she'd seen her neck and the burns that the Devil's Spirit had bestowed upon her. Having built up an image amongst her followers of being untouchable, these injuries served as a reminder to her that she was fallible after all. In response to this humbling thought, Maris' expression hardened once more as she crouched down to pick up the nearest mask that she could grab from one of her soldiers' corpses before returning her focus to Nathan.

"Alas, it's pointless speaking about what-ifs..." she lamented. "The fact is that you are too much of a threat for me to let you live. You've taken me to my absolute limit – hell, I don't even have the energy to conjure up my own magic anymore..." Maris continued, gazing up at the sky which reverberated with the growls of thunder. "But luckily for me, I can still manipulate the natural elements around me..."

She backed up her claim by raising her blemished arm in the air and, in an incredible display, controlled the lightning that was flaring up in the sky. Maris held it high above Nathan's body, the electricity sizzling chaotically while she kept it suspended beneath the clouds.

"Sorry kid, this may seem excessive but it's only fitting that I give someone who was able to wound me a death worthy of the feat..." Maris rationalised cold-heartedly. Once again, Nathan showed no visible reaction to this, as if defeatedly accepting of what would come next.

Meanwhile, knowing that he still had to go back for Nathan, Joshua entrusted the care of his father to the resuscitated Melissa as well as Thomas and Abbie. However, their attention was caught as the damp ground beneath them was illuminated by the intermittent flashes of lightning. It drew their eyes back to the warzone and they were all horrified to see in the centre of it that Maris was looming over a defenceless Nathan.

"No! He's powered down! Nathan!" Joshua cried out, detecting that the Devil's Spirit was no longer shielding him. Thomas and Abbie also picked up on this and the three of them impulsively rushed over to try and save him.

Aware of her surroundings though, Maris noticed that they were making a move to run in. Recognising this, she wasted no more time.

"Rest well kid..." Maris uttered in a low voice, leaving her parting words with Nathan.

With that, she lowered her arm and directed the lightning bolt straight at the boy, leaving Thomas, Abbie and Joshua with their mouths agape in despair during their desperate sprint as the electricity descended from the heavens above.

For Nathan though, just as the shine from the light overpowered his senses, he saw one more image of a woman with red hair – his mother, Victoria. She could see her embracing him and it was like he could feel the touch of her holding him in her arms one last time. It was a blissful experience of peace for him as he closed his eyes, ready for the lightning to consume him and reunite him with his late parents...

⊷⊷⊸◅❮▻⊷⊷⊶

Chapter 25

A deafening roar of thunder rippled through the air and Thomas, Abbie and Joshua automatically came to a screeching halt as the lightning crashed down upon the earth, sending a shockwave throughout the area. The resulting glare forced them to shield their eyes from the blinding flash that illuminated the warzone and swallowed up both Nathan and Maris from their sights.

The flare persisted for several seconds before finally dying down. Sensing behind his eyelids that the glow was starting to diminish, Thomas carefully opened his eyes and peeked through his fingers after wiping the rainwater away. Abbie and Joshua soon did the same once their ears stopped ringing from the effects of the thunderclap, lowering their arms as their feelings of disorientation faded away.

While the terrain ahead of them was still littered with corpses, the ground at the centre of it was now scorched where the lightning had struck. Thomas, Abbie and Joshua searched the area frantically, looking around for any sign of Maris but they quickly found that the mage was nowhere to be seen.

However, Abbie spotted something amidst the deluge of rain that made the colour drain from her face. She grabbed Thomas' and Joshua's attention, their eyes following her arm which pointed out at the heart of the charred earth. The trio were left aghast as they spotted Nathan's body lying there.

Thomas, Abbie and Joshua impulsively rushed back out towards the wasteland, closely followed by Linda who carried Ben in her arms while Melissa and Frank struggled along with the unconscious Clint. The downpour began to settle as the group of survivors got nearer to the middle of the lifeless battlefield, Melissa, Frank and Linda recoiling at the image of the fallen soldiers that they passed as they lagged behind their children.

Once they were feet away from the heap of rubble, everyone was rendered speechless as they approached Nathan. He was lying face up, his eyes closed, his mouth agape and his clothes singed from the thunderbolt. The sight of their friend resting there, unresponsive even with the droplets of water that trickled down his cheek, made Thomas' and Abbie's eyes well up with tears that they couldn't fight any longer. Contrarily, Joshua tried to hold his emotions together as he stepped towards his cousin's side. His lip quivered uncontrollably from looking down at Nathan's face, devoid of expression and yet there was something tragically tranquil about his stillness.

"N-Nathan...Nathan..." Joshua feebly called out to him only to be met with zero reaction. Certain that their friend was dead, Thomas and Abbie closed their eyes and quietly mourned for Nathan as the tears flowed.

Joshua crouched down next to his cousin at the exact moment that Melissa, Frank and Linda arrived with Clint and Ben, finally catching up to the youngsters. Upon seeing Nathan's body, the adults' hearts all sunk as the rain finally ceased. Though they were unable to find the words to console their children, Melissa instinctively hugged Thomas while Frank and Linda stood with Abbie in solidarity.

"I-I'm...I'm s-so sorry Nath..." Joshua gulped. "Y-you saved us all... a-and I just...I w-wasn't strong enough...t-to return the favour..." he stated, his chest tightening at the thought that he'd failed not only his younger cousin but Victoria too.

Joshua reached out towards Nathan's shoulders before dragging his limp body closer to him until he was cradling his head in his arms. Thomas and Abbie stepped forward and knelt down either side of the rookie soldier. Abbie placed a hand tenderly on Nathan's cold cheek while her head rested on Joshua's shoulder for comfort. As the adults sensitively watched the teenagers mourn their friend, Thomas cupped Nathan's right hand in his own palms, wanting to be close to him one more time.

But in that moment, Thomas detected a slight warmth from his flesh. His curiosity piqued by this, he gently rotated Nathan's hand until his palm was facing upwards. Then, learning from his mother's example earlier, he placed two fingers on his wrist to check for a pulse – and his eyes widened when he could feel one.

"Guys, get back!" Thomas blurted out hastily, brushing Joshua and Abbie aside and leaving them both startled by his abrupt outburst. Along with the parents, they observed as Thomas pressed his ear to Nathan's chest, ensuring that he hadn't made a mistake out of blind hope.

Sure enough, just when the first rays of sunlight began to break through the thick clouds above, Thomas' eyes lit up once he felt three soft but undeniable thumps from Nathan's torso.

"His heart's beating! He's still *alive*!!" Thomas announced to the group who couldn't supress their shock at the news.

"A-are you serious?!" Abbie questioned hopefully.

"Th-that can't be possible...h-he was struck by lightning!" Joshua argued, remaining sceptical that his cousin could endure such a concentrated attack. Melissa stepped in to examine Nathan herself and after a few seconds, she gave her verdict.

"There's no mistaking it – it's really faint but he's got a pulse and he's still breathing. Nathan's definitely alive," Melissa confirmed to the relief and joy of the others, although her concern for the unconscious boy remained.

"H-how on earth did he survive all that...?" Joshua wondered in disbelief, regarding Nathan with awe for his resiliency while Melissa and Thomas tended to him.

"D-do you think it was the Devil's Spirit?" Abbie suggested. "I mean, we did see it absorb Maris' attacks..."

"I-I'm not so sure" Joshua acknowledged. "Maris brought that lightning bolt down...b-but I couldn't feel that sinister energy coming from Nathan..."

"W-where is Maris anyway? Y-you don't think she's still lingering around, d-do you?" Frank asked, terrified at the prospect of confronting the mage.

"No, I don't sense her presence anywhere...she must have scarpered..." Joshua reassured him before noticing him struggle to support Clint by himself now that Melissa was preoccupied with Nathan. As he took Clint off Frank's hands, Melissa turned to address the rest of the group.

"We need to get him help immediately!" she insisted. "He's barely alive and I don't how much longer he can hang on for!" Without hesitation, Joshua looked out at the bodies strewn across the ravaged battleground.

"Help!! Anyone!!" he cried out, desperately praying that there were still some surviving soldiers hiding amongst the dead. Joshua did this three times until he realised that his efforts were in vain when no response was returned to him. Just as he was about to give up hope, Abbie spotted something in the sky.

"Looks like help is on its way after all!" she proclaimed to Joshua and the others before directing them to where she was looking.

Just as the sun started to peek out from behind the clouds, everybody watched as around sixty brightly coloured air ambulance helicopters emerged from behind Mount Tamara and hovered into view. While Thomas and Melissa stayed huddled around Nathan, Abbie and Frank jumped up and down, wildly waving their arms in an effort to make themselves as visible as possible to the helicopters. One minute later, the group felt a wave of relief wash over them upon seeing the vehicles descending to the ground before landing.

After the rotor blades finally stopped spinning, several medics exited three of the aircrafts and made their way through the bodies of the fallen towards Abbie and the rest of the survivors. Firstly, at the urging of Joshua and Linda, the medics carefully took the unconscious Clint and Ben off their hands and escorted them into separate helicopters.

They then turned their attention to Nathan, scooping the lad from the earth and carrying him to the nearest vehicle whilst Thomas pleaded with them to be gentle with his friend. As the last warrior standing, the onus fell to a shaken Joshua to relay the events that transpired to the leader of the medical division. He described the wildfire and thunderstorm that had injured his family and friends, confirmed the deaths of Bradley and Victoria, and reported how Maris was responsible for all of them. However, he took care not to mention anything about Nathan's grief unleashing the Devil's Spirit on Chimera's forces – after all, it just seemed too unbelievable to explain, especially when he was still comprehending what he'd witnessed himself.

Most of the medics were focused on clearing the area of the bodies, moving them one by one into the other helicopters. Observing this taking place in the background, Joshua quietly wondered if this is what they had to do with Richard when he was killed. This thought stuck with him as he saw Nathan being placed onto a stretcher, his cousin still unresponsive to what was happening around him. He prayed that Nathan wouldn't share the same fate as his mother and father.

With three helicopters containing Clint, Ben and Nathan, there was only enough space for two more people in each aircraft. Thomas and Melissa agreed to accompany Nathan while Frank and Linda stayed with their son, Ben. Although Abbie was reluctant to be away from her brother's side, she didn't want Joshua to be on his own after everything he'd had to experience today. Thus, she decided to travel with him and entrusted her parents with taking care of Ben.

Once everyone was in their designated vehicle, the three helicopters soared away, leaving the barren wasteland behind. Thomas, Melissa, Joshua, Abbie, Frank and Linda watched over Nathan, Clint and Ben respectively as the aircrafts carried them upwards, the clouds now starting to shift away in the sky. When they'd reached a certain altitude, each person glanced out of their windows. Just before the helicopters flew over to the other side of Mount Tamara, they were all left disturbed by the enduring image of hundreds of corpses lying all across the landscape, all being tended to by the remaining medics. Being unfortunate enough to observe the scale of her destruction from such a height, it served as one last reminder of the unfathomable depths of Maris' strength and how close they'd really come to joining that mass graveyard.

****

Thankfully, it wasn't long before the emergency aircrafts arrived at the nearest hospital. As soon as the helicopters had landed safely, the medics immediately carted Clint, Ben and Nathan away through the corridors for urgent care. The nurses stressed the importance that they be treated as high priority patients due to the smoke inhaled by the former two and the injuries sustained by Nathan thanks to the thunderbolt that struck him.

Throughout the rest of the day, while Clint, Ben and Nathan were undergoing emergency treatment, Thomas, Abbie, Joshua, Melissa, Frank and Linda were also checked over by doctors to ensure that there were no underlying issues suffered from the ordeal. Several different tests were done to monitor this, ones that required the latter six to go in and out of various offices all across the infirmary and bide their time in multiple waiting rooms.

It wasn't until many hours later, long after the sun had set when the medical examinations were completed. Abbie, Frank and Linda were cleared and had gone to look for the ward where Ben was being treated, whereas Joshua went up to the reception to ask for updates on Clint's and Nathan's conditions. Melissa was still being kept under supervision due to suffering a panic attack during the last test.

Thomas was the last of the surviving group to be assessed and he was given the 'all clear' by the doctor. He exited the office and found Joshua seated in the waiting room, his hands cupping his mouth as he anxiously anticipated more information about his family. Thomas understood how he felt – he himself was worried about his mother, having heard about her predicament moments before entering the room for his own examination. So he took a seat next to Joshua who acknowledged Thomas' presence with a glance. The two boys didn't say anything though, as if mutually agreeing to quietly wait in unison for any news about their loved ones. Despite the silence, Joshua's tensed muscles relaxed the instant that Thomas sat beside him supportively.

Minutes later, a doctor from the urgent care department emerged from the corridor. Once he asked the receptionist if, in his words, 'the sons of Mr Griffiths and Mrs Cartwright' were around, Joshua and Thomas shot up from their chairs and made a beeline for him.

"How are they?" both boys asked simultaneously. The doctor was unfazed by the ambush, addressing Thomas first.

"Melissa's settled down now. Given what you've all gone through today, it's a miracle only one of you have experienced a panic attack. Other than that, her vitals are fine, so she's fit to go home tomorrow morning," the doctor explained reassuringly to which Thomas breathed a thankful sigh of relief. The medic then turned to Joshua. "On the other hand, Clint is incredibly lucky to still be alive – the scans showed a lot of soot particles in his airways. Truthfully, I have no idea how he survived that wildfire. That being said, he too will make a full recovery and all being well, he can go home by tomorrow afternoon."

Joshua took a few seconds to let this information sink in, the disbelief slowly turning to gratitude to know that Clint would be okay. After all, there were several times throughout the day where he was convinced that he'd lost his father so to have this update felt wonderfully surreal to him.

"W-what about Nathan?" Thomas wondered about his best friend, snapping Joshua out of his trail of thought. "H-how is he holding up?"

The doctor lowered his head in response to the question. He'd delivered the news about Melissa and Clint with such confident reassurance that the boys instinctively knew from his now sheepish body language that they wouldn't like what they were about to hear. Preparing for the worst, they braced themselves as the doctor opened his mouth to speak.

"The good news is that Nathan's still alive," the doctor stated in a low, serious voice.

"And the bad news?" Joshua replied, sensing where the direction of the conversation was leading.

"He's fallen into a coma…" the doctor revealed to Thomas and Joshua, the arms of both boys dropping despondently by their sides in response to this. "We believe that the bolt of lightning may have shut down his nervous system. We're hoping that this is just temporary and that he'll wake up soon. But Nathan remains in critical condition and we don't know if – *when* that will happen…" the medic clarified, quickly correcting his choice of words in an attempt to not upset the boys further. "I promise you that we're doing everything we can for him and we're keeping him under full surveillance. As soon as we have any substantial updates, we will let you both know," he asserted, bringing back his comforting tone albeit in a much less natural manner this time which didn't escape the notice of Thomas or Joshua.

The doctor was abruptly called for another patient so he had to leave the boys to digest the information by themselves. Once he'd departed from the waiting room, Thomas watched as a pale-faced Joshua lethargically trudged back over to his seat, the sound of his boots clomping down upon the clean hospital floor echoed through the area with each step he took. As Joshua slumped into his chair, Thomas tentatively walked over to him, trying to offer any words of encouragement in spite of his own worries about his best friend.

"Josh, I-I know things are difficult right now…" Thomas acknowledged. "B-but we need to have faith that Nathan will pull through this. He *has* to!" he insisted in an attempt to convince Joshua as well as himself. "Hell, it's because of Nathan and that power of his that we're all still alive now!"

"Not *all* of us…" Joshua muttered glumly.

An awful, chilling sensation of shame permeated throughout Thomas' entire being, flowing through his blood like arctic water as it dawned on him that Joshua was right. In his silent gratitude for his and Melissa's survival, he'd nearly forgotten that there had been a casualty in their ranks – Nathan's mother, Victoria.

"If Nathan does pull through, what's left for him?" Joshua pondered rhetorically while Thomas bit his lip and listened, allowing him to vent. "I mean, it's bad enough that his father died in battle. But now he's lost his mother too – both of them killed by that monster! Victoria shouldn't have been out there and neither should Nathan!" the teenager continued, releasing any anger out of his system which caused him to exhale rapidly. Realising this, Joshua controlled his breathing, slowing it down before letting out one more comment. "And at the end of the day, *I'm* the reason they went out there..." he lamented, the regret seeping through in his voice.

"Josh, you can't think like that..." Thomas told him comfortingly.

"Well it's true," Joshua retorted matter-of-factly. "Nathan came back to rescue me and Victoria went out to save him. I wanted to be a soldier so I could protect people but when my family needed help most, I was completely useless! I couldn't save my aunt! I can't help Nathan! And if it wasn't for him and that...Devil's whatever it was...my dad would have died too! All of us would have!" he ranted on, growing more flustered with every word that he uttered. "Nathan saved us all and this is how he's *rewarded?!* Stuck in a coma with both parents dead?! If there was any justice, Victoria would still be here and Nathan wouldn't be in this position – I would!"

After finishing his self-loathing tirade, Joshua began to hyperventilate. Observing this, Thomas crouched down beside the empty chair until he was eye-level with Joshua.

"Josh, please listen to me!" Thomas urged. "This is not *your* fault, the same as how the school's destruction wasn't your fault! Maris and Chimera are to blame for all of this! Nathan's told you this himself and he wouldn't want you punishing yourself now!" he rationalised.

As Joshua's breaths eventually settled again thanks to Thomas' reassurance, he started to splutter, his mouth dried up from his repeated gasps for air.

"Y-yeah...Yeah, I-I know..." Joshua agreed, knowing that Thomas' claims about Nathan were correct. "A-and then we're the ones left to deal with the aftermath. D-dad doesn't even know that his sister's gone...a-and I have no idea how I'm going to break the news to him..." While Joshua was speaking, Thomas could see his cheeks puff in and out and heard the squelching sounds coming from inside his mouth, trying to generate saliva.

"D-do you want me to get you some water?" Thomas offered. Joshua thought about it for a few seconds before answering.

"Th-that might be good actually..." Joshua conceded.

"Okay, I'll go grab you some. I'll be right back and then we can make a plan together for how we tell Clint..." Thomas established.

With that, Thomas headed off to find the nearest water dispenser which left Joshua by himself. Half a minute passed and as he thought of Nathan's and Clint's predicaments, along with grieving for Victoria, he closed his eyes and couldn't fight the tears away any longer.

Once another thirty seconds had elapsed, Joshua heard some footsteps nearby and could sense that someone was standing right by him. He opened his eyes, expecting to see Thomas. However, he instead found Abbie staring down at him, her face red and from her wet cheeks, it was apparent that she had been crying.

"Looks like I'm not the only one in a right state…" Abbie commented with a forced laugh.

"Hey, what's wrong?" Joshua asked her while wiping his own eyes as she sat beside him.

"Just…just everything…" Abbie responded downheartedly. "M-my parents are squabbling again…over something stupid as usual. I-I just had to walk away from it," she explained to an attentive Joshua, her energy sapped from just talking about it. "Th-then all I could think about was…was how I've had th-three near-death experiences in the last two days…" she recalled, the memories of the fissure, the tunnel collapse and the wildfire still tormenting her – so much so that Abbie had glossed over the fact that she was almost shot by Ranjit eight days ago. "It's like…we've *all* gone through hell…m-my best friend and my brother are in hospital…a-and even now, w-when we should be coming together, all my parents can do is bitch at each other…I-I'm just so done with it all…" she expressed with one last deflated sigh, like a balloon releasing its dying gasp of air.

"Th-that…that's awful, I-I'm sorry you've had to live with that…" Joshua acknowledged empathetically. "I-I was younger back then…b-but I remember my parents didn't get along when they were together either…a-and it was tough to be around…s-so I feel for you…" he added, trying to relate his own past struggles to Abbie's. "A-and how about Ben? H-have the doctors given you any update about him?" Joshua probed.

Abbie's head drooped to face the floor at the mention of her brother's name, something that Joshua picked up on which led him to fear the worst.

"N-no…p-please tell me he hasn't-" he said, but before he could get the rest of his words out, Abbie was quick to assuage his concerns.

"He's alive…and the doctors said his *body* will recover…" she stated bluntly. "B-but they said that Ben inhaled a lot of smoke from the fire… a-and it limited the amount of o-oxygen that flowed to his brain," Abbie detailed, quoting what she had heard from the medics. "Th-they've warned us that because of this…h-he could experience complications for the rest of his life…even potential b-brain damage…a-and only time will tell…how severe it actually is…" she explained, having to stop to compose herself on a few occasions.

"Oh Abbie…" Joshua uttered, devastated for her as she started to weep once more. Seeing her distress, he instinctively held an arm out to her to offer a hug which Abbie quickly accepted, burying her head into his chest.

"I-it's just not fair…why did it have to be Ben?! He's already been through enough…" Abbie sobbed feebly, her voice muffled by Joshua's shoulder.

"Hey, nobody knows how things will turn out for Ben yet. For all we know, he could recover better than anyone expects. If he's as tough as you say he is, I'm sure he'll make it through this," Joshua claimed, reminding Abbie of the words she'd used to champion Ben's resilience during their trek of Mount Tamara yesterday.

For a few moments, Joshua could feel Abbie's breath against his torso and heard her stifled sniffs as she tried to control her crying. He couldn't tell if his efforts to console her were effective, but he remained hopeful once she lifted her head back up to dry her tears.

"H-how…how are Nathan and Clint…?" Abbie queried. "H-have you heard anything…?"

"Dad will be fine. Doctors said they should be okay to discharge him tomorrow," Joshua answered.

"And Nathan…?" Abbie reiterated nervously.

Joshua sighed deeply before responding. "He's in a coma…w-we're not sure when he'll wake up…" he disclosed glumly.

"Oh god…" Abbie gasped, cupping her mouth with her hand out of shock.

"I-I'm sorry…I should have been able to protect him…b-but I failed…" Joshua apologised.

"You did all you could…" Abbie insisted, now holding his hand to comfort him. "Me on the other hand? I should have been at Ben's side…I really let him down. I-I don't know…perhaps if I'd have known CPR like Melissa does…th-then maybe he wouldn't…"

"Hold on, no, I *can't* let you of all people say that about yourself," Joshua interrupted her self-pitying ramble, their heads so close to one another that they were almost touching. "I've never seen *anybody* love a sibling the way you do! You've done everything you can for that lad and then some! You've been twice to Ben what I've been to Nathan so I'm *not* letting you tear yourself down!" he asserted passionately.

"Y-you really think that...?" Abbie murmured, taken aback by what Joshua was telling her.

"Abbie, you're incredible!" Joshua declared. "You're one of the strongest, most loyal people I've ever me-"

Before Joshua could finish his sentence, Abbie leaned in and kissed him on the lips to his astonishment. After a few seconds had passed, the young man pulled away by mere centimetres, wondering whether he should be doing this with how vulnerable they both were in this moment. However, when he stared into her eyes, Joshua felt an undeniable connection with Abbie, one perhaps forged by the pain they each shared. Nevertheless, this mutual attraction that had manifested between the two teenagers spurred them to kiss once more, this time without restraint.

"Uh, guys...?" a familiar voice spoke up from behind Joshua. He and Abbie turned around to find that Thomas had returned with a plastic cup filled with water.

"O-oh, Thomas!" Abbie exclaimed. She and Joshua hastily stood up from their chairs, both flustered at being caught in a compromising position with one another.

"T-Tom...th-this is..." Joshua stuttered, fumbling over his own words as he fidgeted uncomfortably, unsure how to rationalise how he ended up having an intimate moment with one of his cousin's best friends. "W-we can explain..."

"Guys, guys, it's okay," Thomas reassured them, leaving the pair startled by his composed reaction. "We've all been through hell today – I think you're both due some happiness..." he established, approving of whatever was to come between them.

Joshua and Abbie went quiet, at a loss for words at Thomas' acceptance of what he'd seen them doing. They both exchanged a bashful glance though, one that suggested that their feelings still lingered, unhindered by the disrupted moment of intimacy. The silence persisted for several seconds until Thomas took the initiative to break the tension.

"So are you actually gonna take this water? You might need it to cool off now," Thomas joked as he addressed Joshua.

This drew a snigger from Joshua who took the plastic cup off Thomas' hands, while Abbie gave the latter a playful punch on his arm. It felt like the first normal interaction that the trio could recall having in the last two days which seemed to have lasted a lifetime for them given the events that had transpired.

Their peace was soon disturbed however as an urgent news bulletin popped up abruptly on the television screen nearby. Along with any other patients and staff members in the room, Thomas, Abbie and Joshua turned their focus to the monitor.

"Breaking news!" the broadcaster announced in a gravely serious tone, his eyes wide open while facing the camera. "Just an hour ago, we had reports from local citizens that a cavern had opened up at the foot of Mount Tamara! This comes not long after a fierce battle took place earlier this afternoon on the other side of the mountain between our forces and Chimera! The following images and footage show scenes of the aperture as well as a mysterious masked figure emerging from it..."

The trio watched as several photos were displayed on the screen, the first few showing the tunnel that had been carved out in the base of the mountain from different angles. The video that was then aired showed a bird's eye view of someone walking out of the cavern, draped in black garments. Although more snapshots of the individual flashed up before their eyes, including some taken from the ground that revealed a Chimera mask covering the face, Thomas, Abbie and Joshua had already deduced who this was.

"Maris..." Abbie mumbled in a whisper to the others.

"So she hid away in the mountain itself..." Joshua realised, having wondered where she'd vanished to after her attack on Nathan.

"I-is there no limit to that witch's power...?" Thomas gasped with neither Joshua or Abbie able to offer an optimistic answer.

"This person is believed to be the leader of Chimera and extremely dangerous! If you see her, do not approach and remove yourself from the area for your own safety! There is no telling what she is capable of!" the presenter beseeched the general public.

Before Thomas, Abbie and Joshua could finish watching the announcement, their attention was diverted towards the doors of the corridor that were flung open. Three medics stormed through the doorway, politely ordering people to clear out of their path while wheeling a gurney. Abbie heard the doctors stating that they needed to get the patient back to theatre immediately, but it was the sight of the boy on the gurney that raised the concern of the group.

"Nathan...? Nathan!" Thomas called out to his friend. Nathan was carted past his friends in a hurry but from the brief glimpse that they caught of him, Thomas, Abbie and Joshua could see that he was still catatonic.

"Nath, p-please don't leave us!" Abbie cried out in a last-ditch effort to get through to him as the medics escorted his body towards the next hallway. "W-we still *need* you!"

When the medics disappeared through the doors with Nathan, Abbie stepped forward out of pure instinct. However, Joshua grabbed her arm to stop her, knowing that they needed to let the doctors do their job in saving him, no matter how painful it was for them.

The rest of the news broadcast just served as distorted background noise to Thomas, Abbie and Joshua at this point. They didn't need to listen to the rest of it because they'd seen what Maris was capable of with their own eyes – and the lasting image of their unconscious friend being powerlessly wheeled away from them was an agonising reminder of that. As Joshua embraced a distraught Abbie while dealing with his own anguish, they along with a forlorn Thomas kept Nathan in their thoughts while staring resentfully at the television monitor, the bulletin concluding on one final chilling photo of the masked mage before fading to black...

◄──◄◄❰❱►►──►

Chapter 26

After the horrific life-changing events of the last two days, Thomas, Abbie, Joshua and their families soon discovered that the following days would be equally as dramatic.

The next morning, the Sunday news headlines were dominated by reports of what transpired at the now-dubbed Battle of Mount Tamara. The urgent bulletins on television and the newspapers detailed how many soldiers had died during the skirmish, also including an account from Joshua (who was kept anonymous) about how Maris had conjured the wildfire and thunderstorm. It was stated in the articles that the mage had dispensed with Entritica's forces without substantial opposition before carving a path through the mountain itself. Of course, Thomas, Abbie and Joshua knew that this part wasn't entirely true with the latter keeping quiet about Nathan and the Devil's Spirit.

Prior to midday, the backpacks and belongings of Thomas and the other survivors, the ones left behind at the disaster site in their haste to escape, were returned to them at the hospital by the medics who recovered them from the scene. Joshua took the responsibility of identifying which dirt-covered rucksacks belonged to whom, sometimes having to peek at the items inside to do so. He had to do this with Nathan's, recognising it as his cousin's once he pulled out the book titled *'Demons, Dragons and other Servants of the Devil'*. Thomas made a request to borrow this book, wanting to read it to get a better understanding of the Devil's Spirit and whether there was anything else like it that could pose a threat to Maris. Hearing this rationale was enough for Joshua to loan Thomas the hardback.

Once it was confirmed by the doctors that there was still no change in Nathan's condition, Thomas, Abbie and Joshua each tended to their respective families. Thomas accompanied Melissa back home via taxi shortly after she was cleared to leave. Abbie stayed at the hospital with Frank and Linda, ensuring that Ben wasn't alone. Joshua also remained on the ward to visit a recovering Clint who inevitably asked about Nathan and

Victoria. The teenager reluctantly informed his father both about Nathan falling into a coma along with the death of Victoria. As expected, Clint was overwhelmed to hear of his sister's passing, falling quiet while he digested this abrupt and upsetting news. This unsettling silence lasted for the rest of the day, even when Joshua and Clint returned home that night after the latter's discharge from hospital. Despite the former's best efforts to console his dad, Joshua understood that he needed time to grieve by himself.

As the night turned to day again, Monday brought yet more distressing developments with it. Thomas, Abbie, Joshua, their families and the rest of Entritica soon found out how quickly Maris had made her way through the country – it was announced in the early hours of the morning that she had stormed the capital city and slain the king.

Before the nation even had a chance to comprehend this revelation, Maris made a public declaration at noon. She ordered the government and the Entritican armies to surrender to her, citing that if they failed to do so within twenty-four hours, she would wipe them all out with her own power and threatened to do the same to the civilians of nearby towns.

The government and armed forces responded to this by planning an all-out assault on the royal palace which was now inhabited by Maris. Every soldier that the government had at its disposal was sent out to meet at a rendezvous point several kilometres away from the capital. While the platoons were travelling to that destination, the political leaders of Entritica pledged through the medium of television that they would keep fighting for their country, hoping to alleviate the worries of the citizens.

Tensions were naturally high for the remainder of the day, everyone aware that the fate of Entritica would be decided in less than twenty-four hours. As they awaited further news of the attack, Thomas, Abbie and Joshua tried their best to go about their day as normally as they could. There was still no update about Nathan from the doctors, so the trio agreed to meet at the hospital tomorrow to visit him. Until then, Abbie was preoccupied with Ben who was permitted to be taken home by Frank and Linda – although they were advised to bring him to hospital if he experienced any complications. Similarly, Joshua's focus was keeping an eye on Clint while also giving him space to mourn for Victoria.

As for Thomas, when he wasn't tending to Melissa, he was busy reading through the pages of *'Demons, Dragons and other Servants of the Devil'*. He searched through any chapters about mages, hoping to find any weaknesses that Maris might have, and paid close attention to anything related to the Devil's Spirit, intrigued to read about its abilities in detail.

One section that did catch Thomas' eye though was a sub-chapter titled *'Limbo'*. As per the opening paragraph, it was a term used to describe the domain that a person's subconscious entered when they were teetering on the edge of life and death. Given the circumstances, he couldn't help but think of Nathan still comatose in the infirmary, wondering whether he was experiencing this now. If so, he was keen to learn more about it in the hopes that it may provide a clue to reviving his friend.

Thomas' study of the book was interrupted by a text message from his phone. He was fully expecting this to be either Joshua or Abbie, so he was surprised to see that it was actually Lucy. The message read as follows:

Hey Thomas, it's Lucy. The news is really blowing up today! Are you guys all okay? I tried messaging Nathan but I've not heard anything from him so I'm a bit worried. Can you please let me know? X

Realising that Lucy didn't know that their group had been dragged into the Battle of Mount Tamara, Thomas knew he had to break the news to her. He picked up his phone and called her, believing that this would be simpler than trying to explain the whole story via message.

Later that evening, the palace was surrounded by the armed forces. Having anticipated this, Maris stepped out to confront them at the top of the tower, showing the soldiers that they did not have the luxury of a surprise attack. She tried to dent their resolve further by revealing that she had a hostage with her – the princess of Entritica, Jennifer Owens.

The soldiers were rattled when Princess Jennifer implored them to stand down with the use of a megaphone, citing that Maris could wipe them all out with her power. Flustered, the commanding officers hastily resorted to using their trump card early and ordered for missiles to be fired at the castle. There was a mutual feeling of apprehension amongst the privates as the projectiles were launched into the sky towards the tower where Maris boldly stood. Even when the missiles split into cluster bombs on their approach to the palace, the mage did not flinch.

Maris demonstrated that her confidence was warranted by repelling all of the incoming explosives with storm-force winds, sending them back at the platoons. As multiple soldiers tried to flee from the danger, Maris shot multiple bolts of lightning at some of the bombs, causing them to detonate before colliding with the ground. Jennifer closed her eyes, unable to watch as a chain reaction of explosions consumed the soldiers and the grounds that surrounded the palace.

Once the thunderous uproars from the eruptions finally died down, only a quarter of the Entritican army were left alive. The surviving soldiers stared around in horror at what the land ahead of them had been reduced to. Before they could even process how their comrades had perished, Maris made another declaration through the loudspeaker – revealing that she could also repel a nuclear weapon in the same manner, almost brazenly daring them to do their worst. Leaving the officers and combatants in shock at this claim, she gave one final ultimatum: either yield to her or risk more bodies piling up on account of their stubbornness.

One of the remaining commanders called Archie had no other choice but to despondently relay Maris' warning to the Entritican government so that they could make a decision. Knowing how outmatched they were now and that the mage could endanger the entirety of Entritica if they continued to resist, the political leaders reluctantly made the most painful choice.

They surrendered.

****

By the next morning, everyone else in Entritica learned of the dreadful news, including Thomas, Abbie, Joshua and their families.

The mage's takeover of the country was obviously the lead story throughout the day and was all across the media. Newspapers depicted the final stand at the palace yesterday for all to read. Articles either dubbed the soldier's actions as an irrational, suicidal gambit or a valiant, necessary last resort gone horribly wrong, depending on whoever the writer was and whose side they had chosen. Some television platforms and radio broadcasts had already started to align with Maris and Chimera, likely out of self-preservation just as Anil Ali did. Others stuck to their principles and continued to decry them as terrorists and menaces to the world.

Ultimately however, the opinions of the public wouldn't change anything.

Because by Tuesday afternoon, Maris had crowned herself the new empress of Entritica.

This was seen by Thomas, Abbie and Joshua on the television while they were waiting in the infirmary for news about Nathan. Thomas had his head buried in the library book, trying to block out any chatter about Maris and Chimera as he felt too sickened to watch it any longer. On the other hand, Abbie and Joshua held hands for comfort while they gazed at the monitor, though they weren't truly processing what was happening – they just felt too exhausted from the events of the last four days.

"H-how did it all come to this…?" Abbie murmured wearily.

"Entritica really has lost…just like Mr Jones said…" Joshua uttered, recalling the headmaster's prediction.

"I-I just want things to go back to normal…" Abbie expressed while the channel continued to broadcast the news of Maris' coronation. "W-what's going to happen now…?"

"I don't know…" Joshua answered honestly with a sigh. "B-but I was talking with dad earlier. H-he said we should still think about evacuating the country…"

"H-how would we all do that?" Abbie wondered. "The ten of us barely survived last time and Entritica will be crawling with Chimera goons soon. They'd have no problem spotting a group that big…"

"N-no Abbie, dad didn't mean all of us…" Joshua elaborated. "T-the news said earlier that adults shouldn't try to flee…as they'd risk being killed on sight. Kids still can for now though. W-which is why he meant us three – me, you and Thomas…"

"You can't be serious!" Abbie exclaimed, automatically retracting her hand away from Joshua's for the first time since they sat down. "We can't just leave our families behind!"

"That's more or less what I said…" Joshua admitted. "I thought it was the grief talking but he insisted that I think about it…he said our safety is what matters most now…" he relayed to Abbie who fell mute in disbelief at the proposition.

Meanwhile, the reports kept coming in on the television in the background until the receptionist switched it off, fed up of hearing the depressing updates constantly.

"A-and what do you think? About what your dad said…?" Abbie queried curiously.

"I don't know what to think," Joshua replied. "M-my head's a mess. I-I can't just leave dad on his own, especially now he's lost Vic. But he's only telling me to do the same thing Mr Jones would…" he acknowledged, reflecting on the principal's advice to evacuate. "The only thing I am sure of? I have no idea what can stop Maris…"

Hearing Joshua say this, Thomas lifted his head away from the book.

"The Devil's Spirit nearly did," he claimed boldly, catching Joshua's and Abbie's attention.

"What are you getting at?" Abbie probed with a pained scowl on her face.

"I've been reading about it. It makes the wielder invincible and has the power to absorb elemental magic. Plus, it can even kill someone just by touching them," Thomas explained excitedly, a twinkle sparkling in his eye as he talked about it. "Just think, if Nathan was able to awaken to that power one more time, I bet he could-"

"Bet he could what?! Fall into a coma again?! Or worse even?! We still have no idea what kind of toll it's taken on him!" Joshua interrupted indignantly, rising up from his chair and taking both Thomas and Abbie aback. "Besides, we can't rely on that power! We all saw what happened out there – Nathan was possessed! He wasn't in control of it!" he pointed out, something which Abbie nodded in agreement to having seen her friend's eyes rolled back into his head.

"It still saved Clint though, didn't it?!" Thomas rebutted.

"Yes, it did! And I'll always be thankful to it for that!" Joshua acknowledged. "But it also killed hundreds of soldiers in a blind rage! How do we know it won't kill our own forces?! Or even us?! Do you even know what killing does to a person?! It changes you!" he retorted angrily, secretly tormented by having to take the lives of enemy soldiers himself. "Nathan's a sixteen-year-old kid who's lost both parents! He's my *family*! He's your friend! Yet here you are talking about him like he's some sort of weapon when he's got one foot in the grave!!" Joshua reprimanded.

Thomas' head drooped down, now plagued with guilt for thinking of Nathan in such a manner. An uncomfortable silence descended upon the trio after Joshua's outburst, their minds filled with worry for Nathan whose life was hanging in the balance.

Without the volume of the television, it was quiet enough in the waiting room to hear a pin drop. The only discernible sound that the group could hear was the swishing noise the door made when it was pushed open. Thomas, Abbie and Joshua each glanced in its direction, expecting to see one of the doctors arriving to provide an update on Nathan. Instead though, Abbie and Joshua were surprised to see a familiar face.

"L-Lucy...?" Joshua gasped upon seeing her approach them.

"H-hey guys. H-have I missed anything about Nathan?" Lucy asked nervously, gaging the apprehension from Joshua and Abbie.

"What the hell are you doing here?!" Abbie interrogated suspiciously, only to be calmed down by Thomas.

"Guys, guys, it's okay! She wanted to see Nathan, so I invited her!" Thomas informed.

"A-are you sure about this?! Kamran and Anil might have swayed her over to Chimera's side! Can we really trust her?" Abbie wondered aloud.

"I'm *not* with Chimera," Lucy stated in a much more confident and assured tone than her meek greeting. "In fact, if it was up to me, I'd have been leaving Entritica with you guys – only Nathan insisted that I stay, saying I'd be safer with the Alis protecting me..."

"Well, given what we went through, it was best that you didn't join us..." Joshua remarked.

"Yeah, I know...Thomas told me what happened...we spoke yesterday after I'd tried to message Nathan. Once he explained, it made sense why he hadn't replied...I-I can't believe you guys made it through all that..." Lucy expressed in awe at how the three of them had survived an encounter with Maris.

"It was all thanks to Nathan – he saved us..." Thomas reflected earnestly prompting Abbie to elbow him when she thought he was revealing too much.

"Him and that power of his. Nath's saved my life twice now," Lucy commented, reminiscing on how he rescued her from being kidnapped years ago as well as when he pulled her to safety from the chasm days earlier. She turned to Abbie and Joshua knowing that they were still wary of her. "I'm sorry. I know I've not been around for Nathan recently. But I want to be here now. It's the least I owe him..." Lucy professed to the pair.

While Abbie remained standoffish towards her, Joshua's expression softened as he heard this, knowing that he was also guilty of being distant to his cousin in the last few months. Before he could offer any words of encouragement to Lucy though, a doctor emerged from the corridor and approached the group.

"You're Joshua Griffiths, right?" the medic addressed the young man, recognising him as Nathan's kin as well as being the eldest among the quartet. Abbie held Joshua's hand again for comfort as they stepped towards the doctor together. Thomas and Lucy also gathered around to hear the update once Joshua nodded to confirm that he was here for Nathan.

"How is he...?" Joshua asked in barely a whisper.

"This won't be easy for me to explain..." the medic stated, forewarning the group.

"We need to know..." Thomas asserted whilst steeling his resolve for whatever news he was about to hear. As Abbie clutched Joshua's hand tighter, the doctor paused before continuing.

"I'll start with the positives then. Nathan is still alive and his body looks to be recovering from his wounds at an alarming rate. How this is happening is beyond my understanding – he was struck by lightning which, by all accounts, should have killed him instantly. He must have some inhuman resiliency," the doctor explained to the best of his ability.

Thomas, Abbie and Lucy felt a huge relief at hearing this, thrilled to hear that they hadn't lost Nathan. However, Joshua kept his reactions subdued out of intuition.

"There's a 'but' to come isn't there?" he deduced with the doctor confirming his suspicions to the worry of the others.

"I'm afraid that despite Nathan's external recovery, his heartbeat is still really weak. In fact, it's deteriorated bit by bit over the last few days..." the doctor revealed, drawing an audible gasp from Abbie and Lucy. "Again, we're not certain what the reason for this would be. But if he's encountered the leader of Chimera, it's possible that he's experienced some trauma that could be preventing his mind and heart from healing..." the medic theorised openly. Joshua automatically closed his eyes at hearing this and sighed deeply, regretful over the predicament his cousin was in. "Ultimately, if this doesn't change soon, then Nathan's survival chances are very slim. I'm sorry..." the doctor concluded, causing Thomas to avert his gaze as his lip quivered.

Everybody fell quiet as they processed the doctor's diagnosis, Abbie and Lucy starting to tear up while Joshua tried to suppress his emotions. After several seconds had passed, Thomas was the one to speak up first.

"A-are we able…t-to see Nathan now?" he stammered. They had previously been prohibited during the time that the doctors were treating him.

"Yes, it will be fine to do so now. I can escort you all to his ward," the medic kindly offered.

"T-thank you…" Joshua uttered with Abbie and Lucy also nodding to show their gratitude.

Thomas, Abbie, Joshua and Lucy followed the doctor out of the waiting room and through the hospital hallways. They all walked in silence, mentally bracing themselves to see Nathan for the first time since the Battle of Mount Tamara.

After a couple of minutes, the medic brought the group to one of the private rooms outside of the recovery ward. Before he opened the door, he explained that Nathan was inside by himself and that he would need to request for a nurse to remain in the vicinity in case of an emergency. The teenagers accepted these conditions and were allowed into the room.

Joshua and Thomas were the first to enter with the small television in the corner of the room being the initial object in their line of sight. The boys turned their heads to survey the area, noting its plain white walls, the shrubs outside of the window and the heart monitor sporadically beeping beside the bedside table. Finally, just as Abbie and Lucy stepped inside, they all turned their attention to the hospital bed where Nathan was resting.

Thomas and Lucy ambled around to the right side of the bed near the bedside table and heart monitor while Abbie and Joshua placed themselves to the left of it. The latter pair regarded Nathan with expressions of sadness, seeing his eyes tranquilly closed and his lips parted slightly. Had they not known any better, they could have presumed him to be sleeping without a care in the world. On the other hand, Thomas' and Lucy's focus was on the heart monitor, concerned by how faint the signal was and the infrequent beeps coming from the machine, just as the doctor had detailed.

"He's grown so much…and yet he's still so young…too young to be going through all this…" Joshua remarked forlornly as Abbie rubbed his shoulder in support.

"We're all here for you, Nath…" Lucy called out to him in a gentle voice. "We all need you – now more than ever…"

"D-do you really think he can hear us?" Abbie wondered hopefully.

"Who knows at this point? I'm not sure where his mind even is right now…" Joshua lamented.

"I think I might know…" Thomas stated, piquing the curiosity of the others.

"W-what do you mean?" Lucy enquired.

"I've been reading this to find out more about the Devil's Spirit," Thomas clarified, gesturing to the library book in his hand which Lucy also recognised as being in Nathan's possession before the school collapsed. "There was a section in here that talks about where people's minds reside when they're on the brink of death. It's called Limbo," he illustrated to the group as they patiently listened. "I read more about it and apparently, there have been instances recorded where the voices of loved ones have guided lost souls back to the light…"

"Wait, are you saying-" Abbie was about to ask with an optimistic twinkle in her eye but Thomas was already ahead of her.

"Your idea might have some merit – talking to Nath. We might be able to stir him out of his coma…" Thomas suggested, something that Abbie and Lucy reacted favourably to. Joshua was much more sceptical of this notion.

"Are you really sure that we can rely on this book?" he questioned cautiously.

"Well so far, it hasn't got *anything* wrong about the Devil's Spirit. It's nailed the black aura, the extent of its power, how it's triggered by intense emotions," Thomas listed, knowing that they were all characteristics that they'd seen within Nathan for themselves. "You know how the doctor said earlier about Nathan's alarming recovery rate from the lightning? No prizes for guessing what's behind that," he added as he flicked through the book to the relevant page before holding it out for Joshua to read. Sure enough, the extract specified that:

As alluded to earlier in this section, one of the defining qualities of the Devil's Spirit is its supernatural invulnerability. Along with being capable of withstanding elemental attacks, it can rapidly heal the wounds of its vessel and restore the body to full health in a quarter of the time that it would normally take.

"I-I see…" Joshua murmured as he digested the information, seemingly reassured of Thomas' faith in the material.

"If it's gotten this much right about Nathan's power, then maybe the section about Limbo is true too…" Thomas rationalised.

"In that case, there's no reason not to try talking to him!" Lucy asserted.

"C'mon Josh, it has to be worth a shot at least!" Abbie tried to persuade him.

Joshua still had reservations about pinning their hopes on this, especially if it didn't work out. Even with that on his mind though, he knew it was better than doing nothing so he gave his approval with an understanding nod of his head. Now that a plan had been decided, Thomas, Abbie and Lucy leaned in as close as they could to Nathan's ear.

"Nath, concentrate on my voice, okay mate?" Thomas whispered to his unconscious friend. "You're one of the toughest people I know so we need to get you back with us. I need my best mate back so I can't let you die yet."

The quartet each took it in turns to give Nathan words of encouragement, hoping that it could get through to his sub-conscience.

As their soothing voices penetrated his ears, although Nathan's face and body remained unresponsive, they resonated deep within his trapped spirit – which opened its eyes for the first time since Mount Tamara.

In his spiritual form, Nathan lay surrounded by perpetual darkness, so potent that it was barely worth waking from his slumber. His mind was hazy, his memories shrouded in a dense fog that practically reduced him to a vacant hull. The only recollections that were even partly clear were the fractured images of Victoria seconds before her death. Nathan was plagued by these visions, his other senses significantly dulled as a result. Despite this though, he could still feel a faint thumping reverberate in the space all around him.

Suddenly, a warmth started to radiate from the side of Nathan. He caught a luminous glow in the corner of his eye and sluggishly tilted his head in its direction.

There, he watched as a pillar of light opened up before him, forcing him to squint his eyes at its overpowering brightness. Nathan almost turned away from it, however he was compelled to maintain his gaze when he heard noises coming from the beam. When he concentrated hard enough, he not only realised that they were the sounds of people talking, but also that he recognised the voices.

"N-th, c-n you he-r us?" a boy's voice spoke, which Nathan identified as Thomas.

"W-'re all here w-iting f-r you…" a second female voice called out, Nathan recognising it as Abbie.

"We c-n't h-ve you dyi-g on us," a third voice gently yet boldly declared. It took a few moments for Nathan to work out who this was. His memories started to stir slowly until he realised that this was Lucy. Upon hearing his friends attempt to communicate with him, the pulsations around Nathan began to strengthen.

Back in the private room, Abbie was quick to point out to the others that the heart rate on the monitor had improved, generating a slight peak in the reading. Seeing the results for himself, this spurred Joshua to join her, Thomas and Lucy in speaking to Nathan.

In their excitement however, they began talking over one another, overzealously trying to reach out to their friend lost in Limbo. From Nathan's perspective though (or his spirit's at least), the voices blurred into a jumble, triggering a flurry of fragmented flashbacks for him – primarily the ones where his friends were in danger. Visions of Thomas being attacked by Otis and Tobias years ago, Abbie almost being shot by Ranjit, Lucy dangling over the fissure and Joshua marching into battle with Clint rushed through his mind like a blitz. It all culminated in the haunting image of his mother pushing him aside before taking the full force of the lightning bolt. When reliving these horrific incidents, Nathan fixated on the one point of commonality in all of them – himself.

The more he dwelled on these thoughts, the more he mistakenly convinced himself that he was to blame for all the misfortune that they'd suffered. The burden of guilt proceeded to weigh down upon Nathan, his self-loathing reaching its apex when the familiar voice of Ranjit seeped into his psyche with a callous statement:

"You should do the world a favour and just disappear!"

Now at his lowest point with no parents to comfort him, Nathan turned his body away from the pillar of light, away from the voices of his peers. The beam started to flicker, losing its stability as the thumping sensation in the space around him waned once again.

Back in the land of the living, Thomas, Abbie, Joshua and Lucy continued their efforts to revive Nathan until Joshua worked out that the number of beeps from the heart monitor had decreased all of a sudden. He raised his head up from Nathan's bed to look at the screen and saw that the signal was weakening.

"Guys, his heartbeat's gone down again!" Joshua alerted the others who also glanced towards the monitor.

"Damn it! He *was* responding, I'm sure of it!" Thomas insisted.

"W-what do we do now?" Abbie asked frantically.

"Let's calm down first! Pressuring him to wake up won't do him any good!" Joshua stressed.

"I don't think us all talking at once will help either…" Lucy reflected.

"So what do you propose we do?" Abbie questioned.

"H-his heart reacted to the sound of our voices. We need to try that again – just one at a time," Thomas suggested, his words causing Lucy's eyes to light up with inspiration.

"I'm not sure. Maybe we should give him a rest for a bit? He's still recovering and he might not be ready for this yet…" Joshua wondered, still fretting for Nathan.

Suddenly, the group's attention was diverted as the corner television was switched on. Thomas, Abbie and Joshua then realised that this was done by Lucy who had the remote control gripped in her hand.

"What are you doing?" Thomas quizzed in bewilderment.

"You said it yourself Tom – *sound,*" Lucy highlighted. "Nath might not have heard anything since he's been here. Maybe some background noise might help things feel more normal for him. I mean, it's got to be better than us chucking words at him, surely?"

Out of options, once it was apparent that Thomas and Joshua had no objections to the idea, Lucy turned the volume of the television up until it was at a moderate level.

"Can we at least change the channel to something a bit more…upbeat?" Abbie requested.

The others soon saw why she was asking this – news of Maris' triumph over Entritica was still being broadcast. Lucy started pressing the buttons on the remote to try and change programmes, however none of them seemed to be having an effect.

"Oh come on, don't tell me they've only got one channel in here!" Lucy exclaimed out of frustration.

"You've got to be kidding me! Surely they have *something* else?" Joshua griped.

"I'm looking!" Lucy reaffirmed sternly.

The disheartening bulletin continued to blare out about Maris' takeover of the country. While the group tried their best to resolve the problem with the television, they were oblivious to the fact that the sound was reaching Nathan's ears.

His spirit, still coiled up with its back to the quivering pillar of light, tried to block out the noises that came from it. That changed when he heard the closing line of the broadcast before it cut to a commercial:

Coming up when we return, there will be a taped address to the public from the new empress of Entritica, Maris.

As soon as Maris' name was mentioned, Nathan's eyes widened and the fog in his mind began to shift. The tyrant's name echoed repeatedly until his repressed memories were restored – namely the brief moment of consciousness he had prior to being struck down with lightning. And there, now clear as day to him, was the scarred and bloodied visage of his assailant, Maris.

Nathan's blood boiled and the pulsations around him intensified at the sight of her. In that instant, he remembered fully how this demon had killed his parents, causing his hateful emotions to intensify. Although Maris' mouth was moving in Nathan's memory, the sound was still muffled. Following his gut instinct, the boy's spirit turned back towards the sputtering beam, now eager to fill the missing gaps in his mind, no matter how painful it may be for him to hear. As he suspected, her words became audible to him:

"So...you have it too...the Devil's Spirit... To think that there's another like me after all..."

Listening to this, Nathan was quickly reminded of the research he'd done into the Devil's Spirit. The cogs in his head started to whir when Maris compared him to her in terms of power, especially when he regarded the visible injuries on her face that he dealt to her during his possession. As ideas began to take shape in his mind, they seemed to be validated by the next line that he heard from the mage:

"You may be the only person in this wretched world besides my mentor who could pose a threat to me..."

For the first time in three days, Nathan's spirit shifted his position to a seated one. He allowed Maris' voice to play over and over, her statements motivating him and stimulating the thumping beats of the surrounding void each time they were repeated. Nathan established the following things to himself: Maris felt threatened by him; he had this power called the Devil's Spirit that could hurt her; she was not invincible after all – she was fallible, and *he* could so something to stop her.

The final impetus that Nathan needed was the recollection of what he saw before being swallowed up by the lightning. It was the image of Victoria coming between him and the bolt, her soul embracing him one more time.

For Nathan to still be semi-conscious after such an attack, he became convinced of one thing – his mother's spirit shielded him from certain death. In his heart, he knew that this was not just some hallucination because he felt her maternal love for him in that moment. She gave her life for him and he believed that he had a duty to make it count somehow. Thus, when trying to justify why he deserved to still be alive when she was gone, there was one last quote about the Devil's Spirit from Victoria the morning after the incident with Ranjit that resonated in Nathan's mind:

"I can't say whether or not there is some grand purpose behind you having it. But even if there wasn't, that doesn't mean you can't find one. Even though it's caused you a lot of grief up until now, I still believe you can make something positive out of it."

For Nathan, it dawned on him that he now had that purpose. He couldn't just vanish and let things end like this. He knew what he had to do.

His spirit rose to his feet. In response, the pillar of light stabilised and the pounding sensation reverberated across the entirety of Limbo.

Back in the hospital room, Thomas, Abbie, Joshua and Lucy gave up on being able to switch to a different channel. Suddenly their ears picked up the sound of the heart rate monitor beeping and they watched in amazement as the heartbeat reading began to spike up.

"Guys, are you seeing this?!" Abbie exclaimed excitedly.

"I-it's working! I-I don't believe it!" Joshua gasped. Finally shedding his cynical scepticism and relinquishing to hope, he called out to his cousin in an emotional outpouring. "Nathan, can you hear us?!"

Nathan's spirit heard their voices from beyond the luminous column. He placed one foot forward. Then another. And another. His steps gradually added up until he was walking towards the light, undeterred by the pulsations that he felt beneath him. Meanwhile, his friends' optimism grew upon witnessing his heart rate rocket up, prompting them to double down on their messages to the comatose boy.

"C'mon Nath, you can do this!" Thomas asserted confidently.

"We're here for you – come back to us…" Lucy whispered gently.

As their words reached through to the realm of Limbo, Nathan's spirit began to sprint towards the light, letting their encouragement spur him on.

Once he was feet away from the beam, its lustre forced him to close his eyes because it would overwhelm his senses if he didn't.

Nevertheless, Nathan pressed on blindly into the light until he felt its warmth engulf his body and course through his veins...

Moments later, Nathan could detect that the blinding glow was no longer present, yet he could hear his friends' voices clearly. Under the impression that it was now safe to do so, he gradually opened his eyes by a crack, allowing the light to pierce through – something that drew a collective gasp of suspense from Thomas, Abbie, Joshua and Lucy.

"Nath..." Thomas uttered to him before quietly waiting for him to react along with the others. The only remaining sounds in the room were those coming from the television and the heart monitor which displayed stable readings now.

Nathan's eyelids parted further to let more light creep in, revealing the hospital room that he was resting in as well as his friends gathered around him. His head was still in a daze, not fully grasping his surroundings. However, he soon comprehended that he was no longer staring at a vast, empty void on the edge of death. Nathan had returned to the realm of the living. He was alive!

Still feeling sluggish and deprived of energy, Nathan grunted as he shuffled his body about to try and get into a sitting position. It was a relieving and cathartic sight for his friends to see, overjoyed to have their friend back and responsive.

"Welcome back, mate..." Thomas greeted him with a thankful smile while Nathan continued to struggle under the bedsheet, trying to force himself up.

"Take it easy, okay Nath? You've only just woke up," Lucy advised thoughtfully, being careful not to pressure him. On the other hand, Abbie immediately leaned in to hug Nathan, unable to hold back her emotions any longer.

"You had us worried sick, you know?!" she exclaimed with tears rolling down her cheeks as Nathan tried to figure out what was happening around him. "Don't ever scare us like that again!"

"Abs, don't be rough with him! He's just come out of a coma!" Joshua reprimanded her instinctively, even though she wasn't exactly smothering him. "Nath, are you okay?" he asked, turning his attention back to his glossy-eyed cousin.

"Here, let me help you up," Abbie insisted, working to support her friend until he was seated upright.

"I'll pour you some water. You're probably parched," Thomas offered before reaching for the jug of water and empty glass that was on Nathan's bedside table.

"Do you need anything from us Nath? Please, say something…" Lucy begged, noticing that he hadn't said any words to them yet.

Just as Thomas handed Nathan a fresh glass of water, the commercial break ended and promptly returned to the news broadcast. The presenter re-established that they were about to cut to a live audience with the newly crowned leader of Entritica, Maris.

Instantly, Nathan's pupils sharpened as the focus returned to them at the mention of the mage's name. Joshua quickly spotted that the readings on the heart monitor were now skyrocketing wildly. When he listened to how rapidly and furiously his cousin was now breathing, Joshua's intuition told him that something was about to happen.

"N-Nath? What's wrong?" Abbie queried anxiously out of concern, hearing how chaotically the monitor was bleeping.

"Abbie, get back!" Joshua commanded, prying her away from Nathan.

He was right to do so. As soon as the monitor cut to an image of the masked Maris, Nathan surged to life by throwing the glass of water with devastating force directly at the screen to the shock of his friends. Both forms of glass shattered upon impact with the water causing the television to short-circuit and triggering a temporary power outage within the room.

Before Thomas, Abbie, Joshua and Lucy could properly register the destroyed television, Nathan passionately uttered his first words since awakening:

"I'll kill that witch myself! I don't care how long it takes; I swear on my mother's life that I *will* find a way! *No matter what*!!"

Chapter 27

Thomas, Abbie, Joshua and Lucy were rendered speechless by Nathan's startling outburst. They each stared at him with wide-eyed expressions as he huffed and puffed furiously, his own gaze transfixed on the smashed screen of the television where Maris' face was seconds ago.

Before any of the group could say a word, two nurses rushed into the room having been alerted by the sirens tripped by the power cut. They were understandably taken aback at the sight of Nathan awake from his coma, especially since he'd been on the verge of death mere hours prior. The two medics immediately turned their attention to his visitors and began ushering them out of the area.

"I'm sorry but we need to assess him. It'll take time but we'll let you know once we've finished," one of the nurses established.

Abbie was about to protest until she was stopped by Joshua. The eldest of the group quietly assured the nurses that they'd cooperate and led the others towards the door. Thomas, Abbie and Lucy reluctantly shuffled their way to the exit, halting to glance back at Nathan as the nurses started to examine him.

"Let them do their job. He's in good hands…" Joshua mumbled, putting on the best optimistic voice that he could muster.

Knowing that he was right, Thomas and the two girls slinked into the corridor with Joshua being the last one to leave, just as the nurses called for someone to clear away the broken glass of the television. Nathan blankly watched his friends leave the room while barely responding to the nurses' questioning, his thoughts lingering towards Maris and what he intended to do next.

The quartet plodded languidly through the hallways until they were back in the waiting room. Once there, Joshua slumped into the nearest chair with Abbie sitting beside him. Thomas and Lucy placed themselves in the seats opposite, all four of them keeping quiet as they mulled over Nathan's bold proclamation, fretting over his state of mind.

After a few minutes had passed, Lucy was the first one to break the silence.

"D-do you think Nath really *believes* that he can kill Maris?" she questioned curiously. Her words drew a look of derision from Abbie and Joshua.

"Are you for *real*?! Maris has taken over the entire country by herself! Unlike you, we've seen her power with our own eyes!" Abbie chastised.

"Alright, it's not a competition," Thomas pointed out in defence of Lucy.

"Even so, he seemed pretty dead set on it," Lucy stated, recalling the conviction in Nathan's voice. "I've never seen him that determined before..."

"Lucy, he's just come out of a coma. His head's all over the place – he's clearly not thinking straight!" Joshua emphasised, conscious of how scrambled his mind would likely be.

"Josh is right," Abbie agreed. "For all we know, he might even be under the Devil's Spirit's influence. It could be feeding off his hatred for Maris... just like at Mount Tamara..."

"Hm, he did break that TV...and we know it increases his strength..." Thomas added thoughtfully, considering Abbie's idea. Conversely though, Lucy wasn't so convinced.

"No. I'm certain he isn't being influenced..." she asserted.

"Sorry, but what exactly would *you* know about it?!" Abbie quizzed with condescension seeping through her words. This was not lost on Lucy who was growing weary of Abbie's sniping.

"For *your* information, I've seen Nath use that power twice now!" she hissed furiously through gritted teeth, reminding the group of what she had witnessed previously when Nathan had saved her both times. "So I know exactly what energy it gives off – and I didn't sense that energy coming from him this time!"

"What?!" Joshua uttered in disbelief. "How is that possible?!"

"Actually, come to think of it...I didn't feel it either..." Thomas conceded, reflecting on the incident that had occurred moments prior. "Sure, he was angry...but he still felt like *our* Nathan...not just some demonic entity controlling him..." he pondered aloud to the surprise of Abbie and Joshua.

"Hang on…are you saying that Nathan smashed that TV with his *own* power?!" Abbie asked, seeking clarity. "That can't be right! He's not got the strength for that!"

"Like I say, I've never seen him *that* determined before," Lucy repeated. "He said he'd find a way *no matter what*. Doesn't sound like someone who's just going to let that go, does it?"

Neither Thomas, Abbie nor Joshua could offer an argument against this. By Nathan's violent reaction to seeing Maris on the television, it was clear that he remembered all the atrocities that she'd committed. It wasn't unthinkable that he'd get a rush of adrenaline on account of his hatred for the tyrannical mage.

"W-well…I-I suppose a silver lining might be that…if he's looking to *find* a way to stop Maris, it might mean he's not planning to rely on the Devil's Spirit…" Thomas voiced, trying to see the bright side of the predicament.

"But what else could there be? Y-you really think Nathan has an idea of how it could be done?" Abbie queried.

"Whatever *ideas* Nathan's having, we need to talk him out of it!" Joshua stressed. "He's only just escaped the jaws of death; I'm not having him walk back in there!"

"We might not have a say in the matter at this rate…" Lucy remarked, still concerned about how serious Nathan would be about seeing this through.

"Hmph, it's almost like you *want* him to go after Maris," Abbie snorted. "Tell me, is it better for your Chimera allies if Nathan's out of the picture?" she probed brazenly to the shock of Thomas and Joshua.

Infuriated over the passive-aggressive accusations, the typically timid Lucy rose from her seat and strode over towards Abbie before Thomas could stop her.

"Is that what your problem with me is?! I already told you I'm not with Chimera!" Lucy snapped with a face red with anger. In response, Abbie coolly stood up from her chair until she was eye to eye with Lucy.

"You say that, yet you're still protected by the Alis, aren't you?" Abbie highlighted. "How can we trust *anything* you say?"

"Guys, calm down…" Joshua whispered to the two girls as both he and Thomas tried to intervene in the standoff, though to little avail.

"Nathan *told* me to stay with them for my own good! It wasn't *my* choice!" Lucy protested to Abbie.

"So what's stopping you from making the choice now? You really content with others deciding your fate for you?" Abbie barked back.

This remark left Lucy stunned, unable to find the words to form a retort as Abbie glared smugly at her, almost knowing that she'd shattered her psyche. Before Lucy could dwell any further on Abbie's challenge, the receptionist called out to them from behind the desk.

"Hey, no causing a scene or I'll be forced to have you all removed from the premises!" she warned the group, prompting them to settle down with the two girls stepping away from one another. With Abbie dragging up Lucy's ties to the Ali family through her tenuous relationship with Kamran, it raised concerns for Thomas.

"Lucy, d-does Ranjit and the others know that you've come here?" he enquired, snapping her out of her train of thought.

"N-no...t-they don't know..." Lucy confessed sheepishly. Thomas and Joshua exchanged a glance upon hearing this, aware that they were sharing the same opinion.

"If they find out, they might see it as a betrayal. Ranjit did try to kill Nathan after all..." Joshua rationalised. "Listen, I think you should go back home for now. I don't like the idea of you compromising your safety over this..." he advised.

"Yeah, best you go back to your *safe space,*" Abbie added scornfully, something that Joshua frowned at with disapproval.

"I-I can't just leave now – not until I know how Nathan's doing!" Lucy objected, worried for her friend while still feeling bothered by Abbie questioning her autonomy.

"I'll message you later once we get an update. I promise," Thomas assured her.

Lucy turned around to each of the trio, quickly examining their facial expressions as she pivoted her head. She saw the remorseless insistence in Abbie's eyes as well as the sympathetic smiles from the two boys, but she could tell that all of them were mutually insisting the same thing. Feeling outvoted, she eventually conceded.

"Fine...I'll go..." Lucy murmured reluctantly, leading Abbie to exhale out of relief whereas Thomas' and Joshua's shoulders relaxed in response.

"We'll give him your best and tell him you said hello," Thomas pledged.

"Please do..." Lucy beseeched to Thomas before fixing her gaze on Abbie and Joshua. "This isn't me saying goodbye by the way – I want to help Nathan too, so you *will* see me again," she declared unflinchingly, a statement that caused Abbie to fidget uncomfortably while Joshua nodded out of appreciation.

Having had the last word, Lucy left the three of them behind in the waiting room as she walked through the hospital doors and disappeared into the hallways. Once she had gone, Thomas, Abbie and Joshua sat back down in the chairs. However, Abbie's hostile attitude towards Lucy had not been lost on the two boys.

"What was your problem with Lucy back there?" Joshua asked her.

"I don't trust her," Abbie replied bluntly. "As long as she's linked to Kamran and his family, I'm gonna get bad vibes from her."

"You were still pretty harsh with her..." Thomas said to her annoyance. "Lucy's a cinnamon roll, she wouldn't hurt a fly. Are you sure nothing's clouding your judgment on this one?" he wondered.

"Never mind, just forget about it..." Abbie huffed, her eyes shifting away nervously at Thomas' question. Sensing that she wanted to drop the subject, Thomas and Joshua decided it best not to press any further at this time.

Instead, the trio impatiently waited for the next few hours to receive updates about how Nathan was. In that duration, Thomas took the opportunity to call Melissa to inform her that Nathan had woken up from his coma. Joshua did the same with Clint. Abbie phoned up Ben to let him know that she was still at the hospital and spent three quarters of an hour talking to him. As sunset arrived outside, their stomachs started to rumble on account of not having had a proper dinner while being stuck at the infirmary. Joshua remedied this as best as he could by bringing over a bunch of snacks that he bought from the café for him, Thomas and Abbie to re-fuel themselves. When they weren't eating or phoning their families, the trio passed the time by talking amongst themselves, trying as hard as they could to focus their minds away from fretting about Nathan – something that proved very difficult for them.

It wasn't until nightfall when they were finally approached by nurses. Even in their exhausted state, Thomas, Abbie and Joshua sprung up from their seats to hear what they were about to say.

"How is he?" Joshua requested when addressed by the senior nurse.

"It's good news. You'll be happy to hear that Nathan's fit to be discharged tomorrow," she disclosed to the group who were astounded to hear this.

"What?! That soon?!" Abbie exclaimed. "But he's only just woken up!"

"I know, we were surprised too. He has passed all the medical tests though and his body is recovering abnormally well," the nurse explained and despite not being able to provide a rationale for why this was, Thomas was convinced that this was due to the Devil's Spirit accelerating his recuperation.

"Has he been speaking much?" Thomas asked, more worried about his mental recovery than his physical at this stage.

"Only during the examinations when he needed to," the nurse elaborated. "Otherwise, he's stayed quiet but that's understandable given everything he's been through," she informed the group to which Joshua's head automatically drooped to look at the floor, still racked with guilt over his cousin's predicament.

"Can we see him again now?" Abbie queried.

"That's why I've come to find you – despite barely talking, Nathan has requested to see you all," the nurse revealed to the delight of Thomas, Abbie and Joshua. "I can take you to him now so just follow me," she instructed.

On that note, the trio tailed behind the two nurses as they guided them through the corridors. When passing through one of the hallways, Thomas glanced out of the windows and caught sight of the dark starry sky, reinforcing to him how late it really was as well as how long they had been at the hospital for.

Two minutes later, Thomas, Abbie and Joshua found themselves back outside Nathan's ward. The senior nurse opened the door to let them in and said that they could alert her if necessary before leaving to give the adolescents some privacy. The group entered the room to find Nathan sitting upright in his bed, appearing very pensive until he raised his head to see his comrades standing in the doorway while regarding him apprehensively.

"Nath…" Joshua called out to him, worried about how his cousin would react after their experience hours ago.

Thankfully, history didn't repeat itself on this occasion as Nathan greeted them with a warm, comforting smile.

"I'm so glad you're all alive…" the bedridden teenager expressed with a deep sigh, leaving Thomas and Abbie relieved by how much more receptive he was to them now.

Nathan felt at ease when his friends gathered around his bed and even more so once Abbie embraced him. It was a hug which he was all too happy to reciprocate this time around, clutching her tightly in response to the first familiar contact he could perceive having since waking from his coma.

"Trust me mate, the feeling's mutual," Abbie whispered in his ear while shedding a few tears of gratitude. "We really thought we'd lost you for good..."

"Speak for yourself Abs. I knew he'd pull through," Thomas proclaimed confidently, solidifying his faith in his best friend's fortitude as Nathan and Abbie released their grip on one another. As much as he wanted this heart-warming reunion to last, Joshua was aware that there was much to address from the turbulent occurrences of the last three days.

"Nath, how's your head doing? D-do you remember much?" Joshua enquired, trying to subtly gage what details Nathan could recall as a starting point.

"I-I can remember most of what happened," Nathan replied. "I remember trying to help you get Clint away from the smoke. A-and then... Maris took you both out," he described, his voice trembling as he relived the events through his mind while the others listened intently. "I-I tried to save you...so I scarred her...w-with the knife. A-after that...after that..." Nathan continued, straining his way through his account of the incident. Joshua, knowing full well what happened next, attempted to alleviate any pressure that his cousin might have felt in traversing back through the trauma.

"Hey, it's okay, take your time. There's no need to forc-" Joshua reassured but before he could complete his sentence, Nathan interjected of his own accord.

"My mom – Maris k-killed her..." he blurted out.

A sympathetic silence immediately fell upon the room. Abbie's mouth was agape while Thomas closed his eyes and glumly exhaled after hearing Nathan verbally confirm that he'd witnessed Victoria's death. On the other hand, Joshua had his hand cupped over his mouth, quietly questioning his decision to dredge these memories up now as Nathan's head and shoulders slumped downwards, his line of sight avoiding his friends.

"Nath...I-I'm so sorry..." Abbie conveyed. She tried to add something more profound however, her lips merely quivered as she struggled to come up with anything that she thought would be substantial.

"I-I don't know what to say mate..." Thomas confessed, echoing Abbie's sentiments. "I-I really wish I did...I wish I had the words to...to make things right…" Before he could continue with his clumsy, yet earnest speech, Nathan intervened once more.

"Don't worry about it. Words aren't going to change anything now – but actions might," Nathan asserted in an uncharacteristically stern tone, albeit with his eyes still directed at his bedsheets. "So I need you guys to help me with something," he requested.

"W-what is it…?" Joshua replied, concerned about what was to follow.

"I know there's still something missing in my memories," Nathan explained, finally raising his head again to face Thomas, Abbie and Joshua. "Everything went black for me after…a-after my mom's death…" he stuttered, almost getting choked up when acknowledging Victoria's fate, but he powered through and tried to gloss past it which his friends found troubling. "Beyond that point, the next thing I remember is Maris standing over me and striking me with a bolt of lightning," he revealed, stunning Thomas and Abbie when they heard what he'd experienced first-hand. "The gap between those two points – was I under the influence of the Devil's Spirit?" Nathan presumed.

Thomas and Abbie quietly nodded in response, confirming Nathan's suspicions.

"I thought as much. Before I got hit with the lightning, I saw that Maris had burns on her neck which weren't there originally," Nathan reflected. "In that case, I need you to tell me exactly what the Devil's Spirit did. Please, I *have* to know," he pleaded.

At Nathan's request, Thomas and Abbie recounted how the Devil's Spirit had manifested from his body in the form of a giant black dragon. They made sure to mention every important detail, including how the phantom had laid waste to Chimera, fought off Maris and saved Clint's life along with theirs. The more information they provided, the more Nathan realised that their description essentially matched the one in the library book with one particular quote echoing in his mind as his friends were talking:

Yet, there have been claims, though unsubstantiated, from long ago where the user's passions have been excessive enough for the Devil's Spirit to form the shape of a monstrous dragon – one with the ability to wipe out the life force of anyone who comes into contact with it and powerful enough to wipe out populations with ease…

"Nath…Nath? Are you still with us?" Thomas cried out to him.

"Y-yeah, yeah I'm still here…" Nathan responded, blinking rapidly as he snapped out of his daze.

"Okay that's good, you seemed zoned out. Then again, it is a lot to take in…" Abbie acknowledged. "W-what are you thinking right now…?" she asked, detecting the dejected expression on Nathan's face.

"Th-that power…I-I really killed people with it…" he murmured, fixating on the detail about how the Devil's Spirit had effortlessly slain Maris' soldiers.

"That wasn't you who killed them mate," Thomas claimed kindly. "You were possessed by the Devil's Spirit – it's like an entirely different entity to you."

"Thomas is right. You can tell when it's present, too. It gives off a really malicious energy – nothing like the vibe we get from you," Abbie added.

"Besides, you need to remember that it has *saved* lives, too. Without it, I'm pretty sure we wouldn't be standing here now to tell the tale…" Thomas highlighted.

Nathan accepted this fact for the time being, yet he was still disturbed and haunted to think that a power that dwelled within him was responsible for murdering people, even terrorists. Sensing the remorse from his cousin, Joshua felt it appropriate to finally address the topic that had persisted in his mind since Nathan woke from his coma.

"Hey Nath, we need to talk about your outburst earlier…" Joshua stipulated, believing that the shame he felt about the deaths of even his enemies had brought him to his senses regarding his earlier declaration of vengeance.

Unbeknownst to Joshua however, Nathan had already rationalised internally that the victims that he was lamenting were followers of Maris. Once he'd reinforced this to himself, it brought his hatred of his parents' murderer back to the forefront and snapped him out of his stupor.

"I stand by what I said," Nathan insisted boldly to Joshua's shock. "She threw her best shots at me and I'm still alive. I have a duty to bring her down – for *all* the people she's killed!"

"Nathan, Richard and Victoria gave their lives to protect you! It's why your dad joined the army in the first place!" Joshua exclaimed, desperate to make his cousin listen to reason while Thomas and Abbie watched on with concern. "Do you really think they'd want you throwing it away over petty revenge?!"

"I *know* they wouldn't!" Nathan fiercely argued, taking his friends aback. "But *petty*?! Our lives have been turned upside down because of that witch! She rules Entritica! Her presence will be *everywhere*! How the hell are *any of us* supposed to move on from that?!!" he questioned.

Joshua opened his mouth to reply, only to sheepishly close it again when he realised that he had no retort to offer this time. Likewise, Thomas and Abbie remained mute, knowing they also didn't have an answer on how to adjust to life with Maris governing their homeland.

"Guys, I'm afraid we have to face facts – life as we knew it will never return until Maris is gone. That's the *only* way we'll be able to keep our loved ones truly safe…" Nathan stated, continuing to speak from the heart but allowing himself to calm down.

"Nath, going after Maris is a suicide mission," Abbie insisted regretfully. "She's wiped out armies like it's nothing. How on earth are you planning to combat that?"

"Well, I don't *intend* to throw my life away," Nathan emphasised, assuaging Joshua's fears that he'd be running recklessly into the buzzsaw. "And I *do* have a plan – one that doesn't involve just relying on the Devil's Spirit by the way," he divulged, a statement that caught the interests of Thomas and Abbie whereas Joshua raised a doubtful eyebrow in response.

"When have you had time to come up with that?" his cousin wondered aloud.

"Turns out you have a lot of time with your own thoughts when you're being put through medical tests…" Nathan answered matter-of-factly. It seemed that his friends had tentatively accepted this reasoning after a few exchanged glances between them.

"Okay, s-so what are you plotting?" Thomas asked curiously.

"To do what we were going to do – evacuate Entritica. I can't bear to stay here anyway now that Maris is dictating things…" Nathan established as the others listened carefully. "After that, I'm going to do as much research and gather as much intel as possible about mages, Chimera and Maris. I want to learn as much as I can about them to find out what their weaknesses are so I can exploit them," he explained.

"You seem pretty confident in this plan. What exactly are you expecting to find?" Joshua quizzed, suspecting that Nathan already had something in mind from the self-assured tone in his voice.

"Before she struck me with lightning, Maris was talking at me," Nathan informed the trio. "I remember her saying that I was the only person on earth who could pose a threat to her – except her mentor…"

"M-mentor?!" Abbie exclaimed, startled to hear this. "Mentor for what?!"

"That's what I'd like to find out myself, but I have my theory," Nathan replied. "Do you remember when we were in the library doing research online? There was a site that talked about mages and how they were people who inherited or acquired the power to manipulate nature," he reminded Abbie and Thomas.

"S-so you're thinking that-" Thomas was about to infer before Nathan deduced that they were singing from the same page.

"Yeah, I have a strong feeling that this mentor taught her how to use magic!" Nathan conveyed. "Which means that if she can learn it, then maybe I can too…"

"You're hoping to find her mentor, aren't you?" Joshua comprehended.

"It would be ideal, yes," Nathan admitted. "Trust me though, I'm not naïve enough to think I can bank everything on that. That's why I want to explore *all* options before I even think about taking down Maris," he rationalised to Joshua. "I'm sure I'll have more chance of finding the solution outside of Entritica. I may even uncover a way of controlling the Devil's Spirit – who knows? But I know I'll be safer if I'm away from Maris and Chimera…"

Although they didn't say it to him, Thomas and Abbie were quietly impressed with the level of thought that Nathan had put into this strategy. It would have been easy for his plan to be compromised by his vendetta, yet they could see that he was exercising restraint from the calm, logical way he spoke. Even taking this into account, Joshua could sense the unwavering determination emanating from his cousin.

"You're dead serious about doing this…" Joshua recognised.

"I've made my mind up. Once I'm back on my feet, I'm getting away from Entritica like mom wanted. Please don't try and stop me," Nathan reiterated, a fire burning in his eyes that did not go unnoticed by his loved ones.

There was a pause for about ten seconds as everyone mused over what to say next. It was Joshua that broke the awkward silence after reflecting on his own father's wishes for him.

"If that's how you feel…then I'm coming with you…" Joshua decided, only for Nathan to refuse.

"No. Sorry but I need to do this alone. No matter where I go or what I do, disaster seems to follow me," Nathan insisted, still tormented by memories of when his friends and families were in life-threatening danger. "I've lost enough already – I couldn't live with myself if I lost you guys too…"

However, instead of his heartfelt statement being met with further moments of quiet, fuelled by pity, Thomas jumped in with his thoughts on his friend's plea.

"Nath, I know we can't sway you," he conceded. "But you don't get to dictate our actions either. If we want to join you, then that's what's going to happen," Thomas asserted defiantly to Nathan's alarm. "Besides, you're not the only one who's looking to leave this place. I've talked with my mom on the phone earlier. Even though she hates the idea of me being away from her, she agreed that it's in my best interests to get away from Maris' infuence. So surely it's better for us to travel together and have each other's backs?"

"Thomas is right," Abbie echoed. "There's no way we can just let you take on something of this magnitude by yourself…"

Seeing that there was still resistance to the idea from Nathan based on his exasperated grunts and rigid body language, Joshua spotted the rucksack that was tucked away by the side of the bedside table. He plucked it from the floor and held it in front of his cousin.

"Nathan, please keep in mind that I'm not just doing this for your sake and mine. I made a promise to Richard and Victoria that I'd protect you. I'd be letting them down if I just let you go through all of this alone," Joshua stated firmly while patting the backpack. Nathan heard what he was saying, but his gaze was focused on the item in Joshua's possession.

"Th-that bag…i-it's mom's…" Nathan gasped, identifying the rucksack as the one she was carrying on her shoulders during their journey to and through Mount Tamara.

"The medics, they…they recovered it from Mount Tamara…along with the rest of our stuff," Thomas expounded.

"I-I need to…t-to see what's inside…" Nathan stammered, gritting his teeth halfway through to try and control his voice. Again, his friends detected this from him.

"A-are you sure about this?" Abbie probed tenderly, believing it to be too soon. "We wouldn't blame you if you wanted to wait-"

"Please! I *need* to do this!" Nathan snapped adamantly.

Upon realising that he wasn't going to change his mind, Thomas and Abbie turned to Joshua for the final say. The eldest of the group gave a reluctant nod of acceptance, aware that Nathan confronting this was inevitable and that any efforts to delay it were ultimately futile. With that, Joshua placed the rucksack on Nathan's lap.

Nathan hesitated for a few seconds, bracing himself before slowly unzipping the backpack. Thomas, Abbie and Joshua watched on as he began to withdraw some items from the bag, starting with various pieces of food which Victoria had packed for the expedition. Nathan couldn't help but be reminded of the multiple aspects of his mother's personality when regarding certain morsels. Victoria's dutiful insistence that Nathan eat healthy was reflected by fruit like apples, bananas and oranges. Conversely, the presence of beef sandwiches, barbeque-flavoured crisps and caramel chocolates demonstrated her knowledge of her son's favourite snacks and her devoted motherly instinct to indulge him.

These bittersweet sentiments about his late mother continued to wash over Nathan as he rifled deeper into the rucksack, pulling out some of her garments and keepsakes next. While searching through her clothes, it was the sight of her pyjamas that brought back memories of early mornings where he'd wake to find her ironing his school uniform, along with evenings where she would get comfortable and watch television whenever it was Richard's turn to do the chores after dinner.

Then, Nathan came across a collection of photographs held in a protective sleeve. He looked over each of them thoroughly: the first was an image of Victoria and Clint when they were young kids with their birth parents prior to their untimely deaths; second, there was one of the siblings and Richard as teenagers with their foster parents, Sarah and Hannah Yates-Harris; after that were two snapshots of Richard and Victoria together – one of them during their wedding, the other when Victoria was pregnant; the remaining photographs were all ones of Nathan at different ages – from baby to child to adolescent – with the final picture showing him with Victoria and Richard shortly before the latter went off to fight in the war against Chimera.

The boy stifled a sob when looking at the last image, trying his hardest to contain his grief. Seeing this, Abbie instinctively lifted her arm, ready to reach out towards Nathan. However, Joshua mutely placed his hand on her shoulder to stop her. Thomas and Abbie both glanced briefly at Joshua and understood what he was thinking from the stern expression on his face – what would come next would be painful to watch but it needed to happen…

For Nathan, the final gut punch came when he heaved a solid object wrapped up in clothes out of the backpack. He peeled away the garments to reveal what they were concealing as Joshua drooped his head, already anticipating this.

Nathan gulped upon unveiling the gold metallic container – the urn which held his father's ashes…

His lip quivered at the sight of it and the last words he heard from Richard rang through his mind:

"You two are the purest lights in my life. I'll fight to the end to defend you both. Until I come back, please protect one another…"

In that moment, when looking at the urn and remembering his dad's plea, there was only one thought running through Nathan's head – he had failed. The memory of how he froze up against Maris tormented him now more than ever and the urn only served to underline the fact that his parents were both gone from this world.

With this knowledge lingering in his mind, Nathan started to hyperventilate as he reluctantly accepted the truth; his mother and father really were dead. It hadn't truly sunk in for him until now, the urn stealing away any sense of denial that he could cling onto. Other than his hatred for Maris, all that remained now for Nathan was a vast feeling of emptiness.

And then, to the shock and anguish of his friends, tears soon followed.

Nathan didn't allow himself to cry when Richard died. He had placed all his energy in trying to stay strong for Victoria, storing up his emotions.

But now, at his lowest and completely depleted of energy, Nathan wept uncontrollably as he clung to the urn.

"I-I'm sorry dad! I-I…I'm s-so sorry…!" he wailed as he grieved, finally releasing the cork from the bottle that he'd been filling to the brim over these last few weeks.

Witnessing Nathan's breakdown, Thomas, Abbie and Joshua rallied around him before embracing him in a group hug to console the young man.

"I'm sorry too Nath, I really am…" Thomas expressed sincerely, allowing Nathan to cry into his shoulder. "But you still have us and we're not going anywhere…" he maintained.

"That's right, you're not getting rid of us…" Abbie added gently.

Aside from Nathan's muffled sobs, the quartet were united in silent solidarity in the hospital room as Thomas, Abbie and Joshua affirmed to Nathan that he wasn't alone. As much as Nathan didn't want to admit it, he realised in that instant that the journey he wanted to embark on couldn't be done solo after all. In order for him to even have a chance of surviving to face Maris, he would need to accept the company of his friends to both strengthen his resolve and keep him from falling apart...

◄◄►◄《》►►►

Chapter 28

The next morning, a fully recovered Nathan was released from hospital after being visited by Thomas and Abbie and then escorted home by Joshua and Clint. There, he spent the rest of the day trying to properly comprehend life without Victoria around. Whenever there was a moment where he felt numb and despondent with grief, Nathan would switch the television on to hear news aplenty of Maris and Chimera. Aside from messages from his friends regularly checking in, the fury he felt towards Maris was what continued to motivate him.

Over the next few days, reports kept coming in about hundreds of Chimera supporters setting foot in Entritica following Maris' takeover. It wasn't long until videos of civilians being brutally beaten by the terrorists for attempting to resist went viral. Despite the outrage that the people of Entritica felt towards these atrocities, the looming threat of Maris' elemental magic rendered them unwilling to react out of fear for their lives. Instead, Nathan, Thomas, Abbie and Joshua kept their heads down and focused on their plans to evacuate, knowing that playing the long game was their only viable option.

Once Sunday arrived, four days on from being discharged, Nathan was stood in the hallway of his home with his rucksack on his shoulder – he was finally packed and ready to depart.

Before he exited the house though, Nathan took one more opportunity to go around each room in the house to appreciate the cherished memories that he had of simpler times. He reminisced about mornings at the dining table eating breakfast and evenings watching television in the living room with Richard and Victoria. Nathan ventured upstairs for what could be the last time in a while to peer into the bathroom where he'd clean himself up prior to falling asleep. That ultimately led him to the two bedrooms, but he didn't focus on his own this time – in his mind, he had already said goodbye to it days ago. Instead, Nathan stood outside his parents' bedroom and rested his head against the door, quietly weeping tears of grief as a way of bidding farewell to his mother, his father and the home he grew up in…

His moment of mournful silence was then interrupted by a ringtone in his pocket. Nathan wiped his eyes and pulled out his phone to find that Thomas was calling him, so he quickly answered it while ambling back down the staircase.

"H-hey mate, y-you okay?" Nathan asked as he regained his composure.

"Hey Nath, sorry for not calling yesterday. Mom had heard some news about my granddad and I was busy dealing with that," Thomas explained apologetically. "How did everything go with the solicitor yesterday?"

"Y-yeah it went fine, Josh and Clint were also here for support," Nathan stated as he walked out of the hall and closed the front door behind him. "S-she told me that mom left me the house and the money she inherited from dad in her will…" he added sombrely while turning the key to lock the door to that very same house. Knowing that he had given Clint the spare key yesterday, Nathan carefully hid his own underneath the doormat because he wouldn't be needing it outside of Entritica. "They really did everything they could to set me up in case this all happened…" he acknowledged, grateful to both Richard and Victoria.

"They were great parents – and good people…" Thomas commented respectfully, hearing the faint sounds of Nathan's footsteps over the phone as he walked down his driveway. "Nath, I need to ask…are you really sure you're ready to do this now?" he queried.

Nathan reached the pavement as his friend posed this question to him. The young man didn't respond straight away. Alternatively, he turned around to take one final look at his family home. He remembered being in this spot when he said goodbye to Richard before he went off to war; he recalled standing beside Victoria when they prepared to evacuate the first time; both were gone now…

"Yeah, I'm sure…there's nothing left for me here now…" Nathan responded bitterly, committed to his resolution.

"Okay then, I just had to ask," Thomas accepted with compassionate understanding in his voice. "In that case, I'll be seeing you later, mate… stay safe."

"Thanks, you too…" Nathan returned the sentiment. He hung up the phone and directed some parting words at what was now *his* house. "I'll come back one day…" he vowed. "This is just something I need to do…"

With that, Nathan finally left his home behind and made his way down the street, pulling the hood of his jumper over his head. The sky was overcast with grey clouds so there was a chance of showers, however the main purpose was to try and remain inconspicuous to any Chimera soldiers lurking around.

Two streets away, Nathan reached the bus stop and patiently waited for it to arrive. Based on the timetable, it seemed that it would arrive in five minutes.

Before that happened though, he caught a figure in the corner of his eye, approaching him from across the street. Nathan was vigilant at first, fretting that it could be Ranjit or any one of Maris' followers. Once he got a better glimpse of who it was though, he instantly relaxed.

"Lucy...?" he uttered once she was feet away from him.

"Just the man I was looking for..." Lucy huffed as she stepped towards Nathan. "I was on my way to see you, but this saves time at least..."

"I think I know where this is going..." Nathan stated, having exchanged several text messages with her since leaving hospital. However, he didn't get the chance to get the rest of his words out because of Lucy interrupting him.

"Look, just listen to what I have to say!" she insisted. "I know from Thomas that you guys are leaving today. You're not the only ones who are looking to flee though. Dan and Denzel are already on the run with their families – now that Maris is in charge, they're terrified that Ranjit will seek revenge on them for dobbing him into the police," Lucy revealed, reminding Nathan that Drew was ultimately killed two weeks ago. He couldn't help but feel guilt for viewing that tragic loss of life as a minor footnote in the earth-shaking events and numerous casualties that had transpired since then.

"Lucy..." Nathan tried calling out to her, doing his best to mask the exasperation in his voice. Regardless, it went unnoticed by Lucy who passionately continued to plead her case.

"I don't want to stay here either! I can't live a lie with Kamran and the rest of his family anymore, it's just too much! So please let me come with you guys!" she implored.

"Lucy!" Nathan barked to get her to listen.

"What?!" Lucy snapped in response, finally hearing him.

"Look at yourself – you don't even have any bags!" Nathan commented, pointing out how unprepared she was for any journey by her lack of supplies. "Are you sure you want to commit to this? Nobody would blame you for having second thoughts, I just don't want you getting dragged along only to regret it…"

"I won't have any regrets! If you wait, I'll literally go home now, pack what I need and we can meet the others together!" Lucy protested vehemently.

"It's not just about what you take with you! It's also about what you'll be leaving behind – your mom…" Nathan elaborated, reminding her of their previous discussion about her.

Lucy paused for a moment, visibly thrown by Nathan's point of contention. Despite that, she provided a retort a few seconds after.

"S-so what?! I've made up my mind and I can't keep letting myself be weighed down by her choices! B-besides, she's leeched from me and others for long enough – it's about time she learned to stand on her own two feet!" she spat with all the contempt that she could muster. Nevertheless, it wasn't enough to fool Nathan who let out a deep sigh upon hearing her say the words.

"Luce, I know you have issues with her…" Nathan acknowledged. "But she's still your mom. You only get one…" he rationalised, using his own painful experience of loss to give Lucy food for thought.

Although her expression softened, Nathan could see the fire burning intensely in her glaring eyes and it dawned on him that she was not backing down this time. Her stern silence spoke louder to him than her overzealous protests – Lucy was resolute, just like he was and he had to reluctantly accept that.

"Okay…you can come…" Nathan relented with a deep sigh.

"Thank yo-" Lucy was about to say until Nathan interjected.

"On one condition…" Nathan stated, taking Lucy by surprise though she listened intently. "You need to talk with your mom first…at least try and make peace with her before you go…because trust me, you'll never forgive yourself if you don't…" he implored her. Lucy considered his request carefully for a moment before nodding in agreement.

"Very well, I'll do it…" Lucy assured Nathan to his relief. "I'll go say goodbye now, but I won't be long so don't go anywhere," she instructed.

"Fine…" Nathan responded, albeit begrudgingly after a brief pause.

He then watched as Lucy, having taken his answer at face value, turned and crossed the road. After a moment of reflection, particularly ruminating on how he hated the way he'd ended the conversation with her, Nathan tried to get her attention again once she'd reached the other side of the street.

"Lucy!" he hollered out to her, to which she glanced back at him over her shoulder. "I-I'd been meaning to say…T-Thomas said you visited me while I was in hospital…I-I wanted to say thanks…f-for doing that…" Nathan expressed awkwardly as a perplexed Lucy wrinkled her forehead. "I-it never felt appropriate to say over text, I…I just wanted to tell you that in person…" he added, continuing to stumble over his words.

"I-it's cool. I mean you could have just told me that later," Lucy replied, still wondering why he'd bring this up all of a sudden.

"Y-yeah I guess…I-I just wanted to get it off my chest…" Nathan stammered.

"Oh, o-okay then…" Lucy uttered, flashing a small, shy smile out of appreciation. "Well, I'll see you shortly," she established before hurrying down the pavement, keen not to waste any more time.

Nathan observed as Lucy disappeared around the corner to his right and mere seconds later, the black bus came into view on his left. Half a minute later, the vehicle pulled up in front of Nathan who closed his eyes and let out a deep sigh just as it was coming to a halt.

"Sorry Luce…" he mumbled to himself, hopeful that her mother would convince her not to leave. "I'm doing this for your sake too…"

The dark doors opened and Nathan immediately stepped aboard before paying and taking a seat. When the bus accelerated away and turned down another road, Nathan instinctively averted his gaze away from the window, still plagued by remorse for disregarding Lucy's wishes. While he genuinely believed that it was in her best interests, he couldn't help but feel that he'd betrayed her trust…

****

Hours later, after multiple bus journeys, Mount Tamara was finally in sight for Nathan. He kept his hood covering his head as he made his way through the small mountain town which was now teeming with Chimera squaddies policing the area. Nathan made sure to conceal himself amongst other civilians who lifelessly plodded along with their heads hung low, the effects of Maris' oppression already apparent. Last time he was here, Nathan stopped to eat dinner with his family and friends at the Raging Dragon Tavern before climbing the mountain; he denied himself that luxury now though, for he was keen to get as far away from Chimera's menacing presence as possible, not willing to remain in the town any longer than he had to.

Thankfully, Nathan found that it wouldn't be so necessary to rest and restore his energy this time around – because when he reached the foot of Mount Tamara, he came across the cavern that Maris had carved out. Although it served as another reminder of what the tyrant was capable of, it would be a much more efficient detour for Nathan to take. Thus, he wasted no time stepping into the passageway and heading deeper in.

Even walking at a more relaxed pace, Nathan soon found that he could clear this cavern in less than half the time it took to traverse Mount Tamara. Apart from a couple of crags in the walls of the tunnel, there were very few imperfections in the rock surfaces which demonstrated how clean the sculpting into the mountain had been. It was similar to the passageway that had almost caved in on him and the others, only this one had been naturally yet callously parted by Maris' magic rather than the former which was man-made, but carefully crafted over time.

Once he'd reached the halfway point of the tunnel, Nathan could see a few figures that were illuminated by the light ahead. Several more steps closer to them and he was able to distinguish who they were.

"Hey guys..." Nathan meekly addressed Thomas, Abbie and Joshua as they stepped out of the shadows to greet him.

"Funny how the host is late to the leaving party," Abbie joked overenthusiastically to try and lighten Nathan's mood.

"Ignore her, we've not long got here ourselves," Thomas added with a chuckle as he patted Nathan on the shoulder.

"I'm just glad we all got here in one piece..." Joshua remarked. "Entritica's crawling with Chimera goons now – we were lucky to get through the town unnoticed..."

"Y-yeah I saw...we're pretty much going on the run..." Nathan reflected on his own experience in the town roughly an hour ago along with Lucy's account of Dan and Denzel fleeing with their families. "Y-you guys know that this is *my* fight, right? I'd rather you not get dragged into this...after all, you still have your families to think of..." he highlighted, wanting to give them one more chance to bail out if they felt uneasy.

"Nath…you *are* my family," Joshua reminded his cousin. "Dad and I both agreed…he'll be okay and there's no way I can let you go off the grid by yourself" he asserted resolutely.

"Hate to break it to you bud, but this is *our* battle now," Abbie echoed defiantly with an exaggerated grin. "Besides, somebody's got to keep you two in check. Can't have you hotheads charging blindly into danger again, can I?" she rationalised, remembering how both Nathan and Joshua had got themselves into precarious situations against Ranjit and Maris respectively.

Even though she was jesting, Joshua instinctively squeezed Abbie's hand to reassure her that he'd be less reckless. Spotting how Abbie beamed back at his older cousin, it was only now that Nathan noticed that the two were holding hands.

"Um, am I missing something here?" he queried whilst beckoning at their hands.

"Oh…yeah, th-they're an item now…" Thomas clumsily blurted out to Nathan's surprise. Picking up on his wide-eyed expression, Abbie and Joshua glanced at each other awkwardly before releasing their grip on one another, scared that Nathan wouldn't approve of them seeing each other. Instead, after taking a few moments to digest this revelation, Nathan came to terms with it rather quickly.

"Fair enough – as long as you're both happy, it's fine with me," he declared aloofly.

Abbie and Joshua were relieved to hear the sincerity in his voice, however they were concerned by how indifferent Nathan seemed about the subject. From the vacant gaze in his eyes, it was as though Maris and Chimera were the only thoughts running through his mind. They didn't have long to fret over this though because Nathan quickly turned to Thomas to address his oldest friend.

"What about you mate? You really sure you want to leave your mom behind for *my* sake?" Nathan asked, hoping that he could play on his emotions and guilt-trip him into staying with Melissa. However, Thomas was unfazed by this and responded without missing a beat.

"Nath, you're the closest thing to a brother I've ever had. I'm not gonna let you feel alone again…" Thomas professed unflinchingly.

Nathan automatically let out a gasp of shock at hearing Thomas say these words and blinked rapidly to try and stop himself from getting choked up. After being rendered speechless and failing to come up with a retort, he was finally defeated from seeing the determination on Thomas', Abbie's and Joshua's faces.

"Damn you..." he grumbled in Thomas' direction, indicating that he'd accepted the fact that he couldn't change their minds, despite his own misgivings.

With that decided, the quartet continued on their way through the cavern, plodding along the uneven terrain. Thomas walked by Nathan's side as the latter led the group towards the light at the end of the tunnel. Meanwhile, Abbie and Joshua ambled behind them, the former resting her head lethargically on her boyfriend's shoulder. This was noticed by Thomas but overlooked by Nathan who was laser focused on advancing ahead. Feeling the tension in the air, Thomas was keen to break it by making conversation.

"H-hey...th-that was pretty cool of you back there...you know... accepting Abbie and Josh being together..." Thomas acknowledged.

"I'll admit I'm a *little* weirded out by it, but I'm hardly gonna steal their happiness from them – Maris has already done that to enough people..." Nathan whispered bitterly while glancing over his shoulder to see Joshua consoling Abbie. "She was putting on a brave face earlier, wasn't she?" he inferred to Thomas.

"That obvious, huh?" his friend replied. "She's trying to hide it, but it pained her to leave Ben behind...he's still recovering though so it wouldn't be safe for him to travel like this – Abbie knows that and said it's for the best this way..." Thomas asserted, not wanting Nathan to jump to the conclusion that Abbie was pressured into fleeing.

"I see..." Nathan uttered. "At least she has Josh to support her..."

"And us..." Thomas reminded him to which Nathan looked at him before giving a small nod in agreement while treading carefully along the pathway of the cavern.

"By the way, is everything okay with your mom?" Nathan asked gently. "You mentioned earlier that there was some news about your granddad..."

"Yeah, she'll be fine" Thomas confirmed. "The care home told us yesterday that granddad's health is deteriorating. They think he has less than a year left..."

"Oh...wow, I-I'm sorry to hear that mate..." Nathan sympathised as Thomas idly shrugged in response. Nathan took care not to judge this reaction though for he knew of the tenuous relationship that Thomas had with his grandfather. Instead, he posed a different question to him. "H-how did your mom take the news?"

"It was definitely a shock for her. It's the first we've heard about him since she severed ties…" Thomas elaborated, reflecting on how Melissa disowned her father after finding out that he was bullying his own grandson. "She wasn't sure what to do but I encouraged her to try and make peace with him while she still can…" he revealed.

"That's big of you to do that…" Nathan stated admiringly.

"Well, it's not really about me this time…" Thomas pointed out. "I just hope that I did the right thing saying it." Hearing his best friend talk about his mom and granddad's fractured relationship conjured feelings of guilt within Nathan after his interaction with Lucy hours ago.

"I-I saw Lucy earlier…" Nathan confessed in a low voice. "She was asking to come with us, but I said she needed to mend fences with her mom first…a-and then…I-I…"

"You left her behind, didn't you?" Thomas deduced softly, however a hint of disapproval seeped out in his words.

"She'll be safer if she stays with Chimera than if she betrays them. I'm just hoping that her mom can make her see that," Nathan hissed defensively, almost like he was trying to convince himself more so than Thomas. One moment later, as if becoming aware of this, he sought the opinion of his friend. "D-do you think I did the right thing…?" he enquired feebly.

"Do *you*?" Thomas challenged rhetorically, throwing his own question back at Nathan who went silent, struggling to keep justifying his decision regarding Lucy.

He didn't really get the chance to either – before Nathan could even think of an answer, he, Thomas, Abbie and Joshua reached the exit of the cavern. The group stepped out of the shadows to be bathed by the light of the sun that was setting beyond the valley. Ahead of them was the bridge that they never had the chance to cross over one week ago. Thomas, Abbie and Joshua took a deep breath to inhale the open air and brace themselves for the next leg of the journey.

"You ready to do this, Nath?" Abbie enquired before tilting her head to where she believed him to be standing.

However, it was clear that Nathan had other ideas first as Thomas, Abbie and Joshua quickly realised that he was plodding towards the rubble in the centre of the wasteland – the place where Victoria was buried. His three friends hurried to accompany Nathan as he prepared to confront the debris, each step taken feeling heavier than the prior one. Collectively, they tried their best to shut out any haunting memories of the corpses of fallen soldiers that were laid out across the battlefield during their last encounter. Once they were a certain distance away, the quartet could also see where the earth was scorched by Maris' lightning when it struck Nathan. Seeing the charred vein-like pattern etched into the ground with his own eyes sent shivers down the survivor's spine, yet it did not deter him.

Minutes later, Nathan stood beside the tomb and crouched down to place his hand on one of the rocks. Although they remained a few feet behind him, Thomas, Abbie and Joshua gave their friend some space, understanding that this was something he needed to do.

"I'm sorry...I wasn't strong enough to save you mom..." Nathan murmured while tenderly stroking the surface of the wreckage. "But I'm not going to let your sacrifice be for nothing. Come hell or high water, I *will* find a way to stop Maris – I know now it's what I was born to do!" he proclaimed, now believing he had the Devil's Spirit within him for this purpose.

Nathan then pulled the rucksack from his shoulder and began to rifle through it, pushing past clothes, supplies and the library book. He did pause for a moment when he came across his dad's locket – the last time he'd worn the memento was at Mount Tamara; the next time he'd seen it was the day after he'd woken from his coma once it had been returned to him, along with his clothes which had been singed from the lightning. Nathan couldn't bring himself to wear it for he felt the weight of his failure to protect his mom press down on him whenever he looked at it. Yet despite this, he still couldn't bear the idea of parting with it because it still symbolised hope to him, and he refused to cast that aside. Thus, he respectfully left it where it was and continued to rummage through the bag until he found the item he was looking for.

"There's one last thing I can give to you mom..." Nathan whispered.

He then proceeded to withdraw the urn containing Richard's ashes and slowly stand upright before removing the lid from the container.

"Sorry dad, but I'm gonna need you to stay with mom. This is a journey I need to do without you..." Nathan declared.

Then, Joshua instinctively reached out his arm as he watched Nathan tip the urn upside down. Regardless, he couldn't act in time to prevent his cousin from emptying the ashes out onto the rubble and using his hands to spread it across the rocks, covering the surface. Lastly, Nathan placed the hollow golden container onto a flat portion of the debris that he'd located, treating it as a shrine to his departed parents.

"I hope I'll see you both again someday…whether it be right here or in the afterlife…" Nathan lamented, directing his words to where he'd scattered Richard's ashes. "Until then, thank you for everything you did for me and I'll always love you. Goodbye mom, dad…"

With those parting words, Nathan stepped away from the tomb and re-joined his friends. He hesitated at first, conflicted over whether to downplay his sorrow. However, he thought better of it and allowed Thomas and Abbie to console him with a hug before Joshua placed his hand on his shoulder.

"You really okay with doing that?" Joshua questioned Nathan about letting go of his father's ashes, wanting to make sure he had no regrets about it.

"Yeah, I am," Nathan affirmed confidently. "They can be together this way, like they always wanted. Besides, I know they wouldn't approve of what I'm planning to do. Better that I put their spirits to rest than carry them with me…"

Joshua nodded understandingly, already aware of the burden that Nathan believed he was responsible for.

"We'll help you bear the load, mate – together," Joshua assured him.

"Maris, Chimera – *we'll* find a way to bring them all down and take Entritica back," Thomas stated passionately. "The solution exists somewhere – we just have to uncover it!"

"We'll make those bastards pay for what they've done!" Abbie proclaimed.

Hearing his friends' motivating declarations resonated with Nathan's soul, their presence spurring him on when he felt on the brink of despair. Once he'd let their words sink in, he regarded them with a new fire burning in his eyes.

"I'm ready. Let's go!" Nathan announced in one last rallying cry.

On Nathan's word, the quartet turned towards the bridge and departed from the area. They knew that their pilgrimage would be a long and gruelling one, yet their willpower hadn't waned, even with all that they'd endured already. Together, they felt comfort that their resolves would remain strong, no matter what they faced next. Once the sun had reached a certain level, its glare was deflected in the golden urn left behind at the tomb, illuminating the path to the bridge for Nathan, Thomas, Abbie and Joshua. Guided by these rays, the foursome embarked on the next phase of their journey with reinvigorated hope for a cloudy future…

━━━◄❖►━━━

Epilogue

About five minutes after she'd left Nathan at the bus stop, Lucy was stood outside the front door of her home. The lawn was unkempt and littered with pieces of rubbish while the windows looked like they hadn't been cleaned in ages. Bracing herself to tell her mom of her plans, she paused to take a deep, exasperated sigh before opening the door.

Once she'd stepped inside, Lucy could hear giggling coming from upstairs through the wafer-thin walls. With a frown, she called out from the bottom of the stairs.

"Mom? I need to talk to you…" Lucy shouted.

The noises from the floor above suddenly ceased. Lucy listened carefully and could make out some hushed whispers coming from the bedroom. She recognised her mother's voice but could distinguish another one – that of a young man's.

"Oh, not again, mom…" Lucy muttered furiously under her breath. "You've got someone up there, haven't you?!" she accused, raising her own voice so that it carried up the staircase. After no response for five seconds, she addressed her again. "Zara, answer me!" Lucy demanded, using her own mother's name as her tone became deathly serious.

"N-no dear, I haven't…" Zara replied, sounding noticeably flustered. Lucy then heard her hiss something inaudible before bringing her voice back to a normal volume. "I-I've just not…n-not been feeling very well. J-just give me a minute…t-to get changed and I'll be with you shortly," Zara excused herself.

However, Lucy wasn't buying this – she knew her mother well enough and could tell that she was stalling for time. As the ceiling creaked from Zara dawdling her way around her room, Lucy heard a small thud come from outside. She backstepped through the doorway to find that a shoe had fallen onto the ground and raised her head upwards to see who her mother's mystery guest was.

Lucy was left wide-eyed and mortified to discover that it was her estranged boyfriend, Kamran – shirtless and dangling from the windowsill of Zara's bedroom. An influx of emotions washed over her within seconds as it dawned on her what had transpired between her mother and Kamran: shock, hurt, humiliation. Regardless, they were all overpowered by the dominant emotion, one that had been silently building up within her for quite some time – rage.

"You have *got* to be kidding me!!" Lucy bellowed, drawing Kamran's attention to her.

Distracted by the presence of Lucy, Kamran squealed as he tumbled into the overgrown grass. It wasn't long before Zara rushed down the stairs wearing her dressing gown and one slipper upon hearing her daughter's outburst. The colour drained from her face as soon as she saw Kamran scrambling to pick himself up from the ground while Lucy stared her down with an expression of pure disgust.

"L-Lucy…I-I can explain…" Zara squeaked, taken aback by her typically timid daughter's intense glare.

"You really are unbelievable!!" Lucy snarled at her mother, her eyes wild with fury. "And with *him* of all people?! Do you have *any* self-respect?!" she spat while pointing at Kamran who'd finally got to his feet.

"Well, you weren't putting out and you'd been distant for ages – what was I *supposed* to do?!" Kamran shamelessly retorted.

"Why are you *still* here?! You can either hit the road or I can throw you into it…!" Lucy threatened, forcing Kamran to scurry away through the garden gate while holding onto his shirt and his right shoe. "Preferably in front of a car!" she yelled from the edge of the pathway.

"Kamran, hold on! What about our deal?!" Zara hollered as she waddled past Lucy in pursuit of the runaway. Before she vanished around the corner, she turned to her daughter and, even after her treacherous actions, inexplicably gave her the order, "D-don't go anywhere, we still need to talk about this…"

Lucy watched as her mother chased after Kamran, left in disbelief at her audacity with one question running through her mind – *how dare she try to assert her authority after bedding her own daughter's former partner?*

Motivated by her fury and contempt, she instantly made her mind up there and then. Without a second thought, Lucy stormed into her house, headed up to her bedroom and began emptying her cupboards and drawers of any clothes she wanted to take with her. She did it with such haste that it only took her a couple of minutes before she was stuffing her garments of choice into her rucksack.

Lucy then rushed down the stairs and into the kitchen so that she could pick up her purse, along with some morsels of food and drink from the fridge in preparation for the journey. After that, she grabbed a pen and paper from the rickety table and furiously scribbled down a message for Zara:

There's nothing left to talk about. You've taken advantage of me for long enough. I'm done. I'm leaving Entritica to get away from Chimera and you. DON'T try and contact me.

Once it had been written, Lucy opened the door to the back garden so that she could leave through the ginnel to hopefully avoid Zara. However, before she stepped outside, she caught sight of something in the corner of her eye. She recognised an extravagant, black and gold sports bag tucked away behind the table leg – one that belonged to Kamran. It reminded Lucy that it was Sunday, meaning that according to the clock, her ex would be having archery lessons in about half an hour. Wilfully surrendering to her curiosity, she zipped the bag open and peered inside.

As suspected, Lucy found a crossbow with several arrows tucked between Kamran's clothes. Thinking it would be sensible to have a weapon for the journey in case she needed to defend herself, she reached out for the crossbow.

In that moment though, Lucy heard the keys click in the front door – her mother had returned! Aware that she had to act now, she changed tactics and took the entire sports bag with her before jumping out into the garden and slamming the back door shut on her way out.

From there, she ran out into the alleyway and only stopped once she was a decent distance away from her home. Lucy used that brief moment of respite to remove the crossbow and arrows from Kamran's sports bag and shove them into her own rucksack with her supplies and belongings. When she emerged from the ginnel, she took the opportunity to cathartically dump her cheating ex's gaudy bag and expensive clothes into the nearest bin, being sure to properly submerge it in the garbage in one final act of payback.

Lucy then walked away, a newfound confidence swelling up within her as she put her estate behind her. For the first time in her life, she truly felt free – liberated and reborn.

Unfortunately for her, when she returned to the bus stop minutes later, her heart sank to find that Nathan was no longer there.

"Oh...you lying little bastard...!" Lucy cursed to herself out of annoyance once she realised that Nathan had gone against his word to her. Granted, it was not lost on her that it was far from the worst betrayal that she'd suffered in the last half an hour.

Thinking of the devil, her attention was caught by her phone ringing in her trouser pocket. Lucy pulled it out to find that her mother was trying to contact her. There was a fleeting moment where, given this setback, she entertained the idea of answering the call to see what Zara had to say to try and make her stay – would she try to justify her awful actions, or would she make yet another empty promise to change for the better?

Lucy promptly dismissed any interest in finding out the answer to this question when another bus came into view in the distance. She wasted no time in rejecting the call and then blocking Zara's number so that she couldn't contact her, reaffirming her choice.

"Sorry Nath...but you're not shaking me off that easily! Just you wait 'til I find you..." Lucy mumbled aloud, storming over to the bus stop so that she could wave down the vehicle.

As the bus was about to screech to a halt, Lucy grabbed her purse to gather some loose change. While fingering through it, she pulled out a photograph of her father when he was younger. Still tormented by the mystery of his fate, it served to further fuel her goals just in time for the bus to open its doors to her. Lucy stepped aboard with zero regrets, ready to commence her quest to track down Nathan...

⸺⸺◅◦◦▻⸺⸺

With the country of Entritica embroiled in war, Nathan Bennett soon develops an obsession with uncovering the mysterious circumstances of how his father and many other soldiers were killed in battle. As his closest friends Thomas and Abbie try to support him through his grief, Nathan's fixation to gather information soon leads him to grave danger when confronting his childhood tormentor, Ranjit. The encounter results in Nathan succumbing to dark powers that have been dormant since birth – ones he soon becomes aware of following life-changing revelations from his mother.

Days pass by and the continuation of the war brings yet more developments for Nathan and his loved ones: allegiances and betrayals are brought to light; relationships are tested like never before; disasters and tragedies ensue for many. Soon enough, they all learn the identity of their enemies – the terrorist organisation Chimera and their enigmatic leader, Maris ...

Having to contend with so much already and as further catastrophe strikes, Nathan and his friends are forced to make difficult choices to keep their families safe from the invaders. How far will they go to do this? Even with the wildcard that is the power dwelling within Nathan, do they have any chance of surviving against Chimera and Maris? And what will be the fate of Entritica...?